TOO HOT TO HANDLE?

Gary grabbed up the spear, nearly chuckled aloud when he regarded the dwarf, seeming a wild cross between a famished beaver and a lumberjack. Then he fell flat to the ground in terror and shock when all the thick canopy above him erupted suddenly in flames.

He knew he had to run. He got up as high as he could and felt a tug on his arm that put him over the side of the quadricycle for the third time.

Mickey sat low in the seat, looking horrified and helpless. "Suren it's the dragon!" he called out, beckoning Gary to get in beside him.

A tree not so far away exploded from the heat; Gary heard a horse shriek in agony and knew that the thing had been engulfed. He couldn't see Geno, or Kelsey and Gerbil, had no idea at that confusing moment if the others were dead or running. And every second that slipped past put Gary's own escape into deeper jeopardy. . . .

THE DRAGON'S DAGGER

**Thrilling fantasy and adventure from
R. A. Salvatore—bestselling author of
The Legacy, *The Woods Out Back*,
and other acclaimed novels!**

Ace Books by R. A. Salvatore

THE WOODS OUT BACK
THE DRAGON'S DAGGER

SPEARWIELDER'S TALE

THE DRAGON'S DAGGER

R. A. SALVATORE

ACE BOOKS, NEW YORK

This book is an Ace original edition,
and has never been previously published.

THE DRAGON'S DAGGER

An Ace Book / published by arrangement with
the author

PRINTING HISTORY
Ace edition/August 1994

ISBN: 0-441-00078-9

ACE ®
Ace Books are published by The Berkley Publishing Group,
200 Madison Avenue, New York, NY 10016.
ACE and the "A" design are trademarks
belonging to Charter Communications, Inc.

PRINTED IN THE UNITED STATES OF AMERICA

10 9 8 7 6 5 4 3 2

† Prelude

Kelsey the elf ran his slender fingers through his shoulder-length, pure golden hair many times, his equally golden eyes unblinking as he stared at the empty pedestal in Dilnamarra Keep.

The empty pedestal!

Only a month before, Kelsey had returned the armor and reforged spear of Cedric Donigarten, Faerie's greatest hero, to this very spot. What pains the elf had gone through to repair that long-broken spear! The reforging had been Kelsey's life quest, the greatest trial for any member of Tylwyth Teg, the fair elven folk of the Forest Tir na n'Og. Kelsey still carried the wounds of his challenge against mighty Robert, the dreaded dragon, the only creature in all the land who could billow fire hot enough to bind the magical metal of that legendary weapon.

And now, with word just beginning to spread throughout the countryside that the spear was whole once more, the mighty weapon and the fabulous armor were simply gone.

Baron Pwyll entered his throne room through a door at the back of the hall, escorted by several worried-looking soldiers. Nearly a foot taller than Kelsey and easily twice the elf's weight, the big man, gray beard flying wild (Kelsey knew that the Baron had been pulling at it, as was his habit when he was upset), ambled to his seat and plopped down, seeming to deflate and meld with the cushions.

"Do you know anything?" he asked Kelsey, his normally booming voice subdued.

"I know that the items, the items which I placed in your care, are missing," Kelsey snapped back. A hint of anger flashed in Pwyll's brown eyes, his droopy eyelids rising up dangerously. He did not immediately reply, though, and that fact made Kelsey even more fearful that something dreadful had happened, or was about to happen.

"What is it?" the elf prompted, instinctively understanding that the Baron was withholding some important news.

"Geldion is on his way from Connacht," Pwyll replied, referring to the upstart Prince of Faerie, by Kelsey's estimation the most dangerous man in all the land. "With a score of soldiers, a knight included, at his side," Pwyll finished.

"Geldion could not have already heard that the items are missing," Kelsey reasoned.

"No," Pwyll agreed. "But he, and his father—long live the King"—Pwyll added quickly, and glanced around to see if any of his own men was wearing a suspicious expression—"have heard that the spear was reforged. It seems that Kinn . . . King Kinnemore has decreed that the treasure rooms of Connacht would serve better as a shrine for so valuable an artifact."

"Cedric Donigarten's own will bequeathed the items to Dilnamarra," Kelsey protested, against Pwyll's dismissing wave. "You have the documents, legally signed and sealed. Kinnemore cannot . . ."

"I do not fear the legal battle about the placement of the items," Pwyll interrupted. The Baron grabbed at his beard and tugged hard, leaving a kinky gray strand hanging far out to the side of his huge face. "King Kinnemore, even that wretched Geldion, would tread with care before removing the spear, or the armor. But do you not understand? I thought that they had already stolen it, and the fact that Geldion is only now on his way, fully announced, confuses the facts."

"A cover for the theft?" Kelsey reasoned.

"Do you believe Geldion to be that clever?" Baron Pwyll replied dryly.

Kelsey sent his graceful hands through his golden hair once more, turned his questioning gaze to the empty pedestal. If not Kinnemore, than who might have taken the items? the elf wondered. Robert had been defeated, banished by unyielding rules of challenge to remain in his castle for a hundred years. Similarly, the witch Ceridwen had been banished to her island, defeated by the reforged spear itself. No doubt, the conniving witch could still cause havoc, but Kelsey did not think that Ceridwen had had time yet to muster her forces—unless she was working through her puppet king in Connacht.

A clamor by the main door, several groans and the sound of someone spitting, turned Kelsey around. Five soldiers entered, bearing a short and stout character, tied—ankles and wrists, knees and elbows, and neck and waist—to two heavy wooden poles. The dwarf—for it was, of course, a dwarf, though he did not wear the beard typical of his folk—twisted stubbornly every step of the way, forcing his head to the side so that he could line up another man for a stream of gravelly spit.

None of the soldiers seemed overly pleased, and all of them carried more than a few hammer-sized dents in their metal armor.

"My Baron," one of them began, but he stopped abruptly as a wad of spit slapped against the side of his face. He turned and raised his fist threateningly at the dwarf, who smiled an impish smile and spat another stream into the man's eye.

"Cut him down!" the frustrated Baron cried.

"Yes, my Baron!" one of the soldiers eagerly responded, snapping his great sword from its sheath. He turned on the dwarf and brought the weapon up high, lining up the bound prisoner's exposed head, but suddenly Kelsey was between him and his target, the elf's slender sword at the soldier's throat.

"I believe that your Baron meant for you to free the dwarf," the elf explained. The soldier looked at Pwyll, a horrified expression on his face, then blushed and slid his weapon away.

"We cannot free him, my Baron," said the first soldier as he continued to wipe his face. "I fear for your safety."

"There are five armed soldiers around the damned dwarf!" Pwyll replied, tugging at his beard.

The soldier gave the dangerous prisoner a sidelong glance.

"And there were twenty in Braemar!" the dwarf bellowed. "So do let me down, I beg."

Pwyll's big face screwed up as he regarded his troops. He had indeed sent a score of soldiers to the town of Braemar in search of Geno Hammerthrower.

"The others will return to Dilnamarra after their wounds have healed enough to permit travel," the soldier admitted.

Pwyll looked to Kelsey, who turned about and promptly sliced the thongs holding Geno to the pole. Down crashed the dwarf, but he bounced back to his feet immediately and slapped a fist into his open palm.

"I was not among the score of men you battled in Braemar," Kelsey quickly and grimly reminded Geno. "You will cause no further ruckus in Dilnamarra Keep."

Geno held the elf's unyielding stare for a long while, then shrugged, pushed his straight brown hair back from his rough-hewn but strangely cherubic face, and smiled that mischievous grin once more. "Then give me back my hammers," he said.

Kelsey nodded to one of the soldiers, who immediately put his hand on a bandolier lined with a dozen heavy hammers. The man retracted the hand at once, though, and looked from smiling Geno to Baron Pwyll.

"Do it!" Kelsey demanded before the Baron could respond, and so great was the respect carried by the Tylwyth Teg that the soldier had the bandolier off his shoulder and over to Geno in an instant.

Geno pulled a hammer from the wide strap and sent it spinning up into the air. He casually draped the strap over one shoulder, then put his thick hand out at precisely the right moment to catch the descending hammer.

"My thanks, elf," the dwarf said. "But do not presume this capture to mean I owe you anything. You know the rules of indenture as well as I, and twenty against one doesn't make for a fair catch."

"You were not brought back for any indenture," Kelsey explained, and Geno, despite his taciturn façade, let out a profound sigh of relief. The dwarf was reputably the finest smithy in all the land of Faerie, and as such, was almost constantly fending off capture attempts from Barons or wealthy merchants, or simply upstart would-be heroes, all wanting him to craft the "finest weapon in the world."

"The armor and spear are missing," Baron Pwyll added rather sharply, leaning forward in his chair as though he had just placed an accusation at the dwarf's feet. The blustery man backed off on his imposing stance immediately, though, when Geno's scowl returned tenfold.

"Are you accusing me of taking them?" the dwarf asked bluntly.

"No, no," Kelsey quickly put in, fearing one of Geno's volatile explosions. It occurred to the elf for a fleeting instant that his gesture of trust to the dangerous dwarf by giving him back his hammer supply might not have been such a wise thing. "We are merely investigating the matter," he went on calmly. "We thought that you, as the smithy who reforged the spear, should be alerted."

"We are simply trying to solve a mystery here," Pwyll said calmly, wise enough to understand the prudence of following Kelsey's lead. "You most certainly are not suspected of any wrongdoing." The statement wasn't exactly true, but Pwyll thought it an important diplomatic move, one that might keep a hurled hammer off his head.

"Your men could have asked," Geno said to Pwyll.

"We did . . ." the spit-covered soldier started to respond, but Pwyll's upraised hand and Geno's sudden grip on his nearest hammer shut the man up.

"Also, rest assured that you will be richly compensated for your assistance in this most important matter," the blustery Baron went on, trying to sound official.

Geno looked around doubtfully at the rather shabby dressings of the room. It was no secret in Faerie that since Kinnemore had become King, the wealth of the independent Baronies, particularly those such as Dilnamarra who did not play as puppets to Connacht, had greatly diminished. "Are the Tylwyth Teg paying?" Geno asked Kelsey, and the elf nodded gravely.

Baron Pwyll winced at the subtle insult. "Where is the giant?" he asked, referring to Tommy One-Thumb, the giant who had reportedly accompanied Kelsey and Geno on their quest to reforge the spear.

"You think I'd be fool enough to walk a giant into Dilnamarra Keep?" Geno balked. "How'd you ever get to be a Baron?"

Kelsey faded out of the conversation at that point, falling back into private contemplations of the unsettling events. Despite the impending arrival of Prince Geldion, he still suspected that King Kinnemore, on orders from wicked Ceridwen, was somehow behind the theft. The dragon Robert's hand was not as long as Ceridwen's, after all, and who else might have precipitated . . .

Kelsey's musings suddenly hit an unexpected wall and shot off in a different direction altogether, a direction that indicated that this theft might be more mischief and less malice. Who else, indeed?

Mickey McMickey shifted his tam-o'-shanter and rested back easily against a tree trunk at the edge of a glade in the beautiful forest of Tir na n'Og. The leprechaun soon resumed his twiddling with a dagger that Gary Leger, the man from the other world, had inadvertently taken from the lair of Robert. Because of this dagger, because the companions had broken their agreement to the rules of challenge, the dragon's vow of banishment would not hold up to scrutiny.

Mickey's thoughts drifted to his precious pot of gold, bartered to Robert before the leprechaun had ever entered the dragon's lair. How dearly he missed it, and how weak his magical powers had become with the gold lost!

"Not to worry," the usually cheerful fellow said to himself. He looked over his shoulder, to the gorgeous artifacts, the armor and spear of Cedric Donigarten. "This'll bring 'em running."

1 † Smart Bombs and M&Ms

Fiscal month end. Fun time for the finance group at General Components Corporation, a high-tech, high-pressure supplier for the giants of the computer industry. Gary Leger put a hand behind his sore neck and stretched way back in his chair, the first time he had been more than a foot from his terminal screen in over two hours. He looked around at the other cubicles in the common office and saw that everyone else had already gone to afternoon break, then looked up at the clock and realized that they would be back any minute.

Gary let out a profound sigh. He wanted a Coke, could really use the caffeine, but it was already three-thirty, and Rick needed this field service summary report finished before the management meeting at five. Gary looked back to the computer screen, and to the pile of notes—revenue plans, revenue forecasts, and actual monthly figures—sitting beside the terminal. He had to input the data for three more offices, a hundred numbers for each over two pages, then hit the space bar and hope everything added up correctly on the "totals" page.

Gary hated the data entry part of it, wished that Rick would fish out a few bucks from the budget to get him an assistant just one day a month. He loved the totaling, though, and the inevitable investigations that would follow, tracking down missing revenues and delinquent credits. Gary chuckled softly as he thought of the many television shows he had seen depicting accountants as wormy, boring individuals. Gary, too, had believed the stereotype—it had seemed to fit—until, following the trail of bigger bucks, he had inadvertently stumbled into a position as an accountant. His first month-end closing, filled with the seemingly impossible task of making the numbers fit into seemingly impossible places, had changed Gary's perception, had thrown the image of the job as "boring" right out the office window.

"You look tired," came Rick's voice from behind.

"Almost done," Gary promised without even looking over his shoulder. He stretched again and pulled the next office sheet off the pile.

"Did you get a break?" Rick asked, coming over and dropping a hand on Gary's shoulder, bending low to peer at the progress on the computer screen.

"At lunch."

"Go get one," said Rick, taking the paper from Gary's hand. He pushed Gary from his seat and slid into the chair. "And take your time."

Gary stood for a moment, looking doubtful. He wasn't one to dole out his work, was a perfectionist who liked to watch over the whole procedure from beginning to end.

"I think I can handle it," Rick remarked dryly over one shoulder, and Gary winced at the notion that he was so damned predictable. When he thought about Rick's answer to his doubts, he felt even more foolish. Rick, after all, had been the one who created this spreadsheet.

"Get going if you want a break," Rick said quietly.

Gary nodded and was off, crossing by his associates as they were coming back from the break room. Their talk, predictably, was on the war, detailing the latest bombing runs over the Arab capital, and describing how the enemy was "hunkering down," as the popular phrase went.

Gary just smiled as he passed them, exchanged friendly shoulder-punches with Tom, the cost accountant, and made his way quickly to the break room. Rick had told him to take his time, and Gary knew that Rick, always concerned for his employees, had meant every word. But Gary knew, too, that the report was his responsibility, and he meant to get it done.

Someone had brought a television into the break room, turned always to CNN and the continuing war coverage. A group was around the screen when Gary entered—hell, he thought, a group was always around the screen—watching the latest briefing, this one by the French commanders of the U.N. forces. Gary tried to phase it all out as the reporters assaulted the commanders with their typically stupid questions, most asking when the ground assault would begin.

Of course, they'll tell you the exact time, Gary thought sarcastically. Never mind that the enemy command was also tuned to CNN's continuing coverage.

Gary lucked out: it only took five quarters to coax a seventy-five-cent Coke out of the battered vending machine. He moved to a table far to the side of the TV screen and pulled up a chair. He took a pair of hand-grips from one pocket and began to squeeze, nodded admiringly at the ripples in his muscular forearm. Gary had always been in good shape, always been an athlete, but ever since his unexpected trip to the land of Faerie, he took working out much more seriously. In the land of dragons and leprechauns, Gary Leger had worn the armor and carried the weapon of an ancient hero, had battled goblins and trolls, even a dragon and an evil witch. He expected that he would go back to that enchanted land one day, wanted to go back dearly, and was determined that if the situation ever arose, his body at least would be ready for the challenge.

Yes, Gary Leger would like to go back to Faerie, and he would like to take Diane with him. Gary smiled at the notion of him and Diane sprinting across the thick grass of the rolling, boulder-strewn fields, possibly with a host of drooling goblins on their heels. The goblins would get close, but they wouldn't get the pair, Gary believed, not with friends like noble Kelsey and tricky Mickey McMickey on Gary's side.

The image of Faerie waned, leaving Gary to his more tangible thoughts of Diane. He had been dating her for only three months, but he was pretty sure that this was the woman he would eventually marry. That thought scared Gary more than a little, simply because of the anticipated permanence of the arrangement in a world where nothing seemed permanent.

He loved her, though. He knew that in his heart, and he could only hope that things would work out in their own, meandering course.

A couple of MIS guys, computer-heads, infiltrated the table next to Gary, one asking if he could borrow a chair from Gary's table, since most of the other chairs in the room had been dragged near to the TV screen.

"Friggin' war," one of them remarked, catching Gary's attention. "We're only fighting it so we don't realize how bad the economy's getting. Wave the flag and drop it over the balance sheet."

"No kidding," agreed the other. "They're talking layoffs at the end of Q3 if the Sporand deal doesn't go through."

"Everybody's laying off," said the first guy.

Gary phased out of the bleak conversation. It was true enough. The Baby Boomers, the Yuppies, seemed to have hit a wall. Credit had finally caught up to cash flow, and Gary constantly heard the complaints—usually from spoiled adults whining that their payments on their brand-new thirty-thousand-dollar car were too steep.

In spite of the few with no reason to complain, there was a general pall over the land, and rightly so. So many people were homeless, so many others living in substandard conditions. The gloom went even deeper than that, Gary Leger, the man who had visited the magical land of Faerie, knew well. The material generation had fallen off the edge of a spiritual rift; Gary's world had become one where nothing valid existed unless you could hold it in your hand.

Even the flag—drape it over the balance sheet—had become caught up in the turmoil, Gary noted with more than a little anger. The President had called for an amendment to the Constitution outlawing flag burning, because, apparently, that tangible symbol had become more important than the ideals it supposedly symbolized. What scared Gary even more was how many people agreed with the shallow thought, how many people couldn't understand that putting restrictions on a symbol of freedom lessened the symbol rather than protected it.

Gary shook the thought away, filed it in his certainly soon to be ulcerous stomach along with a million other frustrations.

At least his personal situation was better. He had to believe that. He had come out of the dirty plastics factory into a respectable job earning twice the money and offering him a chance to use more talents than his muscles on a day-to-day basis. He had a steady girlfriend whom he cared for deeply—whom he loved, though he still had trouble admitting that to himself. So everything was fine, was perfect, for Gary Leger.

A burst of laughter from the gathering turned Gary to the television just in time to see a truck, in the gunsights of a low-flying jet, race off a bridge an instant before a smart bomb blew the bridge into tiny pieces. The technology was indeed amazing, kind of like a Nintendo game.

That thought, too, bothered Gary Leger more than a little.

He got caught up in the images as the press briefing continued, a French officer pointing to the screen and talking of the importance of this next target, a bunker. A tiny figure raced across the black-and-white image, entering the bunker a split-second before the smart bomb did its deadly work, reducing the place to rubble.

"Poor man," the French officer said to a chorus of groans, both from the reporters at the press briefing and from the gathering around the TV at General Components.

"Poor man?" Gary whispered incredulously. It wasn't that Gary held no pity for the obviously killed enemy soldier. He held plenty, for that man and for everyone else who was suffering in that desert mess. It just seemed so absolutely ridiculous to him that the French officer, the reporters, and the gathering around the screen seemed so remorseful, even surprised, that a human being had been killed.

Did they really think that this whole thing *was* a damned Nintendo game?

Gary scooped up his Coke and left the break room, shaking his head with every step. He thought of his mother, and her newest favorite cliché, "What's this world coming to?"

How very appropriate that sounded now to Gary Leger, full of frustrations he didn't understand, searching for something spiritual that seemed so out of reach and out of place.

Nestled in a mountain valley at the northeastern end of the mighty Dvergamal Mountains, the gnomish settlement of Gondabuggan was a normally peaceful place, lined with square stone shops filled with the most marvelous, if usually useless, inventions. Half the town was underground in smoothed-out burrows, the other half in squat buildings, more than half of which served as libraries or places of study. Peaceful and inquisitive; those were the two words which the gnomes themselves both considered the highest of compliments.

The Gondabuggan gnomes were far from the protection of Faerie's official militia, though, and far even from the help of the reclusive dwarfs who lived within the mountains. They had survived for centuries out here in the wild lands, and though certainly not warlike, they were not a helpless group.

Huge metallic umbrellas were now cranked up from every building, popping wide their deflective sheets and covering the whole of the gnomish town under a curtain of shining metal. Beneath the veil, great engines began turning, drawing water through a score of wide pipes from the nearby river and sending it shooting up into the air.

The dragon roared past, his flaming breath turning to steam as it crossed the spray and hit the wetted sheets of the umbrellas. Robert the mighty was not dismayed. He banked in a wide turn, confident that he could continue his fires long after the river itself had been emptied.

One of the umbrellas near to the center of the small, square town detracted suddenly and as Robert veered for that apparent opening, he heard the *whoosh!* of three catapults. The dragon didn't understand; the gnomes in that area couldn't even see him, so what were they shooting for?

Almost immediately, the umbrella snapped back into place, completing the shield once more.

Robert figured out the catapult mystery as he crossed through the area above that shield, as he crossed through the tiny bits of stinging metal chips the catapults had flung straight up into the air. Flakes ricocheted off the dragon's scales, stung his eyes, and melted in the heated areas of his flaring nostrils.

"Curses on the gnomes!" Robert roared, and his deadly breath spewed forth again. Those areas of metal shielding that were not sufficiently wetted glowed fiercely, and all the valley on the northeastern corner of Dvergamal filled with a thick veil of steam.

Robert heard several umbrellas retract, heard the sound of many catapults firing, and felt the sting of hanging metal all the way as he soared across the expanse above the protected town. The great wyrm banked again, arcing high and wide for several minutes, and then turned in a stoop, just a black speck on the misty southern horizon, but flying fast.

"Pedal! Oh, pedal, pedal, pedal!" Mugwiggen the gnome implored his Physical Assault Defense Team. A hundred gnomes on stationary bikes pumped their little legs furiously, their breath popping out in rhythmic huffs and puffs from the thin line of their mouths under their fully bearded faces. Sweat rolled down a hundred high-browed, gnomish foreheads, down a hundred long and pointy gnomish noses, to drip in widening puddles at the base of the spinning wheels.

Mugwiggen peered into his "highlooker," a long upright tube, hooked horizontally on each end, that could be rotated in complete circles. At the opposite end of the horizontal eyepiece was an angled reflective sheet, catching the images from a similar sheet near the top of the tube, that first caught the images from the horizontal top-piece. This gnomish periscope also featured several slots wherein magnifying lenses could be inserted, but Mugwiggen needed no amplification now, not with the specter of the dragon fast growing on the horizon.

The gnome took a reading on the exact angle of his

scope, then looked to a chart to determine which umbrella soaring Robert would likely hit.

"Fourteen D," the gnome barked to his assistant, a younger gnome whose beard barely reached his neck.

Wearing heavy gloves molded from the thick sap of the Pweth Pweth trees, the assistant lifted the end of the charged coil, connected by metal lines to resistors on the wheels of the hundred bikes, and moved in front of the appropriate slot in a switch box hooked to every umbrella in the city.

"Fourteen D!" Mugwiggen yelled into a tube, and his words echoed out of similar tubes in every corner of Gondabuggan, and warned those gnomes in section fourteen D (and those in thirteen D and fifteen D, as well), that they would be wise to get out of harm's way. Then the gnome went back to his scope, alternately eyeing charts that would allow him to predict the air speed of the soaring dragon, and the timing of the collision.

Robert swooped down over the southern edge of the compact town, narrowed his reptilian eyes to evil slits against the continuing sting of the flak. Like a great ballista bolt, the dragon did not swerve, dove unerringly for the targeted umbrella, which the gnomes had labeled "fourteen D."

"Threetwoone!" Mugwiggen cried rapidly, seeing that his calculations were a split-second slow. His assistant was quick on the draw, though, immediately plugging the end of the coil into the appropriate slot in the switch box.

Metal sheets folded upward as the dragon smashed in, encasing Robert. The mighty wyrm wasn't immediately concerned, knowing he could easily rip his way through the flimsy barrier, shred the metal to harmless slivers.

But confident Robert didn't see the arcing current shoot up the umbrella pole, though he certainly felt the jolt as the charge fanned out along the encasing metal sheets.

Those gnomes nearest to fourteen D were deafened,

some permanently, by the dragon's ensuing roar. Loose rocks in the Dvergamal Mountain range a mile away trembled at the vibrations of the titanic sound.

A hundred sweating gnomes pedaled furiously, keeping the charge steady and strong, and thrashing Robert's nostrils filled with acrid smoke as his leathery wings began to smolder.

Another roar, a crash of metal sheeting, and the dragon burst free, was hurled free, spinning into the air, trailing lines of smoke from every tip of his reptilian body. Two hundred feet up, Robert righted himself, spun right back around and loosed his flaming fury on the breached section of Gondabuggan's umbrella shielding.

Many hoses had already been turned on the vulnerable area, and the steam was blinding, but the town wouldn't escape unscathed. Fires flared to life in several buildings; metal turned to liquid and rolled down the gnomish streets.

"Which one?" Mugwiggen's assistant asked him, holding the loose coil once more.

Mugwiggen shook his head in frustration. "I cannot see for the steam!" the gnome cried in dismay, and he thought that his precious town was surely doomed.

"Free fire!" came the gnomish Mayor's command over the calling tubes. Immediately there came the sound of an umbrella snapping shut, followed by the *whoosh!* of a catapult. A loud *thonk!* thrummed over the network of open horns as a ballista sent a bolt the size of a giant's spear arcing into the air.

But the gnomes were shooting blindly, Mugwiggen knew, with hardly a chance of hitting the fast-flying wyrm. He flipped a few balls on the abacus he always kept by his side and shook his flaxen-haired and flaxen-bearded head at the long, long odds he had just determined.

Robert, though, drifting hundreds of feet above the steam-covered town, couldn't see any better than the gnomes. The great dragon's muscles continued to twitch involuntarily from the electrical jolt; his wings continued to trail dark smoke behind him. He was exhausted, and hurt far worse than he had anticipated from the surprisingly resourceful (even for resourceful gnomes!) defenses.

More flak filled the air about him and several huge spears whipped through the steam, arcing high into the clear blue mountain sky, one spear nearly clipping the dragon's long, trailing tail as it rocketed past.

Robert had seen enough for this day. He angled his wings and swooped away, seeking a perch many miles to the south, confident that when he returned, his wounds would be fully healed, but the gnomish defenses would remain depleted.

"I will feast yet on the flesh of puny gnomes," the dragon snarled, his drool sizzling as it dribbled past the multitude of daggerlike fangs in the great wyrm's maw. "And on man flesh and dwarf flesh and elf flesh, as well! Oh, fool, Kelsenellenelvial Gil-Ravadry! Oh, fool to take the dagger from Robert's lair, to banish wicked Ceridwen while Robert flies free!"

Despite the unexpected setback, the wyrm let out a roar of victory and beat his smoking wings, soaring like the wind to the protective peaks in the south.

On a high plateau, a flat-tipped uprighted finger of rock in the greater peaks four miles to the southwest of Gondabuggan, a handful of gnomes put down their spyglasses and breathed a sincere sigh of relief, a sigh only a bit tainted by the lines of darker smoke rising from the distant city to mix in with the veil of white steam.

"It would seem as if we have held the wyrm back," said Gerbil Hamsmacker, a three-foot-tall, pot-bellied gnome with an ample gray beard, tinged with orange, and sparkling, inquisitive blue eyes. "Heeyah hoorah for Gondabuggan!"

"Heeyah hoorah!" the other gnomes cried on cue, and the group gathered in a circle, all with one hand extended so that their knuckles were all together like a central hub, and giving the thumbs-up signal.

The cheer ended as abruptly as it had begun, with the gnomes turning away from each other and going back to the business at hand.

"Held him back?" came a call from the top of the next plateau, fifty feet west and thirty down from the highest group. The two gnomes down there returned the thumbs-up signal, gave a hearty "Heeyah!" and rushed to the back edge of their platform, calling down to the next group, farther to the west and farther down from them. And so the victory signal was sent to the next group and to the fifth, and final, group, some two hundred feet west and one hundred feet down from the original watchers at the top plateau.

Certainly these five flat-topped and roughly evenly spaced and evenly descending pillars of stone seemed an unusual formation in the wild mountains—until one understood that the gnomes, with their incredible machines and explosives, had played more than a little hand in creating them. Gerbil had needed the pillars for his latest invention, and so the piece, the Mountain Messenger, now stood, a long and hollow tube running from finger to finger, supported by metal brackets at each plateau. It resembled a gigantic Alpine horn, though it was not flared on the end, but instead of issuing booming notes, this contraption spat out packages.

In Gerbil's original proposal to the Gondabuggan Invention Approval Committee, the Mountain Messenger had been designed as a long-range delivery service for parcels to the mostly human towns of Drochit and Braemar on the western side of the rugged Dvergamal Mountains. In truth, though, the Mountain Messenger, like almost every gnomish invention, had been built just to see if it could work. The first trials had not been promising, with dummy loads lost in the mountains and never retrieved, and with one load even clipping the top of the town chapel in Drochit. Constant monitoring and painstaking calculations, fine-tuning the explosive charges along the length of the M&M (as the express had come to be called) and the amount of Earth-pull reversal solution coating the delivery packages, had actually made the contraption quite accurate, cross-winds permitting. At the present time, the gnomes could skid one of their delivery balls down the side of a sloping field north of Drochit, some forty miles across the mountains to the west, eight out of ten tries.

Never before, though, had one of those three-foot-diameter delivery balls been packed with a living creature, let alone a gnome.

"I do so envy you!" young Budaboo, a dimple-faced female gnome with quite a statuesque figure in spite of her three-foot height, said to Gerbil as the older gnome continued to check his packing on the lower hemisphere of the split-open metal ball. "To be the first M&M'onaut!"

"I built it, after all," Gerbil said humbly.

"But you might even be squashed like a fly in one of Yammer's Splat-o-Mallets!" the younger gnome squeaked excitedly, hopping up and down so that her ample chest bounced like the landing delivery balls. "Your name would then be forever etched into the *Plaque of Proud and Dead Inventors* in the University!"

"Indeed," Gerbil said solemnly, and he managed a weak smile as he remembered when he, too, as a younger gnome, had thought that distinction to be the ultimate of gnomish goals.

"Oh, how I would love the honor of being squashed," Budaboo continued.

Gerbil glanced over one stocky shoulder to regard the

excited youngster. Gerbil easily guessed where pestering
and manipulative Budaboo's flattery was heading. She was
an ambitious one, like most young gnomes, and blessed
with an intelligence uncommon even among the exception-
ally intelligent race. "You cannot go," he said bluntly.

Budaboo, thoroughly deflated, slumped her rounded
shoulders and limped away to check on the cranking progress of the huge crossbow, the initial launching mechanism.

When he was finally convinced that he had his traveling
gear, including a quadricycle, properly packed, Gerbil took
out his spyglass and gave one last glance at Gondabuggan.
The steam and smoke had cleared and the gnome could
see the buckled umbrella, and another one with several
metal sheets melted off. At least one of the stone buildings
beneath the opening had been flattened, its wooden sup-
ports charred, but as far as the distant gnome could see,
there appeared to be no casualties. He couldn't be sure, of
course, and even if his hopes proved true, Gerbil suspected
that merciless Robert would soon return.

He shook his head, called to his companions, and curled
into the last open area of the ball's lower hemisphere, se-
curing the flat, sappy ends of a breathing tube around his
lips.

Led by Budaboo, the other gnomes efficiently lined up
the other half of the ball and slowly lowered it into
place—not an easy feat since the ball had two outer layers,
a hard shell for handling the explosions and the impact,
and a rotating inner shell that would soften the spin and
the jolts for contents. Of the intricate details and calculations needed for the Mountain Messenger, the delivery
balls themselves had proven the most difficult for Gerbil,
and had required the assistance of the entire staff of
GAPLA, the Gondabuggan Application of Physical Laws
Academy.

Using a sealed tube with twin earpieces and a hollowed interior, Budaboo listened carefully for all six of the inner hinges to click. That done, the young female set the timer that would release the hinges, giving it an extra three minutes, just to be sure that the ball would have stopped bouncing and rolling before it popped open.

Other gnomes opened a small hole and inserted a hose through both layers of the ball's shell. On cue, two of the gnomes simultaneously opened valves in joining hoses, while a third pumped away on a connected bike. The materials mixed together and rushed into the ball, becoming a fast-coagulating foam that would further secure everything within the capsule, and contained as well the needed potion for keeping the ball aloft.

Then the gnomes gathered together flat-ended levers and rolled the ball up a slope and into place right in front of the cranked crossbow's heavy line. A leather pouch, connected to that line, was wrapped halfway around the ball and the signals began, the duo of gnomes on each of the successive four plateaus scrambling to light torches and insert them into hanging arms on either side of the tube.

"Heavy load," one of the gnomes on the top plateau remarked. "Gerbil has put on some weight."

"The charges have been adjusted accordingly," Budaboo assured him, and she looked to the trigger man.

"Stand clear!" the gunner called through a horn, and the gnomes on the lower plateaus scrambled for trap doors built into their platforms and disappeared from sight.

Budaboo took out her spyglass and examined the lines of torches, four on each side, to ensure that the gusting wind had not blown any out. If only one side of the twin explosives anywhere along the length of the M&M fired, Gerbil's ball would pick up an unwelcome rotation that would curve it wildly to soar far wide of the intended mark, probably to smash into a mountain wall.

"As you will," Budaboo said to the trigger man, seeing that everything was in place. "Lucky Gerbil," she whispered under her breath, wishing that she might have been the first M&M'onaut.

The trigger man heaved a lever and the giant crossbow snapped, rifling the delivery ball down the tube. Bells attached to the tube near to the first plateau tinkled, and the levers holding the torches dropped, flames on each side hitting the tightly packed charges at precisely the moment Gerbil's ball zipped past. Before the sound of the explosions had even begun to ebb, the other six charges went off in rapid succession and with a humongous *thwoosh!* the delivery ball soared out of the M&M and flew out of sight on its trip across Dvergamal.

"Forty miles out and three down to a bouncing stop along the field north of Drochit," one of the gnomes on the top plateau remarked.

"Unless a crosswind catches him and slams him against a stony mountainside," added another.

"Lucky Gerbil," muttered Budaboo, and she could only hope that Gondabuggan would need another messenger when Robert returned.

2 † With Her Face Against the Windshield

There came a measure of freedom for Gary Leger that late August eve, tooling home from work in his Mustang, the rag-top down and the wind snapping his straight black hair back and forth across the sides of his face. Rick had his report and the month was closed, and though the next week promised the hectic time of fine-tuning hundreds of numbers, twenty trips to the copier a day, and several dozen phone calls from District Office Managers, ranging from curious to irate, Gary didn't have to think about that now.

He had left the office a half-hour later than usual and much of the afternoon traffic was far ahead of him, leaving Route 2 west out of Concord clear enough for him to ease the reins on the powerful Mustang. He put his head back, pumped the volume up on the stereo, and cruised down the fast lane at an easy seventy-five, the 5.0 liter eight cylinder hardly working at all. Gary liked the drive home from work when the traffic wasn't too tight. Route 2 was wooded on both sides and wide open to the horizon, where the sun was dipping low, turning the lines of clouds a myriad of colors. Many times on this daily commute, Gary was able to daydream, and inevitably, those dreams took him back five years, to the journey he had taken to the magical land of Faerie.

He remembered Mickey—who could ever forget

Mickey?—and Kelsey, and the chase through Ceridwen's castle and the battle with mighty Robert the dragon. He remembered running scared through the wood called Cowtangle, chased by a horde of goblins and feeling more alive than he had ever felt in this "real" world.

Everybody wants to rule the world, the radio blared, an old Tears for Fears song and one of Gary's all-time favorites. He started to sing along, gave a quick glance at his instruments, and noticed flashing headlights in his rearview mirror. A closer look showed him a red Toyota so close to his ass-end that he couldn't see the thing's front bumper!

Gary immediately looked to the slow lane, instinctively reacting to the flickering signal for him to let the car behind him pass. He noticed that the lane was absolutely clear—why the hell didn't the car behind him just go around on the right?—and noticed, too, that he was pushing eighty.

"Jesus," he whispered, and he took a closer look in the rearview mirror, caught by the image of the young woman in the shiny Toyota, her face up close to the windshield as she issued a stream of curses Gary's way, and every now and then flipped him the finger. Her impatient headlights blinked on and off, her mouth flapped incessantly.

"Jesus," Gary muttered again, and he put the Mustang up to eighty-five. The Toyota paced him, couldn't have been more than a single car length off his rear bumper. Normally Gary, hardly ever in a real hurry, would have just pulled over and let the Toyota fly past.

A horn sounded to accompany the incessant headlights. The Toyota inched even closer, as though the woman meant to simply push Gary out of her way.

Gary backed off the accelerator, let the Mustang coast down to seventy-five, to seventy.

The lips against the windshield of the Toyota flapped more frantically.

Sixty.

Predictably, the Toyota swerved right, into the slow lane, and started by.

"Everybody wants to rule the world," Gary sang along, and as the Toyota's front bumper came halfway up the Mustang's side, he dropped the Mustang into third and gave the accelerator a slight tap. The eager engine roared in response and the car leaped ahead, easily pacing the Toyota.

Now he could hear the crabby woman, swearing at him at the top of her lungs.

Up went the volume on Gary's radio, up went the Mustang's speed, as Gary paced her at eighty-five, side by side.

"You son of a bitch!" she hollered.

Gary turned and offered a cat-got-the-canary smile, then eased the Mustang back into fourth as the speedometer needle flickered past ninety.

The Toyota backed off, and Gary did, too, keeping side by side with her, keeping her in the slow lane, where he figured a nut like that belonged. Curses and a flipping middle finger flew from the Toyota's open driver's side window.

"Everybody wants to rule the ROAD," Gary sang to her, altering the last word and nodding ahead, indicating that they were fast coming up on a perfectly maintained old Aspen—and that could only mean a more conservative driver—cruising down the highway at a perfect fifty-five.

Gary tucked the Toyota neatly in behind the Aspen and held pace for another half-mile, until a line of faster-moving cars came up on his bumper. Understanding that she had been had, the woman in the Toyota slammed her hands hard against her steering wheel several times in frustration and began flicking her headlights, as if the contented Aspen driver had anywhere to go to get out of her way.

"You son of a bitch!" she screamed again at Gary, and he blew a kiss her way, kicked the Mustang into third and blasted off, smiling as he looked back in his mirror, watching car after car zip by the frazzled driver in her Toyota and the contented driver of the Aspen.

Some pleasures in life just couldn't be anticipated.

Two hours later, Gary's Mustang was sitting quietly in the driveway of his parents' home in Lancashire, and Gary was sitting quietly in his bedroom unwinding from the long day and from the ride home. His radio played quietly in the background; outside the window, a mockingbird was kicking up its typical ruckus, probably complaining that the sun was going down and it hadn't found the opportunity to chase any cats that particular day.

Gary moved across the room to the stereo cabinet, opened the top drawer and removed his most precious possession, a worn copy of J.R.R. Tolkien's *The Hobbit*. Gary ran his fingers slowly across the cover, feeling the illustration, feeling the magic of the book. He opened past the credits pages, the introduction by Peter S. Beagle, and the table of contents. Nothing unusual about these, but when Gary turned the next page, he found not the expected, standard typesetting, but a flowing script of arcane runes that he could not begin to identify. Mickey had done it, had waved his chubby hand over the book and changed the typesetting to a language that the leprechaun could understand.

Gary heard a knock on the door, looked out his window to see Diane's Jeep (Gary's old Jeep), parked on the street, in front of the bushes lining the front yard. He dropped the book back in the drawer and slammed it shut just as Diane cracked open the door.

"You in there?"

"Come on in," Gary replied, hand still holding the drawer shut. He watched Diane's every move as she crossed the room to give him a little kiss, watched her dirty blond hair bouncing carelessly about her shoulders, her wistful green eyes, so like his own, and that mischievous smile she always flashed when she first saw him, that I-got-you-Gary-Leger smile.

And it was true.

"What'cha doing?"

Gary shrugged. "Just hanging out, listening to some music." He poked his head under the bottom of the open window, putting his mouth near to the screen, and called loudly, "Whenever that stupid mockingbird shuts up long enough so that I can hear the music!"

"You want to go get an ice cream?" Diane asked when he turned back to her. Again came that mischievous smile, telling Gary that she had more on her mind than ice cream.

It seemed so perfectly natural to Gary Leger, the way things were supposed to be for a guy in his early twenties. He had a decent job paying more money than he needed, the security of home, and a great girlfriend. He had his health (he worked out every day), his minor glories on the softball field, and a car that could trap jackasses in the slow lane on the highway.

So why wasn't he happy?

He was contented, not frazzled like the woman in the Toyota, or like so many of his coworkers who had families to support in a struggling economy, who had to keep looking over their shoulders to see if they still had a job. But Gary couldn't honestly say that he was happy, certainly not thrilled with the everyday tasks and pleasures that life offered to him.

The answer, Gary knew beyond doubt, lay in that cabinet drawer, in the flowing script of a leprechaun he

wanted to speak with again, in the memories of a world he
wanted to see again.

Gary tapped the drawer and shrugged. He and Diane
went for their ice cream.

High and far, the M&M ball flew, through low-hanging
clouds, through a "V" of very surprised geese, and past the
high doors of the holes of mountain trolls, the not-too-
smart creatures scratching their scraggly hair and staring
dumbfoundedly as the missile fast disappeared from sight.

Tucked in tight and surrounded by pressing foam, Gerbil couldn't see out of the delivery ball. If he could, the
gnome might have died of fright as he neared the end of
his descent, came soaring up on the lip of the field north
of Drochit. The load was indeed heavy—too heavy—and
the ball angled in a bit low, diving for the rocky ridge bor-
dering the top of the field.

Good luck alone saved Gerbil, for the ball struck the
turf between two stones, narrowly missing each, and skittered through, spinning into the air again, then landing in
a roll down the descending slope of the long field. The
ball had two shells, separated by independent bearings designed to keep the inner area somewhat stable.

No gnomish technology could greatly soften this bouncing and tumbling ride, though, and Gerbil bit his own lips
many times, despite the tight-fitting mouthpiece, as he
blabbered out a hundred different equations, trying to figure his chances for survival.

Gerbil heard the splat, and he was yanked to a sudden
stop and turned upside-down as the ball bogged down in
a muddy puddle.

"Oh, I hope, I hope, that I do not sink!" the gnome
mumbled around the edges of his mouthpiece. The next
few minutes, waiting for the timers to release the locks,
seemed like an hour to the trapped (and increasingly claus-

trophobic) gnome. As soon as he heard the telltale clicks, Gerbil heaved and straightened with his legs, popping the ball in half, only to tumble over backwards and splat rump-first into the mud.

He was up in an instant, fumbling with the many compartments of the half-submerged ball, trying to salvage all the pieces of the contraption he had brought along. Again, luck was with him, for just a few moments later, he saw a group of Drochit villagers riding down the road on a wagon, coming to retrieve the gnomish delivery.

"Didn't know ye was sending anything," one farmer, the oldest man of the group of six, said when he noticed Gerbil.

"Hey, how'd you get here?" another man asked.

"He flied in the ball!" a third reasoned.

Poor Gerbil had to answer a hundred inane questions concerning his trip over the next few minutes, all the while coaxing the men to help him in his salvage operations. Soon the dry ground near to the puddle was covered with metal tubing, springs, gears, and a box of tools, and Gerbil had to slap curious hands away repeatedly and firmly scold the inquisitive humans.

"Robert the dragon is loose and in a fury!" the flustered gnome said at last. Gerbil had meant to keep that news private until he could meet with Drochit's leaders, but that meeting seemed longer away indeed if these simple men did not leave his equipment alone and let him get on with his assembling.

Six faces blanched, six mouths fell open.

"You," Gerbil said to the oldest, and apparently most intelligent, of the group. "Hand me items as I call for them—promptly, for we have not a moment to lose!"

The farmers were more orderly then, and Gerbil's work progressed excellently, with all the parts fitting neatly together. There came one moment of terror for the gnome, though, until he reached into the bulging pocket of a young man and took out his missing sprocket.

"Thought it'd be good for hitting birds," the young farmer apologized, drawing a slap on the back of his head from the oldest of the group.

"What is it?" Gerbil heard the question fifty times as the contraption neared completion. He figured that it would be easier to show this group than to try to explain, so he waited until he was done, then climbed into the back-leaning seat, tooted the small horn on the four-wheeled thing's steering bars, and began pumping his legs.

For a few moments, he did not move. One wheel had snagged on a half-buried rock and was spinning in the mud. Just as the farmers, scratching their heads like not-too-intelligent mountain trolls, moved near to figure out what the gnome might be trying to do, the wheel cleared the obstruction with a jerk and Gerbil rolled off slowly across the thick grass.

"Well, I'll be a pretty goblin," one man said.

"You wouldn't be pretty if ye was a goblin," answered another.

The first slapped him on the back of the head, and they would have started an all-out fight right then and there, except that Gerbil then turned onto the road, little legs pumping furiously, and the quadricycle sped away.

"Well, I'll be a pretty goblin," they both said together, and the whole group ran off for their wagon. They turned the cart about and shook the reins, spurring the horse into a gallop. But the burdened beast was no match for precise gnomish gearing and well-oiled axles, and Gerbil continued to outdistance them all the way to Drochit.

3 † Mischievous Twinkle

Kelsey stood on a low hill, east of Dilnamarra Keep, watching the sun go down behind the square, squat tower that centered the simple village. The clouds beyond had turned orange and pink with the sunset, and all mud of the town was lost in a rosy hue.

"You just do not understand," the elf said to Geno, who sat on a stone with his arms crossed over his sturdy chest, pointedly looking away from the beautiful scene.

Kelsey turned about to face the dwarf squarely. "Geldion holds Pwyll solely responsible for the missing armor. Connacht has found its excuse to hang the troublesome Baron."

"Why would I care, you dumb elf?" Geno snorted, and he spat on the ground. "I never did any business with Pwyll, or with any in Dilnamarra. I've got no customers there, so I plan to go and watch and enjoy the hanging!"

Kelsey's golden eyes narrowed, but he bit back his angry retort, knowing that gruff Geno was simply baiting him for a fight. "If Baron Pwyll is hung," the elf explained, "then Geldion will appoint an acting Baron, a man, no doubt, who will nod his head stupidly at every edict passed on from Connacht."

"Aren't all humans stupid?" Geo asked in all seriousness.

"Not as stupid as you are acting."

Geno's gaze dropped to the many hammers on his belt. He wondered how many he could put spinning into the air before Kelsey closed on him.

"Stupid, indeed, if you do not understand the implications of losing an ally such as Pwyll," Kelsey added, reading Geno's expression and promptly qualifying the statement. Kelsey needed no fights with Geno, not now with so much apparently at stake. "Only a few of Faerie's human landowners remain independent of Connacht," Kelsey explained. "Duncan Drochit and Badenoch of Braemar are two, but they look to Pwyll for support. King Kinnemore dearly desires to bring Dilnamarra into his fold, craves an outpost so near to Tir na n'Og, that he might keep an eye on the Tylwyth Teg."

"Sounds like an elfish problem to me," Geno remarked.

"Not so," Kelsey quickly replied. "If Pwyll is hung and Dilnamarra taken, then Kinnemore can look east, to Braemar and Drochit, and farther east, to the other two goodly races who have ever been a thorn in the outlaw King's side."

Geno snorted derisively. "That weaselly King would never have the belly for a fight in Dvergamal," the dwarf reasoned, waving his hands as if to brush the absurd notion away.

"But Prince Geldion would," Kelsey said gravely. "And if not Geldion, then certainly the witch Ceridwen, whose hand moves the lips and limbs of Kinnemore." Geno stopped his waving hand, and his smug and gap-toothed smile melted away.

"Even if war did not come to the dwarfs and the gnomes, the trade would surely suffer," Kelsey went on, casually turning back to the sunset as though his proclamations were foregone conclusions. "Perhaps, after Pwyll is hung, you will get the opportunity to clear up your pile of overdue orders, good smithy."

Geno chewed on his lower lip for a while, but had no practical response. He could bluster that he didn't care for the fate of Faerie's bothersome humans, but the men were by far the most populous of the goodly races, far outnumbering the Tylwyth Teg elfs of Tir na n'Og, the Buldrefolk dwarfs of Dvergamal, and the gnomes of Gondabuggan combined. And while the populations of the elfs, dwarfs, and gnomes had held steady for centuries untold, the humans seemed to breed like bunnies in an unhunted meadow, with new villages dotting the countryside every year—new villages needing metal tools, armor, and weapons.

"You have an idea of where to find the armor?" Geno stated as much as asked.

"I have an idea of where to start looking," Kelsey corrected. "Are you coming with me, or will you return to the mountains?"

"Damned elf," the trapped Geno muttered under his breath, and Kelsey smiled, taking the grumbling to mean that he had hooked the tough dwarf into his quest once again.

Kelsey set a course straight north, and when towering trees came into view a short while later, it wasn't hard for Geno to figure out where the elf was heading.

"No, no," Geno stuttered, setting his boots firmly in the turf, shaking his head and his hands as he regarded the majestic forest. "If you plan to walk into Tir na n'Og, elf, you walk alone."

"I need your help," Kelsey reminded him. "As do your people."

"But why the forest?" Geno asked gruffly, if a bit plaintively. "If the witch took the armor, then it would more likely be headed for Ynis Gwydrin, the other way."

Kelsey's eyes narrowed as he listened, getting the distinct impression that Geno would prefer a trip to Ynis

Gwydrin, Ceridwen's dread island, over a walk through the elven forest.

"If Kinnemore took the armor," Geno went on, ignoring the look, "then it would be headed for Connacht, again the other way. Who would be stupid enough to steal something so important to the Tylwyth Teg, then drop it in Tir na n'Og, right under their flower-sniffing noses?"

"Who indeed?" Kelsey mused, and his wry smile sent a myriad of questions through Geno's mind.

"Did you take the damned stuff?" Geno balked, and it seemed to Kelsey as though the dwarf was ready to start heaving a line of warhammers.

Kelsey shook his head, his mane of golden hair bouncing wildly about his shoulders. "Not I," he explained. "Whatever my reasons, I would never act so rashly when so much is at stake."

Geno mulled over the words for a few moments, knowing that Kelsey had put a clue or two in his answer.

"McMickey!" the dwarf cried suddenly, and Kelsey's nod confirmed the guess. "But what would the leprechaun want with armor that is five times his size? What would he want with a spear he could hardly lift off the ground?"

"Those are exactly the questions I plan to ask him, once we find him," Kelsey paused, looking from the now not-so-distant wood to Geno. "In Tir na n'Og," Kelsey finished, and he started off again, motioning for the dwarf to follow.

"Damned sprite," Geno bitched. "I'll pay that one back in hammers for putting me through this."

"Perhaps you will find, after walking the smooth paths of the wondrous forest, that you owe the leprechaun some thanks, Geno Hammerthrower," Kelsey remarked rather sharply. He really didn't expect a dwarf to understand or appreciate the elven wood, but he was beginning to find Geno's grumbling about the place more than a little annoying. "Few of the Buldrefolk have ever seen the wood, and none in centuries. Perhaps your fear of it . . ."

"Shut your mouth and walk on fast," Geno growled.

Kelsey said no more, realizing that advice to be the best he would get out of the surly dwarf.

The sheer vibrancy of Tir na n'Og's primal colors sent Kelsey's spirit soaring, and sent Geno's eyes spinning, as they made their way along the forest paths. It was early summer, and Tir na n'Og was alive, bristling with the sounds of chattering birds and humming bees, the thumping of a rabbit, the splash of a beaver, and the continuing song of a dozen dancing brooks. To Kelsey, to all the Tylwyth Teg, this was home, this was Faerie at its most precious, its most natural and correct state. But to Geno, who lived his life in rocky caves in the rugged Dvergamal range, Tir na n'Og seemed foreign and unwelcoming. In his dwarfish homeland, Geno's ears were filled with the rhythmic sound of hammers ringing on heated metal, and with the unending roar of the waterfalls at the Firth of Buldre. Tir na n'Og's more subtle, but many times more varied, noises kept the dwarf off-balance and on his guard, his gnarly fingers clutching tightly to the handle of a hammer and his blue eyes darting to and fro, searching the impossible tangles to try to discern what creatures might be about.

Birds squawked in the boughs above them, dogging their every step with telltale shrieks.

"They are announcing our presence to my people," Kelsey explained to the nervous dwarf. "The birds are Tir na n'Og's sentries."

The elf had thought that the explanation would put Geno more at ease, but, if anything, the dwarf seemed even more agitated. Every few steps, he would skid to a stop, hop around, looking up, and yell, "Shut your beak!" which only agitated the birds even more. Kelsey was glad that the dwarf was behind him, and could not see his smile, as the chatter multiplied in their wake.

Wider indeed did the elf's smile grow when they came through a small lea, lined by huge pines, and the birdsong reached a new crescendo.

"I told you to shut your beaks!" unnerved Geno roared, but then the dwarf saw through the illusion, saw that the birds were not really birds at all, but were Tylwyth Teg, scores of them, grim-faced and with bows drawn as they watched from the branches.

"Oh," Geno offered, and he said not another word for the next several hours.

After they passed the meadow, Kelsey stopped many times and whistled up trees, waiting for the whistling reply, then starting off once more, often in a different direction. Geno figured that the elf was getting information about the leprechaun in some strange code, but he didn't ask about it, just followed in Kelsey's wake and hoped that the whole trip through the miserable forest would soon be at its end.

It was late afternoon when Kelsey crouched in a bush and motioned for Geno to come up beside him. The elf pointed across a small clearing to a huge tree, and to the leprechaun resting easily against the trunk, twirling a jeweled dagger atop one finger. His hair and beard were brown, fast going to gray, his smiling eyes shining the color of steel in the afternoon sun. His overcoat, too, was gray, and his breeches green. He absently kept the dagger spinning, its tip on the tip of his finger, while he filled a long-stemmed pipe with his other hand and popped it into his mouth. And all the while, the hard heels of Mickey's shiny black, curly-toed shoes tap-tapped a frolicking rhythm on a thick root of the gigantic oak.

Using hand signals and facial gestures, Kelsey communicated to Geno that he should wait for the elf to get into position, then charge straight ahead at Mickey. Knowing how tricky fleeing leprechauns could be, and wanting nothing more than to get out of the forest, Geno readily agreed, though he was more than a little unsettled when Kelsey slipped away, fast disappearing into the brush, leaving him alone.

Just a moment later, though it seemed an interminable period to Geno, the elf poked a hand up from the tangle to the side and back of Mickey. "Damned sprite!" Geno roared again, bursting from the brush, a hammer held high so that he could throw it at the ground in front of the leprechaun's feet if Mickey took flight.

"Ah, there ye are, me friend dwarf," Mickey said easily, not even upset or surprised enough to drop the spinning dagger off his finger. "Suren it took ye long enough. And yerself, too, Kelsey," Mickey said without turning around, just an instant before Kelsey's hand grabbed him by the collar.

Kelsey and Geno exchanged incredulous looks and Kelsey let go, though Geno kept his hammer ready. The elf looked closer at the sprite, wondering if he was merely an illusion, fearing that the real Mickey McMickey was standing on the edge of the clearing, or up in the oak, laughing at them as they stood there confused. None in all of Faerie, not even Robert or Ceridwen, could see through an illusion as well as the Tylwyth Teg, though, and as far as Kelsey could tell, this was indeed Mickey sitting before him.

"You expected us?" Kelsey asked, unsure of himself.

"I called ye, didn't I?" Mickey replied with a huff.

"Then it was you who took the armor and spear," Geno growled.

Mickey glanced over one shoulder, his eyes pointing the way to the leaf-covered items, sitting neatly against a tree at the clearing's edge.

Kelsey grabbed the leprechaun by the collar again and hoisted him to his feet, the jeweled dagger falling to the ground. "Do you realize what you have done?" the elf demanded.

"I have brought ye both out here, as I needed," Mickey replied easily.

"Geldion has come to Dilnamarra," Kelsey growled, roughly letting go of the sprite. "Connacht holds Baron Pwyll responsible for the theft, and thus, he will be hung at noontime tomorrow. You should look farther down the corridors behind the doors you open before you act."

"And yerself should look east, Kelsenellenelvial Gil-Ravadry!" Mickey roared back, and his uncharacteristic tone and use of Kelsey's formal name (which Mickey had never seemed able to properly pronounce before) gave Kelsey pause. He watched curiously as Mickey retrieved the dagger, holding it up for both Kelsey and Geno to see, and wearing an expression which showed that the dagger should explain everything.

To both the others, the weapon seemed out of place in the leprechaun's hand, first because leprechauns rarely carried weapons—and on the few occasions they might, it was usually a slingshot or shillelagh—and second because the man-sized weapon seemed so unwieldy, practically a short sword, to the diminutive sprite.

"Look east, Kelsenellenenen . . . Kelsey," Mickey said again, "to where Robert may have already taken wing."

"The dragon was banished to his castle for a hundred years," Kelsey started to argue, but all the while he stared at the dagger, and began to understand. "Where did you get that?"

"Gary Leger," Mickey explained.

"Stonebubbles," Geno spat, the very worst of dwarfish curses.

"Not the lad's fault," Mickey explained. "He taked it

from the tower, not the treasure room, and taked it for fighting, not for stealin'."

"But the theft releases Robert from his banishment," Kelsey reasoned. "And with Ceridwen banished and posing no deterrent to Robert . . ."

"The wyrm might well be already out and flying," Mickey finished. "And so did I bring ye all together, that we might put the wyrm back in his hole." All the while, Mickey was thinking not of Robert, but of his precious pot of gold, bartered to the dragon in exchange for his life before the friends had ever entered Robert's castle. Mickey didn't think it wise to tell the others that little detail, though, preferring to take the altruistic route this time, knowing that it would more likely appeal to the honorable Kelsey.

"If the dragon has discovered the missing dagger, then he will not likely be easy to put back in his hole," Kelsey reasoned, mimicking Mickey's words derisively.

"Oh, ye should better learn the terms of banishment before ye go insulting me," Mickey replied. "If we get the dagger back to the Giant's Thumb afore the change o' the season, then Robert'll be obliged to return." It was a plausible lie, and one that Mickey hoped would get him near to his pot of gold once more.

Kelsey's fair face screwed up incredulously. He had lived for centuries among the Tylwyth Teg, his people, among the most knowledgeable of races where ancient codes were concerned, and he had never heard of such a rule.

" 'Tis true," Mickey went on, puffing on the pipe to hide his smirk. Leprechauns were the best liars in all the world, but the Tylwyth Teg were the best at seeing through those lies.

"I have never heard of this rule," Kelsey answered.

"If Robert hasn't found the lost dagger and we get it

back, then no harm's done," Mickey replied. "And if he has found it, even if he's taken wing, then he'll be bound to return."

"And if you are wrong?"

Mickey shrugged. "Ye got a better plan? Ye meaning to go off and fight the wyrm?"

"Stonebubbles," Geno spat again.

Kelsey didn't immediately answer, caught in Mickey's web. He certainly did not wish to fight Robert, if that could in any way be avoided.

"And so I bringed ye together," Mickey went on. "It's our own fault that Robert's about, and our own job to put him back where he rightly belongs."

"You could have just asked," Geno grumbled, and he, too, seemed subdued, caught in Mickey's sticky web.

"I needed to get ye all together," Mickey argued. "And I didn't even know where yerself had gotten off to. I figured to let Pwyll do me hunting for me, and it seems like he catched ye good."

Geno grumbled and lowered his eyes, preferring to keep his memories of the wild fight in Braemar's Snoozing Sprite tavern private.

"At what cost?" Kelsey demanded. "Your games have put Baron Pwyll in jeopardy."

Mickey chewed on the end of his long-stemmed pipe for a few moments, thinking it through. "Then we'll just have to take the good and fat Baron along with us," he decided, his big-toothed and pearly smile beaming once more.

Mickey's obvious confidence set Kelsey back on his heels and ended that debate—for the time. "And what of the armor?" Kelsey demanded, determined to find some problem with Mickey's simple reasoning.

"Oh, I'll be filling it soon enough," the leprechaun replied, his gray eyes twinkling mischievously. "Don't ye worry."

4 † Click Against the Window

Diane lay across Gary's bed and Gary sat on the floor, both of them tired as midnight approached. Fleetwood Mac's *Tusk* played softly in the room, and candles burned low while Stevie Nicks rolled through the haunting lyrics of *Storms*.

> *Every night that goes between,*
> *I feel a little less*

She was singing to Gary, about Gary, the young man felt, singing the sad truth that Gary was indeed beginning to feel a little less with every passing day away from the enchanted land of Faerie. Gary remembered it all so vividly, remembered Mickey and Kelsey, and surly Geno. Remembered the vibrant colors of Tir na n'Og and the mud-filled streets of Dilnamarra. Gary thought of Faerie every night as he was drifting off to sleep, usually while this same CD cooed softly at the edges of his consciousness.

"They're hitting Baghdad again!" came a call from downstairs, Gary's father watching the coverage on the late news.

Diane shook her head in disgust. She was one of the few people Gary knew who openly expressed her disdain for the war. You could throw every logical argument at Diane for fighting the war, from oil reserves to the need to defeat terrorism, and she'd just smile and say, "When historians look back on this, they'll see that it could have been avoided, just like every other war." No argument could shake Diane from her convictions.

A tough lady, and that's what Gary loved most about her.

"They're creating their own Robert," Gary mused aloud, thinking of how the media, probably with government's full support, had made the leader of the enemy country out to be the worst criminal since Adolf Hitler. There were no dragons in Gary's world, no real ones, anyway, so it seemed that, from time to time, people had this need to create one. Gary Leger had met a dragon, a real dragon, and his fear of ever meeting a real one again far outweighed his all-too-human need for the excitement.

"What?" Diane asked. "Who's Robert?"

Gary thought long and hard about an answer to that simple response. Many times he had considered telling Diane about his trip to Faerie, about showing her the book and trusting in her to believe in him. "Nothing," he said at length. "Just an evil king I read about somewhere."

The answer satisfied weary Diane, who was already drifting off to sleep. She didn't make it a habit of falling asleep in Gary's room, but the door was open and his parents didn't mind, and the quiet music was so inviting . . .

Something snapped against the window, jolting Diane from her sleep. The candles were out now, the digital clock reading 2:30. The room was perfectly quiet, and dark, except for the dim light of the streetlight coming in through the edges of the front window's shade. As her eyes adjusted, Diane could make out Gary's silhouette, propped against the bed in the same position he had been in when they were awake.

Puk!

"Gary," Diane whispered. She reached out and jostled his shoulder a little, and he responded by shaking his head and looking back to the bed.

"Huh?" he replied dreamily.

Puk!

"The window," Diane said. "Something's clicking against the window!"

"Huh?" Gary rubbed his bleary eyes and looked to the window, just in time to hear yet another click. "It's probably just a squirrel on the roof," Gary announced rather loudly as a yawn intermingled with the words. He pulled himself up and moved across the floor, trying to appear bold. He moved the shade aside and looked out, but the front yard and the street seemed empty.

"There's nothing out there," he said firmly, turning back into the room.

Puk!

Diane reached for the light as Gary pulled up the shade, lifting the bottom half of the window as soon as the weak springs of the old shade had moved it out of the way. "Don't turn the light on!" he told her, knowing that he wouldn't be able to see outside if she did. With nothing revealed, he put the screen up, too, and leaned out, his hands resting on the windowsill as he scanned the front and side yard.

"There's nothing out here . . ." he started to protest, but he stopped in midsentence, the words caught in his throat as he looked down to regard several tiny arrows protruding from the wooden sill.

"No way," the young man breathed. Gary's mind rushed in a hundred different directions at once. Could it be true? Had the fairies come back for him? He knew instinctively that this was a signal, that a sprite was summoning him, probably to go down to the woods out back, to the same spot from where he had once been taken to the enchanted realm.

"What is it?" Diane demanded, coming to within a few feet behind Gary.

It, Gary thought, is time for some revelations. He could tell her now, he mused, could make her believe him with evidence that her stubborn and rational side could not dispute.

"Come here," Gary said, motioning for Diane to join him. He pointed out the little darts and Diane bent low to the sill, shaking her head.

"Some kind of pellet?" she asked.

"Arrows," Gary corrected.

Diane looked at him blankly, then peered low to better regard the darts. "Who could shoot an arrow that small?" she asked incredulously, but then she nodded as if she understood. "Oh, from a blowgun?" she asked, remembering the stories Gary had told her about his blowgun fights at the office.

"No," Gary replied cryptically, trying to build the suspense so that his answer, when he gave it in full, would not be too overwhelming.

"From one of those—what do you call them?—crossbows?" Diane reasoned.

"Nope," Gary replied, working hard to keep the mounting excitement out of his voice. "From a longbow."

Diane looked back to the tiny dart, her face twisted in confusion. "Couldn't be too long a bow," she said with a smirk.

Gary thought of going to his stereo cabinet and showing Diane the leprechaun-transformed version of *The Hobbit*, of showing her the flowing script and blurting out everything that had happened to him.

Take it slow, he reminded himself, thinking of his own doubts even after the sprites had abducted him, even after his first full day in the land of Faerie. Gary had lived the adventure, and yet it had taken him a long time to believe that it had actually occurred—even after it was over and he found himself waking in the woods out back, only the still-transformed book had proven to him that the whole thing hadn't been a dream.

But he had to make Diane believe it, he told himself. It was important to him, vital to him, that someone else, especially Diane, believe his tale and maybe share another adventure with him. He took a deep breath, turned on the room's light, and retrieved the book from the stereo cabinet, handing it over to Diane.

"Yeah," she prompted, not understanding.

"Open it."

Diane's eyes widened as she considered the flowing runes on the strange pages, not at all what she would expect, of course, from a printed book. She looked to Gary and shook her head, totally confused.

"I took that to a professor at the college," Gary explained. "Dr. Keough, who knows Irish history better than anyone else around here. It's Gaelic, as far as he could tell, but a form of the language he had never seen before. He couldn't decide if it was some hybrid of the language, or some pure form."

"You've got Tolkien in Gaelic?" Diane asked breathlessly. "This must be a collector's edition, and must be worth a fortune."

"It's not a collector's edition," Gary replied. "But it's probably worth more than a fortune."

"What are you talking about?"

"Look at the beginning," Gary explained. He went to his book shelf and took out the second book in the series, opening it to the credits page. "Same publisher, same edition, even the same printing," Gary explained, showing Diane the identical information in both books.

She continued scrutinizing the pages, looking for some clue, and Gary wondered if it was time to spring the truth on her. He trusted her, and knew that she wouldn't ridicule him (once she realized that he was serious) even if she didn't believe him. But Gary simply couldn't figure out where to begin. Wild ideas came into his thoughts every time he tried to think of an opening sentence. He imagined his name spread across the headlines of tabloid newspapers:

Lancashire Man Abducted by Fairies
Gary Leger: I Was Impregnated by a Leprechaun

Gary laughed in spite of his dilemma, drawing Diane's attention away from the book.

"What's going on?" she demanded, the perfect cue, but again Gary couldn't find the words to respond.

"I can't tell you," he admitted. He looked back to the open window. "But I think I can show you."

They rushed through the house, out the front door, and Gary led the way down the street, towards the black line of trees, the beginning of the small wood.

"If you wanted to make out, couldn't we have gone for a ride?" Diane asked him, resisting the urgent pull of his hand and not liking the look of those dark and ominous trees.

"This is better than making out," Gary replied excitedly, not taking the time to choose his words more carefully.

Diane tugged her hand free and skidded to a stop on the road. When Gary turned back to her, she was standing with her arms crossed over her chest, one foot tapping on the tar, and her head tilted to the side. The dim light of the distant streetlights did nothing to diminish the appearance of her scowl.

"What?" Gary asked blankly.

"Better than making out?" Diane replied, emphasizing every syllable.

"No, no," Gary stammered. "You don't understand, but come on, and you will!"

"Better than making out?" Diane asked again, but caught up in Gary's overboiling enthusiasm, she accepted his hand once again and followed him down the street and into the woods.

It was pitch black in there, but Gary knew his way, had grown up playing in these woods. They moved down the dirt end of his parents' street, turned onto a fire road, and soon moved through the blueberry bushes, past the wide break atop the high ground overlooking the area that had been cleared for an elementary school.

The view there was beautiful, with the shining dots of stars dotting the sky, and Diane slowed, her eyes drinking it in.

This was the spot where Gary had encountered the fairy ring, but not where he had first encountered the sprite. He allowed Diane a few moments of the grand view, while he snooped around, looked for the telltale lights of dancing fairies.

"Come on," he said at length, taking Diane's hand once more. "Down there." He started along the path once more, heading for where it dipped down the side of a thickly wooded vale.

Diane resisted, slapped at a mosquito that had stung her on the neck. "What's going on?" she asked again. "What does this have to do with those arrows, and that book?"

"I can't explain it," Gary replied. "You wouldn't believe . . . you wouldn't understand it. Not yet. But if you'll just come along, you'll see it for yourself."

"I always pick the nuts," Diane muttered under her breath, and she took up Gary's hand and followed him down the dirt path.

They came to a mossy banking—Diane had to take Gary's word that it was a mossy banking, for she couldn't see a thing. He plopped down, and pulled her hand, patting the ground to indicate that she should sit behind him.

The minutes passed uneventfully, quietly, except for the rising hum of hungry mosquitos gathering about them, smelling human food.

"Well?" Diane prompted.

"Sssh!" Gary replied.

"I'm getting eaten alive," she protested.

"Sssh."

And so they sat in silence, save for the annoying buzz and the occasional slaps. Their eyes adjusted enough to the dark so that they could at least make out each other's black silhouette. Diane nuzzled into Gary's shoulder and he instinctively put his arm around her.

"We should have taken the car," she whispered.

"Sssh." Gary's tone grew more agitated, more impatient, aptly reflecting the frustration building within him.

The minutes became an hour, a chill breeze blew by, and Diane nuzzled closer. A twist of her head put her lips against Gary's neck, and she gave him a long kiss, then moved her head up so that her lips brushed lightly against his ear.

"Do you want some ice cream?" she asked teasingly.

Gary sighed and pulled away, causing Diane to straighten.

"Do you want them to watch us?" Gary asked sharply.

Diane leaned back from him.

"Well?" Gary asked.

"Who?"

"Them!" Gary snapped back, pointing to the empty darkness. He shook his head and closed his eyes. When he had seen the arrows, his hopes had soared. But now . . .

Gary desperately wanted it to be true, wanted the sprites

to come back for him, to take him—and Diane, too—into Faerie for some new grand adventure. To get him out of the world of month-ends and highway games.

Diane looked confused, even a little scared. "Who?" she demanded again.

"The sprites," Gary answered softly and bluntly.

Diane was silent for a long moment. "Sprites?" she asked, and her voice had dropped at least an octave.

"Fairies!" Gary snarled at her, snarled at the obvious doubt in her tone and at his own mounting doubts.

"What the hell are you talking about?" Diane replied. "And why is it that I seem to keep asking you the same questions over and over without getting any real answers?"

"Because I can't explain it!" Gary cried in frustration.

"Try."

"That book," Gary began, after taking a deep breath to clear his thoughts and steady his nerves. "It wasn't printed the way you saw it. It was normal, perfectly normal type-setting."

"Then how did it change?" The obvious doubt in her tone stung the young man.

"A leprechaun waved his hand."

"Cut it out," replied Diane.

"I'm not kidding," Gary said. "That's why I brought you down here. You don't believe me, you can't believe me. Hell, I didn't believe myself—until I saw that book."

Diane started to ask a question, but stopped and held her arms up high to the sides in surrender.

"You'll have to see it," Gary explained. "The words are too impossible."

To Diane's credit, she didn't reply, didn't tell Gary that he was out of his mind, and didn't rise to leave. She took Gary's hand and moved him back beside her.

"Just give me this night," he asked her. "Then, maybe, I'll be able to explain it all."

Diane pulled him closer, put her head back on his shoulder. Her sigh was resigned, but she held her place and Gary knew that she would trust in him, despite the mosquitos, despite the fact that, by all appearances, the young man was out of his mind.

A gentle singing awakened Gary some time later, some time not far before the dawn.

"Diane," he whispered, nudging the sleeping woman. She didn't move.

The fairy song drifted on the breeze, too soft for Gary to make out the individual words, though he doubted that he would understand the arcane language anyway.

"Diane." He gave her a harder nudge, but still she didn't move.

"Come on," Gary prompted as loudly as he dared, and he rubbed his hand across Diane's back, then stopped abruptly as he felt the tiny dart sticking from her shoulder.

"Oh, no," he groaned, and Diane's next snore came as an appropriate reply. The fairies had put her to sleep.

Gary rose into a crouch, saw the flicker of tiny lights, like fireflies, atop the ridge, back near to the blueberry bushes. He half-walked, half-crawled up the slope, the lights and the song growing more intense with every passing foot. And then he saw them, a ring of dancing fairies, like tiny elfish dolls barely a foot tall. They twirled and leaped, spun graceful little circles, while singing in their squeaky yet melodic voices. This was the gateway to the enchanted land.

"Get in," came a chirping voice, the words running so fast that it took Gary a long moment to sort them out. He looked down to see a small sprite standing beside him.

"You came for me?" Gary stated as much as asked.

"Get in!"

"What took you so long?" Gary demanded, wishing that they had arrived hours before. The sprite replied with an incredulous look, and only then did Gary realize that the few hundred yards back to his parents' house must have seemed like miles to tiny sprite legs.

Gary looked back down the trail, to where Diane was sleeping soundly. He needed her to witness this, to come with him to Faerie.

"Get in!" The squeaky voice sounded more insistent with each demand.

"Not without her," Gary replied, looking from the vale to the sprite. The sprite was holding something, Gary noticed, though he couldn't quite make it out in the darkness. His mind told him what his eyes could not, but too late, for then he felt the sting of an arrow against his calf.

"Dammit," he groaned, feeling for the dart and then tearing it free. A few moments later, his vision went double, and through blurry eyes he saw two rings of dancing fairies.

"Dammit," he said again, and for some reason, he was down on his knees. "Diane?"

"Just you!" the now-unseen sprite answered emphatically.

"Dammit!" But despite the protest, Gary was crawling, moving slowly and inevitably for the fairy ring. There he collapsed, his strength drained by the sleeping poison, his legs too weak to support him.

Gary Leger wouldn't need his legs for this next portion of his journey.

5 † The Rescue

He knew as soon as he opened his eyes on a glorious dawn that Diane was no longer beside him. He knew by the vivid colors, almost too rich for his eyes, that he had come again to the enchanted realm of Faerie, and he was not surprised at all a moment later to see Mickey McMickey, Kelsey, and Geno staring down at him as he lay on a patch of thick grass, surrounded by blueberry bushes.

Still groggy from the pixie poison, Gary stretched and yawned and forced himself to sit up.

"No time for sleeping, lad," Mickey said to him. "Baron Pwyll's to be hung at noon, and we've to get ye in the armor and get to Dilnamarra in a hurry."

Gary's stare took on a blank appearance as he tried to orient himself to his new surroundings and tried to digest the sudden rush of news. The Baron . . . the armor . . . Dilnamarra . . .

Geno grabbed him by the shoulder, and with strength far beyond what his four-foot-tall body should have possessed, easily hoisted, flung, Gary to his feet.

"Comes from eating rocks?" a shaken Gary asked Mickey, remembering what the leprechaun had told him of dwarfish power.

"Now ye're catching on," Mickey said with a wide grin. "There's a good lad."

"My welcome, Gary Leger," Kelsey added solemnly,

and from what Gary knew of Kelsey's aloof demeanor, that seemed like the warmest greeting of all.

Gary took a moment to look all around, to bathe in Faerie's preternatural colors and in the continual song that seemed to fill the ear, just below the level of conscious hearing. Music had been an important part of Gary's life in his own world, and the feelings bestowed by the best of the songs that he heard came close, but did not match, the subliminal and unending magical notes that filled Faerie's clear air.

Mickey tugged at daydreaming Gary's belt, pointing out that Kelsey and Geno had already started away.

When they arrived at the great oak tree and retrieved the armor, Gary was suddenly relieved that Diane had not come with him. Up this tree lived Leshiye, the wood nymph, a gorgeous and ultimately seductive creature with whom Gary had shared a most pleasurable encounter on his last visit to Faerie. Inevitably, Gary's eyes now drifted up the wide-spread branches, and he put a hand to one ear, wondering if he might catch a hint of Leshiye's enchanting and enticing song.

Kelsey tapped Gary on the shoulder, and when the young man turned about to regard the elf, he looked into the most uncompromising glare he had ever seen. It was Kelsey who had climbed this very tree to pull Gary from Leshiye's tender, and inevitably deadly, clutches. The elf had been angry then, as dangerous as Gary had ever seen him, and Kelsey's glare now came as a clear warning to Faerie's visitor that he should concentrate on the business at hand and leave any sought-after pleasures for later.

"Why not give back the armor, instead of putting that one in it?" Geno asked suddenly, drawing the attention of the other three. "Geldion would let Pwyll go and I could get back to my home."

"But then Geldion would take the artifacts back to Connacht," Mickey reasoned. In truth, the dwarf's plan seemed simple, but Mickey couldn't let it come to pass, not if he wanted to retrieve his pot of gold. Worried that pragmatic Geno might spoil everything, Mickey found some unexpected support from Kelsey.

"We shall need the armor and spear if it comes to battle with Robert," the elf explained.

Geno snorted. "Let Geldion and Pwyll raise an army to battle the dragon," he said.

Mickey chewed his lip as the situation seemed to hang on a fine wire.

"No," Kelsey said flatly, and Mickey tried hard to keep his relieved sigh quiet. "Robert is our responsibility, since it was our actions that loosed him on the land. It seems a simple thing to return the item to the dragon's lair and force him to honor the terms of banishment."

"The dragon's out?" Gary asked incredulously.

"Just a small issue," Mickey replied, straightening his tam-o'-shanter.

Gary looked to Mickey and shrugged, hopelessly confused, but the leprechaun put a finger to pursed lips, calling for silent patience.

"Your responsibility, elf!" Geno balked, poking a stubby finger Kelsey's way. "The quest was yours, never mine, and you bear the responsibility of the theft."

"What?" Gary mouthed silently to Mickey, though he thought that he was beginning to catch on. The word "theft" led Gary to believe that Mickey had taken something from Robert, something that had broken the dragon's indenture. The notion that the friends had somehow loosed a dragon on the land began to weigh heavily on the young man's shoulders, began to make him think that going right back to the forest behind his mother's house might not be such a disappointment.

"Our responsibility," Kelsey promptly corrected. "And

we, together, shall see it through, shall put the wyrm back in his hole, and perhaps right many other wrongs in the land along the way."

Mickey was smiling easily then, realizing that he had indeed appealed to Kelsey's overdeveloped sense of honor.

"Pretty words, elf," Geno said grimly. "Let us hear them again in the face of an angry dragon." Despite his grumbling, though, the dwarf was the first to move for a metal plate.

Gary felt the balance of the magnificent armor as Geno and the others went about the task of strapping it on. On his initial visit to Faerie, when he had first donned the armor, it had felt bulky and he had felt clumsy in it. Gary had spent the last five years strengthening his muscles, though, preparing himself for this return, and now, as the armor fell into place, his body remembered. When the last piece of metal plating was strapped securely into its place, Gary felt no more encumbered than if he had been wearing a set of heavy clothes and a long leather coat.

Gary lifted the huge and ornate helm and tucked it under one arm. This was the only piece that didn't fit well—Cedric's head must have been huge indeed—and Gary saw no reason to put it on just yet. Then he went for the spear, pausing a long moment to study it, to bask in the view of its splendor. It was long, taller than Gary, and forged of black metal, with a wide tip that flared out back at the top of the handle and turned around on both sides into secondary points, making the whole appear almost like a distorted trident. It looked as if it would weigh a hundred pounds, but so balanced was it, and so heavily magicked, that Gary could easily hurl it fifty feet.

"Well met again, young sprout," came a call in Gary's mind, a telepathic greeting from the sentient spear. Gary let a reply drift from his thoughts, and then, almost as if they had never been apart, he and the weapon were com-

municating continuously, subconsciously, each becoming extensions of the other. It was in this telepathic joining that Gary Leger had learned to fight, that Gary Leger had come to see the land of Faerie as one of Faerie might, and make his battle decisions quickly and correctly when the situation demanded. The spear had given to Gary a different point of reference, and the confidence to act on his newfound instincts. When Ceridwen had caught them on the mountain outside Robert's castle, when all seemed lost, Gary had listened to those instincts and had hurled the spear into the witch's belly, saving them all and banishing Ceridwen to her island home.

"Lead on," Gary said to Kelsey as he took up the magnificent spear. The elf shook his head, put his slender fingers to his lips, and blew a shrill whistle, and a moment later, three horses and a pony burst into the clearing by the oak, flipping their heads about and snorting (Gary almost expected to see fire puffing from the nostrils of the mighty steeds). All four were pure white, and bedecked in an array of tinkling golden bells that rang out in perfect harmony as the beasts jostled about. Rich satiny purple blankets peeked out from under their smooth and delicate saddles.

"A bit noisy, don't ye think?" Mickey asked Kelsey.

"The bells ring only when they are commanded to ring," Kelsey replied. "No mount walks as quietly as a steed of Tir na n'Og, and no mount runs as fast."

"Not likely," Geno grumbled, eyeing the pony with disdain.

Kelsey and Mickey regarded the dwarf for a long while, not understanding what he was talking about, until the pony pawed near to Geno and the gruff and fearless dwarf verily leaped away, his hand snapping down to grab at a hammer.

"He's afraid of horses," Mickey chuckled, but his smile

wrapped tight against his long-stemmed pipe when Geno turned his glare Mickey's way.

"Dilnamarra is many miles away," Kelsey said to the dwarf. "We have no time to walk. You have ridden before," the elf reasoned, for horseback was the primary means of travel in Faerie.

"Ye rode the giant when I made him look like a mule," Mickey added.

"I rode the cart the giant pulled," Geno promptly corrected.

"I don't know how to ride," Gary cut in, looking apologetically to his friends. The young man thought himself incredibly stupid. He had spent five years in his own world preparing himself in case he ever got back to Faerie, and he had never even thought to take a riding lesson!

"Horses aren't so common in my world," he tried to explain.

"And when ye got here the last time, ye didn't know how to fight, either," Mickey reminded him. "Ye learned, Gary Leger, and so ye'll learn again. Besides, don't ye worry, I'll be up in yer saddle beside ye."

Gary looked doubtfully to the horse that had padded near to him, but shrugged and nodded Mickey's way. He started for the saddle, plopped the cumbersome helmet on his head, and put his foot up to the stirrup.

"From the left side," Kelsey corrected.

"Uh-oh," Mickey muttered under his breath.

With a single fluid motion, Kelsey was up in his seat, taking the reins of the riderless horse beside him as well. Gary had to struggle a bit more—the leggings of the armor didn't quite spread wide enough for an easy mount—but he managed to get into place, and Mickey floated up in front of him, taking a comfortable seat between Gary and the horse's muscled neck.

"The lad can do it," Mickey said to Geno. "Are ye not as brave?"

Geno grabbed the pony's bridle and pulled the beast's face right up to his own, nose to nose. The dwarf started to speak several times, but seemed as though he had no idea of what to say to a pony. "Behave!" he barked at last, sounding ridiculous, but when he turned his unrelenting scowl about to regard his friends, they all three quickly bit back their chuckles.

When the dwarf finally settled on the pony's back, Kelsey nodded to the others and clicked his teeth, and the mounts leaped away, hooves pounding as they thundered through the thick brush, bells ringing gaily, though it seemed to the stunned Gary Leger that not a leaf was shaking in their wake.

The wild run through Tir na n'Og was among the most exciting things Gary had ever experienced. The mounts seemed out of control, running of their own free will. Once his mount headed straight for the trunk of a wide elm, head down in a full gallop. Gary screamed and covered his eyes with his arm. Mickey laughed, and the horse veered slightly at the last moment, passing within inches of the elm. Gary fumbled to straighten the helmet, then looked back and saw that Geno's pony, following closely, had taken the same route, and the dwarf, who apparently had tried to jump off, was now struggling to right himself in his saddle, complaining all the while.

"Keep low in the saddle," Kelsey warned from the side, seeing the man upright, and Gary bent as far over as he could. Still, he felt more than one low-hanging branch brush across his shoulders, and the long spear cut a swath in the foliage along the tight side.

Gary heard the singing of running water somewhere up ahead. A moment later, his helmet spun around on his head and he felt as if he was flying, and then he heard the sound of the water fading fast behind him.

"Unbelievable," he muttered, straightening the helm.

"That's the fun of it," Mickey quickly replied, still sitting easily in the crook between Gary and the horse's neck. "Say, lad, ye didn't happen to bring me another book, now, did ye?"

Gary smiled and shook his head. He wished that he had brought several books, the rest of Tolkien's series, at least, so that he might hear Mickey's comments as the leprechaun read them—read them as if they were factual historical books. Gary smiled again as he realized that they just might be, from the perspective of Faerie's folks.

The party charged out of Tir na n'Og just a few minutes later, thundering across the hedge-lined fields, causing the many sheep and hairy "heeland coos," as Mickey called the highland cows, to pause and look up to regard their passing.

It all seemed a wondrous blur to Gary, the miles rolling under him as surely as if he had been flying down Route 2 after work back home. But even with the rag-top down, the sensations in the Mustang could not come close to equaling the thrill of riding this near-wild steed, a beast that Gary might coax, but certainly could not control.

Some time later they came in sight of Dilnamarra, the single stone tower that served as Baron Pwyll's keep poking above the rolling plain and the low wooden shops and cottages. On Kelsey's command, the magical bells stopped ringing, and the elf slowed, bringing them in at an easy and quieter pace.

A crowd had gathered at the muddy crossroads in the center of the small village, gathered around the gallows, to which a trembling and blubbering Pwyll was now being dragged.

Kelsey led the others down around a low hill, where

they left the horses and crept up on foot, pausing to watch from a hedgerow a hundred feet down the north road from the gathering, with the squat tower directly across the gallows from them.

"We've come not a moment too soon," Mickey remarked. "But how're we to get in there and get away?"

"If we had walked, our concerns would soon be at their end," Geno grumbled, drawing angry stares from both Kelsey and Mickey.

"There are a lot of soldiers down there," Gary remarked.

"Aye," Mickey added, "and most o' them wearing the colors of Connacht." He tapped Gary's hand, clutching tightly to the magnificent spear. "We're for needing tricks, not weapons," he said, and Gary nodded and eased his grip.

"What tricks do you have, leprechaun?" Geno asked gruffly. "The fat one will be hanging by his neck in a ten-count." It was true enough; even as they crouched and tried to figure out a plan, Prince Geldion was reading from an unrolled parchment while a contingent of his men prodded and kicked the reluctant Pwyll up the stairs.

"Will the crowd help us?" Gary asked eagerly, picturing some grand revolt with himself at the lead, dressed as Cedric Donigarten, the most famous hero of Faerie.

"Not likely," Mickey answered, bursting Gary's daydreams. "They're commonfolk, and not likely to find the courage to go against Connacht, even if yerself's wearing the armor of their hero of old."

"You must get in close to the Baron," Kelsey said suddenly to Geno, stringing his bow as he spoke. "My arrows have cut ropes before."

Geno laughed at him.

"Geldion and the others will believe that Pwyll is hanging," Kelsey, undaunted, said to the dwarf. Kelsey turned to Mickey with a questioning stare, and the leprechaun understood what role the elf meant for him to play.

Mickey looked back doubtfully to the gallows, where a soldier was putting the hangman's noose around Pwyll's neck. If he had his pot of gold, his source of magical energies, Mickey could have woven an illusion that would have curious onlookers staring at the hanging man for a week. But he didn't have that precious pot, and without it, the leprechaun wasn't sure that his magical imagery would be precise enough to fool half the people around the gallows.

"I see no better way," he answered, though, and he rubbed his plump little hands together and began weaving the words of a spell.

Geno continued to smirk doubtfully and shake his head.

"I will go if you're afraid," Gary offered, and he shifted away as the dwarf's disbelieving and threatening scowl fell over him. With a growl, Geno was up and running, cutting from bush to bush, then darting behind a water trough just a few feet behind the back ring of onlookers. There, Geno spat in his hands and tamped down his powerful legs like a hunting cat, preparing to rush out at the exact moment.

Gary shot a mischievous wink Mickey's way. "A little motivation for the dwarf," he explained.

"It's good to have ye back, lad," the leprechaun replied with a chuckle.

Gary went out next from the hedgerow, slipping closer to the crowd, spear in hand. He heard Kelsey whistle softly and looked back to see the horses walking in behind the elf and Mickey. Then Gary turned his attention fully to the scene ahead, inching up as close as he could get to the anxious crowd. He noted the thickness of the rope and began to doubt Kelsey's plan, began to doubt that any arrow, no matter how perfect the shot, could cut that hemp

cleanly. He heard Geldion complete the damning procla-
mation, labeling Pwyll as a thief and a traitor to the throne.

"And we hang traitors!" the Prince cried out, a pointed
reminder to everyone in attendance. "Executioner!"

A whine escaped doomed Pwyll's thick lips; the executioner's hand went to the long lever at the side of the gallows platform. It all happened at once, suddenly, with
Geno hopping the trough and plowing through the onlookers, cutting a wide wake with his broad shoulders, an arrow splitting the air above him as the trap door dropped
open, and Gary finding himself instinctively heaving the
great spear behind the arrow in its flight.

Kelsey's arrow hit the rope squarely, cutting an edge.
Still the hemp held, and Pwyll's neck would surely have
snapped, had not Gary's spear completed the task, its wide
head easily shaving the rope in half as it flew past.

The crowd roared, a unified groan.

Baron Pwyll felt the sudden, sharp jerk, felt as if his
head was about to be ripped off, and then he was falling,
turning horizontally, and looking up to see himself hanging by the neck!

"I am dead!" he cried, and he was surprised to hear the
sound of his own voice. He slammed against the ground,
but was back up again, seeming to float in the air as he
continued to stare blankly at his own corpse.

"You should be," Geno agreed, grunting under the tremendous weight as he whisked the Baron away.

Poor confused Pwyll didn't know what to think, caught
halfway between what his senses were telling him and
what his mind, what Mickey's illusions, were telling him.

From the far side of the crowd, Gary blinked, for he
hadn't witnessed any of it. Horror and revulsion welled up
inside him as he stared at the hanging and twitching
Baron. But then Gary noticed Geno, his arms full of a sec-

ond Pwyll, rushing out the back side of the gallows, and
Gary remembered Mickey.

He looked through the illusion then, saw the severed
rope, the dwarf running off, and his spear angled out of the
ground twenty feet to the other side of the gallows. No one
else was moving, though, caught up in the illusion, and
Geldion hadn't called for any to block the fleeing dwarf's
path.

A rumble of confusion and a cry of alarm began its inevitable roll through the crowd. Up on the platform,
Geldion and his soldiers glanced all around, trying to see
what the commotion was about, for to their eyes, Pwyll
was hanging securely right below them.

Gary nearly jumped out of his armor when he felt
something tap his shoulder. He turned to see his mount,
down on its front knees, tossing its head anxiously. Gary
hadn't even put his leg all the way over the beast's back
before it took flight, flying around the side of the
gathering.

More and more people were beginning to recognize the
deception, beginning to point this way and that, mostly to
the northeast. Prince Geldion looked down through the
trap door and screamed in shock.

"Cedric Donigarten is come!" one villager cried, spying
the armored rider.

"Woe to Connacht!" cried another.

"Kill him!" Geldion yelled, stuttering over the words,
spittle streaming from his thin lips. "We have been deceived! Oh, devil-spawned magic!"

"The game's over," Gary whispered, bending low and
urging his steed on. He saw Geno link up with Kelsey and
Mickey, the leprechaun up behind Kelsey. The dwarf
heaved Pwyll up on the spare horse, then rushed to his
pony.

A crossbow quarrel clicked off the shoulder-plating of Gary's armor. The road before Gary seemed clear, though, except that one soldier had rushed out of the keep's open door. The man had gone to the spear and was now tearing it from the ground.

"Dammit," Gary growled, and his steed seemed to read his thoughts, veering straight for the man. Gary thought he would have to run the man down, trample him flat, then wheel about and retrieve the spear on the second pass.

"Hurry, young sprout!" he heard in his mind, and he watched in thrilled amazement as a flashing jolt of energy coursed through the spear handle, hurling the soldier to the ground a dozen feet away and sending the weapon flying high into the air.

Gary caught the free-flying weapon in midstride, heard the sitting soldier cry out in terror as the horse bore down at him. But the beast of Tir na n'Og was intelligent indeed and not evil, and it lifted its legs and easily cleared the ducking man, landing solidly far beyond him and thundering about in a tight turn to get away from the occupied keep and catch up to the fleeing companions.

Gary held on for all his life, nearly went flying free as the horse wheeled. He heard a whistle in the air as another quarrel flew past.

"Mounts! Mounts!" one soldier was yelling above the din of the frenzied villagers, the angry shouts of Prince Geldion, and the sudden blare of horns.

Another quarrel zipped past and Gary bent as low as he could go, trying to present a small target. He saw the cloud of dust ahead as his sweating steed approached his companions, heard the tumult behind him fast fading.

He came up between Geno's pony and the horse bearing Pwyll, and nearly laughed aloud, despite the danger, when he saw that the Baron still had the noose and length of rope around his neck. Three long strides brought Gary beyond those two, up beside Kelsey and Mickey.

"The illusion did not hold!" the elf was claiming to the leprechaun.

"Didn't say it would," Mickey replied casually, puffing on his long-stemmed pipe—which Gary thought an amazing feat, given that they were in full gallop. He noted that there seemed to be an underlying tension behind the leprechaun's carefree façade, and thought it curious, as did Kelsey, that Mickey, who had created illusions to fool a dragon for many minutes, had not been able to trick the crowd for any length of time.

"They're coming!" Geno called from behind. Kelsey pulled up his horse and the others followed the lead, turning about to regard the now-distant keep. They saw the dust beginning to rise on the road back to the north and could hear the distant dull rumble of many hooves.

"How come every time we leave that place, there's a Prince chasing us?" Gary asked.

"Oh, my," groaned the thoroughly flustered Baron Pwyll. He growled repeatedly, getting all tangled up as he tried to get the noose off his neck. "Now I am in serious trouble."

Gary blinked in amazement; Geno snorted.

"More trouble than hanging?" Mickey asked, equally incredulous.

"Fear not," Kelsey assured them all, turning his mount back to the open road to the south. "No horse can match the pace of the mounts of Tir na n'Og!"

The elf handed Mickey over to Gary and kicked his steed away. Geno's pony flew past, with Pwyll's horse coming right behind.

"Ready for a run, lad?" Mickey asked, settling into his seat in front of Gary.

"Do I have a choice?" Gary replied, smiling.

Mickey glanced around the man, to the north and the approaching cavalry. "No," he said easily, puffing the pipe once more as Gary loosed his grip on the reins and the powerful steed of Tir na n'Og charged off.

6 † A Sense of Strength

Two score of villagers, peat farmers mostly, gathered on the western road out of Drochit to watch the curious gnome's departure. Gerbil had brought grave news to the Duncan Drochit, Lord of the town; word that mighty Robert the dragon had taken wing again, that darkness would soon descend over all the land. In return, the gnome had been given some news of his own, information about the reforging of Cedric's spear and the subsequent theft of the artifacts.

It didn't take a clever gnome to suspect that the two unusual events might be related (especially since Robert had reportedly been the one to supply the breath for reforging the spear), and so, with Duncan Drochit's promise that Braemar would be alerted, Gerbil had struck out west instead of south, for Dilnamarra and the riddle that might shed some light on the appearance of the dreaded wyrm.

The quadricycle gained speed steadily, despite the mud left over from an early morning rain and the load of supplies Gerbil had strapped into a basket behind his seat. Less than a hundred yards out of town, he had to stop and wait, though, as a shepherd herded his flock across the road, an all-too-common scene that would be repeated four times over the next few hours, with poor anxious Gerbil making sporadic headway to the west. Then he cleared the immediate farming areas near to the village, came into the

68

more wild region between Drochit and Dilnamarra, and made more steady progress.

"I must figure a way to smooth out this road," the easily distracted inventor said to himself, his little legs pumping tirelessly as he bumped and slid along the uneven cart path. And so Gerbil filled the hours with thoughts of extending the Mountain Messenger, or of developing a better road system through the land, or, perhaps, of possible improvements to the quadricycle, such as stronger bump absorbers and a gear ratio designed for mud.

The pursuit lagged behind, but was not given up, as the five companions continued their run down the south road. Soon they came to a crossroads, with four high poles stuck into the ground, one at each corner, and with torn corpses, barely recognizable as men, hanging by the neck from each of these.

This very spot had burned an indelible image into Gary Leger's memory, perhaps the worst memory he had of the land of Faerie. He remembered these very poles, and, he realized a moment later, remembered these very same men hanging by their necks!

They were more bloated now, pecked by the vultures, and one was so badly decomposed that it seemed as if he would soon break loose from the rope. But they were the same, Gary believed, to his horror and his confusion. He reared up his mount in the center of the intersection, staring unblinkingly at the garish sight.

"How long has it been?" he asked Mickey.

"They leave 'em until they fall of their own accord," the leprechaun answered grimly.

"No," Gary corrected. "I mean, how long has it been since I've been gone from Faerie?"

"Oh," Mickey answered. He began silently counting and looked to Kelsey. "Near to a month."

"One moon cycle," Kelsey agreed.

"Why, lad, how much time has passed in yer own world?" Mickey asked.

"Five years," Gary replied breathlessly.

"I thought that you looked older," Geno remarked dryly. "And older are we all getting, sitting here in the middle of this wonderful smell."

"With Prince Geldion coming fast behind!" the fearful Pwyll added, wiping the sweat from his blotchy face.

"Right ye are," said Mickey. "Off we go, then."

"The road to Connacht is surely blocked," Kelsey said. "So we go east, to Drochit and Braemar."

"Right ye are," Mickey said again, and he, too, now looked back to the north, growing fearful that Geldion would soon be upon them. "Off we go, then."

Kelsey wheeled his mount to the left, to the east, and started off a stride, but stopped abruptly as Gary Leger said, in a determined voice, "No!"

"No?" Geno echoed incredulously.

"I came through here once before," Gary explained. "And we let these men hang, fearful that cutting them down would tell Geldion that Kelsey of the Tylwyth Teg had passed through this spot." Gary looked directly at the elf. "For who but the Tylwyth Teg would dare to cut down lawfully convicted criminals?"

"We have not the time," Mickey interjected, guessing where Gary's speech was headed. The leprechaun, too, looked to Kelsey for support, but realized that Gary had cunningly struck a solid appeal to the elf's sense of honor.

Mickey was not surprised to see the elf dismounting, a determined and grim sparkle in his golden eyes.

"We'll make the time," Gary Leger replied to Mickey, throwing his leg over the saddle and sliding down to the ground. "I'm not passing through here and leaving these poor men to hang, not when, by your own words, they did nothing wrong."

"You cannot cut them down!" Baron Pwyll verily shrieked. "That is a crime against Connacht punishable by . . ."

"Hanging?" Gary finished for him, in an unshaking voice. "Well, if I am caught and hung, then I hope someone will do for me what I am about to do for these men."

Noble Kelsey was nodding his complete agreement through it all.

"We have half an hour's lead, elf," the pragmatic Geno said. "No time for digging graves."

"Not even shallow ones?" Kelsey asked, pleaded, and Geno shrugged and hopped off the pony, motioning for Pwyll to come and help him. The Baron seemed hesitant and made no move to dismount, until the dwarf walked over and spoke to him privately—a line of deadly serious threats, no doubt.

Kelsey shimmied up the poles and worked the ropes, while Gary used the butt end of the long spear to gently guide the rotting bodies down. By the time they had the four men cut down and planted in the shallow graves, the cloud of rising dust had reappeared just a few minutes behind them on the road to the north.

"Time for flying," Mickey, the first to spot the dust, remarked. The others were back in their saddles in a moment, Pwyll moaning and looking back in sheer terror, and Kelsey leading the charge to the east.

"Ye've grown a bit in yer five years, lad," Mickey remarked when Gary was back up behind him. The leprechaun gave a squeeze on Gary's rock-hard forearm. "In body and in spirit, so it'd seem."

"Well done, young sprout," Cedric's spear telepathically added.

Gary accepted both compliments in silent agreement.

The fact that he had grown in strength was obvious, and increasingly obvious, too, was his newfound strength of character and confidence. The last time he was in Faerie, Gary hadn't been able to understand the motivations of Kelsey, so noble and so aloof. Kelsey's life was one dedicated slavishly to principles, to intangibles, something not quite foreign, but certainly not familiar, to the young man raised in a world of material possessions, a world that he himself had come to think of as spiritually bereft.

Gary could accept those faults in his own world, the real world, could play games on Route 2 with stressed-out drivers, could smile at the jokes about the latest enemy, the latest "created Robert," and had no choice but to accept the "progress" that was inevitably eating away at the woods out back and at the quality of life in general all about him.

But not in Faerie. The wrongs here were more black and white, more definitive, tainting an air that was too pure to be clouded with smoke. Bringing up the rear as the party charged down the eastern road, clutching tightly to that most mighty spear of legend with an evil prince and his soldiers only a few minutes behind, Gary Leger felt a sense of euphoria, a sense of righteousness.

A sense of strength.

"He will be trouble again!" the raven-haired witch snarled as she stared into her crystal ball, stared at the tiny images of Gary Leger and Kelsey and the others taking flight to the east, past the crossroads.

"Trouble for Lady?" Geek the spindly armed goblin asked, trying to sound incredulous. "Who could be trouble for most mightiest Lady?"

"Dear Geek," Ceridwen purred at him, turning slowly about on the satiny covers of the pillowy-soft bed, a disarming smile on her face. Her hand whipped across, catching Geek on the side of the head and launching him several feet before he crumpled against an ornately carved night table, to fall whimpering on the floor. The goblin quickly scrambled back to the foot of the bed when Alice, Ceridwen's pet lion, leaped up from her bed on the opposite wall, startled by the noise.

"You stupid goblin," the witch growled, looking from Geek to her always-hungry pet. Geek whimpered, understanding what she was thinking, and crawled under the bed. "Trouble like he was trouble for me before!" Ceridwen continued, talking more to herself than to the hidden and cowering goblin. The witch's belly ached with remembered pain as she thought of that fateful day on the mountain outside Robert's castle. She had them, the whole group, at her mercy, until that wretched Gary Leger had thrown the cruel spear.

Ceridwen's wounds had not been mortal, of course. In Faerie, the witch could not truly be killed. But Gary's action had defeated Ceridwen, had banished her to Ynis Gwydrin, her island home, for a hundred years.

The Lady Ceridwen was not a patient witch.

She looked back to her crystal ball, still focused on the crossroads. More horsemen charged into the scene, paused to study the tracks, then veered east, as Prince Geldion continued the pursuit.

Ceridwen's lips curled up in an evil smile. "Geldion," she purred, and then she waved her hand quickly across the ball, dispelling the image to smoky nothingness.

"Geek!" she called, snapping her fingers. A crackle sounded, along with a flash of sparking light under the bed, and Geek rolled out rubbing his smoldering posterior. "Go and fetch Akk Akk," Ceridwen instructed, referring to the leader of the giant monkey-bats that lived in the tunnels far below Ynis Gwydrin.

Geek cringed. He didn't like dealing with Akk Akk, or

any of the unpredictable and stupid (even by goblin standards) monkey-bats. Twice before, when he was delivering similar messages from Ceridwen, Akk Akk had tried to nibble on flat-faced Geek's large and pointy ears.

Ceridwen dropped an angry glare on the goblin, then, and Geek realized that sitting in the middle of the witch's private chambers was not a good place to be when deliberating whether or not to obey one of her unbending commands. Ceridwen's icy-blue eyes flashed dangerously and she snapped her fingers again, and Geek cried out, hopped to his feet, and ran off, skipping about wildly and patting at the igniting sparks crackling across his butt.

As soon as he was gone, the witch ordered her bedroom door to swing closed. "Let us see who will win this time, dear Alice," she said to her pet, now in the form of an ordinary housecat, circling about and kneading at the pillows in its soft bed. "Let us see if Gary Leger and his pitiful friends can escape when I am guiding the pursuit."

Ceridwen's smile grew wider than it had for a month. There were ways to break banishments, the witch knew. Robert had found one, and was out and flying, and, with Gary Leger back in the land of Faerie, so, too, might she.

The witch's eyes flashed again. A second wave of her deceivingly delicate hand and a soft chant brought a new image into focus in the crystal ball, that of the throne room in Castle Connacht, where King Kinnemore, Ceridwen's perfect stooge, sat waiting.

Kelsey led the way down the wide road into the thick forest of Cowtangle. A short way in, the elf paused to get his bearings, then nodded and moved his mount to the side of the road, to a narrower path barely visible behind some thick brush. Kelsey dismounted and motioned for his friends to pass by, then took a wide branch and brushed the narrow trail and the main road clear of tracks.

"This should put Geldion back a while," the elf explained, coming past Gary and Mickey.

"Even if Geldion goes straight through," Gary said grimly, "he'll stay on the east road. Can we afford to have him riding directly ahead of us all the way to the mountains?"

"We will not stay on the road," Kelsey replied, nodding to show that he agreed with Gary's surprising show of reasoning. "We shall parallel it to the east, come to the mountains south of Braemar."

"Where I take my leave," Geno put in.

Gary started to reply to the dwarf, but Mickey tapped him on the wrist and whispered that it wasn't worth the argument.

"There, we will skirt the mountains south, and then east," Kelsey continued, "following our original course through the Crahgs and to the Giant's Thumb."

"If the wild hairy haggis doesn't get you all first," Geno put in with a wicked smile, a smile that turned into a belly laugh when the dwarf noticed how pale Baron Pwyll's face had become.

The dwarf was still roaring when Kelsey took up the lead and started off again down the narrow trail. A short while later, they heard Geldion's contingent gallop by on the main road, and they were relieved.

But it was short-lived, for a notion came into Prince Geldion's mind, an insight sent by a spying hawk serving a witch in an island castle more than a hundred miles away. Soon the companions on the narrow trail heard the unmistakable clip-clopping of horse hooves on the path behind them.

"How'd he know?" Mickey asked incredulously.

"Good fortune," Kelsey replied grimly, before any of the others could utter any more ominous possibilities. The trail forked a short distance ahead and Kelsey veered from the main easterly course, turning southeast.

"Where are we going?" Gary asked Mickey quietly, as the path continued to turn, and soon had them heading right back to the west.

"Kelsey knows the wood better than any," was all that Mickey would reply, though his grave tone sent alarms off in Gary's head. "Keep yer faith." Gary had to be satisfied with that, though he suspected that the leprechaun knew more about their course than he was letting on.

And indeed Mickey did. The leprechaun knew that the path they were riding would take them to the southwestern corner of the small wood, a place of steamy fens and bottomless bogs, and horrid monsters that appreciated having their dinners delivered.

7 † Ghosts in the Wood

What had gone from a gallop down a wide road to a trot down a narrow path soon became a plod along a barely discernible and winding way around steamy wet bogs. The annoying buzz of gnats and mosquitoes replaced the chatter of birds, and low-hanging fog stole the crystal blue from the sky.

"The land of fantasies," Gary Leger remarked quietly, and even his whisper seemed to come back at him ominously.

"And of nightmares," Baron Pwyll put in, sweat covering his thick-skinned face and his eyes wide and darting from side to side as though he expected some horrid monster to spring out and throttle him at any moment.

"Not so bad," Mickey said to keep Gary calm. "She's a quiet place really, even if she's looking like a home for the spooks."

The three of them hardly noticed that Kelsey and Geno, up in front, had stopped their march, with Kelsey turning his mount sideways along the narrow path so that he could look all about. The elf sat shaking his head, golden eyes squinting and lips pursed as though he had just taken a big bite out of a grapefruit.

"What is it?" Mickey prompted.

"I did not believe that Geldion would follow us in here," Kelsey admitted. "Even the mounts of Tir na n'Og

77

have difficulty navigating the treacherous bogs. The Prince is likely to lose more than a few men."

Gary looked all around, confused. "How do you know that he's following us?" he asked, for he had noticed nothing that would indicate pursuit.

Kelsey put a finger to his lips, and all the companions went perfectly silent for a few moments. At first, Gary heard nothing but the endless din of insects, and the occasional nicker from one of the mounts, but then came the unmistakable, though distant, clip-clop of horses plodding through the soft ground.

"I'd lay ye a good-odds bet that our Geldion's got eyes guiding his way," Mickey remarked to Kelsey, and the elf didn't have to ask whom the leprechaun was referring to.

Kelsey clicked softly to his mount and tugged the reins to right the stallion on the path. The elf had hoped to skirt the bogs and come back into the forest proper before nightfall. But now, though the sun was fast sinking in the western sky, he turned deeper into the swamp.

"Damned elf ears," Mickey said softly to Gary. "If he hadn't gone and heard Geldion's horses, we'd be away from this place afore the night."

"She's not so bad," Gary said, echoing the leprechaun's earlier remarks.

"Ye just keep believing that, lad," Mickey replied, and Gary didn't miss the honest look of trepidation that crossed the leprechaun's face as he lit up his long-stemmed pipe once more.

The moon was up soon after the sun went down, and the swamp did not become so dark. The ground-hugging mist glistened, seemed to have a light of its own, starkly outlining the reaching branches of dead trees, and swirling to create images that had names only in the imaginations of frightened witnesses.

Kelsey was glad for the glow, for he could continue to

walk his mount along, but Gary found himself wishing for blackness. Mickey pretended to be asleep, but Gary often saw him peeking out through a half-closed eye from under his tam-o'-shanter. Even Geno seemed fearful, clutching a hammer so tightly that his knuckles had whitened around it, and poor Pwyll fell into several fits of trembling and whimpering, and would have broken down altogether had not the dwarf promptly stepped his pony back to the Baron and whispered in his ear—probably threats, Gary realized.

The young stranger to Faerie couldn't blame the Baron, though, couldn't fault the man for his weakness in this place that looked "like a home for the spooks," as Mickey had put it. Bats were out in force, squeaking and squealing as they darted all about, easily getting their fill of insects. The sucking noises of the horses' hooves pulling free of the grabbing mud came to sound like a heartbeat to Gary, or like the gurgling spittle of a rasping ghoul.

He peered closely into the fog at his side when they passed one fen, watching the edge of an angled log half floating in the stagnant water. Another branch was sticking straight up, just a few inches above the pool, its twigs resembling the dried fingers of a long-dead corpse.

Just your imagination, Gary stubbornly and repeatedly told himself, but that thought held little weight when the supposed "twigs" clenched suddenly into an upraised fist.

"Oh, no," he muttered.

"What is it, lad?" Mickey asked, the leprechaun's gray eyes popping open wide.

Gary sat perfectly still, holding tight to the bridle of his nervous and unmoving horse.

The arm began to rise up out of the pool.

"What is it?" Mickey asked again, more frantically.

Gary's reply came as a series of deep breaths, a futile attempt by the young man to steady his nerves.

"Oh, Kelsey," the leprechaun quietly sung out, seeing no real answer forthcoming.

Nervous Baron Pwyll looked back to discern the problem with the trailing mount, looking from Gary's frozen stare to the pool. The fat man immediately spotted the arm, and then the top of a head, with matted, blotchy hair surrounding many open sores. Pwyll meant to cry out, "Ghost!" but his stuttered cry came out as simply "GAAA!"

The Baron was nearly jerked from his saddle then, as Kelsey rode back, grabbed the bridle from Pwyll's hands and bolted away. Geno acted equally resourceful, skipping his pony past Pwyll's mount (and growing more than a bit frightened as his pony's hooves splashed into foot-deep water), and similarly grabbing at the bridle on Gary's horse.

Gary never saw the face of the ghoulish creature rising from the bog, but he pictured it a hundred different ways, none of them overly pleasant. The group raced off as fast as Kelsey could lead them, and when the commotion had died away, they were all startled once more, this time by the calls of pursuit not far behind them. Kelsey veered into a brush tangle and pulled up there to get his bearings, the others coming in right behind, all of them eager to remain in a tight group.

"They're even following us at night," Mickey whispered to Kelsey. "Who do ye know that'd come through the fens without being chased through the fens?"

"We're being chased through, and I don't want to be here," Gary put in sarcastically.

"The witch," Geno reasoned, to Pwyll's accompanying groan.

"Our pursuit is being guided," Kelsey admitted. "Surely. Perhaps by Ceridwen, but in any case, I do not believe that we will leave them behind."

"We'll leave them behind," Geno promised grimly, pulling out a hammer and slapping it across his open palm.

"Prince Geldion rides with at least a score of men," Pwyll argued.

"Twenty more ghosts for this haunted swamp," the dwarf solidly replied. Geno tossed the hammer up into the air, then caught it perfectly in his gnarly hand.

"More than a score, I'd be guessing," muttered Mickey, poking his chin out to the side, not behind, where the others were generally looking. A line of torches, two dozen at least, was evident through the fog and the trees, moving slowly and parallel to the path the companions had been riding.

"Flanking us," Geno remarked, his surprise obvious.

"And many more behind, would be me own guess," Mickey said. Kelsey ran his slender fingers through his thick and long golden hair, then put a questioning stare on Mickey as he reached for his long bow.

"I can slow 'em, perhaps," the leprechaun replied. "But I'm not likely to be stopping 'em." He closed his eyes then, and began chanting and waggling his fingers in the air before him, in the direction of the flanking soldiers.

A second grouping of torches appeared, farther down the trail from the line of riders.

"There they are!" came a cry, followed by a unified roar and the instant rumble of charging hoofbeats. The torches intersected and became a scramble of lights through the fog. Horses whinnied, complaining of being pulled up so short, and there came several wet thuds, as though mount and rider had gone down.

"Will-o'-the-wisps!" came one cry above the general tumult.

"Not really," Mickey said to his friends, taking another long draw on his pipe. "It's just lookin' that way. A bit o' pixie lights, actually."

The flanking line was soon in wild retreat, most riding, but some men running, and with less than half the torches burning that the companions had previously noted. One rider came splashing through the bogs directly for the brush that held the companions, though he obviously couldn't see them. His cry sounded remarkably like Pwyll's stuttered attempt at "Ghost!" and he was looking too much over his shoulder for such a pace in so treacherous an area.

His horse hit some deeper water and rolled over headlong, pitching the soldier through the air. He slammed heavily into a dead tree and plopped down into the water, springing right back to his feet and running on, trying to wipe the blood and muck out of his eyes.

"They're as scared as we are," Gary reasoned, an idea coming to him along with a smile.

"As you are," Geno gruffly corrected.

"Even better," Gary replied.

"What are ye thinking, lad?" Mickey asked, but the leprechaun would have to wait for his answer, for the fleeing cavalry apparently had linked up with Geldion's main force, and there came the sound of many riders approaching quickly from behind.

"Be off," Kelsey instructed, and his companions didn't have to be asked twice.

Gary Leger had an idea. "When I was a kid, we always threw scary parties on Halloween," he said to Mickey as they tromped along at the back of the line.

"Allhallows Eve?" the leprechaun asked.

Gary nodded. "Everyone was afraid," he explained with a wry smile, "except for the kids doing the haunting."

Mickey took a long draw on the pipe and rolled his eyes as he considered Gary's point. His smile soon outshone Gary's.

* * *

"I told you to get the damned bugs out!" Geno grumbled at Pwyll as the fat Baron slipped a hollowed log over the dwarf's arm. Pwyll immediately retracted the limb and brushed aside a few bugs, then slipped it back over the dwarf's outstretched arm.

"Quietly!" Kelsey demanded, his voice muffled because his shirt was pulled up high over his head and buttoned tight.

"Can you see?" Gary asked the elf.

"Well enough," Kelsey answered.

"Well enough to ride?"

The "headless" elf pulled open a space between two buttons and glowered at Gary. "Just point me at the horse," he growled, his frustration only heightening at the sight of Gary's smirk.

"This will work," Gary said to calm him.

Kelsey nodded, making the whole top part of his tightly pinned torso bob crazily. Despite his frustration— frustration born of fear—the elf approved of Gary's plan and thought it the best way for the companions to escape Geldion without an all-out battle. Gary helped him get to his horse, then, and helped him get up, and soon Kelsey seemed to settle into the saddle.

"Perfect!" Baron Pwyll proclaimed, popping a stubby piece of rotting wood over Geno's head and lining it with brush.

"There ye go, lad," Mickey said, bobbing over to join Gary. The leprechaun cradled a curved piece of bark, a makeshift bowl, filled with some type of golden glistening mud. "Stand still and put yer arms out wide."

"What is it?" Gary asked.

"Something to give ye a ghostly glow," Mickey assured him. The leprechaun rubbed some of the mud on the hip-plate of Gary's armor and indeed, that section of the mail suit took on an eerie golden glow.

"Our enemies approach," Kelsey announced. He kicked his horse away, taking a side route so that he might flank Geldion's force. Pwyll took the reins of the other two horses and the pony and started away, turning back once to remind Geno to "Look like a tree!"

"Geno'll hold this spot," Mickey said to Gary. "And Kelsey will hit 'em on the right. There's a ford across the bog to the left, a place Geldion might know."

"Lead on," the glowing warrior bade the leprechaun.

Soon after, the area was quiet, except for the shuffling feet of Geno the tree as the dwarf tried to get into a better position. The toes of his hard boots stuck out from under the trunk he wore from shoetops to armpits, and his stubby finger couldn't even reach the end of the logs Pwyll had slipped over his arms. Even worse, Geno could hardly see at all, peeking out from under his treelike helmet, through strands of thick brush, and he feared that he might trip and fall, and lie like a helpless turtle on his back until (hopefully) one of the others came back for him.

"Stupid plan," the dwarf muttered, and then he went silent, hearing a group of soldiers moving along the path.

Kelsey took many a stinging hit from low-hanging branches as his horse trotted through the thick brush. He held his seat easily, though, his strong legs wrapped tightly around his mount's back while he clutched his longbow, an arrow notched and ready.

"Find me a wide and safe run," he whispered to his horse when the torches of Geldion's flanking line came into sight. Gary had told Kelsey—and Kelsey thought it good advice—that his only chance was to make quick, fleeting passes at the soldiers, never to give the enemy a good view of him.

A few moments later, Kelsey's mount waited patiently behind a copse of trees, with a clear run before it and

Geldion's soldiers coming along a paralleling course barely twenty feet to the side.

Kelsey held his horse back until the very last instant, then burst from the copse, groaning loudly, as Gary had instructed.

"There's one of . . ." a soldier cried, but his sentence got cut short, turned into an indecipherable gurgle, when an arrow drove into his hip.

The flanking line took up a cry of attack and swung about to charge out and intercept the fast-flying specter. Kelsey thought that the game was up. He fired a steady stream of arrows into the air, having no idea of how many, if any, might hit the mark, and kept his limited vision focused straight ahead, trying to discern an escape route once the wide run ended.

Soldiers crashed their mounts through the blocking brush, a solid line of horsemen at first, but gradually dissipating until those few who suddenly found themselves out in front looked back curiously, then looked ahead to see what had stopped their eager comrades.

"Hey, he ain't got no head!" one man cried—one man and then many.

Kelsey heard the call and smiled under his high-pulled shirt. He dropped the bow across his lap, and in a powerful motion drew out his enchanted long sword, its rune-etched blade glowing a fierce blue that accurately reflected the elf's inner fires. Kelsey pulled hard on the reins, reared the stallion and then swung him about.

"Ring!" he commanded the bells, and a thousand tinkling chimes accompanied his return charge.

"He ain't got no head!" another man cried.

"Give me back my head!" Kelsey answered in a mournful, crooning voice, again as Gary Leger had instructed him.

One of the front soldiers, the captain of this contingent,

sitting right in Kelsey's path, chewed on his lip and rubbed his fingers anxiously, desperately, along the hilt of his sword. He heard some of his forces breaking rank altogether, and didn't know which way to go.

"Give me back my head!" Kelsey growled ominously once more.

"If any's got it, then give the damned thing back!" another soldier, farther down the fast-disintegrating line, cried out desperately.

"Hey," the captain realized suddenly, straightening in his saddle. "If he ain't got no head, then how's he talking?" Thinking that he had uncovered the ruse, the captain turned smugly to one side and then the other.

Only to find that he was sitting out there all alone.

"I ain't got your damned head!" the captain shrieked at the closing horseman, and he threw his sword Kelsey's way, wheeled his horse about and galloped away, screaming, as were his deserting soldiers, of "headless horsemen in the bog!"

"They were here," one of the lead scouts said to his companion, studying the area where the five friends had split up. "And none too long ago." The man bent low to study the fog-enshrouded ground beneath one small tree, his companion right at his back, waiting for news.

Something hard conked the standing man on the back of the head.

"Who?" he stuttered, spinning about.

"What're you about?" the crouching scout asked him, looking back over his stooped shoulder.

"Something hit me on the head," the other man explained.

"This place is scary enough without your imagining things," the scout scolded. "Now, be alert."

The other man shrugged and adjusted his cap, looking back to his searching friend.

Something hard conked him on the back of the head again, harder this time.

"Ouch," he said, stumbling into the crouching scout and grabbing at the back of his noggin.

"What?" the exasperated scout began.

"Something hit me on the back of the head," the man protested, and the fact that his cap was five feet out in front of the two of them added credence to the claim.

The scout pulled a small axe from his belt, motioned for the other man to go around one side of the small tree, while he went around the other.

They hopped in unison around the trunk, coming to a standstill facing each other above one of the tree's two low-hanging branches.

"Nothing here," the scout said dryly.

"I'm telling you," the other man began, but he stopped as the tree suddenly began to shake, its two limbs bobbing, its twiggy clump of branches rustling.

"What in the name of a hairy haggis?" the scout asked, scratching his forehead.

Geno brought his arm, his limb, straight back, clunking the scout on the nose, then shot it forward with all his strength, catching the unfortunate other man under the chin and launching him into the air. He landed in the muck on the seat of his pants, gasping and scrambling to get away.

The tree spun about to face the scout squarely, but the man was not so intimidated. He wiped the blood off his upper lip and regarded it angrily. "Damned haunted tree!" he roared and his hatchet rushed in, splitting the bark and coming to a sudden stop close enough to Geno's face so that the dwarf could stick out his tongue and lick the weapon's razor-sharp edge.

Geno turned quickly, one way and then the other, back and forth, his straightened limbs battering the scout's arms and shoulders. The man let go of his axe and tried to run, but got clipped and fell to the ground. Geno, trying to follow, tripped over the scout's feet, and he, too, came tumbling down.

The tree-dwarf flattened the scout under him, burying the man in the soft muck.

"Now what?" the dwarf muttered under his breath, helplessly prone with the frantic man trying to scramble out from under him. Geno began to shake wildly again, twisting so that his still-widespread arms continued to batter at the man. He added a haunting groan to heighten the effect.

But then Geno was cursing his encumbering suit as the scout wriggled free, knowing that it would take him a long time to get to his feet, knowing that the man had him helpless.

The scout didn't know it, though, for he had seen more than enough. As soon as he came up, spitting mud, he took off in full flight behind his already departing companion.

He never looked back—and soon after, he retired as a scout and took up basket weaving.

The five soldiers approached the ford, and the ghostly limned and impressive figure in the metal plate-mail armor, with due caution, their weapons drawn and the five of them repeatedly looking to each other for support.

"Standing and waiting for us to come and get you?" one of them said as they neared the man.

"I am the ghost of Cedric Donigarten!" Gary Leger growled at them, standing resolute, the wondrous spear planted firmly in the ground before him.

Two of the soldiers backed away, two started to follow, but the fifth, a dirty-faced man with the green cap of a forest tracker, laughed aloud. "Oh, are ye, then?" he asked between chuckles. "Then ye wouldn't happen to be that Gary Leger lad from Bretaigne, beyond Cancarron Mountains? Ye know who I mean, the one who fits so well in old Donigarten's armor?"

"Trouble, lad," Mickey whispered, perched out of sight on a low branch right behind the young man.

Mickey had recognized the speaker, and now so too did Gary, as one of Prince Geldion's personal escorts, one of the men who had been in attendance when Gary had gone with Kelsey and Mickey to originally retrieve the armor from Baron Pwyll, before they had ever set out to reforge the legendary spear. Gary feared that Mickey's estimate was correct, that the game was suddenly over, but some of the whispers behind the confident soldier gave him hope.

"No man, you fool," one of the retreating men remarked. "See how he's glowing."

"Moon-mud," the sly man replied. "He's a man in a suit of metal, is all he is, and no more a ghost than meself. Don't ye know at least Cedric's spear, if not the armor?"

"I am the ghost of Cedric Donigarten!" Gary growled again. "I am invincible!"

"Let's see," the sly man retorted, and he came forward a few steps, two of his comrades tentatively at his sides.

Gary Leger tore the spear from the ground and held it out sidelong in front of him. "NONE SHALL PASS!" he declared in a booming voice, and the two flanking men stopped, causing their sly companion to pause and stare at them incredulously.

"Oh, that's good, lad," Mickey whispered from behind.

"Monty Python and the Holy Grail," Gary whispered over his shoulder. "When he hits me, make my arm fall off."

Mickey started to question that last remark, but the men were advancing again, swords ready. The sly man came suddenly, in a wild flurry, and Gary worked the spear all around, parrying the measured swordthrusts. The soldier quickly grew frustrated, and came ahead with a straightforward thrust.

Gary hopped aside and slapped down with the spearhead, likewise forcing the swordtip to dip. He put his opposite foot forward and turned his body beside his lunging opponent, coming near to the man and smacking him on the side of the head with the long handle of the spear.

"I am invincible!" Gary declared again, hands on hips, as the soldier retreated a few steps to shake the dizziness from his vision.

"Five of us can take . . ." the soldier cried, looking around, only to find that the two men at the back of his group were long gone. "Three of us can take him!" the man corrected. "Together, I say, or face the wrath of Prince Geldion!"

The other two looked doubtfully at each other. The indomitable forest tracker slapped the sword from one man's hand. "I'll not be asking again," the cruel and sly man said evenly.

They came at Gary together, and only through his symbiosis with the magnificent weapon, the lessons the spear had subconsciously taught him, was Gary able to dance about, twirling the spear, and fend off the initial attacks. Fortunately, his enemies' attacks were not well coordinated, though they certainly kept Gary back on his heels. He whipped the spear side to side, brought it up suddenly to stop an overhead chop, then whipped it to his left, knocking aside a darting sword.

Gary didn't know how long he could keep it up. He knocked away the sword to his left again, then the one to his right, and when he brought the spear back in line to halt the sly man's straightforward thrust, he saw an opening.

He could have driven his speartip right through the

man's chest, and with that man—who was obviously the leader—dead, the other two would likely have turned and fled. But Gary had to face the consequences before he made the move, had to come to terms with killing another human being.

His hesitation cost him the opening, and nearly the fight, as the man on his left came in stubbornly again, the sword just missing as the spearshaft deflected it aside.

The man jumped back and whooped with delight, and the sly man turned and punched him victoriously on the shoulder.

Gary didn't have a clue of what they were so excited about—until he looked down to see his armored arm lying at his feet.

"Right," Gary cried, trying to defeat his own shock and remember the script. He lifted the mighty spear in one hand, the one remaining hand that appeared to his opponents to be intact. "Have at it!"

The three soldiers screwed up their faces and looked to each other, then back to the stubborn knight.

"Come along then," Gary growled at them, lifting the spear in his right hand and leveling it in front of him.

"Yield," the sly man replied and he sarcastically added, "ye one-armed ghost."

" 'Tis but a scratch," Gary insisted. "And though the blood may SPURT from my shoulder, it will soon heal," he added, putting a heavy emphasis on the missing visual effect. On cue, a gusher of blood spurted from Gary's shoulder, splashing to the ground.

"I've had worse," Gary said calmly to the disbelieving men.

"AAAAH!"

The tracker found himself suddenly all alone, and even he did not seem so keen for the fight. Gary waved the spear again, and the man advanced a step, but then looked back to Gary's feet, his eyeballs nearly falling free of their sockets, and promptly turned and ran away.

Gary's stomach did a flip-flop when he, too, looked down, to see his severed limb grabbing at his ankle and trying to crawl back up in place.

"Enough, enough," he whispered harshly, gagging in tune with the leprechaun's merry chuckling.

"Oh, a fine plan it was, lad," Mickey congratulated, coming from his hiding place, and privately patting himself on the back for being able to pull off the somewhat simple illusion. "Our tricks'll put Geldion and his men on their heels for sure."

"If the others had similar success, we should get far away," Gary agreed, breathing easier now that the image of his own severed arm was no more.

"Now," Mickey began in all seriousness. "I'm knowing about the holy grail and where the thing is hidden, but tell me who or what this Monty Python fellow might be."

8 † Gerbil's Ride

Mickey and Gary found Geno lying half-buried in the soft ground, spitting curses and spitting muck, with Baron Pwyll standing helplessly over him. It took some effort—the dwarf seemed to weigh as much as an equal volume of lead—but by freeing up Geno's arms from their encumbering logs and using those logs as levers, Gary and Pwyll finally managed to stand the grumpy tree-dwarf upright.

"Stupid plan," Geno growled, smashing wildly at his bark trappings until he had split the log in half. He came out of the suit and scraped the mud from his body, flicked a few confused insects from his arms and shoulders, and ate a few more that looked too tasty to resist. Even the meal did little to improve the dwarf's mood.

"Stupid plan," he said again. On impulse, before Gary could react, the dwarf reached up and slugged Gary in the shoulder, launching him sidelong to land in the muck.

"It worked!" the startled young man protested, louder than he should have. All four went quiet immediately, fearing the consequences of Gary's cry, but when they stopped making so much noise, they heard the general commotion Gary's plan had caused. Screams and shrieks cut through the night fog, calls of ghosts, of headless horsemen, and of the trees themselves turning against the force. Further confirmation of the success came a few moments later, when Kelsey rode up, his head free of the high-laced tunic and a smile wide upon his fair face.

"They are in complete disarray," the elf remarked.

"Stupid plan," Geno said again, under his beetle-tainted breath.

"The Prince was not swayed by the claims of his returning men," Kelsey explained. "He blamed it on demon magics, and said that we would surely hang for our evil tricks."

"Then some of them are still coming," Mickey reasoned.

Kelsey's smile widened as he shook his head. "For all of Prince Geldion's determination, even he was taken aback by a trick that was not of our doing."

The elf paused, inviting a guess, and Mickey's grin came to equal Kelsey's as he caught on. "Geldion passed the swamp with the ghoul," the leprechaun reasoned.

Kelsey laughed aloud. "It seems that Prince Geldion called it an illusion, a magic trick. He even walked up to it as it crawled out of the muck to prove to his men that it was only an image and nothing substantial. The Prince wears a scar on his cheek for his foolishness."

It was all very welcome news, but Gary only half listened as Kelsey went on to explain that the Connacht soldiers had backtracked out of the swamp and would be far from the trail when they exited Cowtangle. Gary thought of the monster, the undead ghoul, they had seen crawling out of the muck, a monster that was, apparently, very real indeed. Now that the tricks were over and the immediate threat had been put off, the hairs on the back of Gary Leger's neck began to tingle. What the hell were they so happy about? he thought. They were in the middle of a haunted swamp, complete with ghouls, on a dark night.

Gary's heart did not slow any when he saw a stilted, leaning form coming slowly through the glowing mist.

"Where are the horses?" he asked, loudly enough to interrupt the continuing conversation.

"I tethered them a short distance ahead," Baron Pwyll explained. "Couldn't have them wandering about in this evil place."

"We should get to them," Gary offered, and he nodded ahead to guide the curious gazes of the others. A rare gust of the wind cleared the mist temporarily, and Gary's mouth dropped open wide. He saw the creature, a badly decomposed body of a long-dead man, skin hanging in loose flaps, one eye fallen back into its head, and, to his horror, Gary Leger recognized the corpse.

"Dad," he mouthed, hardly able to spit the word.

"We weren't for staying anyway," he heard Mickey say, and a moment later, Kelsey grabbed him by the shoulder and tugged at him. Gary resisted, or, at least, his planted feet made no move to help the movement. Kelsey called for help and Geno came over, wrapped his muscular arms around Gary's legs, and hoisted the man clear of the ground. They soon outdistanced the night creature, leaving it behind in a swirl of fog, but that awful image hung heavy in Gary's mind, stealing any words from his impossibly dry mouth, long after they had retrieved the mounts, long after they had picked their way along the muddy paths, long after they had exited the swamp and then the wood altogether.

Sitting in the nook between Gary and the horse's neck, Mickey soon recognized the true source of his friend's distress. "Ye knew the ghost," the leprechaun stated, understanding the tricks of night creatures quite well.

Gary just nodded, couldn't even manage a verbal response, his words caught fast by the image of his father as a corpse.

"They'll do that to ye," Mickey explained, seeing clearly what had happened and trying to put Gary at ease.

"Them spirits're smart, lad. They look into yer head and see what'll most get at ye."

Gary nodded and Mickey fell silent, knowing that he could do no more for his friend. The words did comfort Gary a bit, but that image remained, powerful and horrible. A large part of Gary wanted to be done with this adventure at once, wanted to go back to the other world, the real world, to ensure that his dear father was all right.

They rode hard and fast over the course of the next day, and started out early the day after that, the Tir na n'Og mounts running easily in the low brush not too far from the side of the eastern road. Kelsey had determined that they would go into the small farming and mining community of Braemar, unless Geldion beat them to the place, and learn if the dragon had been spotted out from his mountain home.

With his sharp eyes, the elf, in the lead, spotted a disturbance farther up the road, a commotion he feared might involve the Prince. He veered his mount farther to the side, putting some distance between himself and the road, and bidding the others to follow.

"Something up ahead?" Mickey asked, shielding his eyes with one hand and peering to the east, below the late morning sun.

There came a distant shriek in answer.

"Damned Prince," Geno muttered.

"Or someone in trouble," Gary offered. He looked to Kelsey, almost begging permission to ride out and see what was about.

"It is not our affair," the elf said coolly, but Gary saw Kelsey unintentionally cringe when another cry cut the air.

"Of course it is," Gary said, and he gave a tug on the bridle and sent his mount leaping beyond Kelsey. A whistle and single word from the elf stopped the mount so abruptly that Gary nearly fell from his saddle, and Mickey did topple, popping open an umbrella that came from somewhere, somehow, and floated to the grass, a not-happy expression splayed across his cherubic face.

"You feel no responsibility to check this out?" Gary asked bluntly, turning back in his saddle as soon as he was sure that Mickey was all right.

Kelsey didn't immediately reply—which caught Gary somewhat off guard. "I fear to proceed," Kelsey explained calmly. "There is too much at stake for us to risk an encounter with Prince Geldion."

"Well, you won't have to proceed, elf," Geno offered, pointing past Gary to the road up ahead. "Looks like the fight is coming to us."

It was true enough. Gary turned back the other way to see a cloud of dust rising from the road, and stringing out in their direction. Above it fluttered a group of strange and ugly creatures, appearing as vicious monkeys, dark-furred, with too-wide eyes and red mouths lined by long fangs. They flew about on leathery bat wings, twelve feet across, and even from this distance, Gary could make out the hooked claws extending from their back feet.

The road was up higher than the companions, and from this angle, they could not discern what the monstrous group was pursuing. Gary figured it to be a horseman, though he hadn't yet heard the pounding of hooves, for whatever or whoever it might be was moving with great speed.

"That looks more like Ceridwen's doing than Prince Geldion's," Mickey said, aiming his remark at Kelsey.

"They may be one and the same," the elf retorted, but it was obvious from Kelsey's hurried tone, and from the fact that he had already strung his bow, that the noble elf would not abandon whoever it was that was in peril on the road.

"Surely you're not thinking of attacking those monstrous things!" Baron Pwyll said to him, blanching as he spoke.

"Find a rock to crawl under," Geno said, juggling three spinning hammers as he walked his pony beyond the fat man's mount.

Gary liked what he was hearing, liked the fact that his companions, even surly Geno, seemed concerned with something beyond their specific business. How many times in his own world had he heard about people turning their heads and looking away when someone else was in trouble?

"Let me down, lad," Mickey said unexpectedly. Gary's ensuing stare was filled with disappointment, even disbelief.

"I'll only hinder yer fighting," Mickey explained. "I'll be doing what I can, don't ye doubt, but ever have I been better at fighting from a distance."

A sudden popping sound turned their attention back to the approaching fight. A burst of spinning missiles—they reminded Gary of the blades used on a circular saw—shot up into the air, cutting a myriad of angles that many of the monkey-monsters could not avoid. Two got their wings clipped; a third caught a missile squarely in the face, and dropped from sight.

"It's a gnome," Geno, who had gone up to the edge of the road, called back, and that fact inspired the dwarf to kick his pony into a roaring charge. Gary angled his horse right up to the road and thundered behind, easily catching up to the dwarf's pony, while Kelsey ran full out along the side of the road, holding fast to his mount with his legs, and fast to his drawn bow with his hands.

He had ridden with leprechauns and fought against twelve-foot-tall trolls and mighty dragons, but Gary could hardly believe the sight that greeted him. It was a gnome, as Geno had declared, a creature somewhat resembling the stocky dwarf, but slighter of build and with a face not so carved of granite. The gnome sat low in a contraption that resembled two bicycles lashed side by side, a steering wheel and two panels full of levers encircling him. He pulled one, and Gary saw a coil at the side of the left front wheel unwind suddenly, hurling another handful of circular missiles up into the air.

One monkey-monster, swooping low in an attack pass, caught the whole bunch in its face, wings, and belly, and was torn apart and thrown aside. But a score or more monkeys remained, synchronizing their dives at the frightened gnome.

The monsters never even realized that the gnome had found some unlooked-for allies until an arrow cut the air and drove hard into the side of one monkey. A second arrow followed in quick order, and a third after that, both scoring hits. The monsters sang out with their shrieking voices, looking first to the side, the flying elf, and then ahead, to the fine knight and his long spear and to the dwarf, hammer cocked back over his head, charging side by side down the road.

A few squeals from the largest of the monster band put the monkeys in order immediately, one small group breaking off in pursuit of the elf, another group, including the leader, remaining to dive at the gnome, and the largest band rushing straight ahead at the approaching riders.

"Keep a tight hold!" Geno yelled at Gary. "They'll try to pull you from your saddle!" The dwarf hurled out his first hammer then, but the closest approaching monkey was agile enough to swerve aside. Geno, too, swerved, purposely splitting apart from Gary and going down to the side of the road opposite Kelsey in hopes of confusing the monsters. They were not stupid beasts, though, and while a few turned to follow the dwarf, the bulk kept their focus ahead, zooming for Gary.

He brought the great spear up before him, resisted the urge to hurl it into the face of the closest monster. Keep your nerve, he thought, and told himself to trust in his armor and in his mount, and to follow the warrior training Donigarten's spear had given to him.

Still, Gary Leger thought he was surely doomed as the group of more than ten of the winged monsters closed on him. They were larger than Gary had thought from a distance, fifty to eighty pounds apiece, surprisingly agile and swift, and with long and pointy white teeth, and hooked claws that certainly could, as Geno had warned, pull Gary from the saddle. Gary remembered the time when, as a kid, he had cornered a raccoon under his best friend's front porch. He'd put on some work gloves and thought to climb under the porch and catch the critter, a cute little raccoon like the kind he had seen on TV. When that wild animal reared up on its hind legs and bared its formidable teeth, young Gary Leger had been smart enough to turn tail and scramble out.

So how come I'm not that smart now? he wondered, and then the time for wondering was over as he and the monkeys made their first pass. Ducking low, Gary poked ahead with the spear, nicking the lead monkey as it spun completely around in midair to avoid the strike.

Riding past, Gary tried to bring the weapon back in line ahead of him, but he was into the gauntlet too fast. He took a hit on the shoulder, a wing buffeted him, spinning his helmet about so that he could not see, and his horse grunted as a claw opened a deep scratch along its muscled neck.

Still, the pass was not nearly as bad as Gary had thought it would be; he took less than half the hits he had expected. He managed to right himself in the saddle, managed to right his helm, and looked back to find that many of the monkeys had swerved to either side of him and were now hovering some distance down the road, looking curiously Gary's way.

And no wonder, for riding right beside Gary, one on either side, were two exact replicas of the man, complete with spear and armor.

So surprised was Gary that he nearly charged on blindly right into the approaching gnome contraption. He found his wits, and realized the company to be Mickey's handiwork, in time to begin his turn to the side of the road.

The six monkeys that went for Kelsey were met by a seemingly solid line of arrows, coming out so rapidly from the fast-riding elf that his hands were no more than a blur. The terrain was rough on the side of the road, though, and Kelsey bounced about, many of his shots going wide and wild.

He scored three hits, two on the same beast that took that monkey down altogether. The other five came stubbornly on, though, even the one sporting an arrow shaft from its shoulder. They shrieked eagerly above the clapping pounding of their bat wings, and were almost upon Kelsey, wicked claws extended as they angled down for a swooping pass.

Kelsey's horse cut so sharp a turn, right back towards the monkeys, that the elf was forced to grab on, hands and legs, just to keep in the saddle. Surprised, too, were the monkeys, and the horse dipped its head low, and Kelsey fell flat across its back as they passed right under the beasts, who were still too high to attempt any raking attacks.

Kelsey straightened immediately and reared up his mount, readying his bow as he turned about and getting off several more shots before the monsters were able to reverse direction and come at him again in any coordinated fashion.

* * *

The four monkeys that went after the smallest of the new foes were surprised indeed when a barrage of flying hammers—it seemed like there were at least twenty of the missiles—came out suddenly as they closed the final few yards. Metal slapped hard against leathery wings, crunched monkey bones, and took all the front teeth, top and bottom, from one hooting maw.

Geno's pony came around, following the dwarf's call for a charge. Smiling that mischievous, gap-toothed smile, Geno took the bridle firmly in one hand and stood up on the pony's wide back, his stubby legs cocked for a spring.

The closest monkey had just recovered from the hammer attack when its eyes widened once more in surprise, this time as the hammer-thrower, and not a hammer, soared its way.

Geno hit the monster squarely, wrapping his powerful smithy arms about it and hugging as tightly as he could. The monkey clawed and bit, and beat its wings furiously, but even if those wings had not been entangled by the dwarf's ironlike grasp, they would not have supported Geno's solid weight. Down came the two, Geno twisting so that the beast was below him.

The monkey stopped thrashing, stopped breathing, when they hit. Geno bounced off the flattened thing and hopped about. Just in time, for a second foe was in full flying charge, swooping for the fallen dwarf.

"Catch!" Geno politely roared, whipping a hammer the monkey's way. The sharp crack as the weapon bounced off the creature's skull sounded like a gunshot, and the aimed plummet became a dead drop.

A third flying beast, following the charge, wisely turned aside, though the fourth of the group continued on. This one was walking, however, not flying, with one wing tucked tight against its back and the other, shattered in the initial hammer barrage, dragging on the ground beside it.

Geno's mischievous smile did not diminish. He flipped his hammer repeatedly into the air, catching it with the same hand, while his other hand beckoned the monsters to come and play.

A monkey dove for the low-riding gnome—Gary thought that the little man, who already showed a line of blood across his high-browed forehead, was surely doomed. A tug on a lever and a metallic umbrella sprang up, angled above and to the side, and the monkey-monster bounced harmlessly aside.

A second monkey, coming the other way, was closer, though, and Gary saw the gnome frantically reach for another, similar lever, probably designed to complete the umbrella covering. The gnome pulled, and there came a clicking sound, but nothing happened—nothing except that the gnome's face drained of blood as he looked at the swooping menace.

Purely on instinct, Gary let fly the spear. It skewered the diving monkey and carried it away, launching it far over the back of the speeding quadricycle.

Gary's horse thundered past the gnome a split-second later, Gary just catching the thumbs-up sign as he galloped past. Back up over the bluff and onto the road, his steed charged, and Gary bent low to the side, reaching down in an effort to retrieve the spear, lying with its dead quarry along the top of the bluff on the opposite side. He saw that it was just beyond his fingertips as he came near, and so he reached lower.

Too low.

The world become a spinning blur, filled with solid bumps and ringing armor, over the next few horrible seconds. When Gary finally stopped his tumbling fall, he found himself sitting against the base of the bluff. He heard his horse nickering, calling, from the road up above and behind him, and he instinctively struggled to stand, though he hardly remembered the fight in that confusing moment, and hardly remembered that there remained many monsters yet to battle.

He got almost halfway up before the ground seemed to writhe to life, to leap at him and swallow him.

Geno's muscled legs twitched, launching him ahead suddenly, and he barreled into the walking monkey. They wrapped arms and went into a roll, each biting hard into the other's neck. Geno's maw was not as strong as the beast's, but his neck was as hard as granite, and he did not fare badly.

He looked up over the monkey's shoulder and saw its companion rushing in. Smiling, his mouth full of monkey flesh, the dwarf waited until the unsuspecting monkey was almost upon him, then jerked his arm free and met the charge with a flying hammer.

The monkey tumbled to the ground, stunned but not dead, and the dwarf used that free arm to promptly pull it into the pile.

They rolled about, all three thrashing wildly, the monkeys clawing and biting and Geno punching, kicking, head-butting and biting, and doing whatever else seemed to work. Blood, dwarven and monkey, mixed with dirt, caking all three in grime.

Geno grabbed a tuft of hair on the back of one monkey's head and pulled the thing perpendicular across his chest as he rolled once more. Yanking as they came over, Geno managed to plant the facedown monkey's forehead firmly against the ground. With a growl, the dwarf forced the pile to continue to roll and the monkey screamed out in agony, its head bending over backwards and its neckbone snapping apart.

With surprising strength, the beast jerked free of the dwarf's iron grip and went into a series of wild convulsions. It was out of the fight, though, twitching on the ground and fast dying.

That left Geno one on one, and he looked down to see that the remaining monkey had used the distraction to its seeming advantage, its strong maw clamped tightly around Geno's bleeding forearm. The dwarf grunted and flexed his muscles, and his right arm, his smithy-hammer arm, tightened and bulged, forcing the monkey's mouth wider.

Wider, too, went the disbelieving beast's eyes.

"You think that hurts?" Geno asked it incredulously. He looked to the gnawing monkey, then to the hand of his free and cocked arm. "That doesn't hurt," he explained, and he extended his pinky finger and his index finger. "Now this hurts!"

Geno's free arm shot about, his fingers diving into the monkey's eyes, driving the beast off his forearm. Geno's arm recoiled immediately, his hand balling into a fist, and he punched the creature square in the face.

The monkey seemed to bounce to its feet, but stood there dazed, offering no defense as the dwarf stalked in and slammed it again. It bounced, but still stood, and then Geno's forehead splattered its nose all over its face and it flew away.

It never hit the ground, though, as a strong dwarven hand caught it by the throat and held it up.

Geno looked to his bloodied arm, wondered if the wound might slow his smithing business for a while.

"You shouldn't have done that," he explained to the semiconscious beast, and his powerful hand began to twist.

* * *

In the span of six seconds, and a like number of zipping arrows, five monkeys had become two.

Kelsey dropped his bow and drew out his sword, kicking his mount into a charge to meet headlong the next stubborn attack. The monkeys came at him together, one to pass on either side of his mount.

Kelsey veered to the side at the last moment, trying to put them both on his right, but the monkeys were just as quick, and turned accordingly. Undaunted, the elf lifted his sword up and over to the left, angling for that beast. Predictably, the frightened thing opened its wings for drag and fell back, and Kelsey's blade whipped across to the right, deflecting a diving claw and severing half the monkey's foot.

Kelsey knew instinctively that the one to the left was diving for him, had him vulnerable, so he continued to the right, falling all the way over the side of the horse. The monkey's hooked claws caught nothing but air.

Kelsey did not fall from his seat, as had Gary. The Tylwyth Teg were said to be the finest riders in all of Faerie, and Kelsey did not diminish that reputation in the least. Right under his steed's belly, between the pumping legs, he rolled, tugging himself back up the other side, and tugging tight to the bridle, rearing his mount. He had won the first pass, but the monkeys were coming back the other way for the second.

Kelsey kicked his mount into a charge, happy to oblige. Again, the monkeys tried to flank him, one on either side, and this time, Kelsey went right through the gauntlet, his sword snapping left, right, and left again, so quickly that he took only a minor nick on his forearm.

He was better prepared, his cunning warrior mind working fast, as he brought the mount around for the third pass, this time turning before the monkeys had even come about.

Down the middle, Kelsey started again, but then he lifted one leg over his horse's back, standing at the side of the charging beast, using the horse's body as a shield between him and the monkey on the right. Again, Kelsey perfectly anticipated his opponents' reactions. The monkey on the left swerved wide, having no desire to face the elf head-on, and the one to the right cut in for the horse, thinking the elf concerned with its companion.

Kelsey started left, then jumped back across his horse's back, sword leading in a straightforward thrust. The weapon suddenly weighed an extra fifty pounds, exploding through the monkey's chest, but Kelsey managed to hold on to it, taking the skewered monkey along for the ride. He heard a shriek close behind, and knew that the monkey which had fled the pass had come around quickly. Lying sidelong across his running horse's back, his sword stuck fast in a dead enemy, Kelsey was not in an enviable position.

With few options, the elf heaved the dead monkey out behind him. It slipped free of the blade, right into its flying companion's path, and the charging monkey had to kick off from the body, its momentum stolen by the ploy. By the time the living monkey recovered, recovered, too, was Kelsey. He turned his horse about once more and began yet another charge. Alone, the monkey wanted no part of the elf, and its wings beat furiously, trying to get it out of harm's way.

Kelsey's sword slashed its wing, and its flight became an awkward flutter. It swooped and rose, turned sideways and rolled right over in midair, finally fluttering down to the ground. The frightened monkey ran on, but it was no match for the speed of Kelsey's powerful mount. The horse ran it down, monkey bones crackling under the pounding hooves.

The monkey lay in the dirt and dust, its backbone shattered, and watched helplessly, dying, as Kelsey turned his steed once more.

But Kelsey had no time to finish the unfortunate beast. He looked back to the road, saw Gary's horse trotting, suddenly without a rider, and saw the gnome on his curious contraption rolling fast into a snapping and slashing tangle of nearly a dozen monsters.

And Kelsey's bow lay on the ground many yards away.

Gary had saved Gerbil, but the gnome realized that the reprieve would not last for long. A handful of monkeys still pursued him, and several others, the band that had rushed past Gary Leger, were now coming at him from the other direction.

"Drat'n'doggonit, drat'n'doggonit!" the gnome cried, his little legs pumping the pedals furiously, and his hand working the jammed umbrella lever.

"Not to be pretty," Mickey McMickey, watching from some distance away, muttered. It appeared as a strange game of "chicken," with Gerbil leading one band of monkeys at top speed one way, and a larger band flying fast the other.

Monkeys shrieked, Gerbil screamed, and at the last instant before the collision the gnome grabbed the steering bar in both hands, jerked it sharply one way and then back the other, sending the quadricycle into a spin, its skidding wheels shooting a swirling cloud of dust into the air.

Gerbil yanked yet another lever as the groups came crashing together, this one dropping his seat flat, getting him down as low as he could go between the contraption's high wheels.

Monkeys smashed together, smashed into the quadricycle, and slammed against poor Gerbil. The whole of the group seemed to hang motionless—a communal stun, it seemed—and then the quadricycle rolled slowly out the side of the group. The monkeys, beginning to recover, had the gnome helpless.

Nets flew up from the road, flying in at the throng. Monkeys shrieked and scrambled and would have battered each other into complete chaos, but Mickey, his powers at a low ebb, couldn't hold the illusion and the nets dissipated.

More real were the arrows that suddenly flew in, and the hammers that came spinning from the other side. The gnome was helpless, unconscious actually, but not so helpless was the grim-faced elf, rushing in on his shining white steed, or the running dwarf, laughing wildly, his little legs rolling under him, his arms heaving hammer after hammer.

One of Geno's hammers and one of Kelsey's arrows got the large leader of the group at the same time, blasting its breath from its lungs and then turning that burst of breath into a whistling gurgle through a neat hole in its neck.

Those monkeys that could still fly did so, and seven of the nine got away, the other two falling prey to Kelsey's bow. The three living monkeys on the ground joined together in a unified defense against the charging dwarf . . . and were summarily buried where they stood.

9 † Braemar

The huge red-bearded man walked slowly down the rocky mountain trail, great sword resting easily over one shoulder. Below him, nestled beneath the veil of rising mist in the secluded mountain dell, lay the quiet town of Gondabuggan.

Robert's hand clenched tightly about his swordhilt. He hated being in the confining human form, wanted to be out soaring on the high winds, feeling the freedom and feeling the strength of dragonkind.

But Robert had lived many centuries and was as wise as he was strong. He suspected that the resourceful gnomes had sent word of his coming, figured that the tough dwarfs in the mountains and the puny humans across the towering range were well into their preparations to battle him. Even with the euphoric knowledge that the witch, Ceridwen, his principal rival, had been banished to her island, Robert would not forget due caution.

If he were to rule the land, he would have to do it one village at a time, and Gondabuggan had the misfortune of being the closest settlement to the wyrm's lair.

Though he was in human form, Robert retained the keen senses of dragonkind, and he sniffed the gnomish sentries, and a different scent that he had not expected, long before they suspected that he was anywhere about. He moved to a rocky outcropping, some fifty feet from the gnomes, and perked up his ears, hearing their every word.

"Kinnemore's army is on the field, by one report," said a dwarfish voice.

"It is truly amazing," replied an excited gnome. "Truly amazing!"

"Of course the meddlesome king is involved!" the dwarf replied. "The spear and armor of Donigarten have been stolen, by the elf who defeated Robert (with the help of Geno Hammerthrower, of course) and the hero of Bretaigne. Kinnemore is nervous, and all the land is in chaos."

"Truly amazing," the gnome said again. "To think that Gerbil Hamsmacker simply flew through the mountains! Truly amazing!"

"Oh, he will go down in gnomish records," another gnome agreed, clapping pudgy hands together.

The exasperated dwarf groaned. "The artifacts and the king's army are more important!" he tried to explain.

"Yes," agreed a booming, resonant voice as a huge and muscled red-haired, red-bearded man stepped into view. "Do tell me about the artifacts and the king's army."

An hour later, Robert was a dragon again, gliding easily on the warm updrafts rising from the cliffs on the eastern edge of Dvergamal, waiting for his meal of two gnomes and a dwarf to settle—dwarfs had always been so indigestible! The news of events in the west had saved Gondabuggan, for the time being, for Robert now understood that there was more about all of this than his being free and Ceridwen's being banished.

Robert knew as well as any that Kinnemore was Ceridwen's puppet, and that, guided by the witch, the king would certainly cause him trouble. And there were heroes in the land now, for the first time in centuries, for the first time since the days of Cedric Donigarten. Dragons, whose power was as much a fact of intimidation as actual strength, did not like heroes.

Gondabuggan would have to wait.

Gerbil opened bleary eyes to see the sculpted features of a golden-haired, golden-eyed elf looking back at him. A leprechaun sat on the front right wheel of Gerbil's quadricycle, puffing on a long-stemmed pipe and saying, "Hmmm," repeatedly as he studied the gnome.

Gerbil quickly straightened himself in his seat, tried to put on his best greet-the-visitors face.

"Gerbil Hamsmacker of Gondabuggan at your service," he said as politely as could be, and indeed, Gerbil meant every word to this troupe that had rescued him from certain doom. "I pray that none of your most helpful party was too badly injured."

"The laddie, there, got a few lumps, is all," Mickey answered, motioning to Gary, who was kneeling in the road while Geno and Baron Pwyll tried to hammer a fair-sized dent out of one shoulder plate.

"The armor," Gerbil breathed under his breath, his gnomish eyes, typically blue, shining brightly and his head bobbing as if it all suddenly made sense to him. "Oh, I do say that I thought Sir Cedric himself had come a'bobbing to my rescue! Of course, of course, I do know better than that. Humans do not live so long, and Cedric . . ."

"Of course," Mickey replied. "But I'm agreeing that the lad has come to wear the armor well."

"Yes, yes," Gerbil said excitedly. "That is why I came west, you know, because the word is spread that the armor and spear were missing . . . stolen, actually."

"What concern would that be to a gnome of Gondabuggan?" Kelsey asked gravely.

"None and lots," Gerbil answered. "You see, Robert the Wretched was the one who reforged the spear."

Kelsey and Mickey looked to each other and seemed not to understand the connection, at least not as far as Gondabuggan was concerned.

"Well, the missing spear and armor might offer some clues as to why Robert has come out on wing, so to speak," Gerbil explained at length. "The two events were too closely related . . ."

"What do you know of the dragon?" Kelsey interrupted, his voice stern. Kelsey knew, as did most of Faerie's folks, that a gnome could ramble for hours if not properly guided through a discussion, and from what Gerbil had just referred to, Kelsey wasn't certain that he had hours to spare.

"What do I know?" Gerbil balked. "Indeed, what do I? Of course, that depends mostly on the subject matter. Take explosives, for instance . . ."

"About the dragon," Kelsey clarified.

"He was over Gondabuggan, that is what I know!" Gerbil said. "Just . . ." He paused and lifted his plump gnome hand, counting on the fingers so that he could be precise. "Just fifty-one hours ago."

"What do ye mean by he 'was over' Gondabuggan?" Mickey asked. "Did he attack the town, then?"

Gerbil nodded rapidly. "With fire and talon!" he replied. "Of course, that is what one must expect from a dragon, unless the dragon is one of the lake variety. Then the expected attack mode . . ."

"Ye're sure?"

"I am, if the dragon treatise is correct," Gerbil replied.

"Not about water dragons!" Mickey retorted. "Ye're sure that Robert flew over yer town, just fifty-one hours ago?"

"I watched it with my own two eyes, of course," replied Gerbil. He nodded a greeting as the other three walked over to stand beside Kelsey. "Oh, he came down in a tirade, breathing and kicking," the gnome went on, and his level of excitement seemed to rise accordingly with the rising audience. "We held him at bay, but I would guess that Robert is not yet finished with Gondabuggan! Oh, woe to my kin!"

Some of the others began to whisper; Pwyll's remarks were filled with forlorn, but Kelsey steeled his gaze, seemed to find something not quite right with Gerbil's dire tale.

"You were in Gondabuggan for Robert's attack just two days ago?" the elf asked. As soon as Kelsey put it so plainly, Mickey went silent, understanding the elf's quite reasonable doubts.

Gerbil counted quickly on his fingers again. "Fifty-one hours," he replied with a nod.

"You have come a long way in fifty-one hours, good gnome," Kelsey remarked. "Even though the weather has been fine and your . . ." He looked to the weird contraption.

"Quadricycle," Gerbil explained.

"And your quadricycle is swift," Kelsey went on, "Gnome Pass is many days from Drochit, and Drochit is still a day's ride from here."

"Oh, I could not take the quadricycle through the mountains, of course," Gerbil retaliated. "Too many rocks and trails too narrow, after all! Oh, no, I did not ride. I flew."

"On Robert's back, then?" Mickey asked sarcastically.

"On the Mountain Messenger," Gerbil replied without missing a beat. "It is a long descending tube, packed at precise points . . ."

"I know of yer M&M," Mickey assured the gnome. "Are ye telling me that ye climbed into one o' them balls and got shot across the mountains?"

"Landed in the field north of Drochit," Gerbil replied with a proud smile. "Of course, if I had been splattered, then I would have had my name etched into the *Plaque of*

Proud and Dead Inventors." The gnome gave a long sigh. "Better to live at this time, though," he conceded. "With the dragon about, after all."

Gary, confused and intrigued, couldn't take any more of the rambling. "What are you talking about?" he demanded.

"It's a big cannon," Mickey answered before the gnome could get into a lengthy explanation. Mickey was more familiar with Gary's world than any of the others, having often snatched people from that place, and he knew how best to put the M&M in terms that Gary Leger would understand.

"And he climbed in a hollow ball and got blasted across the mountains?" Gary asked incredulously.

"Something like that," Mickey replied. He turned back to the gnome, wanting to hear more of Robert, but Gary wouldn't be so easily satisfied.

"How far?" he asked.

"The distance has never actually been measured," Gerbil was happy to explain. "My calculations approximate it at forty miles, give or take seven hundred feet."

Gary leaned back to consider this. He knew of battleships in his own world that could throw two-ton projectiles more than twenty miles, but, as he found the proper perspective, the prospect of hurling a ball with a living gnome inside twice that distance—and have the gnome crawl out alive—seemed absolutely ridiculous. He tuned back in as Gerbil was describing Robert's attack on Gondabuggan, how the gnomes put up a wall of water, and metallic umbrellas to fend off the attack.

"Impossible," Gary cut in as soon as the gnome paused to take a breath.

"No, really," Gerbil came right back. "Umbrellas of properly folded plates, just like this." He reached for the handle to his smaller versions of similar umbrellas on the quadricycle.

"Not the umbrellas," Gary explained. "There's no way you can hurl a ball that far."

"No way?" Gerbil cried, throwing his hands up in absolute disgust.

"Never be saying 'no way' to a gnome, lad," Mickey whispered to Gary. "Puts them all in a tizzy."

And indeed, Gerbil Hamsmacker was in a tizzy. If Gary Leger had called the gnome's mother a thousand dirty names, or had called the race of gnomes thick-headed, it would not have upset the proud M&M inventor any more than this. Gerbil blustered and threw his hands this way and that. He rambled off a series of calculations, followed by a series of curses at the thick-headed, dim-witted, slow-to-learn, never-to-understand humans.

"I just don't believe that you can launch a projectile that far," Gary began, wanting to explain that the speed and the impact would surely kill any passengers. "How high up was the cannon? That ball would have to travel at . . ."

"Two hundred and seventy-two miles per hour," Gerbil proudly interjected. He looked sidelong at Kelsey. "Two-seventy-three and you clip the overhang at Buck-toothed Ogre Pass."

Geno tugged at Kelsey's tunic. "I saw one hit that overhang once," he said. "At night, and the sparks were far-to-see!"

Kelsey nodded, not doubting the tales, but Gary shook his head, finding it impossible, even amidst this land of impossibilities, to believe a word of it.

"But the landing," he started to protest, hardly able to find the words to properly express his whirling thoughts.

"Of course the target area was the descending slope of a field," Gerbil cut in. "Peat mostly, and cow droppings. The trick, you see, is for the valves to release the precise amount of Earth-pull reversal solution at precisely the moment to slow the flight and soften the landing."

"Earth-pull reversal solution?" Gary had to ask.

"Flying potion," Mickey quickly explained.

"I don't believe it."

"Ye don't believe in leprechauns either, lad," Mickey remarked. "Remember?"

Gary stuttered over a few responses, then turned back to Gerbil, armed with more questions.

"He'll have an answer for anything ye ask," Mickey said before Gary could get on a roll. "He's a gnome, after all."

Gary's determined look faded to resignation. "Precise amounts at precise moments?" he asked the gnome.

"Precisely!" Gerbil proudly cried, his cherubic face beaming as only the face of a gnome who had been praised for an invention could beam.

Gary Leger let it go at that, just sat back and listened as the intriguing little gnome finished his tale. Then Gerbil stood up straight in his seat, looking all around as though he wasn't sure of where to go, or of where he had been.

"What were those nasty things?" he asked.

"Some witch-mixed monsters, by me guess," Mickey replied, and he looked gravely at Kelsey as he spoke. Had Ceridwen extended her evil hand once more? they both wondered, and both, inevitably, knew the answer.

"I do not believe this to be a chance meeting," Kelsey added, speaking to Gerbil. "You may find the road to Dilnamarra difficult, at best."

"Well, I am not so sure, not at all, that I have to go there anymore, though I would like to speak with the fat puppet, Baron Pwyll, to see what I might learn of the theft," Gerbil answered, but then he looked at Gary, obviously in possession of the supposedly stolen items, and gulped loudly.

"Then speak with him," Mickey offered with a mischievous grin, "for to be sure, the fat puppet's but a few feet away."

"At your service," Pwyll remarked dryly, and Gerbil gulped again. But Pwyll took no real offense, and the overdue introductions were not strained at all. Kelsey was already figuring that they might have to go to Gondabuggan, and in that case, Gerbil would prove a great help. Leprechauns got along well with gnomes, as did dwarfs, and even Geno put on a genuinely warm expression as he clasped the gnome's little hand.

In the end, it was decided by all that Gerbil would remain with the group, backtracking to the east. The gnome spent a long while milling over the proposition, looking east and west repeatedly as though he wasn't sure of how he should proceed, but when Mickey reminded him of the airborne attack, he nodded his agreement and turned the quadricycle about.

The group of six came to a ridge above Braemar, a small village of two dozen mostly single-chambered stone houses, late the next afternoon. There was no keep here, as there was in Dilnamarra, just a large central building, two stories high—which Mickey called the "spoke-lock," the hub—surrounded by a cluster of town houses, including a blacksmith and other craftsmen, a trader, a supplier, and, of course, the infamous Snoozing Sprite tavern, wherein Geno had been captured by Baron Pwyll's men. Beyond the central cluster of town rolled rock-lined fields of grazing sheep and highland cows, dotted here and there by the customary squat stone houses with their thick thatched roofs.

"We're sure to make a stir if we walk right in," Mickey reasoned. "Especially if Geldion's got men down there."

Kelsey looked around, in full agreement with the leprechaun. He didn't know how to weigh the potential reaction of Braemar to the disturbing news. Badenoch, the village's leader, was one of the few independent Barons in Faerie, often showing more support for Pwyll than for the emissaries of Connacht. But certainly, this unusual troupe would attract much attention. Geno could go in relatively safely, as dwarfs were not uncommon to Braemar, and though Geno might be recognized, he could easily concoct a story of escape from Pwyll's bumbling soldiers. Gerbil had already been to the sister town of Drochit, twenty miles to the north, and gnomes often visited Braemar, as well. The Tylwyth Teg were not common this far from Tir na n'Og, not in these days of King Kinnemore's reign, but Kelsey, too, could probably go into Braemar without too much difficulty.

Both humans would be more than welcome in the friendly town, except that if Pwyll was recognized, the word of his passing would spread throughout the countryside. And the armor, more fabulous than anything in all the land, would keep a crowd milling around Gary for every step. Few knights rode the fields in this dark time, and even the wealthiest of those who did had no metal plating to match the craftsmanship of Donigarten's legendary suit. Word of the theft had come this far north, according to Gerbil, and with it, undoubtedly, word that King Kinnemore wanted the armor retrieved. Who knew what friends of the throne, and independent bounty hunters perhaps, might be about, ready to seize the opportunity to get into Kinnemore's good graces and abundant treasures?

Mickey would have the most difficulty of all in going into Braemar, though. Braemar was primarily a human settlement, and few men would look upon a leprechaun and not make chase, seeking the famed pot of gold. Mickey rarely ventured into any town, and never without using a clever disguise. Kelsey couldn't be certain, but it seemed to him that the leprechaun's illusions were not carrying the same strength as in the past.

"I doubt that Geldion has come this far," Kelsey said at length. "And I wish to learn more of Robert's movements. Perhaps the dragon has been seen on this side of the mountain, and if not, we will need supplies to properly cross Dvergamal."

Mickey nodded, but was not in agreement—not with the elf's planned course, at least. Kelsey was talking about chasing the wyrm, but Mickey wanted only to get back to the Giant's Thumb, Robert's castle, and get back his precious pot of gold.

"Send in a couple, then," Mickey offered. "Dwarf and gnome, and even . . ." Mickey put his stare on Pwyll, but shook his head suddenly and looked to Gary instead. ". . . Gary Leger, as well," the leprechaun finished. "But leave the spear and armor here," Mickey said to Gary. "Ye'll not likely be needing them in the peaceable town."

Few eyes turned with anything more than passing curiosity when the three companions wandered down the dirt streets of Braemar an hour later, Geno at the lead with Gary and Gerbil right behind. Many people were about, rushing mostly, and several approached the strangers with "Have you heard of the dragon?" or "Good gnome, does Gondabuggan survive?"

Gary would have liked to stop and question these villagers in more depth—that was why they were in town, after all—but Geno gruffly excused himself from any budding conversation (usually with a stream of spittle heading the villager's way), and pulled the others along, moving with purpose towards the large central structure, the spoke-lock. Gary thought that the dwarf meant to go and find Lord Badenoch, Braemar's leader, and so he did not argue, but Geno went right past the main house, into a long and low building. Gary couldn't make out the runes on the sign outside the place's wide door, but the accompanying painting, that of a small pixie curled up peacefully amidst a patch of white clover, confirmed to him that this was the Snoozing Sprite tavern.

The place was bustling, mostly with villagers, men and women, having their supper and talking of the dragon, and of the missing armor.

"Where should we sit?" Gary asked, but he realized when he looked down to his sides that he was talking to himself. Gerbil had scooted off to the side, to talk to a tall and lean barkeep, and Geno was making his way through the crowd, spreading stumbling people in his wake, towards a far table where sat three other dwarfs. Gary started to follow, but remembered what he had learned of dwarven manners—mostly that the four would probably pick him up and heave him away if he interrupted them— and so he went to find his own table instead.

He wound up along the far wall, well past the bar, at a round table built for four, and still covered with the bowls and spoons of the previous occupants. Gary looked around, saw no one objecting to his choice, and slipped into a chair, defensively putting his back against the wall. He leaned this way and that, trying to keep an eye on his friends among the crowd.

Geno was still with the dwarfs, apparently they were friends, and Gary had to wonder if perhaps the dwarf's part in this adventure had just come to an end. Geno was ever the reluctant companion; if he had found some allies and was inclined to be done with the group, not Kelsey's sword nor Mickey's tricks would get him away.

Across the way from Geno, Gerbil was sitting atop the bar, chatting easily with the barkeep, and with a crowd of curious men who had gathered around the gnome. They were seeking information about the dragon, Gary figured, and Gerbil was undoubtedly trying to find out what more, if anything, had happened to his town.

"That's me dad," came a sweet voice at Gary's side.

Acting as though he had been caught Tom-peeping, Gary straightened suddenly in his chair—too suddenly, for he overbalanced and nearly toppled to the floor. Standing beside him, tray in hand, was a young lass of not more than twenty years, with shining red hair and a fresh complexion that no makeup could ever improve. Her eyes sparkled innocent, childlike, and Gary got the distinct feeling that she had grown up in a field of wildflowers, smiling at the simple pleasure of the warming sun.

"Sorry to startle ye," she offered, catching hold of Gary's shoulder and helping him to regain his balance. That done, the lass started to load the used bowls onto her tray. "Me name's Constance, and that's me dad talking to yer little gnome friend."

"Oh," Gary replied, trying to digest it all. He extended his hand, pulled it back in to wipe the grime of the road off it, then held it out again. "Pleased to meet you, Constance," he offered lamely with a strained, still-embarrassed smile.

"I've not seen ye before in Braemar," Constance noted. "Are ye passing through, or have ye come to find a hiding place from the dragon?"

"What do you know of the dragon?" Gary asked, trying futilely to hide his anxiety. "Has he been seen near to here?"

"Some say they've seen him, but I think they're just trying to make themselves more important than they are," Constance replied with a mischievous wink—a wink that sent a shiver along Gary's spine. This was a beautiful girl, and though she was polite and proper, there remained something untamed about her, something that could melt a man's willpower.

"The only trusted word we've heared came from Drochit," Constance went on. "A gnome was there, so 'tis said, with word that Robert had attacked Gondabuggan.

Last we heared, the gnome went west, to Dilnamarra, to speak with fat Pwyll and find out what had happened to Donigarten's suit. The two're related, so 'tis said."

Gary nodded and pretended that it was all news to him.

"Anyway, it is exciting, isn't it?" Constance asked, and her smile nearly knocked Gary off his chair as he nodded his agreement. "And who might ye be?"

It took Gary a moment to even realize that he had been asked a question. "Gary Leger," he replied without thinking.

"A strange name," Constance remarked offhandedly, and her delicate face screwed up as though she was trying to place the name.

"From Bretaigne, beyond Cancarron Mountains," Gary quickly added, using the alias that Mickey had concocted for him on his last trip through Faerie.

"Ah," Constance mewed. "Ye're the one who came to Dilnamarra for the armor!"

Gary suddenly realized his error, knew that it was not good for him to be connected in any way with the events in Dilnamarra—not with Prince Geldion hot on their trail.

"No," he said, trying vainly to sound calm, and trying vainly to weave a believable lie. "That was a different man, a cousin, I believe, though if he was, he was not one I've ever met."

Constance's doubting expression showed him how ridiculous he sounded. "Oh," was all that she replied.

"Yeah, not one that I ever met," Gary said, and he glanced around to Geno and Gerbil again, wanting nothing more than to crawl out of that place.

"What might I be getting ye?" Constance asked unexpectedly, her smile genuine, and enticing once more.

Too many stutters escaped Gary's mouth.

"The leek soup's hot and warming," Constance suggested.

"Good enough," Gary replied, and Constance turned away. Gary realized that he might have a problem, though, so he grabbed frantically at her elbow.

"I'm sorry," he said suddenly, letting go as Constance abruptly spun about to face him, and realizing that he probably shouldn't have done that. The girl, though, seemed to take no offense. "I mean . . . I have no money," Gary quickly explained.

"Oh." Constance seemed truly perplexed. "Ye're traveling with not a pence?"

"My friends . . ." Gary started to reply, but he wasn't sure what he might say about those two, so he didn't continue.

"Go and see then," Constance offered. "And if they got nothing for ye, then let me talk to me dad. He's got something needing done around here, don't ye fret. I've not ever seen him turn one away without a proper meal in his belly!" Constance spun and kicked away, a young foal in an open field, and Gary slumped back in his chair, thoroughly charmed.

His smile did not last, though. Not when he noticed that another group had taken an apparent interest in him. Four men, wearing the clothing of villagers, but with long dirks at their sides, were looking his way, their stubbly faces grimly set. They stopped Constance as she walked past, and asked her some questions, all the while looking back at Gary as he sat there, feeling very conspicuous.

Constance went by them without incident and they talked among themselves for a few moments, as though everything was perfectly natural. Every now and then, though, one of them would look Gary's way, locking stares with the stranger.

Gary felt the tension mounting as the minutes slipped past, felt all alone and dangerously out of place in a suddenly unwelcoming town. He tried to figure out what his next move should be, and only realized then that he did not have the sentient spear and the armor.

"Hurry up, Geno," he muttered under his breath, hoping that if it came to sudden blows, the dwarf and his tough companions would rush to his aid. But to Gary's shock, when he looked to the table, Geno and the others were not to be found. Gary groaned quietly; he could only believe that the dwarf had quit him and the whole adventure, had left him vulnerable.

All four of the men were staring at him intently then, and his instincts told him to jump up and run for his life. The men whispered among themselves, started towards him.

A hand clasped on Gary's shoulder, and he would have fallen to the floor had not the dwarf grabbed a tight hold and hoisted him to his feet.

"Come on," Geno said, and Gary really didn't have much choice but to follow, bending low in the unyielding grip, as the dwarf stormed away, for a side door that Gerbil was holding open leading to the wing of private rooms.

"Here come some," Mickey remarked, and Kelsey and Baron Pwyll came up to the crest of the bluff, lying in the grass beside the leprechaun.

Mickey pointed to the road, but it was obvious what he was talking about as six horsemen approached the town, some sporting longbows over their shoulders and others with sheathed swords at their hips.

"We must expect that the people of the surrounding areas will flock to the town, prepared for battle," Kelsey reasoned, trying to figure out what significance, if any, this group indicated. "Lord Badenoch may have put out a call to arms."

Mickey nodded hopefully, but Baron Pwyll was not convinced. "In that case, he could not expect this group,"

the large man whispered. "There, the one in the lead." He
pointed to a large square-shouldered man with a bushy
black beard, riding a tall roan stallion. The man carried no
bow, but had an immense broadsword strapped to his back,
its pommel rising up high behind him, higher than his
head.

"Ye know him?" Mickey asked.

"That's Redarm," Pwyll explained. "Named for a
wound he got in a sword fight, a wound that would have
defeated a lesser man. He's one of Geldion's lackeys, by
all that I've heard." The Baron shook his head. "No, this
group would not have come to Badenoch's call."

Mickey and Kelsey exchanged serious glances, both
then instinctively looking to the unoccupied armor lying in
the brush behind them at the base of the bluff.

10 ✝ Midnight Ride

"Wake up." The whisper, accompanied by a repeated tapping on his shoulder, sounded harsh, urgent, in Gary's ear. The young man was well settled into a wonderful dream, of a walk through beautiful Tir na n'Og with Diane beside him, of bringing some of his other friends to Faerie and letting them see this different side of Gary Leger, this heroic side.

"Wake up!" This time the call was accentuated by a finger snapping against Gary's cheek. He opened his eyes, saw that it was Gerbil standing in the dim light beside him. The gnome appeared anxious, but Gary couldn't figure out what might be wrong. The room was perfectly quiet, and the night outside the open window was dark, no moon this night, and still.

Gary stretched his shoulders; the room had only one bed, claimed by Geno (though Gary couldn't figure out why, since the dwarf had flipped it over so that he could sleep across the hard slats), and Gary had fallen asleep sitting on the floor with his back against a wall. His accompanying yawn was too loud for poor Gerbil's sensibilities, and the gnome slapped a hand across Gary's open mouth.

Gary pushed him away. "What?" he demanded in a soft, but firm, whisper.

Gerbil looked nervously to the door. "We have been discovered, it just very well might be," the gnome replied.

Gary sat up straighter and rubbed the sleep from his eyes as Gerbil climbed up on a chair and dared to light a single candle sitting in a tray on the room's small desk. Only then, in the quiet light, did Gary realize that Geno was no longer in the room.

They heard a commotion in the hall, a scuffling noise followed by several bumps, and looked to each other curiously. Gerbil hopped down from the chair and padded over to the door, glancing back at Gary, and then taking a tentative hold on the high knob.

The door burst open; poor Gerbil came right off the floor, hanging onto the knob with his little feet kicking as he and the door swung about.

"The window!" Geno cried, rushing into the room. The dwarf skidded to a stop and spun about, hammer swiping low. Gary winced at the resounding crack as the weapon connected on the kneecap of the man pursuing the dwarf. He howled and pitched headlong, grabbing at his crushed joint.

"Window!" Geno cried again, and he grabbed Gerbil's freely waving hand and pulled the gnome from his doorknob perch. Gerbil's other hand immediately tugged a bottle from his belt. He brought it up to his mouth, bit off the end, and splashed its contents all over himself.

"Get me there!" he bade the dwarf, and Geno was already thinking along those very lines. With a single, powerful arm, the dwarf twirled the seventy-pound gnome about his head once and then again, and hurled Gerbil across the room.

Gary blinked in disbelief at the gnome's flight. Gerbil started fast, but soon lost momentum and seemed as though he would crash to the floor. He continued to float, though, turning several perfect somersaults and winding up in a straight-armed, slow-motion dive that slipped him through the open window without a scratch against the wooden frame.

Geno turned back to the hall, facing four more dirk-wielding opponents—the same four men Gary had seen earlier in the tavern.

"Window!" the dwarf shouted to Gary. Gary looked that way, then looked back to Geno curiously, surprised by the dwarf's uncharacteristic altruism. Geno was under no debt to protect Gary, or even to accompany them at all on this journey. And yet, here he was, fighting furiously, telling Gary to run off while he held the enemy at bay.

Gary began to understand, then, the urgency of it all, the apparently desperate situation that Faerie had been placed in with the return of the dreaded dragon. But he would not run away from the dwarf, he decided. For perhaps the first time in his life (no, the second, he realized, counting his first trip to Faerie), Gary Leger felt as though he was part of something bigger than himself, something more important than his own life. He would go to Geno's side, use fists if need be against the daggers.

"Waiting . . . the window."

The silent call came into Gary's mind, a voice he recognized clearly. How it had gotten there, he didn't know, but the spear of Cedric Donigarten was leaning above the rosebushes under his room's window, waiting for him to retrieve it.

Geno cut a wide swath in front of him with his heavy-headed hammer, but came nowhere near to hitting the three agile men who had fanned out before him. Daggers thrust in behind the flying weapon, but the dwarf reversed his grip quickly and started with a reverse backhanded cut that forced the men to hop back once more.

This time, though, Geno did not hold onto the hammer. It spun from his grasp, slamming one man in the chest and knocking his breath from his lungs. He staggered backwards, slamming into the door and then tripped to the floor, dazed.

A companion, seeing the dwarf's weapon fly, snarled and thrust ahead more forcefully, but quicker than he anticipated, Geno pulled another hammer from his belt and snapped it across, slamming the man's fingers.

The dagger, stained with the blood of the dwarf, fell to the floor. Geno had only been scratched, but when the newest of the wounded men fell away, the dwarf found the fourth of the party waiting for him, daggers in each of his hands, cocked back over his head.

Geno went into a frenzy, started to charge, but got hit by the other man standing near to him. The dwarf blocked one of the daggers, but the other dug into his thigh. He shot a death-promising glance towards the thrower, only to see that the man had two more daggers up and ready.

Geno fell to the side, threw his hammer up before him, and somehow managed to escape the deadly throws. He was vulnerable, though, off-balance and with the remaining uninjured man, the man who had gotten back up from the floor near to the door, and the man with the broken fingers, coming back in at him.

The huge black tip of an enormous spear slashed the air between the combatants, forcing the three men to fall back. In stepped Gary Leger, grim-faced, whipping his powerful weapon about furiously, using its length so that the men, with their much shorter weapons, could not get anywhere near him or Geno.

"Window!" the young hero cried to his dwarfish companion.

A fifth man staggered through the crowd unexpectedly; Gary had to pull back on his cut to avoid disemboweling him. It didn't matter anyway, for the man looked at Gary plaintively, then fell to the floor, an elfish arrow protruding from his back, just under the shoulder blade, and through, Gary realized, the back of the dying man's heart.

Gary's stomach did a flip-flop, but he determinedly swallowed the bile and continued his defensive frenzy.

Geno patted him on the hip and was off and running, pounding across the room while issuing a long scream, then leaping headlong out the window and into the night.

Gary heard Pwyll shriek from outside and figured that the dwarfish missile hadn't missed the fat Baron by far.

"Up!" The sentient spear's warning came in time for Gary to snap the tip upward and knock aside a flying dagger. Instinctively, Gary came back the other way, covering his exposed flank, and he grimaced in anger as his spear cut deeply into an opportunistic enemy's side. Down the man went, screaming in agony, and Gary yelled, too, if only to block out the man's cries.

"No!" Gary growled as he noticed again the man Kelsey had shot, now lying perfectly still in the unmistakable quiet of death. Gary's denial was useless, helpless, and realizing that, the young man buried his own frailties under a curtain of sheer rage.

Now the spear came flashing across with renewed fury, Gary driving the remaining men backwards. He stopped a cut in midswing and gave a short thrust that forced the closest of the group to suck in his gut and hop up onto his toes, falling backwards a moment later and tangling with his companions.

Gary turned and ran for the window. He smiled in spite of his revulsion, conjuring an image common to old Errol Flynn movies. As he came towards the window, Gary dipped the tip of his spear, thinking to fancifully pole-vault his swashbuckling way outside.

His calculations weren't quite correct, though, for the enchanted spear's tip sliced right through the flooring, shifting Gary's angle and stealing his momentum. He came up in the air, up even with the vertical shaft, then went nowhere but down, to one knee on the floor just beyond the stuck weapon.

He saw his enemies regrouping back by the door, and they saw him, and quickly came to understand his dilemma.

Gary pulled hard on the spear, bending the metal shaft his way, but making no progress in freeing it. He thought of fleeing, of diving out the window, but he couldn't leave the spear behind—not to these men, who were obviously working for Prince Geldion.

But still, what choice did Gary have? Three of the cruel men charged at him, verily drooling at the thought of such an easy kill, and a fourth hopped on his one good leg behind the pack. Gary tugged hard until the very last moment, then cried out and let go.

The bent shaft sprang back the other way with tremendous force. The nearest enemy lifted a forearm in front of himself defensively, then howled as his bone snapped apart, jagged edges of it cutting out through the skin right before his disbelieving eyes. He flew away, into a companion, and both of them tumbled backwards, tripping up the man with the shattered kneecap.

Gary could hardly believe his luck, went desperately for the spear as the remaining man came in around the quivering weapon. Gary almost reached his spear, but then he fell back, thinking that he had been punched in the side.

Wide did Gary Leger's eyes go when he looked down to see not a fist, but a dagger, above his hip, to see his blood gushing out through torn skin.

I've been stabbed! The thought rocketed through Gary's mind, horrified him and confused him, for he honestly still felt as if he had only been punched; the pain was dull and not too intense. Still, the image was more than Gary could rationally take, and he didn't think of his actions, didn't hear the primal cry of sheer survival instincts escape his lips.

His opponent was well balanced, crouching with the bloodied dagger held ready. He got the weapon up to block Gary's furious left hook, but Gary didn't even wince as his hand and arm scraped across the blade, continuing on to slam the man in the face. A right cross followed, coming in under the surprised man's rolled shoulder, finding an open path to the man's chin.

The next left hook met no resistance at all until it smashed the man's cheek, whipped his head across the other way.

This was pure street-fighting, not delicate boxing, and wild Gary didn't look, didn't aim, as he continued to swing, left and right, left and right. His own yelling prevented him from hearing the solid smacks, or the cracking bones in knuckles and cheeks alike.

The man fell away, but Gary kept swinging, four more punches flying freely through the empty air before he even realized that he had knocked his opponent down. He regained his composure then, and saw the man on the floor, trying to crawl, trying to get up, apparently trying to remember where and who he was. He managed to get to his hands and knees, and Gary started to kick at him, but he rolled over to his side of his own accord, lay still and groaned.

Gary put a hand to his side, wincing as he brought it up and regarded the generous amount of blood. It had all happened in mere seconds—the other three in the pile hadn't even sorted themselves out yet. Gary dove for the spear, grabbed its shaft in both his aching hands, and heaved with all his might.

The back-and-forth action of the weapon had loosened the floor's hold on it, and it came out more easily than Gary anticipated. Spear in hand, he stumbled backwards,

pitched head over heels in a backward somersault out the
open window, his toes smashing glass and snapping the
bottom wood on the window frame, and fell heavily into
the thorny rosebush.

"Dammit!" he groaned and he looked up from his natural prison to see an enemy come to the window—and
then go flying away with a hammer tucked neatly into his
face.

"About time ye're getting here, lad," Gary heard
Mickey say. He tried to turn his head about to regard the
leprechaun, but a thorny strand tugging painfully against
his neck changed his mind.

Baron Pwyll and Gerbil were at his side in an instant,
pulling him free, while Geno lined up the window with another readied hammer.

"Hurry, then," Mickey implored them. "We're to meet
Kelsey down the south road, and the elf's not in any mood
for us being late!" Behind the leprechaun, the two horses
and the pony whinnied nervously, but did not scatter. One
of the horses, Gary's, had a large sack strapped over its
back, bulging with the metal plates of Donigarten's armor.

They finally got Gary untangled—Geno heaved another
hammer into the room to turn away the two men stubbornly continuing the pursuit—and went for the horses.
Pwyll hoisted Gerbil, who didn't seem thrilled at the prospect of riding so tall a beast, up to his mount, but before
the little gnome had even swung his leg over, he pointed
down the road and whispered, "Trouble, oh, yes."

"Oh, yes," Gary echoed when he looked that way. Half
a dozen riders lined the road a short distance from the tavern, regarding the friends and seeming almost amused by
it all. One of the men wore full metal plating, like the armor of Donigarten, and carried a long lance tipped by a
pennant bearing the standard of the lion and the clover, the

emblem of Connacht. On his back was strapped a huge sword, one that Mickey and Baron Pwyll had seen before.

"Yield or be killed!" the knight declared.

"Five on six," Geno muttered mischievously. "Even up, if the damned elf would get here."

"I'm thinking that Kelsey's got his hands full of fighting already," said Mickey.

"Oh, well," replied the dwarf without the slightest hesitation. "Then Kelsey will miss all the fun."

"Not so quick," Mickey whispered back, sitting easily in his place in front of Gary's saddle. "I'm knowing that knight, and knowing that he didn't have the armor when he rode into town, not so long ago."

"So?" Geno's question reflected no doubts and no fears.

"He's got friends in town," Mickey reasoned. "More than we've seen, don't ye doubt."

"Archers in the hedge," Gary whispered, nodding to his right, and even as he spoke, they heard several voices from men congregating in the room behind them.

Baron Pwyll groaned.

"You got anything to trick them?" Gary asked Mickey.

The leprechaun shrugged. "Me magic's not so good," he answered honestly. "And the knight'd see through it, if none o' the others would."

It seemed to Gary as if they had few options other than the demanded surrender. But to do so would surely doom Baron Pwyll, and in looking at the precious spear he carried, Gary realized that the cost might be much higher than that.

"Yield or feel the tip of my lance!" the knight bellowed. "I have no time and no patience for your delay!"

Gary recalled all that he could about chivalry and codes of behavior, knew that this man was driven by a sense of honor, warped though it might be. Gary's smile widened;

what his friends needed was a distraction. He hoisted Mickey from the horse and set him down on the ground.

"Get up with Geno," he explained quietly. "You'll know when to ride."

"What're ye thinking?" Mickey demanded, sounding not too pleased.

Gary was already climbing up to his seat, and paying the leprechaun little heed.

"My friends will yield," Gary called to the knight.

"When gnomes fly," Geno growled, but Gerbil threw him a reminding smirk to defeat that protest.

"If you can defeat me in a challenge of honor," Gary finished. He couldn't see the knight's face for the faceplate, but he imagined a wide smile curling up under that metal.

"My dear Gary Leger of Bretaigne," the knight began, chuckling with every word and slowly lifting the grilled faceplate up onto his head.

"These guys don't miss a thing," Gary, surprised at being so easily recognized, whispered to Mickey.

"You have been blinded by your pride," the knight continued. "For have you forgotten that you wear no armor?" His comrades broke into laughter—too loudly, Gary noted, and that told him just how much they respected this knight. One of the men, though, trotted his horse up beside the knight and whispered something in his ear that the armored man apparently did not like.

"I remember!" the knight roared, and he slapped the man away.

"They want him alive," Gary heard Mickey remark to Geno. The leprechaun continued to whisper to the dwarf, but Gary could only make out the name "Ceridwen" in the ensuing moments.

"What's the knight's name?" Gary mumbled over his shoulder.

Mickey directed Gary's gaze to Baron Pwyll.

"I don't know his proper name," the Baron said. "But he is called by Redarm."

"Have I forgotten?" Gary balked incredulously to the knight. He held the spear of Cedric Donigarten up high. "Good Redarm, have you forgotten that my spear will cut through your feeble armor more easily than your lance will pierce my skin?"

"My thanks, young sprout," came a call in Gary's head. The laughter down the road stopped abruptly.

"Don't mention it," Gary whispered to the sentient weapon.

"Laddie," Mickey warned.

"Are these horses as fast as Kelsey says?" Gary asked.

"Faster," answered the leprechaun.

"Then get ready to prove it," Gary whispered. "These guys, the archers, too, and especially Redarm, are going to be more interested in the joust than in you."

"Laddie," Mickey said again as the dwarf verily tossed the leprechaun atop the pony. Both Geno and Mickey understood what Gary Leger had in mind.

"Laddie," Mickey muttered again, not so sure that he liked the decision.

"Have a good ride to the netherworld," Geno said evenly to Gary, cutting Mickey's concerns short. "Though I hate to lose the spear."

"Hey, Geno," Gary replied, smiling as wickedly as was the dwarf. "Suck pond water."

"Thanks," the dwarf answered. "I have, many a time. Nothing like it after a hot day at the forge."

Gary unstrapped the sack of armor and handed it over to Pwyll, who nearly fell from his horse as he tried to secure it. "By the way," Gary asked the dwarf, needing to know before he went for his apparently suicidal ride, "how did you throw the gnome so far?"

Gerbil started to answer, "Earth-pull reversal . . ."

"Never mind." Gary cut him off, holding his hand up high and shaking his head.

"I am waiting, Gary Leger of Bretaigne!" growled Redarm, seeming larger and more ominous as his huge horse plodded out away from the other.

"We're all to die," muttered Pwyll.

Gary ignored the gloomy Baron and trotted his mount out from the group. He looked to Redarm, to the road and fields around the man, and knew that his was a desperate choice. Perhaps Baron Pwyll was correct, at least as far as Gary was concerned, but even so, the young man would not despair. He felt again like something larger than himself, like a part of a bigger whole, and if he died allowing his friends to escape, then so be it. Gary paused as he fully contemplated those thoughts; never once in his own world had he felt this way.

Gary lowered the mighty spear.

"If I win, then my friends are allowed to ride free," Gary declared.

"As you wish," Redarm replied exuberantly, and Gary knew that cocky knight didn't mean a word of it—not that Redarm expected Gary to win anyway.

It was, perhaps, the hardest thing that Gary Leger had ever done, something that went against his very instinct for survival. But he gritted his teeth and kicked his horse into motion, commanding the bells to "Ring!" and charging off down the road. The thunder of hooves doubled as Redarm similarly charged, that long and deadly lance dipped unerringly Gary's way.

Gary moved to the left side of the road, opposite the archers, held the spear across his body with his left hand, and clutched the bridle tightly with his right. Only with the bouncing of the charge did the young man realize how severe the wound in his side might be, and his battered knuckles ached so badly that he feared he would simply drop his weapon. He squinted against the sudden sharp pains, kept his focus straight ahead.

"Oh, valiant sprout!" came the spear's cry in his head, a cry that showed the spear to be thrilled to be in a joust once more.

"Oh, shut up," frightened Gary growled back through a grimace, working as hard as he could to hold his balance while keeping the spear out in some semblance of an attack posture.

The combatants closed, weapons leveled (though Gary's spear had begun to dip), elfish bells ringing and horses snorting for the exertion. In Gary charged, grim-faced, roaring in rage and pain.

And then he veered, at the last moment, away from the knight, turned his horse to the side of the road and charged off into the darkness.

"Young sprout!" came a cry of telepathic protest.

"Shut up!" Gary yelled back.

It took Redarm several moments to understand what had just happened in the pass. "Treachery!" he roared, in the direction of the diminishing sound of elfish bells. "Coward! Kill him! Kill them all!" The infuriated knight looked back towards the tavern wall, to the dissipating illusion of a horse and a pony where Gary's friends had been.

The surprised archers put a few wild shots the way Gary had fled, then came out of the bushes, scratching their heads.

The wind in Gary's face, the wind of freedom, almost erased the continuing pain in his side. He had outsmarted the enemies, used their strict adherence to codes against them, knowing that they would believe that he would not avoid a challenge of honor. But Gary would not confuse honor with stupidity. He had no armor on, hadn't even a shield to turn aside Redarm's deadly lance.

He heard one arrow cut the air not so far away, but was more concerned with the sound of hooves as his enemies took up the chase. He bent low in the saddle, told the bells to stop ringing, and trusted in his steed.

Kelsey had not lied; the sound of pursuit fast faded behind Gary as he flew on across the rolling fields. He heard the distant ringing of similar elfish bells and took it to be a signal from his friends. His mount apparently thought so, too, for the horse veered and snorted and took control of the ride from Gary. A few moments later, Gary saw a dark line up ahead, a stone wall probably. Whether he held doubts or not did not seem to matter to the horse, for the beast picked up its pace and did not turn to the side.

Equestrian jumping looked so easy on television. And indeed, the mount of Tir na n'Og easily flew over the low wall, clearing it on the far side by more than a dozen feet.

They had to land, though, and Gary Leger immediately gained tenfold respect for the straight-backed riders he had watched in equestrian competitions. He jerked forward, almost flying over, as the horse's forelegs slammed down, then went straight down, though of course he could not go straight down, when the horse came fully to the field.

His breath long gone, Gary thought that he should reach up and feel his throat to see just how high his testicles had bounced.

He was still leaning when he caught up to the others, Kelsey included, his horse trotting in beside Baron Pwyll's mount.

"Well done!" shouted the sincerely relieved Baron, and he clapped Gary hard on the shoulder. The dazed and wounded Gary would have fallen right off the other side of his horse, except that Geno was there to catch him and toss him roughly the other way.

The others watched in confusion as Gary struggled to gain an unsteady seat on his mount. "I think I need some help," the young man explained, and this time he did fall, between his horse and Pwyll's, the blood running freely from the knife cut in his side.

11 † Spirituality's End

"Why did you bring him?" The voice was distant to Gary, but he recognized it as Kelsey's, and the elf did not sound happy.

"I told ye before," Mickey replied. "It's bigger than yer spear and yer armor, bigger than Robert himself."

"Enough of your cryptic babble," Kelsey demanded.

"He did get us out of there," offered another voice, Baron Pwyll's.

"He dishonored himself, and us!" Kelsey snarled back.

Gary had been trying to convince his sleepy eyes to open, trying to shift his prone, weary body so that he could get up and join in the conversation. But now he knew what his friends were talking about, who his friends were talking about, and he was not so eager to join in.

"Ye couldn't expect the lad to fight it through," Mickey reasoned. "He didn't even have on the armor!"

"He challenged the man," Kelsey declared, and his words sounded with the finality of a nail being driven into Gary Leger's coffin. "Honorably."

"He fooled the man," Mickey corrected. "Fittingly. Besides, ye're the only one o' the group who's angry with the lad. Even Geno, who'd fight yerself to a draw, feels he owes the lad his thanks."

"Dwarfs don't mix honor and stupidity," came another voice, Geno's voice, from a different direction. "That's an

142

elfish trait, and one for humans, though you cannot trust any human, even on his word."

Gary blinked his eyes open. He was lying flat on his back, sunk deep in a thick bed of soft clover and looking up at the most spectacular display of twinkling stars he had ever seen. To his left, he saw the horses, and saw Geno and Gerbil ride up on the gnome's quadri-contraption. Across the other way sat Gary's remaining companions, circling a pile of glowing embers, Baron Pwyll eagerly digging the remaining food out of a small bowl.

"Is he alive?" Geno asked with his customary gruffness as he and the gnome crossed by Gary's feet.

"Oh, sure," Mickey answered. "His wound's not too bad, and the salve should fix it clean."

Gary instinctively dragged his hand to his side, felt a poultice there, and realized that the sharp pain had become no more than a distant and dull ache.

"Did you note any signs of pursuit?" Kelsey asked.

"Plenty of signs," Geno replied with a chuckle. "But all going in the wrong directions. Geldion's bunch lost the trail altogether when Mickey made the horse bells sound back to the north."

Gary had seen and heard enough of the leprechaun's tricks to understand what had occurred. Redarm and his minions were probably twenty miles away by now, chasing illusionary bells through dark fields.

"And we can keep goin' to the south," the leprechaun reasoned.

"East," Kelsey bluntly corrected. There came a long pause, as all of the others waited for Kelsey to explain. Gary wanted to hear it, too.

"We shall cross Dvergamal," the elf decided. "The dragon was last seen near to Gondabuggan. Perhaps he will still be about, or perhaps some of your folk"—Gary knew that Kelsey was speaking to Geno—"have seen him crossing the mountains."

"Oh, yes, yes, a fine plan," Gerbil interjected, above the stuttered protests of Baron Pwyll. "If Robert is still about my town, then won't he be surprised—oh, his dragon eyes will pop wide!—when a whole new group of heroes arrives to battle him!"

"If the wyrm is still about your town, then your town is no more a town," Geno put in, and from his tone, it didn't seem to Gary that the dwarf was particularly fond of Kelsey's plan.

"Have you a better idea?" Kelsey demanded, apparently thinking the same thing.

"I have an idea that chasing a dragon, a dragon that can fly," the dwarf emphasized, "across mountains, will get us nothing more than tired. Besides, whoever said that the plan was to catch up to the damned wyrm?"

"We have not the time to go all the way to Robert's lair," Kelsey reasoned, his voice firm and even.

"And you won't catch a flying wyrm crawling along mountain trails!" Geno said again.

"He's right," Mickey interjected. "We won't be catching Robert by going where the dragon's last been seen. We'll find charred trees and charred bones, to be sure."

Gerbil groaned.

"But not a sight o' the fast-flying wyrm," Mickey finished.

Gary chanced a look to the group, saw Kelsey, obviously agitated, jump up to his feet and stalk a few steps away.

"More than that," Geno said roughly, "the dragon is nowhere near to Gondabuggan anymore."

"What do you know?" Kelsey demanded, spinning about.

"The Buldrefolk have seen him," Geno answered. "In a

foul mood, soaring across the peaks of Dvergamal. Robert is out and flying free with Ceridwen banished to her island for the first time in centuries. He has a lot to see, elf, and a lot to conquer. Did he destroy the gnome town? Will he go for the Crahgs next, try to find some allies out of the pile of monsters lurking in there? Or might he go straight for Connacht, to burn the castle and the King? Robert knows as well as we that Kinnemore is Ceridwen's puppet. With the witch banished, if he can bring down the throne, then what might stop him?"

How true rang every one of Geno's suppositions, and how hopeless the desperate task seemed then to Kelsey. His scowl became a look of dread and resignation, and he turned back away, staring out into the empty night.

"We'll catch him," Mickey said to him. "But not by going where he's been—by going where he's sure to be."

Kelsey turned about once more, his eyes, shining golden even in the dim light of the embers, narrowed with an expression that seemed to Gary half anger and half intrigue.

"Oh, we'll go east, like ye said," Mickey went on, lighting his long-stemmed pipe. "But not 'til we get south around the mountains."

"To Giant's Thumb," Kelsey said.

Pwyll groaned again, and Geno's stream of spittle sizzled as it hit the embers.

"Dragons don't like thieves walking into their empty lairs to their backs," Mickey said with a conniving smile. "Robert'll come rushing back as fast as his flapping wings'll fly him when he senses that we're there. And when he sees what we bringed back to his hoard, then he's bound to stay put for a hundred years."

"What you brought back," Geno corrected.

"You have decided not to accompany us?" Kelsey asked.

"I never decided to accompany you!" the dwarf corrected. "I came east because east is my home, to get away from that stupid Prince Geldion and from yourself!" He poked a stubby finger Pwyll's way. "Don't you think that I've forgotten who put me in this trouble in the first place!"

The fearful Baron blanched.

"Ah, a load o' bluster," Mickey said, and Gary half expected Geno to leap up and spring across the embers to throttle the leprechaun. The dwarf did some mighty glowering, but kept his seat.

"Ye're here because ye got put in the middle of it, that much is true," Mickey continued. "But ye've stayed because ye know ye have to stay. Like our friend gnome, there. He'd like nothing more than to get back to Gondabuggan and his own, but he won't go, not if our best plans don't take him there."

"True enough, I figure. I figure," Gerbil replied, stroking his gray beard, shining more orange in the firelight than Gary had noticed before. "I figure?"

Geno sent another stream of spittle sizzling against the embers, but he did not openly dispute the wise leprechaun's reasoning. The dwarf knew more than the others, though, knew that Prince Geldion and his small band were but a tiny fraction of the resistance stemming from Connacht. Geno's companions in the Snoozing Sprite had told him that the King's army was on the march, northeast across the fields, drawing a line between Connacht and Braemar.

"South and east it is, then," Kelsey agreed. "To the Giant's Thumb, to lure the wyrm and to trap the wyrm."

A series of clucking noises issued forth from Baron Pwyll's twisting mouth, obvious protests against the seemingly suicidal course.

"You can stay here and wait for Geldion," Geno offered, punching the Baron in the arm. The dwarf spat again and rolled over, propping a rock for a pillow. "Too fat and slow anyway."

Gary shook his head, tried to lift his arms to clasp hands behind his neck, but found that he could only lift his right arm, his bound left side being too sore for the maneuver. He grimaced and tucked his left arm against his side, hoping that it would heal before he found himself in another battle.

That thought led Gary's gaze down between his feet, to the pile of armor and the long black spear, resting easily against it. Gary propped himself up on his elbows—gingerly—and reached his toe down to tap against the weapon.

A blue spark erupted from the butt end of the spear, singeing Gary's toe and coursing through his body, sending his thick black hair into a momentary standstill atop his head.

"Hey!" he exclaimed.

"Coward!"

The message stole all the surprise from Gary's body, stole his strength and just about everything else, as well. He stared blankly at the mighty weapon, confused and distressed.

"I'm not a coward," he replied, quietly aloud, but with the protest screaming in his thoughts.

He waited, but the spear did not dignify the declaration with a response.

"Problems?" Mickey asked, skipping over to sit in the clover beside the young man. Gary looked to the spear.

"Damned thing zapped me," he explained.

"Coward!"

"I am not a coward!" Gary growled.

"Ah," muttered Mickey. "The proud spear's not liking yer choice to run from Redarm."

"I didn't run from Redarm!" Gary snapped back, more

angrily than he had intended. "I mean ... I just ... we were trying to get away."

Mickey stopped him with a low whistle and a knowing wave of his little hand. "I know what ye were doing, lad, and you did well, by me own guess," the leprechaun explained. "The spear's a proud one, that's all, and not liking missing any fight, needed or not."

"Coward!"

Gary growled at the spear; images of heaving it over a bottomless ravine in Dvergamal came into his thoughts. The spear responded by imparting telepathic images of Gary going over the edge, and of the spear plunging down behind, chasing him, point first, all the way down the sheer cliffs.

And then the connection was broken, simply gone. Gary looked around curiously, suspecting, but not certain of, what had occurred. Had the spear rejected him? Would it refuse his grasp in the morning, and forever after?

"How stubborn can a weapon be?" the young man asked Mickey.

"Less bending than the metal they're forged with," the leprechaun replied.

"Then we might be in trouble."

Mickey nodded and took a long draw on his pipe, then blew a large smoke ring that drifted the length of Gary's body and settled around the tip of the mighty spear.

"Have it your own way," Gary remarked to the spear, and he lay back down in the clover, head in his hand and looked again to the wondrous nighttime sky of Faerie. Hundreds of stars peeked back at him, pulled at his heart. He wanted to fly up there suddenly, to soar out into the universe and play in the heavens.

" 'Tis a beauty," Mickey agreed, seeing the obvious pleasure splayed across Gary's suddenly serene features.

"Better than anything I've ever seen in my own world," Gary agreed.

"The same sky," Mickey replied.

Gary shook his head. "No!" he said emphatically, and then he took a moment to figure out where that firm denial had come from. "It's different," he said at length. "My world is too full of cities, maybe, and streetlights."

"They burn all the night?"

"All the night," Gary answered. "And dull the sky. And the air's probably too dirty for the stars to match this." Gary chuckled resignedly, helplessly. It was true enough, true and sad, but there was even something more profound that made Gary believe that even without the night lights and the dirty air, the stars of his own world would not shine so brightly.

"It's different," he said again. "We have a different way of looking at stars, at all things." Yes, that was it, Gary decided. Not just the actual image of the night sky, but the perspective, was very different.

"We have science and scientists, solving all the mysteries," he explained to a doubtful-looking Mickey. "Sometimes I think that's the whole problem." Another pitiful chuckle escaped Gary's lips. He considered the demise of religion in his world, when the mysteries of faith became not so mysterious. He thought of the Shroud of Turin, long believed to be the actual cloth covering the body of Jesus. Only a few days ago, Gary had watched a show on PBS where scientists had dated the cloth of the shroud to sometime around a thousand years AFTER the death of Christ.

It was an inevitable clash, science and religion, and one that Gary was just now beginning to understand that his people had not properly resolved or accounted for. Religions hung on to outdated myths, and science ruthlessly battered at them with seemingly indisputable logic.

"Explaining everything," Gary said again, and again, he

laughed, this time loudly enough to attract the attention of Kelsey and Pwyll, sitting by the glowing embers. "Do you know what it feels like to be mortal, Mickey?"

"What're ye talking about?" the leprechaun replied sincerely, honestly trying to understand this thing that was so obviously distressing his friend.

"Mortal," Gary reiterated. "You see, when you take the mysteries away, so too goes the spirituality, the belief in something beyond this physical life."

"That's a stupid way to live."

Gary chuckled yet again and could not disagree. But neither could he escape, he knew. He was a product of his world, a product of an era where science ruled supreme, where no balance between physical truths and spiritual needs had been struck. "It's . . ." Gary searched for the word. ". . . despairing. When the physical world becomes explained to a level where there is no room . . ." Gary let the thought drift away and simply shook his head.

"Ye think yer scientists got all the answers, then?" Mickey asked.

Maybe not for this trip of mine, Gary thought. Whatever the hell this placed called Faerie might actually be.

"There is no magic in my world," Gary answered solemnly.

"Oh, there ye're wrong," the leprechaun replied, taking the pipe from his mouth and poking Gary in the shoulder with its long stem. "There ye're wrong. The magic's there, I tell ye—yer people have just lost their way to seein' it!"

"No magic," Gary said again, with finality, and he looked away from Mickey and stared back up at the incredible night canopy.

"Can yer so-smart scientists tell ye then why yer heart leaps up at the sight o' stars?" the leprechaun asked smugly, and he snapped his little fingers right in front of Gary's nose.

"Thought not!" Mickey continued in the face of Gary's incredulous stare. "Yer science won't be telling ye that, not for a long while. It's a magic common to all the folk— never could a man or a sprite or even a dwarf look up at the stars and not feel the tug o' magic."

Gary wasn't sure that he bought Mickey's description of it all, but the leprechaun's words were, somehow, comforting. The man from the other world stole a line from a song, then, again from that haunting *Tusk* album, a quiet song by the group's other woman singer. "Oh what a wonderful night to be," he half sang, half chanted. "Stars must be my friends to shine on me."

"Ah, the bard McVie," Mickey said with obvious pleasure.

Gary's forthcoming reply stuck in his throat. The bard McVie! How the hell could Mickey . . .

Gary shook his head and let out a cry that startled Mickey and sent Kelsey leaping to his feet. Seeing that nothing was askew, no enemies nearby, the elf threw a threatening glare Gary and Mickey's way and slowly eased himself back down.

"What?" Mickey started to ask, but Gary cut him short with a wave of his hand.

"Never mind," was all that he cared to say at that time.

"As ye wish, lad," Mickey answered, hopping to his feet. "Get yerself some rest, then. We've a long road in the morn."

Gary continued to look at the stars for a long time, thinking hard. The bard McVie? The last time Gary was in Faerie, when he had brought *The Hobbit* along with him, Mickey had hinted that the author of that book, J.R.R. Tolkien, had probably crossed into Faerie, as Gary had done, and that the books that Gary considered so fantastical might be the true adventures of that remarkable man, or adventures told to him by another visitor to Faerie, or by one of Faerie's folk.

Now the leprechaun had inadvertently expanded upon that possibility. Could it be that many of the artists, the sculptors and the painters, the musicians penning haunting songs, the writers of fantastical works, had actually crossed into this realm, had found the magic and brought a little piece of it back with them to share with a world that so badly needed it? Might the artists of Gary's world be people who could find the magic beneath the dulling cover, who could see the stars despite the city lights?

It was a comforting thought, one that led weary and wounded Gary Leger into a deep and much-needed sleep.

12 † Arrayed for War

Mickey's salve worked wonderfully, and most of the pain was gone from Gary's side when he awakened the next morning, despite the fact that moisture hung thick in the air, grayed by a solid curtain of heavy clouds. There remained some uncomfortable pulling in the scar tissue when Gary stood up and stretched, and a soreness when Geno and Baron Pwyll began strapping on the armor, but it was nothing too bad.

Gary spent most of the minutes looking over to the spear, lying prone on the grassy field. There had been no mental contact, at least none that Gary could consciously sense, since he had awakened. It seemed to him that the spear was brooding—he got the feeling, too, that it didn't like the fact that he was donning its complementary armor—and he feared that he might have to find himself another weapon.

Even more worrisome to Gary was the fact that Kelsey, who also had labeled him a coward, was giving him the proverbial cold shoulder. The elf looked his way several times while the armor was being put on, always locked gazes with Gary for just an instant, and then his golden eyes would narrow and he would brusquely turn away.

Not that Gary was overly thrilled with Kelsey at that time, either. He kept seeing images of the man stumbling into the room at the Snoozing Sprite, an elfish arrow dug into his back. Gary understood the necessity of fighting, understood the grim consequences of not winning, but it seemed to him as though Kelsey could have achieved the same margin of victory by shooting the man in the leg instead, or in the shoulder, perhaps. Gary knew well how marvelous a shot the elf was with that deadly bow; if the arrow was sticking through the man's heart, it was only because that was exactly where Kelsey had meant it to be.

The armor was on, then, and Gary worked his arms about in circles, stretching this way and that to try to better the fit. Kelsey walked by him, on his way to the horses, again throwing an angry, dangerous glare Gary's way.

"Did you have to kill them?" Gary asked reflexively, grabbing at something, some accusation, with which to shoot back at the judgmental elf.

"Of what do you speak?" Kelsey replied to him, seeming honestly confused. Mickey and Gerbil, over by the gnome's quadricycle, and Pwyll and Geno, already readying their mounts, paused and looked Gary's way.

"The men back at the inn," Gary pressed, trying to ignore the elf's cavalier attitude about it all and the continuing concerned stares of his other companions. "You shot to kill."

"Perhaps we should have stopped to reason with them," Kelsey said sarcastically, coming up to stand right before Gary.

"You didn't have to kill them," Gary said sternly.

"They came at us," Kelsey pointedly reminded him, and the elf snorted derisively and turned away, as though he felt that the conversation wasn't worth continuing.

"I am not a coward!" Gary growled at his back. Gary never considered his next move, never took a moment to think things through. He slammed his hands against Kelsey's back and shoved as hard as he could.

Kelsey flew several feet, diving headlong. He was agile

enough to tuck his shoulder, and wise enough not to fight against the undeniable momentum, and he rolled right back to his feet, spinning as he went so that he came up facing Gary. In the blink of an eye, Kelsey's sword came out and he rushed Gary's way, launching a swing.

Gary hardly flinched, reminding himself that Kelsey would not kill him. He instinctively brought his arm up to block, caught the sword on his forearm as it whipped to a stop barely inches from his neck. The two stared unblinkingly for several moments. Gary realized a throbbing ache in his arm, believed that he might be bleeding under the armor, but he did not relent his hold, even growled and pushed the weapon farther from him.

"I am not a coward," he said again.

"But are you a fool?" Kelsey asked dangerously and Gary heard Mickey suck in air and hold his breath.

Gary didn't blink, didn't flinch at all, just held the pose, and the weapon, as the long seconds slipped past.

"You fled," Kelsey remarked at length.

"Wasn't it Kelsey who led the flight from Geldion in Dilnamarra?" Gary replied coyly.

"I made no challenge of honor!" the elf snarled, snapping his sword away and slipping it into its scabbard so quickly that Gary could hardly follow the movement.

"To hell with your challenge," Gary replied without hesitation. "I had to get my friends out of there. Their lives were worth more to me than any false conceptions of honor. Brand me a coward if you choose, Kelsenellenenen . . . whatever the hell your name is, but you know better."

Kelsey's visage softened somewhat for just a moment. The elf seemed to realize his slip, though, and his scowl returned as he turned away to go to his horse.

Gary only then realized that he was trembling—with anger and not with fear.

"I am waiting, young sprout," came a call in his head,

slightly reluctant perhaps, but Gary realized then that his
bold words had deflected more than Kelsey's outrage. He
went over and roughly grabbed up the spear, and, under
the continuing gazes of his surprised friends, walked
steadily to his horse. He hoisted Mickey up first, then
moved to put his foot in the stirrup.

The white steed shied away and Gary understood that it
was smart enough to react to Kelsey's emotions.

"Tell the stupid horse to behave," Gary demanded of the
elf. Kelsey scowled at him and said nothing, but the horse
did not shy away when Gary took hold of it a second time.

At Geno's insistence, they rode out at a leisurely pace.
Kelsey didn't offer much argument against that, since he
wanted to learn much more about what Robert had been
up to before they ever got near the Giant's Thumb. They
kept mostly to the south, skirting the towering rocky peaks
of Dvergamal, and only occasionally skipping away from
the mountains' protective shadow to ride up to lonely
groupings of farmhouses and see what they might learn.

For the most part, the group remained quiet, each caught
in his own private swirl of worries and contemplations.
Gerbil did not even know if Gondabuggan had survived,
Baron Pwyll felt that he surely would not, and Kelsey's
fair features were clouded by the weight of tremendous responsibility. Geno kept looking every which way, as
though he expected the dragon, or something else, to
spring out at him at any moment, and in watching the
dwarf, Gary recognized that Geno's insistence that they
ride more slowly had nothing to do with a sore backside.

For Gary Leger, the enormity of the situation around
him, the incredible danger, far beyond anything he had
ever experienced in his own world, kept his mind more
than occupied. Again there was that strange sense of calm
accompanying it all, though, that feeling that he was part
of something bigger, the feeling that his actions, whatever

the personal cost, held a profound effect on something more important than his own mortality.

More important than his own mortality!

But it was true; Gary knew that to be truly how he felt. He wondered how many people of his world had ever experienced this sensation. He thought of the war raging back home, of the fanatical, suicidal people facing off against the United States-led coalition. Were they really so altruistic, so believing in their religion, that they were not afraid of death itself?

The thought sent a shudder along Gary's spine. He feared people so fanatical. But also, Gary envied them, for their purpose in life, however Gary might judge the merits of their religion and loyalties, was larger than his own, was larger than the next fifty or sixty years, or however long he had left to live.

An inevitable smile cut through the trepidation, and Gary glanced around at his five companions. He saw Gerbil sitting low, casually pumping the wondrous quadricycle, and felt sympathy for the gnome, and prayed that Gerbil's fears for his homeland would not come to pass. He noticed Geno, glancing about again, and knew that the dwarf was up to something. He felt for Kelsey, so noble and proud, and inadvertently the cause of this terrible strife.

Gary's gaze lingered long on Mickey. The leprechaun sat before him on his horse, resting easily against the beast's high-held neck and holding his pipe (though it was not lit) between his teeth. Gary had seen this same faraway look in Mickey's gray eyes before, a sadness and a longing.

"What are you thinking?" he eventually asked the sprite.

"Of long ago," Mickey answered quietly. "When all the

goodly races were as one. Maybe there's not enough true evil in the world today, lad."

Gary thought the comment odd, especially considering the company Mickey was now keeping: two men, an elf, a dwarf, and a gnome, all riding side by side towards a common goal.

"It would seem as if they're united again," Gary remarked.

Mickey shrugged and made no comment.

"Why did you bring me here?" Gary asked bluntly, and for the first time in the talk, the leprechaun looked directly at the young man. "I need to know," Gary explained.

Mickey's huge smile erupted. "I needed a body to carry around that armor," the leprechaun remarked coyly. "Couldn't be leaving it in a bush, and wouldn't want to sack it and lift it over me shoulder!"

"No," Gary said seriously, somberly. "It's more than that."

"Well, ye've fought the dragon once already . . ."

"And more than Robert," Gary interrupted. "I might help against the dragon, but not enough to make it worth your while to pluck me from my own world."

"Ye don't want to be here?" Mickey asked evenly.

"I didn't say that," Gary quickly replied, refusing to let the tricky leprechaun deflect the conversation.

Mickey let out a deep sigh and clasped his hands behind his hairy head, the tip of his tam-o'-shanter dipping low over his sparkling gray eyes. He looked away from Gary and off into empty air. Gary waited patiently, understanding that the leprechaun had something to say, was just trying to weigh every word carefully.

"Ye know it's more than the dragon," Mickey began. He motioned for Gary to slow the horse, to put some ground between them and the others. "Ye knew last time ye came here that bad things been brewing between Connacht and Dilnamarra."

Gary nodded, remembering the confrontation between Baron Pwyll and Prince Geldion when they had first gone for the armor, a time that seemed like several years before to Gary (and from his perspective, it was!).

"And so goes Dilnamarra, so goes Braemar," Mickey went on. "And Drochit as well, and a dozen other hamlets that have so far resisted King Kinnemore's greedy hands."

"Kinnemore is Ceridwen's puppet," Gary remarked. He had heard this much before.

Mickey nodded. "Aye, and with the witch stuck to her island, and Robert flying free, she's been forced to play out her hand, to take the aces outa her sleeves," the leprechaun explained, in language that he knew Gary would fully comprehend. "That's why Ceridwen went for the armor, and went for Pwyll when the armor could not be found. And she'll be going for more before all's ended, lad, and so'll greedy Robert."

Gary sat back in his saddle. He had suspected those very things, of course, both from Robert's reported raids and the actions of stubborn Prince Geldion. But to hear Mickey put it so plainly nearly overwhelmed the young man. There was a tug-of-war going on here, between Ceridwen with her puppet king and the dragon, and all the commonfolk of Faerie, and the dwarfs and gnomes and Tylwyth Teg, and even the leprechauns, were caught squarely in the middle of it.

"That's why Geno's coming along," Mickey remarked, easily understanding the train of Gary's thoughts. "And Gerbil, too, though the little one hasn't figured it all out yet. Yerself played a part in bringing it to this point, lad, and so there might be things that only yerself can do. I thinked it proper and right that ye should get to help in finishing the tale."

Gary wasn't so sure that he liked where this particular tale might be headed, for his own sake and for the sake of Faerie's goodly folk, but he nodded his appreciation to Mickey, for he did indeed want, and need, to be an active participant in the writing of the tale.

The armored captain fidgeted impatiently atop his armored warhorse, looking to his lightly clothed servant and the great black bird perched upon the man's upheld arm. With a squawk to cut the morning air, the crow lifted off and flew away furiously, swiftly becoming a black speck among the ominous gray of the heavy sky.

"What did the damned bird say?" the captain demanded, obviously not thrilled in dealing with supernatural creatures. By the edicts of his own dear King, magic had been declared demonic and outlawed, and here they were, the army of Connacht, talking to birds!

"We must not be straight for Braemar," the servant informed the captain. "The outlaw Pwyll and his renegade band, along with the stolen artifacts, are making south along the mountain line. We need veer to the east and intercept them. King Kinnemore has declared that they must not make the Crahgs."

The large and straight-backed captain scowled. The outlaw Pwyll, he thought, and the notion didn't sit well with him. He and many of his soldiers had gone to Connacht from Dilnamarra, and they had never known Baron Pwyll, for all his bluster and love of comfort, to be anything short of generous.

But Kinnemore was King, this lowly captain's King, and to this man's sensibilities, that placed Kinnemore just one rung on the hierarchical ladder below God himself.

"What of Prince Geldion?" the captain asked.

"The Prince and his force are riding west of the outlaws," the servant explained. "We will join on the field."

The captain nodded and motioned for his sergeants to get the force moving once more. He didn't like dealing with supernatural creatures on a superstitious level, but in all practicality, the information being passed between the crows was proving invaluable to the mission, and thus, to the King.

"Friends of yours?" Gerbil asked Geno when the party had broken for a midday meal. The gnome motioned across the camp, beyond the tethered horses and the parked quadricycle, to the foothills, where a group of dwarfs fully arrayed for battle were marching in a single line along a narrow trail, just under the low-riding layer of thick gray clouds. Gary and Pwyll turned in unison with Geno to regard the dwarfs, noticed Kelsey crouching behind a stone, bow in hand. Mickey was nowhere to be seen, but Gary knew the leprechaun well enough to realize that he had certainly spotted the dwarfish marchers.

"Better go to them," Geno remarked dryly. "Before the elf gets himself clobbered." He jumped up and brushed the biscuit crumbs off him, then spotted a large one that had fallen to the ground and greedily scooped it up, along with a good measure of dirt, and stuffed it into his mouth.

It struck Gary as more than a little curious that Geno did not seem the least bit surprised by the appearance of the dwarfs.

"Put the puny bow away!" they heard Geno rumble at Kelsey, and he kicked a stone the prone elf's way as he ambled past. He and the dwarfs exchanged signals of greeting, and then they all disappeared over a ridge.

Kelsey came back to the group, then, obviously fearful, and Mickey came in right behind him.

"What is it?" the leprechaun asked as soon as he saw the elf's darting eyes.

"We may have just lost Geno's aid," Kelsey replied.

"Or worse." The way he kept glancing about revealed to Gary, and to fearful Pwyll, that Kelsey almost expected the dwarfish band to attack. In an instant, the Baron's eyes went this way and that, more anxiously than Kelsey's.

"The dwarfs're not our enemies," Mickey offered calmly to Kelsey, and to nervous Pwyll. "Ye'll know that soon, me friend. The dwarfs're not our enemies, and Geno's not for leaving."

"What do you know?" Kelsey demanded.

Mickey nodded to the ridge, to where Geno had just re-appeared, stomping his way back to the campsite. Kelsey nodded, too, calmed by the sight, and Pwyll let out a profound sigh of relief. Gary tossed the man a curious glance, and wondered, and not for the first time, how Pwyll had ever become a Baron.

"They are out searching for the dragon?" Kelsey reasoned hopefully.

"Dwarfs are too smart to go out looking for dragons," Geno grumbled back.

"What about you?" Gary remarked, seeing the obvious fault in Geno's logic. Hadn't Geno, after all, already accompanied them once to Robert's lair?

"Shut your mouth!" came the predictable response.

Gary did.

"Then why?" Kelsey asked, and it seemed to Gary as if the elf already knew, had known all along.

"I learned it in Braemar," Geno replied. "From friends at the Snoozing Sprite."

"Learned what?" piped in Gerbil, stroking his orange-and-white beard and appearing more openly anxious than he had previously let on.

"Oh, it is King Kinnemore!" Baron Pwyll, knowledge-able in the politics of the land, wailed. He threw up his hands and verily danced in circles, crying that they were all doomed.

Geno nodded grimly. "A force rides from the south-west," he confirmed. "Five hundred strong by some reports, larger than that by others."

Gary could understand that, knew how badly Ceridwen, and thus the King in Connacht, wanted to get her hands on the armor and spear of Cedric Donigarten. "Why are the dwarfs out?" he had to ask, somewhat confused by where Geno's folk fit into all of this. "Do they care that much for us? For him?" Gary added, pointing to Baron Pwyll.

"They care that little for Ceridwen's king puppet," Geno corrected.

Gary looked to Mickey, who only shrugged and nodded, seeming not surprised in the least by the sudden turn of events. More than ever, Gary Leger understood why Mickey had brought him back to Faerie, and though he was terribly afraid, more than ever did Gary Leger appreciate the leprechaun's choice.

He had helped to bring things to this point, for better or for worse, as Mickey had said. He felt duty-bound now to finish the tale.

For better or for worse.

"Lord Duncan Drochit and Badenoch of Braemar should be told," Kelsey reasoned. "If so large a force is coming this way, then they'll likely not stop at catching Baron Pwyll and retrieving the artifacts."

Baron Pwyll let out another of his increasingly annoying whines.

Geno nodded grimly to Kelsey and pointed back to the north, where a cloud of dust was just beginning to climb into the midday air.

"The King has come!" Pwyll cried out. "Oh, woe . . ."

"Shut your mouth," Geno barked at him.

"Badenoch and Drochit," Kelsey reasoned. "With the combined militia of the two towns."

"Still not a third of what Connacht has sent," Geno replied grimly. "Riding plowhorses and carrying wood axes and hay forks."

Gary looked at his own armor, his own mighty weapon, and could well imagine what those poorly outfitted common farmers might soon meet in the field.

Baron Pwyll continued to wail; a shudder ran along Gary Leger's spine.

13 † Hold Yer Breath, Lad

The companions caught up with the ragtag militia of Drochit and Braemar a few hours later, on the high edge of a field looking down across the rolling hills to the west and south. Despite Geno's assurances concerning what his dwarfish kinfolk had told him, Kelsey kept the companions outside the ring of farmer-soldiers, unsure of where the lines of alliances had been drawn. By all reports and all previous actions, Duncan Drochit and Lord Badenoch would seem to be friends, but in these confusing and dangerous times, and with so much hanging on the success of their quest, the friends had to exercise all caution.

The sentries within the camp, too, seemed unsure, eyeing the riders with some concern and clutching tightly to their pitchforks and axes. Finally, a contingent of dwarfs came marching out of the rocky foothills, and Geno, Kelsey, and Gerbil fell into step beside them, going with them to meet the militia leaders.

"They'll have no trouble," Mickey assured Gary, and Baron Pwyll, whose fate seemed to hang so precariously in the balance. "We're all looking for the same thing, to stop the dragon and Connacht."

"Unless Badenoch and Drochit think it safer to hand me over to Prince Geldion," Baron Pwyll said gloomily, but there was a trace of accepting resignation in the large man's tone that Gary had not noticed before.

"They won't hand you over," Gary said firmly, to comfort the troubled man.

"Ye should have more the faith in yer friends," Mickey added. "How many times have both Badenoch and Drochit looked to yerself with support, mostly in matters concerning the witch-backed throne?"

Pwyll nodded, but the grim expression did not leave his round face. "Perhaps we would all be better off if I just surrender to Prince Geldion when he arrives," the Baron said with unexpected altruism.

"Better for all?" Mickey quipped. "Not so much better for yerself, unless ye're fancying hemp collars."

Pwyll shrugged, but his mounting determination did not seem to ebb. It appeared to Gary as though the man was fighting an inner battle, conscience against cowardice, mustering his courage and looking beyond his own needs, even his own survival. Pwyll was formulating his own secret agenda, Gary knew, one that might well send him running to Geldion.

"Besides," Mickey quickly put in, apparently beginning to understand things the same way as Gary, "Geldion's not really looking for yerself."

Both men cocked curious eyebrows Mickey's way. "For the spear and armor?" Gary asked.

"That's a part of it, by me guess," Mickey replied, eyeing Gary directly and grimly. "But he's wanting yerself, lad, and that we cannot let him get."

Gary was about to ask what in hell Prince Geldion might want with him, but he thought things through silently instead, remembered from where the King, and thus the Prince, was being directed. Beautiful, raven-haired Ceridwen was the power behind Faerie's throne, and Gary was the one who had put a spear through the witch's belly, had banished her to her island home for a hundred years.

It was not a comforting notion, and hung heavily in

Gary's thoughts for the rest of that day, even after a group of men rode out from the encampment and bade the three companions to come in.

Baron Pwyll was immediately summoned to join the conference with Kelsey, Badenoch, and Drochit. Seeming more assured than before, the big man squared his shoulders and walked with a confident stride.

"He was thinking of surrendering to Geldion," Gary remarked to Mickey, though he realized that the leprechaun had already figured that much out.

"That one'll surprise ye," Mickey replied. "Pwyll, above all the other lords, has held out against Kinnemore. Just the fact that Geldion's taking the trouble to come out after him shows Pwyll's strength."

Gary nodded, but had a hard time reconciling what he knew about the fat Baron—particularly how Pwyll seemed to spend more time trembling than anything else—against the obvious respect the man commanded from friends and enemies alike. The guards standing on opposite sides of the command tent, wherein Kelsey was meeting with the two lords, beamed happily at the sight of Pwyll, as though their salvation was at hand, and straightened their posture as he passed between them.

Gary sighed, and figured that Pwyll must have been something more spectacular when he was a younger man. He looked to Mickey again, and found the leprechaun walking away, towards a small cook-fire where Gerbil, Geno, and a few other dwarfs were gathered.

"What's the matter with the little one?" Gary heard Mickey ask as he rushed to catch up with the sprite. One look at Gerbil, head down and a pained expression upon his normally cheery expression, told Gary where that question had come from.

"Word has spread of casualties from the dragon attack on Gondabuggan," Geno informed them. The beardless dwarf gave a surprisingly sympathetic look Gerbil's way, then piped in heartily, "The gnomes beat him off, though! Sent Robert fleeing to the mountains to lick grievous wounds." Geno reached over and gave Gerbil a swat on the back, but the gnome did not visibly react.

"But not without cost," another dwarf, one with a blue beard tucked into a wide, jeweled belt with a golden buckle, added. "An entire section of the town was destroyed and a fair number of gnomes killed. And it is said that Robert came back, but did not go into the town."

"A gnome patrol is missing in the foothills," Geno added. "Along with one of my own kin."

Pangs of guilt turned Gary's stomach. He had been part of the group that had gone to Robert's lair, an act that had apparently coaxed the dragon out. And Gary had been the one to banish Ceridwen, a good thing by one way of thinking, but the act that had upset the balance, had given Robert the Wretched the confidence to fly free so far from his mountain home.

Gary had found that he liked Gerbil, and if Gerbil was typical of his race, as Mickey had said, then the loss to Gondabuggan was surely a loss to all the world.

"They're going to send us around the fighting, if there is to be any fighting," Geno remarked, pointedly changing the subject. "If Geldion blocks the way, then we are to go around while Badenoch and Drochit hold him at bay."

Mickey nodded, apparently in agreement, but something discordant tugged hard at Gary's sensibilities.

"We all want the same thing," the young man replied angrily. "How can we think about battling the Prince with the dragon soaring about? Why don't we all just band together against the dragon, then worry about our personal feuds?"

There came no immediate response, the simple logic of Gary's words seeming to steal the words from Geno and

Mickey and all the others. At first, Gary took this to mean that he might be on to something, but he soon came to realize that he simply did not understand the depth of the budding feud between Connacht and the outlying baronies.

"Who's going on to the dragon?" Mickey asked Geno.

"Same as before," the dwarf replied. "Though we might bring a few of my kinfolk along, and Pwyll might be asked to stay behind."

"He'd hate that," Gary remarked sarcastically.

"And the little one," Geno went on, patting Gerbil again. "His path is his own to choose. He might want to get back to Gondabuggan and help with the repairs."

"No," Gerbil said resolutely, lifting his head so that the others could see the determination in his inquisitive eyes. "No, no! I go to sting the dragon's home, I do, just as he attacked my own! Be afraid, wretched wyrm!" the gnome proclaimed loudly. "Oh, do, if you are half as smart as the legends say. You have never had an angry gnome in your nest, I would guess, and when you do, you will not be so happy a wyrm!"

Gary was just coming to terms with Geno's unexpectedly sympathetic posture when Gerbil launched his uncharacteristic tirade. He stared at the suddenly fierce gnome incredulously, then to Geno and the other dwarfs, lifting their mugs in a toast Gerbil's way.

"Slow to anger, but fierce as a badger when they do," Mickey whispered to Gary, referring to Gerbil and the race of gnomes in general. Gary did not argue; standing there, one foot up on a log, his head tilted back proudly, Gerbil seemed almost four feet tall.

Geno was the only dwarf accompanying Kelsey, Gary, Mickey, and Gerbil as they walked their mounts (and Gerbil pumped his quadricycle) to a ridge above and to the side of the field where the opposing forces would meet.

Kelsey and Geno moved behind a brush line overlooking the field, while Gary, with Mickey tucked in front of him, stayed back, and Gerbil found a level and out-of-the-way place to park his rolling contraption. With all that was happening, politically and militarily, the village leaders had decided that speed and stealth would be absolutely necessary if the small group was to have any chance of getting through to the Giant's Thumb to replace the stolen dagger. Thus, Badenoch, Drochit, Pwyll, and Kervin of the dwarfs had determined that the other dwarfs would not accompany the band, that the responsibility fell upon the shoulders of those who had taken the dagger, and upon Gerbil, who insisted that he be allowed to go along. Surly Geno, hoping for a little dwarfish companionship on the hard road, hadn't stopped grumbling since.

Neither would Baron Pwyll accompany the friends, for Lords Badenoch and Drochit had begged the man to remain with them (right before Pwyll had begun to beg to be allowed to remain with them), to lend support and wisdom as they tried to fend off Connacht's encroachments from one side, and Robert's impending appearance from the other. That left one Tir na n'Og horse free, Gary noted. He was about to ask about that, wondering if they should perhaps take the mount along as an extra, when he got his answer. Up padded the proud horse, bearing a short but stout and heavily muscled man with an impossibly thick black beard and tanned arms the size of Gary's thighs. He wore a sleeveless jerkin and simple breeches (that were too small for him), and carried an immense hammer over one shoulder. His skin was darkly tanned and seemed darker still, with patches of soot ground in against the brown flesh. His beard and thick-cropped hair were matted with the dirt and sweat of hard labors.

"Well met," Kelsey called to him, apparently expecting the ally. Geno and Mickey greeted the man as well, though

Gerbil seemed too consumed by his private thoughts to even recognize that another had joined them.

The huge man started for the ridge, then noticed Gary and gave a fierce tug that promptly wheeled his horse about, aiming it straight for the armored man. "Cedric," he said, extending a calloused hand Gary's way and flashing a huge, broken-toothed smile.

"Cedric?" Gary echoed.

"Cedric the smithy," the man replied. "Best shoer in the world."

"Gary Leger," Gary replied, and he was nearly pulled from his saddle when the man grabbed his extended hand and pumped it vigorously.

"An honor, spearwielder," the man growled, and Gary was surprised by the obvious admiration in his tone. The smithy let go—Gary unconsciously wiped his now-grimy hand on his side—and jerked his horse about roughly. He nodded once more to Gary before padding up towards the crest of the ridge to join Kelsey and Geno.

"They're to meet in the field," Cedric explained loudly, and then Gary could make out no more as the powerful smithy moved in close to the others.

"Cedric?" Gary asked Mickey.

"All the smithys—the human smithys—are named Cedric," the leprechaun explained. "In honor of Donigarten. Ye couldn't find an ally more loyal, lad. Ye're carrying the spear and wearing the suit of the man's idol. That's why he was given the extra horse. Cedric'll die for ye, die for the spearwielder, smiling all the while if he thinks he's helped yer noble cause."

It sounded crazy to Gary Leger, and he wasn't so sure that he liked having a man so willing to die for him. He started to mention that fact to Mickey, but changed his mind, suddenly realizing those thoughts as condescending. Who was he to determine another man's motivations? If

Cedric the smithy would die smiling for the noble cause, then Cedric was a noble man, and Gary was the fool if he confused that sense of honor with foolishness.

"A good thing to have him along," Mickey remarked, and Gary nodded sincerely.

They saw Kelsey's arm jerk out suddenly, pointing to the field below, and Mickey bade Gary to walk the horse over so that they might see the arrival of Geldion.

The Prince came in from the southeast, the soldiers of Connacht arrayed behind him in the even lines of a well-trained army. Geldion rode out from the ranks on a black horse, flanked by three soldiers on either side. Redarm was not among this guard, Gary noted, and nowhere to be seen among the front ranks of Connacht soldiers, though what that might mean the young man could not discern.

Gary focused his attention on the Prince instead. Geldion looked far from regal, looked almost haggard, actually, his skin too browned from the long road and pulled tight to his bones. He wore his worn brown traveling cloak, tied only at the neck, and a suit of armor that had seen many, many encounters. Jeweled scabbards at his side held sword and dagger, though, and Mickey assured Gary that Geldion was well versed in the use of both weapons.

In response to Geldion's bold approach, Badenoch and Duncan Drochit trotted their mounts out from their ragtag force, Kervin the dwarfish leader running along beside them.

"Well met, Prince Geldion," the friends heard Badenoch call. The wind was behind the Lord, blowing in the faces of the hiding companions, and they heard the words clearly. "Glad are we that Connacht came to us in our time of need," Badenoch went on, "for mighty Robert has taken wing and threatens all the land!"

Geldion rocked back in his saddle; he seemed a bit surprised to Gary.

"Will you and your forces ride to Braemar beside us?" Badenoch continued, his tone anything but hostile.

"Is Geldion to become an ally?" Gary whispered to Mickey. For a moment, the young man thought that his earlier words might prove true, that these supposed enemies would band together against a common foe more powerful than either of them separately.

"Badenoch uses diplomacy to force Geldion to move first," Kelsey explained grimly, and Gary was somewhat surprised, and certainly pleased, that the elf was apparently talking to him again. "The lords feign friendship so that Geldion will have no excuse to attack."

Prince Geldion sat atop his mount, eyeing the lords suspiciously. His father had told him of the conspiracy, had even hinted that outlawed magic was being used to bring the lesser towns into line against Connacht. The thought did not sit well with the Prince of Faerie. Geldion was an extension of Kinnemore's throne, the most loyal of sons, but a part of him had been thrilled, and not so angry, when the ancient spear of Faerie's greatest hero had been reforged. His father, though, had been purely outraged, a fact that bothered and confused Geldion more than a little.

That confusion would not deter him from executing the duties Kinnemore had given to him. Not at all. Geldion would not let this Gary Leger of Bretaigne steal the repaired spear away, even if he had to kill the man personally!

"We may ride to Braemar," he replied in his shrill voice. "But not for any defense against Robert. The dragon is only one of our concerns, and not the most immediate one."

"Surely the dragon . . ." Badenoch began, but the always impatient Prince cut him short.

"I demand the return of the outlaw, Pwyll, and the stolen artifacts!" Geldion explained. "And there is a young man, a Gary Leger from Bretaigne, a spy from beyond Cancarron Mountains, who desires to bring the precious items back to his homeland."

"Now, that'd be a trick," Mickey remarked quietly, seeming not at all surprised by the lie.

"Where the hell is this Bretaigne place?" Gary asked him.

"Beyond Cancarron Mountains," came the predictable answer, which told Gary, who had no idea of where the Cancarron Mountains might be, absolutely nothing.

"Are you so certain of his intent?" Badenoch asked. "Was it not Gary Leger who accompanied Kelsenellenelvial Gil-Ravadry . . ."

"Well said!" Mickey exclaimed, and he winked at Gary. "He got that damned name right." The leprechaun's smirk drew a glare from Kelsey.

". . . to Robert's lair to reforge the spear?" Gary heard as Badenoch continued. "Was it not Gary Leger who banished evil Ceridwen to her island fortress?"

"All by himself," Geno muttered sarcastically.

"Well done, young sprout," came the telepathic call in Gary's head.

Badenoch's last comment forced a visible wince from the haggard Prince, a wince that none of the friends on the not-too-distant ridge, and none of the three leaders facing Geldion, missed.

"Reforging the spear increased its value to Bretaigne," Geldion argued. "As for any fights with Ceridwen, they were merely incidental, and not looked for by any of the traitors."

"True enough, except for the 'traitors' part," Mickey put in dryly.

"Connacht seems eager to brand traitors," Badenoch replied.

"Hold yer breath, lad," Mickey remarked at hearing the firm response, and even Geno gulped in some air.

Geldion verily shook from boiling rage, his anger fueled by confusion. This was not how the kingdom was supposed to respond! His father was King, after all, the rightful King. How dare these lessers speak ill of Connacht! "You seem eager to place yourself among that list!" he snapped at Badenoch. "I demand the return of the traitors, and of the stolen artifacts!"

Cool Badenoch, sitting tall on his proud stallion, his neatly cropped salt-and-pepper hair blown across his face from the breeze off the mountains, slowly glanced around from one side to the other, then looked directly at the opposing Prince.

"We do not have them," he answered calmly.

Geldion wheeled his black horse about, jostling a couple of his escorts, and galloped back to the Connacht line.

"Hold yer breath, lad," Mickey said again.

"The bells must not ring," Kelsey said to the others, turning his mount away from the bushes and walking the horse down to the side of the ridge. Geno and Cedric followed immediately, and Gerbil pumped his quadricycle into position right beside the group.

Gary waited a moment longer, though, sensing that the storm was about to break and unable to tear his gaze from the field.

Geldion took a position in the center of the front rank. He stared across the field, his features grimly set, his right arm upraised. Badenoch, Drochit, and Kervin had not returned to their force; they sat far out from the lines, talking easily, and this seemed to upset Geldion all the more. Gary could hardly believe their courage, and understood that their apparent indifference to the coming storm was merely to give the unmistakable appearance to all witnesses, even the Connacht soldiers, that it was Geldion and the throne, and not the eastern villages, who precipitated this battle.

Whatever the appearance, Prince Geldion would not be deterred. He moved as if he meant to call out again to the opposing leaders, probably to speak the accusation one final time, but the first word came out as a growl and Geldion just snapped his arm down to his side.

Gary nearly jumped out of his seat, so surprised was he by the sudden thunder, the shaking of the ground beneath him, and the roar of a unified battle-cry, as five hundred horses and five hundred soldiers charged to battle.

Prince Geldion sat very still in his saddle, letting his soldiers flow out around him in their wild charge across the field. "So be it," Geldion muttered grimly. "So be it."

The three leaders in the field were not surprised in the least, though. They wheeled about and started off, Kervin accepting Drochit's extended hand and half climbing to the side of the horse, flying with all speed for their own ranks.

14 † A Mind of Its Own

"Ride on!" Kelsey commanded, starting down the side of the ridge behind the smithy Cedric, leading the group to flank the impending battle on the western side.

Geno, alone among the companions, seemed hesitant, looking back to his left, back where his dwarfish comrades stood to face the overwhelming odds. His torment was obvious, and not unexpected to Kelsey, and the elf quickly reversed direction, sidestepping his mount around the rolling quadricycle and slapping Gary's pony on the rump as it trotted by. A few words to Geno, reminding the dwarf of the importance of the mission, brought Geno along, though many times did the beardless dwarf look back over his left shoulder.

The field was lost from sight almost immediately as the companions went low in a gully. They heard the continuing thunder of pounding hooves, the cries of battle, the wails of the wounded and dying, but it seemed not nearly as intense as Gary had expected.

"Our allies are in flight back to the foothills," Mickey explained to him, seeing his quizzical look. "That was the plan all along, to bait Geldion in and keep him running the opposite way from us."

Gary looked back, using one hand to adjust the too-big helmet with his head as he turned. He heard shouts of frustration from Geldion's hungry force, confirmation of the

177

leprechaun's claims, and was glad. The whole thought of
the battle—especially with a greater common enemy, the
dragon, free to terrorize the land—made bile rise in Gary's
throat.

Cedric was still leading the way, driving his horse hard
along the gully, then into a perpendicular trail running
straight west and even lower from the battlefield. They
went around a hillock, turning back to the south, now with
a wall of grass between them and Geldion's force, the cries
and thunderous hooves fast fading into the background.

It seemed not enough distance to the eager smithy, and
he kicked his big boots against his mount's flank, spurring
the horse full out as they rounded yet another bend, this
one wrapping right behind the battlefield, back to the east.

"What ho, with ease good smithy!" Kelsey warned. "We
have put them behind us."

Gary understood where Kelsey's words were leading.
The elf knew that Geldion's main force could not catch
them, but he feared—and rightly so, Gary believed—that
scouting parties, or groups held back to flank the enemy,
had been deployed in the region.

Around the bend went reckless Cedric, and his horse
whinnied immediately and skidded to a stop in the soft
turf. All the others broke stride as Cedric's horse backped-
aled, the smithy yanking hard on the reins, trying not to
fall backwards off the mount.

Cedric reappeared fully from around the bend, a stunned
expression on his bushy-bearded face and an arrow sticking from his chest.

Kelsey, in full charge, fitted an arrow and ducked low,
his mount galloping with all speed around the back of the
wounded Cedric, using the smithy as a shield. As soon as
he came clear on the other side, the elf let fly his arrow,
then dropped the bow across his saddle horn and drew out
his gleaming sword.

Geno, ever hungry for battle, charged right behind, and Gary followed. Gerbil skidded the quadricycle to a stop and pulled open a compartment to the side of his seat, removing a long metal pole, a crank, and two iron balls secured to either end of a four-foot length of hemp.

Cedric was still up on the horse when Gary caught up to him, the smithy's mouth still wide with surprise, and his hands tight around the reins. Hardly thinking of the movement, Gary lifted Mickey across to the man's horse, yelled for the leprechaun to help him, and kicked his mount away, following Kelsey and Geno.

Eight Connacht soldiers had been positioned in the gully, looking for potential flanking maneuvers from this very direction. That number was now seven, with one man slumped low in his saddle, face against his horse's mane, and an elfish arrow sticking diagonally into his collar.

But the scouts, still twenty yards away and with bows in hand, had not been taken by surprise. A line of crimson appeared on Kelsey's neck as an arrow narrowly missed its deadly mark. Another bolt would have hit the elf squarely, except that Kelsey fell to the side and threw up his sword, luckily tipping the missile wide. Those same two bowmen were the closest foes for the elf, and he roared in, hoping to get to them before they were fully prepared for close melee.

The hiss of metal on metal split the air as broadswords slipped free of their scabbards. One of the soldiers foolishly kicked his mount ahead, relinquishing the two-on-one advantage for the first attack routines.

Kelsey's sword, blue-glowing with magical fires, slashed across as the horses came side by side, and the broadsword intercepted it and forced it wide. Quicker than the soldier believed possible, Kelsey let go the sword, flipped his hand around and caught its hilt with an upside-down grasp. He jabbed it back, daggerlike, into the man's knee.

The soldier howled, his horse reared, and Kelsey, already going to the side, turned his mount further and called into its ear. The intelligent beast readily complied, lifting its haunches from the ground and kicking out with both hooves, blasting the wounded soldier from his saddle.

Kelsey continued the turn, came around a full circle, moving behind the now-riderless horse to bide some time as the second soldier bore down on him, broadsword slashing through the air.

Gary worked hard to catch up with Geno. The gully was not wide—just a few horses could fit side by side, and with Kelsey already in tight against the enemy, Gary knew that poor Geno would take the brunt of the remaining bow attacks.

One arrow went wide, at least one other hit the charging dwarf with a popping thud. But Geno hardly seemed to flinch, bent low over the side of his pony, a hammer cocked and ready.

It wasn't until he felt the smack against his chestplate that Gary Leger realized his error in focusing his attention on the fate of his diminutive friend. It took him many moments to get past the shock of being hit so that he could even realize that the arrow had splintered harmlessly against his fabulous armor, its stone tip barely scratching the marvelous suit. Still, the shock had broken Gary's momentum, had sent Geno rushing far out ahead of him.

Gary looked up ahead and prodded his horse forward, but then reared his mount as another archer drew a bead on him and let fly.

One soldier, the only knight among the group, lowered a long lance and charged out for the approaching dwarf.

Geno straightened as though he meant to come across on the pass as if in joust. But the dwarf on his pony was barely half the height of the armored man on the tall black stallion. Geno had come to Gary's defense when the young man had tricked Redarm, and now the dwarf proved that he, too, would not confuse stupidity with honor. The knight came thundering on, thinking to skewer the apparently helpless dwarf and charge past to the next rider. Before he ever got close, though, Geno's arm whipped out, one, two, and three, and a line of hammers twirled in low, clipping the front legs of the knight's horse.

The beast stumbled with the first hit, began to pitch with the second, and the third only ensured that it was going down head first. The surprised knight did not react nearly quickly enough as the tip of his long lance dipped and then caught into the ground. The weapon's butt end slammed hard into the man's armpit, and he pitched forward in a fumbling pole-vault. He nearly went up vertically before the lance snapped, dropping him hard to the ground, where he lay, dazed and weighted by the heavy armor, and unable to crawl or even roll out of harm's way.

Geno tightened his muscular legs around the pony's sides and forced the mount to veer sharply, hooves slamming atop metal plating, driving the wounded knight deeper into the soft turf.

Another arrow hit the dwarf then, in the left shoulder, but Geno only growled and snapped his legs around the other way, making a tight turn towards the archer.

The arrow tore a gash in his horse's ear, continued on to deflect off Gary's armored side, stinging him though it could not penetrate the enchanted metal.

The man was already reaching for another bolt, and now eyeing Gary's horse dangerously.

Gary knew that he couldn't give the archer that next

shot, that the man would likely kill his mount and leave him sprawling helplessly in the grass. He had just seen Geno's maneuver, and the thought of being crunched under fifteen hundred pounds of horse and rider didn't seem overly appealing.

Gary cocked the mighty spear over his shoulder and brought his arm forward as if to throw.

"Do not!" screamed a voice in his head, and to his amazement, his fingers would not loosen from the black shaft.

Gary's horse bolted away, apparently of its own accord, charging straight for the archer. Instinctively, Gary leveled the spear at his hip, while desperately clinging to the reins of the out-of-control beast.

The archer's face paled. He fumbled with his arrow, then seemed to realize that he could not possibly ready the bow and fire in time. He threw the bow aside and grabbed at his swordhilt.

Gary knew that he had the man dead.

Dead!

Gary Leger was about to kill a human being. His conscience screamed at him, his heart missed many beats, but his horse, nostrils flaring and head down in full charge, did not sway an inch.

At the last moment, Gary flipped the balanced spear around in his hand. He nearly toppled off the side of his galloping mount for the effort, and clicked himself painfully in the shoulder with the mightily enchanted speartip. Somehow he managed to get the butt end of the spear out in front, though, and it cracked off his terrified opponent's raised forearm, blasted through as Gary's mount rushed by, and smacked full force into the man's chest, knocking him flat out on his back across his horse's rump.

Gary heard him groan as he rushed past, was grateful

for the sound, though he winced as he heard the man drop heavily to the ground.

Gary's horse swung about sharply, unexpectedly, and Gary lurched in the saddle, rolling far to the side.

"Slow down!" he called helplessly to the horse. He focused ahead just in time to see another archer, arrow nocked and eyes set on Gary, pull back on his bowstring.

The horse jostled over an uneven patch of ground, and Gary's poor-fitting helmet dropped down over his eyes.

"Oh, God!" he cried, thinking that he was about to die. Something slammed his forehead, dented his helm, and he saw little stars explode behind his eyelids.

"Oh, God!" he said again, but he realized that he was still alive, still on his horse. He grabbed blindly across the mount's back and pulled himself as upright as he could, and spotted the archer under the top edge of his fallen helm, fast moving off to the side.

Gary realized that he couldn't go by the man, couldn't give him any more clear shots. He fell over the other way, tugging hard on the reins. The horse apparently had the same idea, and turned more easily, and at a sharper angle, than Gary expected.

And at a sharper angle than the archer had expected, Gary realized as he brought his forearm up to bat the troublesome helm so that the slit somewhat aligned with his eyes.

"Oh, God!" Gary cried a third time, just as his horse rammed full force into the archer's.

It wasn't pretty, it wasn't graceful, but somehow it proved effective as the enemy soldier and horse toppled sideways, the horse crushing the man's leg as they slammed down to the ground. Gary's agile mount quickstepped, bucked and hopped, among the tangle, and came out beyond, Gary still holding the reins and still holding the spear, though his helmet had flown completely around on his head.

"You do not fight to kill," the spear remarked—accused?—in Gary's mind.

Thinking that the weapon was belittling him, Gary started to respond with a stream of silent curses.

"That is good, young sprout," the spear went on, ignoring the ranting man. *"You value life, even the lives of your enemies."*

Gary had no more time to pay attention to the telepathic barrage. More enemies remained, and he couldn't see them!

"But I'll not let you get killed," the sentient spear imparted. *"Not yet."*

The thought seemed curious to Gary, and he was too muddled and afraid to put two and two together when, an instant later, his mount cut a nasty turn (and again, Gary had to hold on for his life) and leaped away, running full out. Gary tried to get a hand free so that he could at least figure out where he was going. Not that he was sure he wanted to see ahead, for he feared that he would find another knight with a lowered lance, patiently waiting to skewer him.

Just as he let go the reins with one hand, his horse leaped high and long, coming down with a jolt that forced Gary to grab on with both hands again. Grab on and tighten his legs about the steed's sides, lying low in the saddle all the while.

It took Gary another long moment to discern that the sounds of battle were fast fading behind him, that he was running free and far away from enemies and friends alike.

His first thoughts went to Ceridwen, the troublesome and dangerous witch. Had she taken control of the horse? Was she reeling Gary Leger in to her like an angler with a hooked fish?

"Help me!" Gary cried, his shout ringing inside the helmet and inside his own ears. He yanked on the reins with all his strength, but the horse pulled back, kept its head low and flew on across the rolling fields.

Kelsey and the swordsman continued their fight across the back of the riderless horse, the agile elf easily parrying the lunging attacks of the angry fighter. The elf would have liked to play this out longer, to take no chances against an opponent he could obviously defeat, but he heard Geno's arrow-inspired grunts and saw Gary Leger bolting about wildly, dangerously.

The fighter gave a straight thrust across the horse's back, his sword diving for Kelsey's thigh.

Confident in his mount, Kelsey let go the reins altogether and caught the man's wrist, shifting himself about and tugging hard, drawing the overbalanced man right across the riderless horse's back. The elf's sword was free, and his opponent was trapped and helpless.

Surprisingly, to Kelsey, an image of Gary Leger came into his thoughts. The tip of Kelsey's blade was just an inch from the helpless, terrified man's exposed forehead when Kelsey turned it aside, sent it snapping into the man's biceps instead so that he cried out in pain and lost his grip on his own sword.

Kelsey let go the wrist and grabbed the man by the hair, tugging him fiercely, pulling his face down towards the ground. His sword came in again, this time hilt-first, slamming the man on the base of his neck. The soldier struggled no more, went limp under Kelsey's grasp and slowly slid over the back of the riderless horse and fell to the ground.

Kelsey took care not to trample the unconscious man, sidestepped his mount around the back of the riderless horse, and looked for his companions.

He saw Geno, two arrows already sticking from the dwarf, charging the two remaining opponents, both archers, sitting composed, side by side, bows drawn and ready.

"Now you die, dwarf!" one of them cried, as much in fear as in anger.

A horn blast to the side—not the winding horn a knight might carry, but a curious beeping sound—turned all eyes.

Gerbil's quadricycle rushed and bounced along the steep slope of the gully's side. One of the gnome's arms worked frantically on the contraption's steering bar, while the other pumped wildly on a crank, turning a high pole tipped by spinning bolas. Gerbil tried to watch the rough path ahead, while eyeing a sighting device attached to the pole.

"Oh, yes!" the gnome cried, letting go the crank and flicking a trigger. The bolas flew free, spinning fiercely, looping about the nearest archer. The hemp wound fast, iron balls cracking the unfortunate man about the shoulders and pitching him sidelong into his similarly surprised companion.

"Oh, yes, yes!" Gerbil shouted in victory, but he should have paid attention to his own precarious perch instead. The front left wheel of the quadricycle slammed against a rock and bounced up high, taking the whole side of the gnome's vehicle off the ground.

Gerbil's victory shout turned to a shriek as he tried to hold the quadricycle steady on two wheels. He lost the valiant fight when his right front wheel plopped into a ditch and got yanked sidelong. Poor Gerbil and his contraption pitched head over heels, crunched down in the soft turf, and slid to a stop at the base of the gully's slope.

Geno wasn't watching the gnome, more concerned with the tangle of enemy archers before him. The one who had been hit with the bolas went down hard between the horses, one shoulder obviously broken, wailing loudly and trying to keep his own horse from stepping on him. The other archer was still in the saddle, though, righting himself and trying to ready his bow. Sheer terror covered his face when he looked up to see the charging dwarf, face contorted in rage and a hammer high above his head.

The archer fell backwards, fell away from the chopping hammer, as Geno's pony slammed in. Geno leaped right from his mount, dove forward into the leaning man and forced them both off the back side of the archer's horse. The man twisted about so that he did not land flat on his back and tried to break his fall with outstretched arms. One wrist exploded with a tremendous crack, and the surprising weight of the short but compact dwarf drove the man facedown into the turf.

Geno grabbed a handful of hair and jerked the man's head back, then face-slammed him into the soft grass. Seeing a better target, the dwarf yanked him back again, shifted the angle slightly, and rammed him into a half-buried rock.

The man's ensuing scream came out as a blood-filled gurgle. His nose and cheek shattered, but that only seemed to urge the ferocious dwarf on. Geno slammed him again, then hooked an arm under the man's shoulder and tugged so fiercely that he dislocated the arm. A dwarfish knee crunched the half-turned man's stomach, rolling him right over to his back, his arm garishly wrapped behind him.

Geno was up to his feet in an instant, deadly hammer ready to do its grim work.

"Do not finish him," Kelsey advised, trotting his mount over. Both elf and dwarf looked around to see that, amazingly, not a single opponent had been killed, though the man whom Geno had trampled with the pony was grievously wounded.

"Go to the gnome," Kelsey ordered. The elf turned about to see Mickey steering Cedric's horse forward. The huge smithy sat very straight in the saddle, caked with sweat, his dark eyes unblinking.

"Whatever ye're to do, do it fast," Mickey advised, and he looked to poor Cedric, then back to Kelsey, shaking his head.

The man on the ground flopped about, jostling Geno, and the dwarf's hammer came up in an instant.

"Geno," Kelsey said slowly.

"Bah, good enough for you!" the dwarf yelled at his wounded victim, and he followed the growl with a stream of spittle, then stomped off to extract the fallen gnome.

Kelsey looked around, was somewhat relieved to see that no other enemies were in the area. But neither was Gary Leger.

"Where'd the lad run off to?" Mickey asked.

Kelsey shook his head, having no answers.

"There's suren to be other enemies about," Mickey remarked.

Again, Kelsey had no answer for the leprechaun. He, too, was concerned for Gary, and he was concerned for himself and the others as well, for Cedric seemed to be hovering near death, and Gerbil and his gnomish contraption had gone down hard.

15 † In the Name of Honor

Gary finally righted his helm enough so that he could see, but with the dizzying blur of the broken landscape rolling beneath, he almost wished he hadn't. Stifling a scream, the young man who wished he had taken some riding lessons tucked the magical spear tightly under his arm and held on for all his life. His horse leaped across shallow ravines, zigzagged through boulder-strewn fields, and splashed across several small streams. Gary sensed that enemy soldiers were about, even saw one group, resting under a widespread tree at the base of a hillock, eating a meal. One of them noticed Gary as well, pointed and called out.

But Gary was a white blur, a trick of the eyes, gone from sight before the other soldiers even reacted to the cry.

Still, the young man knew that he was vulnerable, and if the clopping of hooves, the rattle of armor plates, and the occasional snort from the fiery horse weren't enough, the elfish bells began to ring!

I didn't command them to do that! Gary thought, trying to sort out what in the world was happening to him. He hadn't thought about the bells at all, actually, and yet they were ringing. He couldn't control the horse, couldn't control the bells, and that led him to the inevitable conclusion that someone else had taken command of everything around him.

Gary Leger had met the witch Ceridwen on his last journey through Faerie; he figured that he knew who that someone else might be.

He had to jump off. As terrifying as that thought seemed, Gary believed that he had no practical choice. It had to be Ceridwen, after all, and Gary figured that anything would be better than meeting her again. Jumping was easier thought than done, though, for the armor prevented Gary from making a clean leap, and the ground, turf-soft in some places but boulder-hard in others, promised to smash him apart.

"You have to do it," he whispered grimly to himself, and he forced himself to make the first move, to bring the spear out from his side so that he could toss it away from him as he went.

Gary's arm jerked, but he found, to his disbelief and his horror, that his fingers would not let go.

"Do not throw me away, young sprout!" came the mental command.

Gary's thoughts rushed back in a jumbled blur, too fast for him to clearly spell out to the sentient spear what he believed was happening. He took a deep breath, forced himself to slow down at last, and pointedly imparted, *I did not command the elfish bells to ring!*

"I did," came the surprisingly calm response.

Gary nearly fell out of the saddle; under his helm, his mouth drooped open. What the hell was going on?

The horse bounded around another bend, leaped a low hedgerow, and padded to a quick stop, and Gary Leger had his answers.

"Restore my honor!" the spear commanded.

Gary was as surprised as the three men facing him across the way—two Connacht soldiers centered by the knight, Redarm.

* * *

The surprisingly resilient quadricycle rolled away, Gerbil taking care to avoid the groaning forms of the fallen Connacht soldiers. Carefully, too, went Kelsey on his horse, leading the horse bearing Mickey and Cedric. The leprechaun had done his best in binding the wounded smithy, and Kelsey had helped as well, the elf, like all the Tylwyth Teg, being greatly versed in the healing arts. Gerbil had even added a potion and healing salve, from yet another compartment in his amazing vehicle. They had not been able to dig the arrowhead out of Cedric's chest, though, and despite the warm blankets they wrapped about the man, cold sweat continued to stream down his face.

"We won't catch Gary Leger tugging him along," Geno grumbled to Kelsey.

Kelsey had no rebuttal, except to ask, "Would you prefer that we leave the man behind?"

Geno thought that one over for a long while, even nodded a few times. "Stonebubbles!" he cursed at last, and he walked his pony out ahead of the slow-moving elf, taking the point position.

Mickey took a deep draw on his long-stemmed pipe, feeling more helpless than he had ever before. The continued absence of his pot of gold, his source of magical energy, had depleted the leprechaun to the point where he practically hadn't been able to help out at all in the last fight. He called upon what little magical energy he had remaining now, though, imparting to the grievously wounded smithy images of a spreading chestnut tree, a hot forge, and glowing metal. Better for Cedric to rest easily with the thoughts that would most comfort him, Mickey figured, and he watched the man's muscled chest, expecting that each shallow breath would be Cedric's last.

His face alone could frighten the heartiest of men. Redarm sat atop his great stallion, the hinged faceplate of his plated armor up high on his head. Despite his obvious delight at seeing Gary, his expression was grim, his skin ruddy and scarred in a dozen places. He wore a thick black moustache that covered both his lips when his mouth was closed, and his similarly thick eyebrows converged above the bridge of his oft-broken, crooked nose. Even from twenty yards, Gary could tell that Redarm's eyes were dark, black actually, and bloodshot. Angry eyes, Gary thought, always angry.

The man forced a smile, a curiously evil sight. "Geldion relegated me to the back lines," he said, a coarse chuckle accompanying his gravelly voice, "in punishment for my obvious eagerness to kill you! And here, by the fates, do you come to play."

Not so fateful, Gary thought grimly.

"Restore my honor," the spear commanded.

Eat shit.

The sentient spear had no response to that, seemed somewhat confused to Gary, and that gave him some pleasure—muted pleasure, of course, since the young man believed with all his heart that he was about to die.

"By Prince Geldion's word, this man from Bretaigne is to be taken alive," the soldier to Redarm's right reminded the knight, placing his hand over Redarm's wrist as the knight reached for the hilt of his sword.

"Geldion did say that," Redarm agreed calmly, and the soldier removed his hand. Redarm had the sword out in the blink of an eye and slashed across, smashing the cruel blade downward into the side of the man's neck, nearly decapitating him. The soldier sat very still in his saddle, his expression frozen. Then, as though the residual energy of the tremendous hit had rolled down to his feet and come storming back up, he seemed to leap out of his saddle, falling dead to the grass.

The now-riderless horse nickered and pawed the ground in helpless protest.

Redarm swung about the other way, but the remaining soldier had already kicked his horse into a run, fleeing with all speed.

Gary looked on dumbfoundedly, felt his stomach churning and his pulse pounding in his temples. He had seen battle in Faerie, had even seen men cut down, but never so ruthlessly and never by another man.

"Now it is as it should be," the scarred knight said to Gary. Without even wiping away the blood, Redarm replaced his sword in its scabbard and took up his lance.

"Have you made your peace with whatever god you serve?" the knight asked politely, and before Gary could stutter an answer, Redarm dropped his faceplate, set his lion-and-clover-emblazoned shield, and dipped his lance atop its concave-cut corner.

What the hell do I do now? Gary asked the spear.

"Restore my honor!"

"Will you say something else!" Gary cried out, and Redarm straightened in his saddle, lifting his faceplate once more.

"What else is to be said?" the knight asked confusedly. "Prepare to die, Gary Leger of Bretaigne, impostor of Cedric Donigarten!" Down came the faceplate, down dipped the lance.

"Son of a bitch," Gary groaned.

"You say the most curious of things," remarked the sentient spear.

"Eat shit," Gary told it again.

"Indeed," replied the spear, and Gary could sense that it was not happy. *"We will talk of that comment again, young sprout."*

At that moment, Gary Leger didn't think that he would get the chance to talk of anything ever again. He looked around, wondering where he might run, but remembered that the spear, and not he, was in control of his horse. He groaned again, realizing that he didn't even have a shield, and dipped the speartip Redarm's way.

"No shield," Gary whispered to himself, thinking that he might bring that up to the knight, might at least get Redarm to relinquish the unfair advantage, might get the honorable knight to throw his own shield aside.

Gary never got the chance to mention it, though, for his horse kicked away suddenly, and Redarm's did likewise, and the thunder of hooves and the jingling of elfish bells filled the air.

It seemed to Gary a macabre game of chicken, a game of nerves as much as skill. He saw Redarm's approach, saw mostly the deadly tip of the knight's lance, lined perfectly with his breastplate. Gary tried to shift about, tried even to turn his horse more to the side, for the two mounts seemed as though they would collide head-on.

All that Gary could do was hold on, though, and hold tight to the spear, bracing it against his hip. With only a few strides to go, Gary understood another disadvantage of jousting with a spear, however strongly magicked.

Redarm's lance was at least three feet longer.

Prince Geldion's force continued the pursuit long after the eastern militia had cleared the field. Duncan Drochit, Badenoch, and the dwarf Kervin had urged their forces on as fast as Geldion had urged his—the other way. The three leaders had no intention of battling Connacht's well-armed and well-trained army on an open field and had never planned to do so. They had come out to meet Geldion only to keep him from their towns, and to keep him distracted while the small party slipped around.

Now they rode and ran with all speed, back into the foothills of rugged Dvergamal. Stragglers who could not keep up, or those who inadvertently turned down the wrong narrow trails and wound up blocked from further retreat, were mercilessly cut down.

Kervin's dwarfs offered the only real resistance to the Connacht army. They had secretly dug trenches, carefully replacing the top turf so that Geldion's riders would not see the traps. They had rigged small rockslides in the lower hills, both to hinder and crush pursuing enemies and to block off some of the trails used by their fleeing allies. Half the dwarfish force, ten sturdy warriors, had crouched among a rocky outcropping at the lip of the wide field, and when Geldion's lead riders came rushing past, intent on those men in full flight, out they came, battleaxes and warhammers chopping, a hearty song on their lips. They died, all ten, in bloody heaps, but not until they had taken down four times their own number in enemy soldiers.

And so the tumult died away on the wide field, the thunder of hooves, the flying mud, and shouts of battle and agony, rolling away to be swallowed up in the diminishing echoes of rugged Dvergamal. The field bore the scars, quick though the charge passed, with lines of broken, churned turf, and with its northeastern corner bloodied by more than three score casualties.

The instant of impact, when the tip of Redarm's lance poked hard against Gary's chestplate, seemed to move in slow motion for the terrified young man. He felt the hard jab against his breast, saw the lance bend, its tip sliding to the side, to find a niche in the crease of his armor at the front of his shoulder.

Gary felt himself being pushed back, knew that his mount would not slow, and could not break momentum or turn away fast enough to save him. On came relentless Redarm, driving hard, roaring in victory.

The lance bowed and snapped, and suddenly the magi-

cal spear was the longer weapon. Its tip flared with energy
as it battered Redarm's ornate shield, turning it around on
the man's arm. Any lesser weapon would have been deflected, but Donigarten's spear was the mightiest in all the
land, and was angry now, determined to win back its
honor.

Gary felt the magic throb up his arm, telepathically
compelling him to keep the weapon level and keep his
course straight, the horses passing barely six inches apart.
Gary flinched, knowing that he would surely be hit again
by the remaining portion of the lance. But again, it all happened in the span of an eye-blink, and Gary had no time
to formulate any logical arguments against the sentient
spear's demands.

He watched through the slit in his helm, his green eyes
widening in blank horror, as the spear fought through the
blocking shield and dove for Redarm's chestplate. Metal
armor curled up beneath its killing touch, tore apart and
rolled inward as the spear bit at the knight's flesh hungrily,
ate into the man's broad chest.

Gary felt the crunch as the remaining portion of
Redarm's lance slammed him in the belly, but there was
no strength behind the blow, no strength left at all in his
opponent.

The spear continued its plunge, through the man's lung
and spine, bloodied tip driving out his back.

The horses passed and both men, connected by the
spear, were jerked about to face each other. Gary felt as
though his arm would be pulled from its socket, but he
held on stubbornly, and was promptly yanked half out of
his saddle, lying sidelong across his mount's bouncing
rump. He hooked his free arm under the front of his saddle, watched as his helmet fell bouncing to the ground.

Redarm, too, fell back, and tumbled off his horse altogether. Gary could not support the sudden weight and had

not the strength to tear the imbedded spear from the dead man. He let go and tried to right himself instead, figured to turn his horse about and somehow retrieve the bloodied weapon. And all the while, black wings of guilt flapped around Gary's ears, told him what he had just done, made him look at the fallen, broken knight.

Redarm lay on his side in a widening pool of blood, the spearshaft protruding from one end, its tip sticking out the other. He was not moving, would never move again, Gary knew.

Gary winced in pain as he started to shift his weight closer to the center of his now-trotting mount. Both his shoulder and belly had been hit hard and he knew without looking that blue-black bruises were already widening in those areas. He could only hope that he was not bleeding under the armor.

When he had found his balance, he caught the bridle again and slowed the horse even more. For the first time since the pass with Redarm, Gary managed to look ahead of him, to look where he was going.

Two twelve-foot-tall giants, their legs as thick as the trunks of old oaks, their chest broad and strong, stood side by side, a few feet apart, holding a thick net between them and grinning stupidly through pointed and jagged greenish-yellow teeth.

Gary knew them, had seen mountain trolls on his last journey through Faerie. He gave a yell, tried hard to turn his mount aside, but the surprisingly quick monsters shifted with him, and both he and his horse plunged headlong into the net.

The powerful trolls were moved backwards no more than a single step by the impact, and they quickly wrapped their captured prey so tightly that Gary's terrified horse could not even continue to kick and thrash.

Gary thought that he would surely be crushed in that

pile. He strained to get his face out to the side so that he could at least try to draw breath.

"Horsie for supper," a third troll remarked happily, coming over to join its companions. He poked a huge and dirty finger into Gary's face. "But none fer you!" he laughed. "No food fer you all the way!"

"All the way?" Gary whispered. This had not been a random stroke of bad luck, he knew then. Someone else, not Prince Geldion or even King Kinnemore, had guided these monsters, and Gary, already fearful of a certain witch, had little trouble in figuring out who it might be.

He took some small comfort when the band started away, realizing that the trolls had been too stupid to even go over and retrieve the magical spear.

Small comfort.

16 † The Deal

An enormous smacking of lips bade Gary to awaken. Before he ever opened his eyes, he realized that he was no longer netted beside his horse, no longer in crushing quarters. He found that his arms were bound tightly together behind him, though, the edges of the metal armor digging painful creases into his shoulder blades.

" 'Orsie's a good supper," he heard a resonant troll voice declare.

"Arg, but me'd like a bit o' man-meat," said another, and Gary's eyes popped wide and he let out a tremendous shout when the troll reached over, caught an exposed piece of skin between two huge fingers and twisted so brutally that Gary soon after felt warm blood oozing from the spot, just above his hip.

There were five of the monsters, giant and appearing human, except that their ears were far too small, and their eyes and noses too large, and their skin was the color of granite, as was their long and dirty, tangled hair.

"That waked the little feller up!" roared another of the group, and when he laughed, a thousand elfish bells that he had draped around his body began to jingle.

Gary winced and looked away, understanding what had happened to his courageous mount. The tinkling bells did not seem so gay to him anymore, mixed in with the smacking sounds of trolls devouring the beautiful horse.

It went on for many minutes, trolls slobbering and talking to each other in their typically unpleasant way. Every once in a while the same one of them near Gary would beg for just a bite of man-meat, and Gary seemed to always wind up getting sorely pinched at least once. The other trolls were adamant against that, though, and after a few occasions, seemed to tolerate their too-hungry companion less and less. At one point, the troll gave Gary a pinch, but was hauled away by another, lifted to his feet, then punched right in the eye. He tumbled back, hitting the ground hard just a foot away from prone Gary's head. He leaped up immediately, surprisingly fast given his half-ton bulk. Gary looked at the deep depression the thing had left in the ground and nearly fainted away, imagining what his head might have looked like if the troll had fallen atop him.

"Yer turn to carry!" one of the trolls growled, picking his teeth with a horse bone.

"Arg, he can't carry!" protested another, the fattest of the group, with black eyes and a tongue that didn't quite seem to fit inside his mouth. " 'E'll eat the man, and then the witch'll eat us!"

"Troll-bunny pie," another remarked, nodding stupidly.

Gary did not miss the obvious reference to Ceridwen.

"Then you carry 'im!" snarled the tooth-picker. The fat troll protested more, but the tooth-picker whipped the horse bone off his head, then set on him, punching and biting. Two others joined in, the fifth staying back so that he wouldn't damage his precious elfish bells, and soon the fat troll relented.

"You wiggle and I'll squeeze ye good!" the behemoth promised as he easily lifted Gary with one hand and tucked him under his round, though still rock-hard, arm.

The strength of the thing horrified Gary. He had fought trolls before, a couple of times, on his first visit to Faerie, but he was still surprised at how solid these monsters were. He felt as though he had been lifted by the steel shovel of a backhoe and tucked tight against the side of a brick wall. He was facing forward, at least, and the wind felt good in his face as the trolls ran off with long strides that could match the pace of a race horse.

Gary settled into a bouncing rhythm as the minutes became an hour. His shoulders ached with his arms bound so tightly behind his back, but he knew that if he complained, the trolls would probably just rip his arms off so he wouldn't have to worry about them anymore.

"Caught by trolls on your way to see the evil witch," Gary whispered sarcastically under his breath. "You've done good."

A huge hand came across in front of his face, the nail of the troll's middle finger held tight against its thumb.

"Arg, stop the spellcastin'!" the creature demanded, and it snapped the finger into Gary's forehead. Gary's head jerked back, his vision blurred, and he felt as if he had been kicked by a horse. He lay limp in the troll's grasp for a long while, watching the pretty stars that had suddenly come up, though night was still far away.

Geno was not gentle as he pushed the magical spear the rest of the way through the dead Redarm.

"There," Mickey, obviously upset, spat at Kelsey. "Did the lad get his honor back in yer own stupid way o' seein' things?"

Holding the empty helmet, Kelsey nodded gravely. "Gary Leger has done well," the elf admitted. "On almost every occasion."

"Damned good spear," Geno proclaimed, examining the incredible wound, with Redarm's metal armor folded into his chest around the gaping hole.

Mickey looked from the spear to Kelsey, and took an

impatient draw on his pipe. He knew that Kelsey, in his typically understated way, had given Gary about as great a compliment as anyone could expect from one of the haughty Tylwyth Teg, but it didn't seem enough to the leprechaun at that grim time. Mickey had brought Gary back to Faerie, was leading a quest through dangerous lands by holding to a lie. The leprechaun felt responsible now, one of the few burdens the carefree Mickey hadn't been able to simply let roll off his rounded shoulders.

"Well, he won the fight," Geno said, hands on hips as he regarded the ground around Redarm. The other soldier, the one Redarm had cut down with his sword, lay in a pool of blood to the side, his horse and Redarm's grazing easily on the grassy field in the distance. "So where in the name of a stupid gnome did he go?"

Gerbil glared at the dwarf.

"Just a saying," Geno grumbled. "No such thing."

"Indeed," replied the gnome. "And can we conclude that this other unfortunate soldier was killed by the knight?"

Geno drew out Redarm's bloodied sword. "Seems that way."

"Thus did the knight and the soldier come at odds," reasoned the gnome, determined to prove Geno's insulting "saying" far from the truth. "Might we conclude that the disagreement came from the sight of Gary Leger?"

"Redarm wanted him dead," Mickey put in. "But the others had orders to take him alive."

"Others?" Geno and Kelsey said together, that thought sparking new lines of reasoning. The two of them went into a search immediately, certain that other clues would not be far away.

They found their answer not far to the south of the dead men, in the form of the huge tracks of bare-footed monsters right where the tracks of Gary's horse abruptly ended.

"Trolls," Kelsey announced grimly, looking to the south as he spoke, for he understood the potential implications.

"What?" Geno asked in surprise.

"Trolls," Kelsey said again, turning to regard the dwarf. Only then Kelsey realized that Geno hadn't been addressing him at all. The dwarf stood unblinking, staring at the spear he held in his hands. He looked over to Kelsey and Mickey a moment later, a stupefied look on his normally unshakable features.

"Damned spear just told me that they're taking him to the witch," the dwarf announced. He beamed a helpless smile a moment later. "Been good to know you, Gary Leger!"

The spear responded to that unfaithful farewell by jolting Geno with a burst of electrical energy. The dwarf growled, his straight, sandy brown hair standing up on end, one eye twitching uncontrollably. He spun the spear about in his hands and planted it deep into the ground, then prudently hopped away. "Damned spear."

"We've got to go and get the lad," Mickey said to Kelsey, recognizing that the elf was truly torn. In truth, Mickey, too, did not like the prospects. Trolls could move with incredible speed, and would not tire for many days. They already had a head start, and even without it, would get to Ynis Gwydrin, Ceridwen's enchanted island, long before the companions.

Kelsey sighed and looked around. The mounts from Tir na n'Og were certainly up for the run, and Gerbil had done well to keep pace in that curious contraption of his, but what of Cedric?

The smithy had managed to ease his way down from the horse, but leaned heavily against it. Sweat covered his face; his breath came in shallow, forced gasps. He seemed incoherent, staring away into empty air, but he apparently understood more than the others realized, for he announced, "I am dying," and bade them to leave him there.

Mickey and Kelsey believed the man's claim, but even so, neither of them could simply leave the brave smithy behind.

"Geno and I will go for Gary," the elf decided. He looked to Mickey. "You and the gnome can get him to cover." He indicated Cedric, looking that way as he spoke, and was surprised to see the man walking away from the supporting horse.

"No!" Cedric declared in a voice that amazingly did not quiver. He strode, defiant of his garish wounds, over to the spear and, somewhere finding the strength, roughly tore it from the ground. The huge man's eyes glistened as he held the magnificent weapon before him, seeming to draw strength from simply holding the artifact that was so dear to one of his trade. Cedric nodded and smiled, as though he was holding a private conversation with the sentient weapon. This was the spear of his namesake, an item most holy to smithies all across the land of Faerie, and never before had Cedric of Braemar been so serene.

"Can he ride hard?" Kelsey asked Mickey.

The leprechaun shrugged, not even chancing a guess about what was going on, about where this grievously wounded man had found the sudden burst of strength.

"I understand," Cedric said to the spear. He came out of his private conversation then, and looked to the friends and nodded. Then, to their surprise and horror, the altruistic smithy turned the spear suddenly and plunged its tip into his breast, smiling with supreme contentment.

He held the pose for a long, horrible moment; then his legs buckled under him and he went down in a heap.

"Oh, oh, oh!" a stunned Gerbil uttered repeatedly, a stubby gnome finger poking out from the low seat of the quadricycle to the spectacle of the dead man. "Oh, oh, oh!"

"I'm not getting that out!" Geno roared in rage, pointing to the again-imbedded spear. The gruff dwarf turned and walked away, spitting curses about "stupid peoples!"

"Oh, you should have a plaque for that," the gnome offered in all sincerity.

"Indeed," Mickey muttered, and took another long draw off his pipe.

They were in the mountains, and the daylight was fast disappearing. This was not Dvergamal, Gary knew, for these peaks were not quite as tall and rugged as in the dwarfish homeland. The trolls were carrying him through the region called Penllyn, whose heart was Ynis Gwydrin, the isle of glass.

Ceridwen's isle.

Act fast, Gary told himself. He stretched and yawned loudly, gaining the attention of the troll carrying him.

"How long have we been running?" he asked, trying to sound calm, even relaxed.

The troll's other hand came around again, middle finger tight against the thumb, and Gary thought he was about to take another nap.

" 'Ere, shut yer mouth," the monster growled, and it shook its free hand dangerously, but did not snap Gary in the head again.

Gary knew that he had to speak directly, had to say something that would immediately attract the dim-witted troll's attention—else the stupid thing might knock him cold before it ever realized that he had something important to say. He squirmed a bit so that he could look around, tried to find something that might lead the conversation forward. He found himself thinking of *The Hobbit*, and of Bilbo's encounter with similar trolls, and of how those adventurers got out of their rather sticky predicament. He heard the elfish bells ringing gaily, draped about one of the monsters.

"Why does he get the magical bells?" Gary asked suddenly, without even thinking.

The troll carrying him slowed noticeably. Its hand, finger cocked, started around towards Gary, but it held back, apparently intrigued.

"Magical?" it asked as quietly as a troll could, which meant that Gary was not quite deafened.

"Of course," Gary replied. "The bells make a horse run swifter, make the wearer stronger."

"Stronger?"

"Of course," Gary whispered, his eyes flashing excitedly. "Stronger" was the perfect buzz-word for any troll, the word that brought drool to the bully's lips. Gary knew from the troll's tone that he had started something important here. "The troll wearing the bells . . ."

"Petey," Gary's bearer interrupted.

"Petey," Gary continued, "will soon grow much stronger. As he absorbs the magical energy of the elfish bells, he will likely become the strongest troll in all the world."

There came a long pause as the troll considered the news. "Hey, Petey," he called a moment later. "I wants to wear the bells."

The ringing stopped as Petey stopped, looking around to consider his garment. "They're mine, they is," he snarled. "I tooked 'em, and I'm keepin' 'em."

"Gimme the bells!" Gary liked the urgency of the troll's tone as the monster stepped towards stubborn Petey. He would have liked it even more if his troll had thought to put him down first.

"Go pick a goblin's nose!" Petey yelled back.

The troll reacted the only way trolls ever react—with violence. The monster wasn't close enough to punch Petey in the eye, so he hurled something instead, the only thing he had in his hands at the time.

Gary's cry ended with a guttural grunt as he connected on Petey's blocking forearm and was roughly deflected off to the side. He spun down to the rocky ground, dazed and battered, his thoughts screaming all the while that he had to get up and get away.

Predictably, the troll fight soon became a general row, with all five of the monsters rolling and clawing, biting each other and landing some incredibly heavy punches. One rolled Gary's way, nearly rolled over him, and that surely would have been the end of him!

"Get away!" he whispered under his breath, and he, too, rolled, over the side of a rock into a short drop. Then, when he found his breath again, he began to crawl on his knees, stumbling and tumbling across the broken land-scape. He managed to get up to his feet, but soon tripped back to the ground.

He took some comfort in the continuing thunder of the troll battle. But that ended soon enough when one of the monsters, Petey, Gary believed, yelled out above the din, "Hey, where'd he go to?"

"Oh, damn," Gary muttered, and he forced himself up again, running with all the speed he could manage, hoping he wouldn't fall blindly into a deep ravine in the fading light. He bounced off rocks, clipped his shoulders and head on low-hanging branches as he disappeared into one copse, and finally tripped facedown over the roots of a scraggly bush. Dazed, he rolled to his side, looking for some place to crawl into and hide.

He saw the giant, smelly foot of a troll instead, and a moment later felt as though he was flying. He stopped his ascent even with, and looking into, a bruised troll face, contorted with frothing rage.

" 'Ere, don't kill him!" one of the monsters ordered

from the side, and Gary was glad to hear those words, for he thought that this troll certainly meant to kill him.

"Yeah, the witch says that we don't kill him!" another troll emphatically agreed.

"Little sneakster's gonna run again!" the troll holding Gary declared.

"Bite 'is feets off," another offered, and the troll holding Gary smiled wickedly and turned him upside-down. An instant later, Gary felt the pressure of troll jaws against the sides of his sneakers.

"Ceridwen wouldn't like that!" he squeaked frantically. He felt the pressure ease, but not relinquish, and knew that he had to concoct some story, some excuse to save his feet, at once.

"I'm already bruised and cut," Gary stuttered. "Ceridwen won't like that, but these wounds will heal. If you bite my feet off, though, they won't grow back!"

"What's that got to do with it?" Petey demanded.

"Yeah, yous's just a prisoner," added another.

Gary laughed—it wasn't an easy thing to do in his predicament. "Just a prisoner?" he asked incredulously. "Don't you know why Ceridwen wants me?"

"Duh?" came the common response as the trolls, having no idea of what the man was babbling about, looked around at each other.

Gary considered the best way to put this. He had no idea of what horrid trolls understood of love and sexuality. They seemed to be carved out of stone, not born, and he had never seen a female troll, after all.

"Ceridwen thinks I'm cute," he announced. "She wants me as a husband."

"Duh?" Gary went up into the air, coming to a stop hanging upside-down right in front of the troll's confused face.

"I don't think the witch—whom I've seen turn trolls

into bunnies," he added quickly, "would like a husband with no feet."

The troll looked to its companions and shrugged heavily, Gary bobbing three feet with the movement. A moment later, he was tucked under the troll's arm, every limb still intact, and the group headed off.

Gary thought of *The Hobbit* again, but came to the conclusion that he was not quite as sneaky as the wizard in that tale, and so he kept his mouth shut, all the way to the crystalline lake.

Geek and some other goblins were waiting for them there. They tied Gary down in a rowboat, then finished their business with the trolls.

Despite his grim situation, Gary Leger twisted about to stare with admiration at the castle that came into sight as they neared the distant island. Its walls were of glass, sparkling wondrously in the first light of twinkling stars. It was beautiful and icy, a palace fitting for Ceridwen, Gary decided as he remembered the witch, so alluring and so dangerous.

Beautiful and icy.

Gary had been in this room before. He had battled a demon here, which had caused many of the scorch marks that marred the otherwise beautiful decor. The doors had been repaired, as had Ceridwen's canopy bed, and the large leatherbound book—the book that had distorted time itself—was no longer out in plain view on the carved desk.

Gary continued his scan of the witch's bedroom, pointedly keeping his gaze away from the wall to the right of the door. There sat Alice, Ceridwen's pet. She appeared as a normal house cat now, but Gary had seen her in more ominous trappings. When he and his friends had escaped Ceridwen's castle, Alice had taken on the form of a lioness and attacked them. Gary had skewered the cat with the magical spear, a vicious fight that the young man remembered all too well.

Alice apparently remembered it also, and recognized Gary. From the moment Geek had escorted him into the bedroom, Alice had eyed him like he was a field mouse come to play. Geek had quickly departed, leaving Gary feeling oh, so vulnerable.

He was almost relieved when the door opened—almost, until he saw Ceridwen enter the room, her posture typically perfect, seemingly taller and more ominous than Gary remembered her. She verily floated across the way, Geek the goblin cowering in her wake, her icy-blue eyes locked into Gary's gaze.

Gary had met a few women at least with black hair and blue eyes, a somewhat unusual combination, in his own world, but that mixture paled when measured against this standard. Ceridwen's eyes burned with an intensity Gary could hardly believe, an intelligence that transcended her human trappings. The luster of her thick and long hair showed every other color within its general blackness, like a raven's wing shining in the sunlight.

She sat on the bed next to Gary, and he unconsciously brought his suddenly sweaty palms in close to his sides. Ceridwen had made romantic overtures towards him before. Only her evil reputation, and the fact that Gary knew she was looking for no more than a conquest, had given him the strength to keep the witch at arm's length.

He could resist her now, he knew, for all the previous reasons and for the fact that he had a marvelous friend waiting for him should he manage to get out of Faerie alive. Still, he couldn't deny the powerful allure of the witch.

"Again, you have done well, Gary Leger," the witch said, and Gary was surprised by her tone, seeming almost subdued.

Gary nodded but did not reply, fearful that anything he might say would give the witch too much information. Ceridwen looked down at him, nodded in the face of his nod, as though his silence, too, had proven revealing.

Gary wanted to crawl under the bed; he knew that he was outmatched here.

Ceridwen motioned to a mirror on the wall. She waved her hand and spoke a word and the glassy surface clouded, and then reformed into an image of the field on the southeastern edge of Dvergamal. Geldion was there, in the midst of Connacht's encamped army, along with several dead dwarfs and dead farmers, butchered in the field as they tried to flee. Several human prisoners sat in a heavily guarded area, looking thoroughly miserable, their expressions hopeless. Gary remembered the high poles at the crossroads, and could easily guess what Geldion had in mind for them.

"You may talk freely, Gary Leger," the witch explained. "I know all that I need to know." Ceridwen waved her hand again and the image in the mirror disappeared.

Gary tried not to show his revulsion for the brutal scene. He couldn't help but think how much like his own world Faerie could sometimes be. But why had Ceridwen chosen to show him that particular view? he wondered.

He looked over to her, sitting perfectly straight, eyeing him closely and licking her red lips in anticipation. Then Gary understood. The gruesome battle scene had overwhelmed him, mainly because he had played such a large part in bringing it about. He was indeed one of the authors of this tale, as Mickey had said, and Ceridwen wanted to show him the flip side to the adventure and the glory, the harsh price of victory. Inevitably, Gary's shoulders began to slump, but he straightened immediately, reminded himself that to show such weakness now could only help this alluring enemy sitting beside him.

"Do you know why I have brought you?" the witch asked calmly.

"The spear and armor," Gary replied indignantly, and his eyes narrowed, for he did not possess the spear. Fortune had aided him in getting one up on Ceridwen.

Ceridwen chuckled softly. "I could have had that and left you dead on the field," she reminded the young man. "And did you not think it odd that my trolls took you and did not bother to retrieved the spear?"

Gary fought hard to hide his surprise. Ceridwen knew about that! Suddenly none of this was making any sense to him. He believed that the witch must be bluffing, at least in part. She had not ordered the trolls to specifically bring her the spear, and so it had been left, but Gary could not believe, for whatever reason Ceridwen needed him, that the witch would not want the precious spear, possibly the only weapon in all of Faerie that could even hurt her, in her clutches.

So that might have been part of it, but if not for the artifacts, then why had Ceridwen taken such trouble to get him alive? Only one thought came to Gary, and it was not a pleasant one: revenge.

"You do not know our ways," Ceridwen said, rising from the bed and moving over to Alice, who was curled up in a purring ball. Gary tensed, fearing that the witch was about to send the vicious feline his way.

"You understand the general principles of the land," Ceridwen continued, absently draping a hand over the furry ball. "That much you proved in your first fight—in your flight—from the knight Redarm. It is the particulars that you need a lesson in, Gary Leger." Ceridwen rose again and turned suddenly on Gary, her blue eyes flashing with the first indication of eagerness Gary had seen.

"The particulars," she said again.

Gary had no answer for her, didn't even have a clue about what she was talking about.

"You were the one who banished me," the witch said. Gary's mind whirled in several different directions, most of them holding terrible implications. Might it be that Ceridwen could reverse the banishment by killing him?

The witch calmed again, apparently realizing the young man's distress. "Let me explain it differently," she offered. "Robert is free upon the land, more free than in centuries, since I do not stand to oppose him."

"The two evils kept each other in check," Gary remarked, and then he thought his choice of words incredibly stupid. Still, Ceridwen seemed to take no offense at being referred to as an "evil."

She nodded, as if to say touché, and went on. "In your victory, you and your pitiful friends have inadvertently plunged the world into dire trouble," she said. She waved at the mirror and an image of Gondabuggan came into view, many parts of the town still smoldering from Robert's initial attack. Ceridwen didn't let the image hang for long, though, and Gary saw through the propaganda, sensed that the gnomes had gotten off fairly well.

"This will be but the beginning," the witch proclaimed. "Robert will fly unhindered from one end of Faerie to the other, his breath burning a swath of destruction. And when he is fully convinced that his day has come, he will bring out his lizard soldiers."

Gary shuddered, remembering all too well Robert's strange and dangerous troops, the lava newts.

"Farewell, then, to Braemar," Ceridwen remarked. "And to Drochit and Dilnamarra, and all the towns and hamlets within the dragon's long reach."

"We'll stop that," Gary declared, and he caught himself one step shy of revealing the whole plan to the witch.

"No," Ceridwen replied. "Nor will I, banished as I am

on my island. In a hundred years I will come out to find all the land under Robert's shadow."

"What are you getting at?" Gary demanded, his anger pushing aside all fears. If killing him would have released Ceridwen, then the witch would have already done so. This elaborate explanation, apparently trying to convince Gary that no scenario could be as bleak as having Robert flying free in Faerie, told Gary much about what was going on, told him that Ceridwen needed his willing assistance.

"Faerie does not have a hundred years," the witch snarled back at him, but she quickly put her dangerous frown away, taking on an innocuous appearance once more.

"You want me to release you," Gary replied, finally catching on. "I banished you, so by your rules, the particulars of which I do not know," he had to add, "I am the only one who can release you from that banishment."

Ceridwen did not answer, did not have to, for the firm set of her sculpted features told Gary that he had hit the mark.

"Not a chance," the young man said smugly.

"Consider the consequences," Ceridwen replied, her voice deathly calm. "For Faerie, and for yourself."

The threat certainly made an impression on Gary Leger, altruistic though he wanted to be. Ceridwen could hurt him; he could boast all he wanted to and pretend to hold the upper hand in this meeting, but he couldn't forget for one moment that Ceridwen could utterly destroy him with a clap of her deceivingly delicate hands.

"There is one evil upon the land, and you advise me to loose another to counter it?" Gary asked incredulously, trying to put this conversation back into the hypothetical.

"I advise you to consider the consequences," Ceridwen said again. "For Faerie, for yourself, and for your pitiful friends!" With that, the witch cried out at her mirror. Again an image formed, this time of the passes in Penllyn near the lake.

Gary saw his companions—four at least, for Baron Pwyll and Cedric the smithy were not with them—moving slowly along the trail, Kelsey carrying the magical spear and Gary's lost helmet.

Ceridwen muttered under her breath and the scene shifted, scanning the rocky ridges in the companions' wake, where lurked many, many trolls.

"Two score of them," Ceridwen remarked. "Awaiting my word to descend upon your friends and destroy them."

Gary forced himself to sit up straight. "How do I know that you're telling me, showing me, the truth?" he asked, though the obvious quiver in his voice proved that he believed what he was seeing. "I'm sure that your mirror could show me whatever you wanted it to."

Ceridwen didn't justify the remark with an answer. "You are the one who can end my exile," she said coldly. "You alone, Gary Leger. Consider the weight that has been placed upon your shoulders." Ceridwen looked to the mirror, showing again the four companions moving slowly along the winding trail. "A pity that friends so loyal should perish." She looked to Geek and started to say something, but Gary, his nerves at their end, cut her short.

"We can deal," he said.

"Deal?"

"You let me go, and my friends," Gary explained. "Guarantee us safe passage out of Penllyn." Gary paused, to study Ceridwen's reaction as well as to carefully weigh the confusing thoughts that were rushing through his head. What should he do? The answer was obvious, as far as he and his friends were concerned, but what would truly be the best course for Faerie? Would the land be better off if

Ceridwen were allowed to come forth and help put Robert back in his hole?

"I'll reduce the terms of your banishment to one year," Gary finished, as good a compromise as he could think of on such short notice.

Ceridwen laughed at him. "A year?" she balked. "In a year, Robert's hold on the land will be nearly absolute."

"Unless my friends and I can stop him," Gary was quick to put in.

"And if you cannot?" Ceridwen asked simply, revealing Gary's dilemma.

Gary didn't know how to respond. He thought of Mickey's words when the leprechaun had explained why he had retrieved Gary. "There might be things that only yerself can do," Mickey had said, and that made perfect sense to Gary now, though it did little to show him which choice was the proper one.

"Two weeks," Ceridwen snapped, seeing nothing forthcoming.

"Six months," Gary shot back, instinctively bargaining for every advantage. "Not so long a time to one such as Ceridwen."

"Three months," the witch replied. "I will be free before the onset of winter, that I might find my wintry allies to battle against Robert."

Gary thought long and hard, his eyes never leaving the dangerous situation revealed in Ceridwen's mirror.

"My friends and I run free?" he asked.

"For whatever good that will do," Ceridwen agreed.

Gary felt as though he was forgetting something—until he thought of the previous image in the magical mirror. "And you retract the army of Connacht," he said. "And let those prisoners go free."

Ceridwen acted surprised. "I?"

"Get off it, witch," Gary snarled. "Everyone, even a

newcomer to Faerie, knows that you pull Kinnemore's strings. Badenoch, Drochit, their men—all their men—and the dwarfs can return to their homes unhindered, while Geldion and the army go back to Connacht, where they belong."

Now it was Ceridwen's turn to carefully consider the deal. She was not an impatient witch, and three months certainly was not a long time. "King Kinnemore's army will be recalled to Connacht," she agreed.

"Three months," Gary said grimly, and he was surprised to hear the words, surprised that he and Ceridwen had come so quickly to a deal. Surprised that it was, suddenly, over. "On condition that I have your word that you will no longer interfere with my progress," he quickly added, wanting everything to be exactly spelled out.

"Interfere?" Ceridwen asked, feigning surprise. "I?" Gary scowled and Ceridwen cackled like a crow. "Agreed," she said quickly, before anything more could be tagged on.

Gary nodded, hoping that he hadn't forgotten anything else, hoping that he had made the best deal he could—for himself, and for the land.

"But why would I interfere, my dear Gary Leger?" the witch asked a moment later, her tone sincerely incredulous.

Gary thought that somewhat surprising question over, but had no answer, even had no answer as to why Ceridwen would ask it.

"I will go so far as to tell you something, my unwilling associate," the obviously thrilled witch purred on. "Robert knows of your return, and of the missing armor and spear. The dragon is onto your little game, Gary Leger, and if you think that Connacht and Prince Geldion are the worst of your troubles, then think again!"

Gary's face was twisted in confusion—both at the news and at why Ceridwen would offer it to him.

"Do you not understand?" Ceridwen innocently asked him. "I hope that you and your friends are successful. That way, when I walk free in three months, Robert will not be there to oppose me.

"But you cannot change your mind and not go after Robert, now, can you?" the witch teased. "He will lay waste to all the land."

Gary chewed on his lips, wondering how badly he had fared in this meeting. He had followed his heart, and had, indeed, put a secondary plan of action into effect should he and his friends fail in recapturing Robert, a plan that could save many lives across the land. But at what cost? Gary had to ask himself. He didn't know the particulars, as Ceridwen had said, and he had been forced by a desperate situation to make a quick decision that he was not fully prepared to make.

He looked to the mirror, to his friends, and realized that others, and not he, would suffer the consequences if he had chosen badly.

17 † Cackling Crow

"There's trolls all about us," Mickey said softly.

"Well, why don't they just come out and play?" Geno growled, slapping a hammer across his open palm. He looked towards a pile of rocks two dozen yards away, suspecting that several trolls were concealed behind it, and let out an angry snarl.

Kelsey's hand was on his shoulder in an instant, bidding him to calm down. The elf, above all the rest of them, understood just how many trolls were circling about them, and the last thing he wanted was a fight.

"We may have to leave," he whispered to Mickey.

"What about the lad?"

Kelsey shrugged helplessly, and Mickey couldn't really argue. He knew that the others wanted to rescue Gary as much as he, but the young man had obviously already been taken to Ynis Gwydrin, and with these trolls looming all about, they would have a hard enough time even getting close enough to see the surrounding lake.

Kelsey glanced around, scanning their options. Geno and Gerbil sat atop the rugged pony (the gnome's quadricycle wasn't much good in rough mountain terrain), while Kelsey and Mickey shared Kelsey's steed. The riderless horse, Cedric's, was tied behind, the magical spear and helm strapped upon it, waiting for Gary.

Kelsey looked back to Mickey and shook his head

grimly. He wasn't one to quit easily, but this trek seemed foolhardy. Even if they could get to the lake, how would they get out to the island? And even if they got out to the island, how might they deal with Ceridwen?

But all the logic in the world couldn't overrule the fact that one of their companions, a trusted friend, was in dire trouble.

"We cannot leave him to her," Mickey said firmly, grabbing the elf's wrist. Kelsey looked to Geno and Gerbil, and both responded with a nod ahead, to the path that would take them to the lake, and Kelsey nodded, too, thinking then that if they died in their foolhardy attempt, then so be it.

Kelsey just turned his attention to the path ahead when out stepped a surprising, and welcome, sight. "Troll!" Geno screamed, hoisting his hammer as if to throw.

Gary Leger looked back over his shoulder. "Where?" he asked innocently.

"Laddie!" Mickey cried.

"What in the name of a smart goblin are you doing here?" Geno demanded, lowering the deadly hammer. "I thought you were a damned troll!"

"Trolls are taller," Gary replied sourly. He caught some movement to the side out of the corner of his eye. "Like those over there," he growled and picked up a stone. "Get out of here!" he cried, pegging the missile into the tumble of boulders. "Before Ceridwen turns you all into bunnies and puts you into a pie!"

The stone skipped off several boulders, might have hit a troll or two (for the sound wouldn't be much different from that of a stone hitting boulders), and a group of the monsters skittered away, boulders rolling about in their blundering wake.

Mickey and Kelsey exchanged incredulous looks.

"What've ye been doing, lad?" the leprechaun asked slowly, cautiously.

"Arguing, mostly," Gary replied, moving up to the riderless horse and seeming in no mood to talk about anything. Indeed, the young man was deeply troubled by his meeting with the witch, terribly afraid that he had acted wrongly in reducing Ceridwen's sentence. He put one foot in the stirrup and started to hoist himself up, then changed his mind, realizing that someone was missing.

"Where's Cedric?" he asked anxiously, privately guessing the answer.

"He died happy," Mickey replied solemnly.

"Son of a bitch," Gary muttered, burying his face into the side of the saddle. He died happy, the young man thought. That meant he died thinking that he was helping Gary, the spearwielder.

Gary was surprised a moment later to feel the cold tip of Kelsey's sword pressed tightly against his shoulder blade, in a crease in the armor. He understood the elf's doubts and fears, and knew enough not to make any sudden moves.

"How did you come out?" Kelsey asked evenly, positioning his horse so that Gary was cut off to the right.

"Ceridwen sent me out," Gary answered.

Kelsey poked him. "Do not play me for a fool," he warned. Geno walked the pony around to the side, blocking off any escape to the left, as well. Gary could not see Kelsey, but he could see the dwarf and gnome, and while Gerbil seemed almost as confused and shocked as was Gary, there was little compromise in the sturdy dwarf's stern expression.

"Ceridwen let me go," Gary declared, his voice firm and confident. "She wants me to slay Robert."

"That makes sense," Mickey offered, but Kelsey kept the swordtip in tight against Gary's back.

"You're hurting me," Gary remarked.

"I will kill you," Kelsey replied in all seriousness, "if I find that you are not who you appear to be."

"How did you chase off the trolls?" Geno asked, and the question seemed more like an accusation.

"I didn't," Gary snapped back.

"Then who?" the elf demanded, prodding him again.

"They were working for Ceridwen," Gary explained. "Before she ever sent me out of her castle, she sent word to the trolls that we were not to be harmed, or bothered at all." Gary snapped his fingers as an idea popped into his head.

"The spear," he started to explain, reaching across the saddle. What he had intended was to take the weapon, re-establish a telepathic bond, and let it inform the others that he was indeed who he claimed to be.

What he got instead was the smack of an elfish sword off the side of his head, and a flying tackle from an outraged dwarf. The next thing he knew, he was sitting on the ground facing Kelsey's horse, his arms wrenched up high behind his head by the snarling dwarf.

"Should I break them off?" Geno asked in all seriousness, and it seemed to Gary as if the powerful dwarf wasn't waiting for an answer.

Kelsey slid down from his seat and put his sword to Gary's throat. "Who are you?"

"Someone who wants to go home," Gary said to Mickey. He tugged hard against Geno's grasp, but the dwarf's viselike hands did not loosen. "Someone who's feeling unappreciated."

"Enough of the cryptic answers!" Kelsey demanded.

"I'm Gary Leger, you stupid elf!" Gary shouted. "Ceridwen let me off of her island because I dealt fairly with her, and she told her trolls to leave us alone because that was part of the deal!"

Geno let go, stood staring blankly at Kelsey.

"Deal?" Kelsey asked.

Gary ran his hand through his thick black hair and sighed deeply several times. He didn't want to admit what had happened on Ynis Gwydrin, but he didn't see any other way to gain back the trust of his friends—friends he dearly needed now, perhaps more than ever.

"Ceridwen will walk free in three months," he admitted.

"Stupid . . ." Geno stammered. He spun and punched the horse, and it snorted and leaped away. "Stupid! You really are a coward! You'd just do anything to save your worthless bones!"

Kelsey's forlorn, disappointed stare hurt more than the dwarf's tirade. The elf's swordtip dipped slowly to the ground.

"Oh, shut up," Gary said to Geno, though he never blinked in the face of that elfish stare.

The dwarf was upon him in an instant, curled fist only inches from Gary's face.

"I didn't do it to save my life," Gary said firmly. "Ceridwen wasn't going to kill me, anyway." He didn't know if that last statement was true or not, but it sounded good, and Gary needed something that sounded good at that moment. "I did it to save the four of you," he said.

"What are you saying?" Kelsey asked.

"She showed me your progress," Gary explained. "In a . . . magic mirror, or something."

"A scrying device," Mickey helped, more versed in the ways of witches than the man from the other world.

"Whatever," Gary said. "I saw you, and saw the trolls." Gary eyed Geno directly. "Dozens of trolls."

"We would have willingly died," Kelsey boasted. "Rather than . . ."

"Rather than what?" Gary snapped at him. "If you had

died, and I was captured, and Kinnemore's army was on the field, and Robert was flying free . . ."

"The lady paints a glum picture," Mickey offered.

"Any worse a picture than having that witch out and about?" Geno asked.

"Oh, yes," Gerbil piped in unexpectedly. All eyes turned on him, and the gnome sank low in the saddle. "I mean, she was out before, after all, and things didn't look so very bad. Not like now, I mean."

"True enough," remarked Mickey.

"I had to make a choice," Gary said resignedly. "I don't know if it was the best one—maybe I should have let her out right away so that she could go against the dragon and save us the trouble." He shrugged and ran his fingers through his black hair once more. "I did the best I could."

Kelsey took hold of Gary's hand and hoisted him to his feet. "It was a difficult choice," the elf admitted. "You said that Ceridwen would let us out of the mountains?"

Gary nodded. "I made her agree that she would not hinder us in any way in our quest to put Robert back in his hole."

"Why would she want to?" Mickey asked in all seriousness.

"Exactly," Gary agreed. "But I also made her agree to send Geldion and his troops back to Connacht. I figured that would give Pwyll and the others some time to regroup, maybe put up some defenses."

Kelsey was nodding approvingly, and Gary relaxed somewhat. "'I did the best I could," he said again.

"You did well," Kelsey replied.

"Just fine, lad," agreed the leprechaun.

"But what are we to do next?" Geno put in. "If we put the wyrm back in his hole, then the witch runs free."

Gary didn't miss the curious way Mickey's face seemed to pale.

"The dragon must be stopped!" Kelsey and Gerbil said together, and they both looked at each other, surprised.

"Owe me a Coke," Gary said for both of them, though neither of them knew what the hell he was talking about, or what the hell a "Coke" might be. "Never mind," was all that Gary offered in reply to their curious stares, and he turned to his new mount.

Any levity that Gary had managed to forge, any relaxation that had come over him in learning that his friends approved of his desperate choice on Ynis Gwydrin, was washed away the moment the young man laid eyes on that riderless horse.

Cedric had died happy.

For the spearwielder.

Gary gritted his teeth and pulled himself up into the saddle, roughly taking the reins and turning the horse the other way on the trail. "Let's get the hell out of here," he said angrily, and he started the steed at a swift trot and then a gallop, playing his own anger out in the strong movements of the willing horse.

They came out of Penllyn later that afternoon, the sun fast disappearing behind the mountains. As Ceridwen had promised, no trolls, or any other monsters, blocked their way or hindered them in any manner at all.

They retrieved Gerbil's quadricycle, stuffed under a bush for safekeeping. The gnome immediately opened yet another of the thing's seemingly endless compartments, pulling out a pile of badly folded parchments.

"Maps," he explained to the curious onlookers. "The most up-to-date and detailed in all the land. I know that I have one in here, oh, yes I must, showing the trails between Penllyn and the Giant's Thumb."

Kelsey nodded in deference to the gnome, knowing that Gerbil needed to feel helpful, needed to believe that he was doing something to take revenge on Robert for what Robert had done to his village. In truth, Kelsey already knew the route they would take—the very same route he, Gary, Mickey, Geno, and the giant Tommy One-Thumb had taken on their first trip to the dragon's lair.

Kelsey waited patiently for the gnome to sort through the pile, though, and Mickey took that opportunity to leave Kelsey's saddle and go up to his customary position in front of Gary Leger.

"We will ride out a few miles from the shadow of Penllyn," Kelsey explained, as they regrouped and prepared to start away once more. Gerbil nodded eagerly and fumbled with the pile of parchments, narrowing down the possibilities. The light was fast fading, and none of the companions wanted to remain near to the witch's mountains after dark, but again, Kelsey waited patiently for the gnome.

"Then we set a short camp," he explained. "In the morn, we ride northeast until we reach the Crahgs, then cross them as best as we can."

"Not so best," came a cackling reply. The companions all looked to each other for a moment, until they realized that the source of the response had not been any of them.

"There," Gary said a moment later, pointing to a large crow sitting on the low branch of a lone tree not far from the bushes where they had stashed the quadricycle.

Instinctively, Geno's arm came up, a hammer at the ready, and Kelsey, his glare unrelenting, went for his bow.

"Don't shoot it!" Gary growled at both of them. "The bird seems to know something."

"Spy of Ceridwen," the dwarf remarked, for it was no secret among the peoples of Faerie that the talking crows were in alliance with the witch. Rumors had it that Ceridwen bought the birds' alliance by enchanting them with the gift of speech.

"And no friend to us," Kelsey added grimly, fitting the arrow to his bowstring.

"But an ally of our quest," Gary remarked.

"Crahgs are blocked," the crow cackled, and the actual sight of a talking bird gave even the stern elf pause. "Wolves and haggis, dragon friends."

"That'd make sense," Mickey agreed, looking to Kelsey to lower his bow. "Robert's sealin' off the eastland for his own uses."

"Or he's looking for us and thinking that we'll go through the Crahgs," Gary added. Three grim faces turned on him (four when Gerbil took a moment from his map-watching to look up and figure out that something was amiss), none of his friends appreciating him speaking out that little possibility.

"Robert has more to think about than this bunch," Geno put in derisively, wanting to fully dismiss Gary's thought. The dwarf threw a smirk Gerbil's way, and the gnome responded in kind, but then went right back to his tangle of maps.

"And that crow is working for the witch," Kelsey added, lifting the bow once more. "For no better reason than to deter us, than to keep us confused until Ceridwen might come forth."

"Robert knows about us," Gary said immediately, before either Kelsey or the dwarf could take any rash action. Again, the grim gazes descended over the young man.

"Ceridwen told me," Gary explained. "The dragon knows about the armor and the spear, and knows that I've returned."

Geno looked hopelessly to Kelsey, as if to say, "Now what?" but the elf seemed to have no answer.

"Even if that's true," Mickey put in hopefully, "he'd not expect us to go walking of our own free will back to his stronghold."

"Unless he thought we had something which could put him back in his hole," Gary remarked.

Kelsey looked questioningly to Mickey.

"It's a little-known detail of honorable challenging," the leprechaun said smugly, striking flint to steel to drop sparks into his long-stemmed pipe. "Robert'll never guess the truth." Mickey wasn't nearly as confident as he appeared. The last thing the leprechaun wanted, either out here or in the caverns beneath the Giant's Thumb, was an encounter with Robert. Mickey wanted his pot of gold back, nothing more, but his original lie seemed to have taken on monumental proportions suddenly, with so many side-players and kingdom-wide intrigue.

Kelsey looked to the northeast, as though he was spying out the distant Crahgs. He looked back to the smug crow, sitting confidently on the branch.

"Do you believe the bird?" the elf asked Gary suddenly.

Gary nodded. "I don't think that Ceridwen would have any reason to lie," he replied. "It's like she said, our victory over Robert will only make things easier for her."

"I'm starting to hate this," Geno remarked, impatiently slapping his hammer across his open palm. His pony nickered and started to rear, but the powerful dwarf tightened his legs around the beast and it went still.

"Your point is well made," Kelsey said. "And the Crahgs will offer us little cover from the flying dragon." Kelsey turned his gaze more directly east, south of the distant hills.

"What're ye thinking?" Mickey asked him grimly, guessing exactly what Kelsey had in mind.

"There is a wood near here," the elf replied. "Dark and tangled. It might provide us cover for the next portion of our journey."

"There!" shouted the gnome, poking a finger so forcefully into the map that he drove it right through the parchment. He retracted the digit and looked at the map, scratching his head curiously. "Readwood?" he asked.

"Dreadwood," Geno corrected, the dwarf's gravelly voice grave. "You poked out the first rune."

From Mickey's intake of breath, Gary could tell that this Dreadwood was not a nice place.

"I see no choice," Kelsey said to the leprechaun. "Not if the crow speaks truthfully about the Crahgs."

"Wolves and newts," the bird cackled.

"Shut your beak!" Geno roared, and he hurled his hammer the bird's way. The heavy weapon smacked the branch near the bird and ricocheted away, the crow taking wing into the dark air, shrieking in protest all the while.

"Shut your beak!" the dwarf roared again. "If I wanted to hit you . . ." Geno let it go at that, just spat up into the darkness after the long-gone bird.

"How bad is this Dreadwood?" Gary asked Mickey privately when the commotion died away.

Mickey shrugged, seeming nonchalant about the whole thing. "We'll get through, lad," he answered. "Don't ye fret."

Gary took faith in that, believed in his friends and in himself. "And once we get the dragon put away," he reasoned, a new idea popping into his head, "I'll make a deal with him."

"Full of deals that don't even concern you," Geno grumbled, crashing around in the brush to find his hammer.

"What are you thinking?" Kelsey asked, pointedly ignoring the dwarf, and his visage unexpectedly stern.

"I reduce Robert's time of banishment," Gary answered, smiling widely. "To three months, as I did with Ceridwen. Then they both come out together and neither of them has any advantage." Gary thought his idea perfectly logical, and he wasn't prepared for the heightening intensity of

Kelsey's glower. From that unyielding stare, Gary almost believed that the elf would trot his horse over and strike him down.

"Ye're forgetting something, lad," Mickey whispered.

"What?" Gary asked, to the leprechaun and the elf. Kelsey let his stare linger a few moments longer, then turned his mount away.

"What?" Gary asked again, this time straight to Mickey.

"It was not yerself that challenged the wyrm," Mickey reminded him, and Gary's breath hissed as he sucked it in through his gritted teeth. He hadn't even thought of that, hadn't even realized that he might be overstepping his bounds and insulting his proud friend.

"Kelsey," he said, as apologetically as he could. "I didn't mean . . ."

"It does not matter," Kelsey replied, turning his mount back around.

"Of course, you are the one who can reduce the dragon's banishment," Gary offered. "You're the only one who holds any right to deal with Robert. I just got carried away."

"You just might," Geno remarked dryly, and Gary glared at him, thinking that the dwarf might be enjoying this awkward situation just a bit too much.

"It does not matter," Kelsey declared again, his melodic voice firm. "We must worry first about putting the dragon back in his hole. Then we will decide which is the best course for the good of the land."

Gary agreed with the elf's choice of priorities, as did the others, but Mickey's thinking was following a slightly different course. Mickey understood the dragon better than any of them, and he knew that if Ceridwen's claims were correct, if Robert was on to them, then they could expect to meet him long before they ever got near his castle. Mickey understood, too, that Robert the Wretched had long kept spies in the dark forest of Dreadwood, and that those thick boughs might not provide as much cover as Kelsey hoped. Robert was going to have to be tricked— not an easy task—and the cost might be high.

But leprechauns were the best in the world at deception. In truth, Mickey was deceiving his own companions even now. And so Mickey tuned out of the conversation altogether, began to plot as only a leprechaun can plot.

Whatever the cost, he meant to get back his pot of gold.

18 † Dreadwood

Even the hardy mounts of Tir na n'Og nickered and whinnied and flipped their heads side to side, shying away as the group approached the dark and tangled forest. Dreadwood started abruptly, a thick clump of trees in the middle of the plain between the mountains of Penllyn on the south and the rolling Crahgs on the north. Kelsey took them near to the Crahgs, the narrowest expanse of the forest, but still the wood seemed dark and wide to Gary Leger.

He had spent many days of his youth in the woods, even after sunset, with no fears beyond the very real possibilities of mosquito bites or of inadvertently stepping on a bees' nest. Now, though, as his horse approached the tangle, a feeling of dread rose up within Gary, a feeling that there was more evil within this place than biting bugs.

Already he knew that whoever had named this forest had named it right.

It didn't seem possible to Gary that they would even find a path through the forest. The twisted trees seemed a solid wall, gnarled and writhing, a living barrier that would not permit visitors.

Kelsey held up his hand for the others to stop, and sat atop his horse, eyeing the wood suspiciously. He motioned to the side, and the whole troupe shifted.

"There is a road," Mickey remarked to Gary, and to

Gerbil, who seemed nervous about the possibility of getting his quadricycle through. "The trees just aren't wanting to show it to us."

Again Kelsey motioned, back the other way, and the group followed accordingly. They reversed direction again, several more times, Kelsey studying the trees, looking for hints of the path.

"None better at spotting illusions than the Tylwyth Teg," Mickey said quietly, trying to keep his less informed friends patient and comfortable.

Finally, Kelsey sat up straight on his mount and sighed deeply. He gave a look Mickey's way that seemed to say that he was pretty sure of the path, but also that it was only a guess. He reached down to the back of the saddle and drew an arrow out of his quiver, examining the fletchings. Apparently not finding something he needed, he shook his head and replaced it, drawing out another.

After a similar examination, Kelsey put his mouth against this arrow's tip, whispering to it as though it could hear. He then produced a length of cord, fine and silvery as a spider's web, from his saddlebags, and threaded it through a tiny hole near to the arrow's fletchings. Then Kelsey fitted the arrow to his bow and lifted it towards the forest, closing his golden eyes.

Again he whispered—some sort of an enchantment, it seemed to Gary—and he moved the bow slowly, first to the right, then back to the left. Seemingly at random, the elf let fly, and the arrow cut through the air, making for a huge elm. It didn't hit the tree, though, and Gary had to blink, thinking his vision had deceived him.

The fine cord continued to unwind for some time, Kelsey holding its other end and nodding Mickey's way. At last, it went slack and the elf slipped down from his saddle and took it up, walking his mount as he collected the cord.

"What just happened?" Gary had to ask.

"Arrows o' the Tylwyth Teg have a way of finding their way around the trees," Mickey explained with a sly wink. "They'll not hit a living thing if telled not to by their makers."

They were near the forest by then, near the living, seemingly impenetrable wall, when Gary, to his surprise, noticed a break in the trees, wide enough even for Gerbil's quadricycle to pass through. Why hadn't he seen that from the field? he wondered, and he shrugged his amazement away, reasoning that Kelsey's arrow magic had countered the forest's own magic.

No matter how many times he returned, or how long he stayed, Gary Leger knew that he would ever remain a stranger to the land of Faerie.

Kelsey disappeared into the dark forest, the shadows swallowing him as soon as he crossed the threshold. Right behind the elf, Geno's pony shied away, but the dwarf grunted angrily and with a single powerful tug put the beast back in line and kept it moving.

Gerbil went next, his quadricycle bumping up one way and then the other as he passed over the nearest tree roots, and Gary came last, eyes determinedly straight ahead. It seemed to the young man as if he had walked into the night. Rationally, he knew that he was no more than a few feet from the entrance, the sky outside sunny and clear, but when he looked back, he saw a distinct hole of only dim light, as though the sun itself feared to peek into Dreadwood.

"Easy," Mickey coaxed, to the horse and to Gary. "Easy."

"Some light, leprechaun," Kelsey called back as he retrieved his arrow, sticking at an angle from the forest path, and climbed into his saddle. Mickey gave a grunting response—it sounded more like a groan to Gary—and began a long chant, which seemed strange to Gary, since on his last visit to Faerie he had seen the leprechaun merely snap his fingers to produce globes of glowing light.

Finally, Mickey did snap his fingers and a tiny ball, barely a candle's flicker, appeared atop them, hovering in the air and weaving wildly back and forth as though it would soon go out.

Then it diminished even more and Mickey shrugged helplessly. "Me magic's not so good against the weight of Dreadwood," he explained.

Kelsey, who had just put an arrow through the trees' illusion, eyed the leprechaun suspiciously, and Gary understood the elf's obvious doubts. Something was wrong with Mickey, with Mickey's magic at least, for the leprechaun's bag of tricks had been far less helpful this time around than on Gary's first trip through the enchanted land. Gary remembered his first encounter with the sprite, when Mickey had tricked him repeatedly, when Mickey had him plucking giant mushrooms out of the ground, commanding them to take him to their pot of gold. Most of all, Gary remembered Mickey's cocky swagger, the leprechaun's sincere belief that tricking a human, or a monster, was a matter of course and nothing to get overly concerned about.

Where had the leprechaun's confidence, and his magic, gone to? Gary wondered, and his look Mickey's way reflected his confusion.

Mickey only shrugged and brought the brim of his tam-o'-shanter low over his eyes, as deep an explanation as Gary or any of the others was going to get. The little faerie light winked out altogether a moment later, and with the dim portal fast fading behind them the friends soon found themselves fully engulfed by the gloom.

In truth, the road inside the forest was flat and clear, and wide enough so that Gary could walk his horse beside the gnome's rolling contraption. Gary's eyes soon adjusted to the darkness, and he found that it was not so bad. Some sunlight did make its way through the leafy boughs, diminishing as it wove down to Gary's level, but enough so that he could distinguish general shapes around him, could see Kelsey and Geno, leading the way on their mounts. On the road beside him, Gerbil was at work again, fumbling with some items too small for Gary to make out, and absently pumping his little legs, his quadricycle easily pacing the horses. Gary realized that, though he and Gerbil had been traveling companions for several days now, he hadn't really gotten to know the gnome. He noticed Mickey, resting easily against his horse's neck, hat still low, long-stemmed pipe in his mouth, and little legs crossed at the knee, and realized that he wasn't going to find much company there.

"What are you making?" Gary asked the gnome.

"Light," came the polite, if short, answer.

Gary nodded, but then screwed up his face. "You're making light?" he asked. "You mean, you're going to light a torch?"

"Torches are for dwarfs and elfs, and the human folk," Gerbil replied, again pointedly not elaborating. "Even for goblins, I suppose."

Gary considered the condescending tone for a few moments. "How do gnomes make light?" he politely asked.

"Potions."

Now Gary was intrigued, but he understood that the typically talkative gnome obviously didn't want to be bothered at that moment. He continued to walk his horse even with the quadricycle, watching Gerbil's every move. Soon the gnome had a pole erected in the front section of the contraption, its top a tube, rotating end around end in tune with the turning of the pedals. Gerbil had a funnel between his working knees, its narrow end connected to the bottom of the tube, and in his hands he held two beakers.

"Potions?" Gary asked.

"Ssssh!" the gnome hissed.

"Ye take a chance on blowin' yerself up if ye distract a workin' gnome," Mickey quietly added, and Gary went silent, having no doubts of Mickey's claims and having no desire to blow himself up. He watched curiously as Gerbil poured specific amounts of each potion into the funnel. A moment later, a glow came from the turning tube atop the pole, intensifying with each rotation.

Kelsey and Geno both looked back curiously, and neither seemed pleased.

"Ye're makin' yerself into a target," Mickey remarked to the gnome.

"I cannot work in the dark, of course!" the flustered gnome shot back. A bit more of the contents of one beaker went into the funnel, and the light brightened accordingly.

"Suit yerself," was Mickey's casual reply.

Gary sat mystified. He had seen rings that used chemical reaction to produce light, but he hardly expected to find such a process utilized in this enchanted place. He was about to question Gerbil, and to congratulate him for his fine light, but then a tree branch reached down suddenly and plucked the gnome from his seat, lifting him up, kicking and squealing, into the dark boughs.

Gary tried to call out, but found his voice stuck in his throat. He lunged over to grab at Gerbil as the gnome shot by, was overbalanced to the side when another branch swung down the other way, bashing him in the shoulder and sending him flying from the saddle to crash halfway over the side of the quadricycle. Gary turned back in time to see the same branch, a foot thick, slam straight down on the back of his horse, narrowly missing the purposely falling leprechaun. Gary heard a tremendous cracking sound as the poor horse's legs buckled, and the beast went right down to the ground.

A hammer spun through the air, whacking off of the low branch, but doing no real damage. It was soon followed by a flying dwarf as Geno leaped from his mount, wrapping his powerful arms about the limb of the attacking tree. With a growl, the dwarf bit hard into the branch, tearing off a large piece of bark.

Kelsey was already up the boughs, scampering along writhing branches to get near to the caught Gerbil. Smaller branches whipped at the elf as he passed and his sword flashed, often dropping pieces of tree free to the ground.

"Get up!" came the call in Gary's thoughts, and he was already on his way. He fumbled to get his helmet straightened, then searched out the spear and hoisted it in eager hands.

But where to hit a tree?

Geno spat out another hunk of branch above him; Kelsey had reached Gerbil and was hacking mightily at the entrapping branch, but hadn't yet begun to free the gnome.

Gary roared and went for the trunk, driving the spear straight ahead, its tip plunging through the hard wood. The tree went into a shaking frenzy, and poor Gerbil whined in pain.

Gary turned and readied the spear for a throw, thinking to sink it into the branch holding the gnome, thinking that Gerbil would surely be squashed before too much longer. Another branch swung about first, though, slamming Gary's armored back and launching him through the air, where he landed, again, half across the quadricycle.

"Are ye all right, lad?" asked Mickey, sitting low in the contraption's seat.

"I've been better," Gary replied, forcing himself back up to his knees. He heard a crack above him and had to shift aside as Geno and his branch came tumbling down, the wild dwarf having bitten clear through the limb.

"Not half bad!" Geno proclaimed, quickly biting off another chunk. And off he ran, leaping straight into the trunk, throwing a hug about it and chomping away with dwarfish ferocity.

The branch hit Gary again, but not so hard, since the tree then seemed to focus on the dangerous dwarf. An instant later, back to his knees yet again, Gary understood the effectiveness of the dwarf's tactics, for the tree could not easily get at Geno when he was in so close.

And Gary was glad for Geno's efforts, because, for the moment at least, he had been left alone. He immediately looked above him, to the squirming gnome and the battling elf, and knew that he had to react.

Don't miss, he thought, to which the spear gave an indignant reply, as though it had been insulted.

"I'm talking to myself!" Gary explained gruffly, and he let fly.

The spear cracked into the branch just a foot away from the gnome, nearly splitting the limb down the middle. Another great tug from Kelsey pulled the gasping Gerbil free, and then the elf and the gnome simply hung on as the branch cracked apart, dropping the spear straight back to the ground and sending its passengers on a wild swing that ended in a free-fall into a thick bush far to the side of the path.

Gary grabbed up the spear, nearly chuckled aloud when he regarded the dwarf, seeming a wild cross between a famished beaver and a lumberjack. Then he fell flat to the ground in terror and shock when all the thick canopy above him erupted suddenly in flames.

Horses whinnied and fled, wood crackled and burst apart. At first, Gary thought that Mickey had pulled off a clever illusion, but when he took a moment to think about it, it made no practical sense. How do you visually fool a tree?

Besides, Gary realized as flaming brands began to fall

all about him, as the air began to burn his lungs and sting his eyes, this was no trick.

He knew he had to run. He got up as high as he could and felt a tug on his arm that put him over the side of the quadricycle for the third time.

Mickey sat low in the seat, looking horrified and helpless. "Suren it's the dragon!" he called out, beckoning Gary to get in beside him.

A tree not so far away exploded from the heat; Gary heard a horse shriek in agony and knew that the thing had been engulfed. He couldn't see Geno, or Kelsey and Gerbil, had no idea at that confusing moment if the others were dead or running. And every second that slipped past put Gary's own escape into deeper jeopardy.

He scrambled in beside Mickey and found, to his relief, that the clever gnomes had put a notched and sliding adjusting bar on the seat (though even sliding it all the way back did not allow Gary to straighten his legs). Gary gave a scream as a branch fell into his face, and batted the thing away, then kicked hard with one foot, hoping just to start the quadricycle moving on such rough and uneven ground. To Gary's amazement, the contraption leaped away. He didn't know whether incredible gearing, or magical potions, enhanced the ride, but merely a few pumps later, he was flying free of the fiery zone, rushing down the wide path.

"Ride on!" the leprechaun commanded when Gary slowed and looked back to find his friends.

"We can't leave them!" Gary retorted, surprised by Mickey's callous attitude.

"Go!" came a call from back down the trail. Gary looked to see Kelsey emerging from the blazing region, waving him away.

"The dragon is on to us," Mickey explained. "Our only

chance is to separate and lead him in two different directions at once."

As if on cue, Gary heard a whoosh of air from the canopy over his head, looked up to see a huge shadow cross above him.

"Ride on, for all our lives, lad!" Mickey implored him, and Gary put his head down and pedaled with all his strength, sending the quadricycle careening down the winding road as fast as any Tir na n'Og horse could run.

He was more than a mile away before he even realized that Kelsey—the Kelsey who had told him to go—had not a bit of soot on his fair elven face.

Soot-covered, his golden hair singed, and the gnome tucked unconscious under his arm, Kelsey crawled out the side of the bush, looking back helplessly and wondering if any of his friends or any of the precious mounts had survived. Gerbil groaned repeatedly, at least, and the elf knew that he was still alive.

As was Geno, Kelsey learned a moment later when he heard the dwarf grumbling and growling and smacking his hammer off any nearby tree. Following the sounds, Kelsey was soon beside the dwarf.

"Where are the others?" he asked.

"Stonebubbles!" was all that Geno would reply.

"I thought that you had surely perished," Kelsey remarked.

Geno snorted. "I work at a dwarfish anvil, elf," he explained. "It would take more than a bit of dragon fire to burn through this hide!"

"But what of the leprechaun and Gary Leger?" Kelsey asked, and gruff Geno could only shrug and curse, "Stonebubbles!" once more.

The three kept low (and, with Kelsey's begging, Geno kept quiet) for the next half-hour as Robert continued to pass overhead, every now and then setting another section of the forest ablaze. Finally, the dragon seemed to tire of the game and swooped away, and Kelsey led his companions off. They found the pony, at least, wandering terrified to the south of the disaster, and then, when they hit the road, found the unmistakable tracks of the quadricycle, dug deeper than usual, as though the contraption was carrying more than the normal weight.

"They escaped," Kelsey proclaimed, deciding, as much on hope as on what his tracking skill was telling him, that both his friends must have been aboard. The elf's initial excitement ebbed as the three followed the tracks and came to realize that their companions were long gone.

"How fast does that thing go?" Geno asked Gerbil, the dwarf obviously angered that Mickey and Gary had apparently run off.

"How fast?" Gerbil echoed, scratching at his soot-covered beard. "Well, indeed, with the added weight . . . I put it at two hundred and fifty pounds . . . but then, of course, Gary Leger is much stronger than the average gnome . . ."

"How fast?" the dwarf growled.

"We cannot catch them on foot," Gerbil quickly replied. "Or even with the single pony."

Geno kicked a nearby tree and swung about to face Kelsey—then looked back over his shoulder to make sure that this particular tree wouldn't kick back. He looked back to the elf, then back to the tree right away, eyeing it suspiciously. Finally, convinced that this one was quiet, like a tree should be, Geno focused on the elf, and was surprised to see Kelsey taking a parchment from the trunk of a nearby tree. Geno thought it more than curious that none of them had spotted that note before.

"From the leprechaun," Kelsey said, and that alone explained many things. Kelsey read on and nodded, then held the parchment out for the others to see.

Under control. Meet you at Braemar.

"Braemar?" Geno roared. "Why Braemar? I thought we were going to Giant's Thumb, to put the damned wyrm back in its damned hole."

"But now the dragon is out," Gerbil reasoned.

"The dragon was always out!" Geno growled. "On to Giant's Thumb, I say, and let's get this business finished!"

"You forget that we do not have the stolen dagger," Kelsey interjected. "If Mickey has returned to Braemar, then so must we."

Geno wiped some soot off his unbearded face and shook his head helplessly. To all of them, it seemed as though they had been defeated, been turned around at the first sign of trouble. "Damned stupid sprite," the dwarf muttered. "What did he go and turn around for?"

Kelsey nodded, but his thoughts were heading in a different direction. Why indeed would Mickey turn back at this time? They were as close to Giant's Thumb as to Braemar, and would likely face Robert again whichever way they turned. Kelsey chuckled, understanding it all, understanding that Mickey had turned them around as a decoy, to hopefully turn Robert around as well.

"What is it?" Geno demanded.

Kelsey shook his head. "I am only glad that we are all still alive," he lied, and he waited for Geno to look away before he turned his gaze back to the east, where he now knew that the leprechaun and Gary Leger were in full flight.

19 ✝ Pot o' Gold

"Keep it rollin' straight," Mickey assured Gary, the leprechaun standing in front of the quadricycle's steering bar and peering intently ahead. Gary looked at the leprechaun's back incredulously, for all he saw ahead of them was a wall of thick trees blocking the exit from Dreadwood.

"And keep it fast," Mickey remarked, with absolute confidence.

Gary didn't disagree with that second request. Many times over the last two hours, sentient trees had reached down to grab at them, and only their great pace had gotten them through. But now, Gary didn't see how they could go on. He closed his eyes, as Mickey had previously suggested, and trusted the leprechaun to guide him past the forest's illusions. He sensed the wooden wall coming up fast, though, and had to look, nearly screaming aloud when he saw that the wall of trees loomed just a dozen feet away.

Instinctively, Gary threw up his arms in front of his face, locking the steering bar with his knees. He thought a crash unavoidable, but suddenly a break appeared as the road bent around one wide elm. In the split-second it took the rambling quadricycle to rush past, that break widened, and then it was as though someone had switched on a

244

powerful light as the gnomish contraption burst out of the tangled wood.

Lathered in sweat from his run, Gary let the quadricycle roll to a stop. He looked back to the forest, simply amazed that they had gotten through. Lines of black smoke continued to rise in the west, a reminder that though they were out, they were far from safe.

"What are we going to do?" Gary whispered harshly, as though he expected the dragon to descend on them at any moment.

Mickey peered up into the sky in all directions, then settled a firm and unblinking gaze on the young man. "We're going to get to Giant's Thumb," he announced. "And finish our business."

"How far is it?" Gary asked.

"How fast and long can ye pump this thing?"

Gary had no honest answer. He was tired from his wild rush, but again, whether it was the incredible gearing or some hidden magic, the quadricycle had outperformed his wildest expectations, had taken him farther and faster, and with far more ease, than the most expensive racing bikes of his own world ever could. "What about the dragon?" he asked suddenly, looking back to the smoke, remembering that most of the land between here and their destination was open and barren.

Mickey shrugged and seemed to Gary, for perhaps the very first time, very much afraid.

"We can go back through the forest," Gary offered. "Maybe we'll find Kelsey and the others."

"No!" The leprechaun's tone was cutting-edge sharp, and an angry light flared in the normally cheerful sprite's gray eyes. "We're on to the mountain," he declared. "To finish our business. Now, if ye've got the wind and the strength left in ye, get this thing running fast."

"What about the dragon?" Gary asked again, more firmly.

"Robert's tired," Mickey reasoned. "He's been flying a long way, by me guess, else he'd not have let us out o' Dreadwood alive. That's the weakness o' dragons, lad. They're all fire and muscle and killing claws, but it takes a mighty effort to move that mountain body about, and they do get tired."

"He'll be rested long before we get to Giant's Thumb," Gary replied ominously.

"Aye." Mickey nodded. "But will he know that we're well on our way? Kelsey and Geno'll have a trick or two to keep Robert busy back here, don't ye doubt, but if ye plan on sitting here talking, their efforts will go for nothing."

Gary took a deep breath, adjusted himself as well as he could in the low and tight quarters, and started to pump his legs. He stopped abruptly, though, and snapped his fingers, then began unstrapping the metal leggings of his armor and the bulkier plates along the rest of the suit.

"I don't think this will help much if we meet up with Robert," he explained.

Mickey nodded gravely.

Barely fifteen minutes later, the quadricycle kicked up a trail of road dust in its wake.

Kelsey nodded to the north, to a high perch on the nearest Crahg, where sat Robert, his great leathery wings wrapped about his gigantic torso and his reptilian eyes closed to evil slits.

The three companions were still under the thick cover of Dreadwood, still back near the eastern entrance of the wood.

Kelsey took an arrow from his quiver and fitted it to his bow. He nodded to Geno and Gerbil, as if asking their opinion, but he knew in truth that they could not disagree with this action. Gary and Mickey were out of the forest, headed for Robert's lair by Kelsey's reckoning, and that gave Kelsey, Geno, and Gerbil the unenviable job of keeping Robert's eyes away from the east, of keeping Robert's eyes focused on them.

"Find some cover," Geno whispered to Gerbil, and he pushed the gnome off, then scampered in a different direction. Kelsey gave them a good start, then lifted his bow the dragon's way and drew back on the bowstring. He knew that he couldn't really hurt the beast, not from this distance and probably not even from a point-blank position, but he could certainly get Robert's attention. The trick, Kelsey reminded himself, was to be far, far from this spot before the arrow ever clicked against Robert's thick armor.

He fired and never watched the projectile, running with all speed in a direction different from the ones taken by Geno and Gerbil. A moment later, the ground rumbled under the thunder of a dragon roar, and then a shadow crossed over that section of Dreadwood and all the trees went up in a line of furious fire.

Robert made several passes, but, as Mickey had said, the dragon was weary and could not sustain the assault. He dropped into one group of trees and thrashed them into kindling, then lifted away to another perch near the eastern end of the wood and sat back, watching, waiting.

"Your cover will not last!" Robert's roar promised. "I will burn away all the trees and then where will you hide, puny enemies?"

Gerbil, in a deep hole under the roots of a great oak, Geno, comfortably flattened under a boulder, and Kelsey, farthest from the sight of destruction, heard the dragon's reasonable claims and each of them, even the sturdy dwarf, wished at that time that he was back in his homeland, many miles from Dreadwood.

The miles rolled out behind them, Gary pedaling relentlessly that morning of the first day out of Dreadwood. For an hour, the bumpy horizon of the Crahgs remained north of them, but it soon gave way to flatter plains.

Mickey's spirits soared that day, with no sign of the dragon apparent and the Giant's Thumb fast approaching. The leprechaun could feel his magical energies returning as he drew ever nearer his precious pot of gold. "Keep it straight and keep it fast," he would often say to Gary, always careful to temper his boiling excitement, always remembering that Gary Leger didn't know the whole truth of the matter.

Gary seemed not so happy. He was glad, of course, that Robert was nowhere to be seen, but his thoughts were behind him, not ahead, back to the tangled wood where he had left his three companions, where black lines of smoke were still rising into the sky. Even if they succeeded in putting Robert back in his hole, Gary would consider it a hollow victory indeed if Kelsey, or Geno, or Gerbil had perished in the process.

Still, barely hours later, after a short midmorning rest, Gary could not deny his own excitement when they came around the southern edge of the ruined forest and saw the great solitary obelisk that was the Giant's Thumb protruding from the dragon-ravaged plain.

On Mickey's orders, Gary veered to the north and came in by the dry lake bed of Loch Tullamore, up to the lip of the valley before the mountain, sheltered by the few living trees east of the Crahgs.

"Now where?" Gary asked, realizing their dilemma as he began strapping on his armor once more. He saved the helmet for last, and wound up simply strapping the bulky thing to his back, realizing that he could not possibly climb with it bouncing about his head. With that thought, Gary looked up again to the towering obelisk, to the castle walls that seemed to grow right from the stone, several hundred feet above the vale.

The last time they had come to the mountain, they had gone in through a cave above the red waters of a steamy pool, hidden around a rocky outcropping not so far away. But Gary and his friends had a giant with them on that occasion, a giant who was able to carry them across the deep water to the cave entrance. Even if they could now get to that entrance, which Gary doubted, the tunnels would only take them so high. And again, it had been the work of Gary and Mickey's companions, and not of either of these two, that had allowed them to scale the rest of the way and get over the walls.

"Leave the gnome's contraption here," Mickey explained. "There's a wide and easy road around the other side of the mountain that's fit for walking."

There was indeed an easy way up, Gary knew, but he knew, too, that the road the leprechaun spoke of led right between rows of barracks, right through the heart of Robert's army, lizardlike humanoids called lava newts, as tall and strong as a man, that would swarm the intruders at first sight.

"Don't ye worry," Mickey casually remarked into Gary's doubting expression. "I'm feeling me magic today. We'll get through the stupid lizards." Mickey gave a cocky chuckle, which seemed odd to Gary, considering the leprechaun's almost pitiful use of magic thus far on the adventure.

The young man only shrugged and followed, though, when Mickey started away, for he had no better ideas and he didn't want to remain anywhere near this dangerous place a moment longer than necessary.

It took them more than an hour to make their careful way around the south of the mountain to the long sloping road up the eastern side. Many times, Gary thought he saw movement on the high walls, lava newt soldiers, probably, halfheartedly manning their positions.

To Gary's amazement, Mickey faded into invisibility. Gary realized then that this was the first time the leprechaun had done that on this adventure. The last time through the land, Mickey had faded away every time danger loomed near, but this time, even when Gary had faced the soldiers in the haunted swamp, Mickey had taken to a more ordinary form of hiding.

Now the leprechaun was gone, though, and he floated up to a comfortable perch on Gary's shoulder, seeming more like the old, at-ease Mickey, seeming confident that he could get them out of whatever trouble came their way. Gary saw a spark in the empty air and knew that the leprechaun had lit his long-stemmed pipe.

"Now ye walk right up the path, lad," Mickey explained. "Big, proud steps, like the kind that Robert'd take. With yer sword over yer shoulder."

Gary was beginning to catch on to what the leprechaun had in mind. He smiled in spite of his trepidation and reached for his helm, then changed his mind, remembering that Robert had not worn one. "Trust in the illusion," Gary whispered to himself, and he hoisted his spear in one hand, bringing it towards his shoulder.

"Not that shoulder!" Mickey snapped at him. "Ye trying to skewer me through?"

Gary quickly brought the spear around to the other side, thinking how hard it was to ignore such a blatantly illogical thing as an invisible leprechaun. Gary could feel Mickey atop his shoulder—if he stopped and thought about it—but he couldn't see the leprechaun there.

"You're making me look like the returning Robert," Gary reasoned.

"Already have," Mickey replied. "Be a good lad and run yer fingers through yer red beard."

Gary looked down, looked for the illusion, then brought his hand tentatively through the image. He could almost feel the thick and tangled hair. His cheeks itched, he realized. His cheeks itched! Gary half believed that Mickey had magically grown a beard for him.

Gary smiled again and chuckled nervously. He could hardly believe that he was about to openly walk through Robert's army, and so he tried not to think about it, just took a huge breath and strode off forcefully, up the inclining path.

"Proud and stern," Mickey told him. "Don't ye talk to any o' them, and don't ye let any o' them talk to yerself!"

Gary glanced over at the invisible sprite—and noticed a line of white smoke drift lazily into the air, coming from, seemingly, nowhere.

"The pipe, Mickey, the pipe," he whispered. "The smoke is showing."

"So it is," came the reply a moment later, but the line of white smoke continued.

"Put it out," Gary ordered.

"Ye can hardly see it," Mickey argued. "Besides, shouldn't there be some smoke beside a dragon? Go on, then."

Gary grumbled, but decided not to argue the point. He was, after all, depending on Mickey more than Mickey was depending on him.

Rows of wooden buildings lined the trail higher up and Gary, and Mickey's illusion, got the first test before they even reached the area. Two ugly lizards, humanoid lizards with red scales and reptilian eyes, rushed down to greet him, their eager tongues flicking repulsively from between yellow-stained fangs. Each had a shield strapped about its arm, a loincloth about its slender waist, and a short sword on one hip. Other than that, the lizard soldiers were naked, though their scaly skin seemed a solid armor.

They garbled something in a hissing language which Gary could not understand. He growled from deep in his throat and pushed them aside, striding by and not bothering to look back.

"Well done," came Mickey's whisper.

Gary barely heard the sprite. He expected the two lizard soldiers to rush up from behind and cut him down at any moment. *Are you ready?* he asked telepathically of the spear.

Gary felt his hands tingling with the unspoken response and knew that the weapon was more than ready, was eager, to begin the bloodletting.

Having more to lose than did the spear, Gary hoped it wouldn't come to that.

And it didn't. Lava newts approached, and fell away at sight of Gary's uncompromising scowl. The great doors on this end of the castle swung wide before Gary ever got near them, and he passed between the portals without even a look to the soldiers. The road before him was cobblestoned now, continuing on this level inside the castle's outer wall, overlooking the steep cliff, and forking to Gary's right, up an incline to another set of doors that would lead him into the inner, and upper, bailey.

"Which way?" Gary whispered to Mickey, for he still wasn't sure where they had to go, and what this item was that they had to put back.

"Get to the great hall," the leprechaun replied.

Gary thought it over for a moment, then headed to the right. Again the doors swung wide at his approach, lizard soldiers scrambling to keep out of scowling Robert's way. Inside the inner wall, Gary immediately turned right again, and headed for the oaken door of a long and low structure facing him from the nearest corner.

"Hey," Gary quietly mouthed. "What happens if Robert is already back here? And will you put out that freaking pipe?"

"Don't ye worry," said Mickey in as calm a tone as he could muster. "Lava newts can't count to two."

Gary nodded and started to say, "Good," then realized the absurdity of the leprechaun's reply.

They had no trouble entering the building, coming into a narrow but short corridor. The wall to the right was solid and bare stone, but the one to the left was thickly curtained. More guards appeared at a break to the left, but Gary waved them away forcefully and they fled from sight.

Gary turned the corner, to the left beyond the curtain, and sighed profoundly when he saw that the dragon was not at home. Still, many soldiers watched his every move intently, and the young man believed that the battle-hungry spear might soon get its fight.

"Byuchke hecce," came a telepathic call.

"What?" Gary inadvertently spoke loudly, and several lava newt heads turned on him, though whether they were suspicious or simply awaiting commands, the young man could not know. How does one discern the meaning of a lizard's expression? Gary wondered with a shrug.

"Byuchke hecce," the spear implored him more forcefully. *"Tell them, Byuchke hecce!"*

Gary had no idea what the sentient thing was talking about, but, like during the successful walk up the path, the young man felt it better to trust in his more knowledgeable companions. "Byuchke hecce," he called to the soldiers.

They regarded him with curiosity, almost disbelief.

"Say it like ye mean it," Mickey whispered.

"!" the spear agreed.

"Byuchke hecce!" Gary roared, and the lizard soldiers looked at each other and then ran from the room.

"What did I tell them?" Gary asked when he was sure that they were far out of hearing distance.

"Ye said ye were hungry," Mickey explained, and he popped back to visibility, his cherubic features turned up in an approving grin.

"Hungry for lizard meat," the spear added.

"Though how ye thought to say a thing like that, I'm not for knowing," Mickey went on uninterrupted, for he, of course, had not been a part of the telepathic communication between Gary and the spear.

Gary hoisted the spear off his shoulder, held it before Mickey and shrugged, the leprechaun nodding accordingly. Mickey led on, then, to the great hearth at the opposite end of the room. Gary shuddered at the sight of Robert's immense sword, resting in its customary place against the wall beside the hearth. At first, he thought that the sword indicated the dragon to be at home, but then he realized that if Robert had "taken wing" as everybody had said, he probably wouldn't have brought the weapon with him. Still, whether the dragon was home or not, Gary found the sight of that monstrous sword, taller than Gary and with a blade nearly six inches across at its base, completely unnerving. He had seen Robert, in human form, wielding the weapon and could not bear to imagine having that incredible sword swung his way.

The nimble leprechaun fumbled about the hearth's brickwork, easily locating the mechanism to the secret door within the fireplace. To Gary's surprise, the eager sprite then led the way in, rushing into the tunnels, and pulling Gary along en route to the dragon's treasure room. They came to many twists and turns, many forking intersections, but Mickey never slowed, as though he knew this place intimately, or, Gary suddenly came to think, as though something was leading the leprechaun on.

All in all, Mickey's behavior struck Gary as strangely out of sorts. The leprechaun verily leaped in joy as they burst through a curtained portal, coming into a chamber piled with gold and gems, armor and weapons, and other treasures too great for Gary to comprehend. He stared in blank amazement as Mickey rushed past it all, ignoring the gem and jewel baubles, some bigger than the leprechaun's chubby hand, and scrambled up the pile, kicking a shower of gold in his wake.

"Oh, I know ye're here!" Mickey chirped, and those simple words told Gary more than anything the leprechaun had said since he had brought Gary back to the land of Faerie.

Gary had suspected it all along, and now he knew for sure that Mickey had a secret agenda, that the leprechaun's claims that all this was "bigger" than Robert had another element in them, an element that Mickey was telling no one.

Gary followed Mickey's trail up the pile, trying not to be overwhelmed by the wealth splayed before him. He crested the hoard just in time to see Mickey wrapping his little arms about . . .

"Your pot of gold!" Gary cried.

"And isn't it fabulous?" the leprechaun squeaked back, and then Mickey suddenly seemed nervous to Gary, like a kid caught with his hand in the proverbial cookie jar.

"I'm not normally bringing it forth," Mickey stammered, as unsure with words as Gary had ever seen him. "I'm just thinking that it'll be a good thing to have on hand should Robert come walking in."

"I'm just thinking that the pot was here all along," Gary replied evenly. Gary thought back to his last journey through Faerie, to all the clues that might now lead him to believe that Mickey had arranged a secret deal with Robert, a deal that included the leprechaun's fabled pot of gold. Gary had seen Mickey making arrangements with a sprite on the road, soon after the leprechaun had learned that Kelsey would take him along all the way to the Giant's Thumb. And Mickey had used illusions to fool the dragon in these very caves, something that, by the reputation of dragons, should not have happened. When Gary had asked Mickey about it, the leprechaun had claimed that he only showed Robert what Robert thought to be the obvious truth, and that Robert had been too busy fighting with Kelsey to look carefully at the trick. Mickey had even gone so far as to say, "Besides, me magic was at its strongest in there."

Those words echoed in Gary Leger's mind, and now he understood them as a slip of the tongue, as a vague, probably unintentional reference to the fact that Mickey had secretly bartered his pot of gold to the dragon.

So many things came clearer and clearer to Gary Leger, and most of them did not shed a positive light on the leprechaun. Gary thought of Cedric, who had died, and of so many others who had suffered. And for what? the young man now wondered.

He looked on incredulously as Mickey lifted the pot from the floor and folded it! Then folded it again, and a third time, as though it was no more than a piece of paper! Soon, it was all but gone, and Mickey prudently tucked it into a deep pocket, then turned, beaming, at Gary.

His smile went away in the face of Gary's scowl.

"Was it?" Gary asked sternly.

"Was what?"

"Was the pot here all along?" Gary asked, speaking each word with perfect clarity.

"Why, laddie . . ."

"Was it?" Gary's yell set Mickey back on his heels.

"Not all along," Mickey replied, and Gary could see that the leprechaun was squirming.

"All along since we last left the dragon's lair?" Gary clarified and qualified, understanding Mickey's semantic games.

"Well, laddie, what are ye getting at?" the leprechaun asked innocently.

"What am I getting at?" Gary echoed softly, shaking his head and chuckling. "You said we were coming here to return something, to put the wyrm back in his hole."

"Aye," Mickey agreed, leading Gary on.

"You took the pot."

"It's me own pot."

"You gave it to Robert."

"I done what I had to do," Mickey argued, and admitted. "But I'm not to let the wyrm keep me pot. Suren I'm a leprechaun, lad, and suren I'm to die without me pot in hand!"

"That's not what I'm talking about!" Gary roared. "You said we were coming to put the wyrm back in his hole, but we never were. We were coming so that you could get back your precious pot of gold!"

"How do ye know we're not here to do both?" Mickey asked coyly, flashing his cherubic smile.

"Because you're taking the stupid pot!" Gary screamed. "And even if we put back whatever it is we came to put back, it won't work, because you're taking something else!"

"Good point," Mickey agreed casually.

Gary wanted to pull his hair out—no, he decided, he wanted to pull Mickey's hair out! He roared again at the futility of it all, at Cedric's death and at the loss of those killed on the field southwest of Dvergamal. He remembered that he had bargained to let the witch loose on the land again, had freed Ceridwen because he believed that this trip to the Giant's Thumb was of the utmost importance.

Mickey did not continue his innocent act. His scowl soon matched Gary's and he pulled a jeweled dagger out of another of the seemingly endless supply of pockets in his gray jacket and threw it at Gary's feet.

"What ..." Gary started to ask, looking down at the weapon, at first thinking that Mickey had actually thrown the dagger at him. Then the truth hit Gary, though, like the slap of a wet towel in his face. Gary knew this dagger, had seen it in this very castle, had taken it from this very castle!

"Don't ye get thinking that ye're any better!" Mickey yelled at him. "There it is, lad. There's the item that was stolen from Robert's lair. There's the missing piece that let the wyrm fly free."

Gary found his breathing hard to come by. The souls of a hundred dead fluttered about his shoulders, threatening to bend them low under their burdening weight. He, Gary Leger, had taken the dagger!

He had freed the wyrm!

"I didn't know," he breathed. "I didn't mean ..."

"Of course ye did not," Mickey agreed, his tone honestly sympathetic. "It was a mistake that not a one could blame ye for."

"But if we put the dagger back, then Robert is bound?" Gary asked as much as stated.

Mickey slowly shook his head.

"Then it's true," Gary snapped, his rolling emotions putting him back on the offensive again. "We came here for no more than your pot of gold."

"Aye," Mickey admitted. "And that's not as small a thing as ye're making it to be."

"People died," Gary snarled.

"And more will," Mickey answered grimly. "I did not

do this just for meself, lad," he went on, his tone grim and rock-steady. "I came for me pot, lied to ye all to get ye to help me, but it's for the better of us all. Yerself and Kelsey, the gnomes and the folk o' Braemar, have got a dragon to fight, and the fighting'll be easier now that I've got me pot. Ye seen it yerself, seen how little I helped ye in the swamp and on the road. And ye seen how much more I helped when we neared me pot. We walked right through Robert's army, and walk through 'em again we will, without a one of them thinking anything's outa place!"

Gary could not deny the leprechaun's reasoning, and he found that his initial anger was fast fading.

"Ye'll need me in the trials ahead," Mickey added. "And now I'm ready to be there to help ye out."

"What about the dragon?" Gary asked. "I could go back to Ynis Gwydrin and let Ceridwen out now. We could just let her and Robert go back to their own fighting."

Mickey thought it over for a minute, then shook his head once more. "Even the witch'd not stop Robert until all the eastland was in flames," he reasoned. "With Dilnamarra already under Kinnemore's evil grasp, Ceridwen'd like to see Braemar and Drochit burned. She'd like to have Robert get the pesty gnomes and the mighty Buldrefolk out of her way. No, lad, Robert's got to be fought, and got to be fought soon—sooner than the witch'd have a mind to do it."

Gary sighed and nodded and looked around. "But not here," he said. "We won't fight the dragon in the middle of his stronghold."

"Then we're to be fast flying," Mickey reasoned. "Dragons know their treasure better than a babe knows its mother, and Robert's sure to soon figure out that we're poking around his own."

Gary had no objections to Mickey's suggestion. "We

should take something to lead the wyrm on," he reasoned, looking eagerly at the glittering mound.

Mickey tapped the pocket wherein he had dropped the pot. "We already have, lad," he muttered grimly. "We already have."

Gary didn't disagree, but then a thought came to him, a perfectly conniving thought.

Before the sun had set that same day, Mickey and Gary were back in the quadricycle, zooming across the barren lands west of the Giant's Thumb. On one side of Gary rested the spear of Cedric Donigarten—on the other, Robert's huge sword.

20 ✝ Broken Trees and Burning Homes

Wearing again the mantle of a large, red-bearded man, Robert stalked into the ruined edge of Dreadwood, casually batting aside blackened, still-smoldering trees with mighty arms that suffered no pain from the heat. He grabbed one large log up in his hand and heaved it away, smiling with evil pleasure as it smashed against another standing tree, its ember-filled inner core exploding into a shower of sparks.

"Are you in here, little elf?" the dragon-turned-man bellowed, crunching through the hot area without the slightest regard for the minor fires.

No fire could ever harm Robert the Wretched.

"Do come out and play, Kelsenellenelvial Gil-Ravadry!" the dragon called. "Else I will have to burn down the rest of the forest."

There came no reply, not even the chirp of a bird in the ruined area. Robert's eyes narrowed, and he scanned the immediate region carefully, looking for some sign. He had hit the woods a third time, again with all his strength and fiery fury, and he had figured that Kelsey and his friends, including that puny impostor Gary Leger from Bretaigne, were probably already dead. Thinking about it now, though, with no sign of charred corpses anywhere about, the dragon believed that he might have erred in attacking so openly and in such a straightfor-

261

ward manner. Robert had let his fury get in the way of good sense, and now he was tired—too tired to spread dragon wings and search out the countryside, too tired to summon his killing breath anymore and lay waste to the rest of the forest.

He wasn't worried, though. Even in this human form, Robert knew that he was more than a match for the elf and his friends, was confident that they had nothing which could truly harm one as powerful as he.

The dragon continued his search for more than an hour, finally stumbling upon the tracks of a horse, and beside them the light bootprints of an elf, running northwest, back out of the woods the same way Kelsey and his friends had entered.

"So a few escaped," the dragon mused, thinking that they would not escape for long. Robert followed the trail right towards the edge of Dreadwood, saw that it continued on in the same direction, cutting a line across the rolling fields to the southern tip of Dvergamal. The dragon nodded; he had turned Kelsenellenelvial and his friends around, at least, and it seemed as though their numbers had been diminished.

Robert briefly considered a quick pursuit, but the sun hung low in the sky before him, and he was tired. He might spend the entire night searching, without luck, and then the morning would leave him more weary.

"Running home," the dragon said, and his wicked smile returned tenfold, for Robert knew where "home" might be.

"How long can you keep that up, elf?" Geno asked, and the dwarf seemed more amused than concerned, watching Kelsey half running, half flying along the side of the fast-trotting pony. Behind the dwarf, Gerbil, bouncing wildly and wishing for his quadricycle, moaned in sympathy.

"We will continue long past the sunset," the elf informed Geno. "And I will run as long as I must."

"Do you believe that the dragon will be following us?" Gerbil asked nervously, glancing back to the southeast. "They are reportedly stubborn, after all, but this one seems to have his nose pointed in many different directions all at once, if you know what I mean."

"Robert will be out in the morn, if not before," Kelsey replied. "We can only hope that he finds our trail and not that of our companions."

"Now there's something to hope for," Geno put in sarcastically, and just for the fun of it, the dwarf let the pony's bridle out a bit more, picked up the pace so that Kelsey, holding a rope attached to the mount's neck, was more flying than running.

Their camp was restless and nervous that night, with Kelsey pacing all the while, and Gerbil too nervous to even close his eyes. Geno, though, was soon snoring loudly, something that disturbed both the elf and the gnome more than a little. Having no luck either waking the dwarf or turning Geno's body over, Kelsey wound up splitting a small stick and pinching it over the dwarf's nose.

The three were moving again before any hint of dawn found the eastern horizon, with Kelsey constantly glancing back over his shoulder, as though he expected the dragon to swoop upon them at any time. This, of course, unnerved poor Gerbil more than a little, and the gnome finally just wrapped his arms as tightly as possible around the dwarf's waist and buried his face in Geno's back.

Dawn did little to brighten anyone's mood, for the three felt vulnerable indeed trotting across rolling and, for the most part, open hills under the light of day.

"Is that the witch's crow?" Geno asked a short while later. Kelsey turned his eyes back to the trail ahead to see the large black bird standing calmly on the grass, and to see the dwarf lifting a hammer for a throw, Geno's icy-blue eyes sparkling eagerly.

"Hold," Kelsey bade him, drawing a disappointed, even angry, look. "We do not know what news the bird brings."

"What lies it brings, you mean," Geno corrected, but he did bring his hammer back down, slowing the pony so that they might stop and speak with the bird.

"Dragon, dragon," the crow cackled. "Get away!"

"We did," Geno answered dryly.

"It could be that the bird means that the dragon is coming and that we should NOW get away," Gerbil intervened.

"Dragon, dragon, get away!" the crow cried and it flew off, cutting a fast track for a small but thick copse of trees not too far to the south.

"I don't see any dragon," Geno huffed, looking back behind them.

"By the time you saw Robert, Robert would see you," Kelsey warned. "And then it would be too late."

"Dragons are bigger than dwarfs," Geno argued.

"But they see better than eagles," Kelsey shot back. He was already heading for the south, tugging the rope so that the pony turned to follow.

From the shadows of the trees, they watched Robert's passage. The dragon came by incredibly low, barely twenty feet off the ground, his nostrils snuffling and his eyes as often turned down as ahead. The beating of his wings crackled and rolled like thunder, and the wind of his wake shivered the trees of the copse, though they were fully fifty yards away.

"He's hunting," Geno remarked.

"Us," Gerbil added, and Kelsey nodded grimly. Both the dwarf and the gnome took some consolation in the fact that Robert had zipped by, and was already long out of sight, but Kelsey's expression remained grave.

Geno looked around to the boughs of the trees. "I hope that crow is still about," the dwarf admitted. "When that dragon does not find us on the road ahead, he'll be sure to turn around."

Kelsey shook his head and began, to Geno and Gerbil's dismay, to lead the pony back out of the trees. "Robert will not be back," the elf assured them. "Not for some time."

Kelsey winced at his own words, though the claim seemed to brighten the moods of his two companions. They were safe enough for the time being, Kelsey sincerely believed, but he also believed that he knew the price of that security.

Like Kelsey, Robert was heading for Braemar.

The dragon sensed that the trail had gone cold, understood that the elf and his friends had probably turned aside and let him pass. He thought to turn about and hunt the group down, but other instincts argued against that move. Robert's hunger was up; his course had him speeding straight for Braemar.

He beat his wings more fiercely, climbed into the air, then stooped low again, gaining momentum, gaining speed. He forgot his weariness in those minutes, his dragon-hunger urging him on, urging him to begin the destruction.

Robert whipped past the first low foothills of Dvergamal, cut in behind the closest mountain peaks so that the helpless folk of the village would have less warning. The sky about the mountains was heavy with dark clouds, but as far as the dragon could tell, it had not yet rained.

The thatched roofs and wooden planks of the houses would still be dry.

Soon Robert saw the chimney smoke rising to meet the overcast, drifting lazily into the air above Braemar, and an anxious growl escaped the dragon's maw as he thought of how much thicker that smoke would soon become.

The lone bell in Braemar's small chapel began to ring; Robert's keen ears caught the cries of the distant villagers, rousing the town, calling out the approach of the dreaded wyrm.

The dragon cut a sharp turn around a jutting wall of stone, leveled out with the town in sight, and began his swooping descent.

Arrows zipped out at him, bouncing harmlessly from his armored body. Robert's snarl came again, for these were simple farm folk and miners, and not the clever gnomes of Gondabuggan. No metallic shields would come up to stop the dragon this time; no catapults would send stinging flak into the air to hinder Robert's passage.

Barely thirty feet up, he swooped over the edge of the town, loosing his fiery breath in a line that sent one, and then another, and then another, thatched roof up in flames. The dragon began his turn before he even passed beyond the cluster of houses, his great tail snapping about to clip the second floor of the spoke-lock, collapsing one corner of the building.

Below him, the people were in a frenzy, rushing about with bows and spears, others running with buckets of water to fight the fires.

"Useless!" the proud dragon bellowed as the missiles continued to bounce away. Useless, too, were those battling the fires, their buckets a pitiful sight against the flames leaping high, so high, into the air. Already one of the houses was gutted, the fires dying low simply because their incredible intensity had consumed the thatch and wood fuel.

It took the huge wyrm a long while to bank enough to

make a second pass, and this time, Braemar's defense proved more organized. Robert came in over a different section of town, from the west, finding no resistance as his breath consumed yet another farmhouse. As Robert passed the central area, his tail taking another swipe at the two-story structure, he met a wall of arrows and spears, fired nearly point-blank. Again, the dragon's sturdy armor deflected the brunt, but one missile nicked Robert's eye.

His roar split stones a mile away, deafened those near him, as he banked suddenly up into the air, then dropped to his haunches upon the ground.

A second volley shot out at him from behind a long and low building, the Snoozing Sprite tavern. More than one arrow knifed into the dragon's mouth, and stuck there painfully, until Robert's breath came forth, disintegrating the missiles and lighting the corner of the building. Despite the unexpected pain, the evil dragon hissed with pleasure when he heard the screams of several archers, when one man, engulfed in flames, came rolling out from behind the Snoozing Sprite.

Robert's continuing hiss was cut short, though, as a score of hardy villagers, accompanied by Kervin and his rugged dwarfs, charged out from another hiding spot, axes, hammers, swords and spears, even pitchforks and grass scythes, going to vicious work on the sitting dragon.

Robert snapped his tail about, launching a handful of enemies away. A lasso hooked about his foreclaw, and when the dragon instinctively jerked against it, he found that the thick rope was secured to a huge oak tree.

A dwarfish hammer smashed the dragon's ankle. Robert lifted his foot and squashed the troublesome dwarf into the dirt.

But the sheer fury of the villagers' response had surprised the wyrm. While Robert crushed the poor dwarf, a dozen other weapons smashed hard into his armor plating.

One great axe cut a slice through the lower portion of the dragon's leathery wing. Robert buffeted with the wing, sending the axe-man flying away.

The dragon's breath melted another man to his bones; Robert's tail whipped again, and three dwarfs flew through the air.

From the other end of the burning tavern came yet another volley of arrows, the whole group concentrating on the area of the dragon's face. Robert's rage multiplied; his thrashing sent more men and dwarfs spinning away. And then he set his wings to beating, leaped off the ground, forgetting about his hooked foreclaw.

The rope jerked him around, and he stumbled, crashing headlong into a stone house, smashing the place to tiny bits of rubble. Up leaped the outraged dragon, issuing another stone-splitting roar. He spun and tugged, and the great oak tore from the ground. Stubborn villagers came at him once more. Another volley of arrows sent stinging darts into his reptilian eyes.

Robert leaped into the air, his wings pounding furiously.

The ground ripped wide open as the tree was pulled along, its roots tearing free until Robert, tiring, turned his maw about and breathed again, disintegrating the thick rope.

A group of men fled screaming, and the shadow of the dragon covered them, Robert swooping low and snapping up more than one of them in his great maw.

All of Braemar would have been leveled and burned, every person in the town would surely have perished, except that the wyrm was tired. The defense had been stronger than Robert had anticipated, and since his last true rest, he had burned half a forest and had flown a hundred miles.

He gave another roar, its tone triumphant, and soared

away to find a mountain perch, confident that when he had rested, he would return and finish the town.

Good fortune was on the side of the village that day, for soon after the dragon attack, the low clouds opened up and sent heavy rains to quench the dragon fires, and to soak the remaining thatch and wood.

"Rain is no friend to a dragon," one villager remarked hopefully, but the encouraging words rang shallow in light of the destruction and the dead.

From the empty window of another building, the glass blown out by the sheer thunderous force of the dragon's passage, Badenoch of Braemar and Baron Pwyll looked on helplessly.

21 † Sobering Return

"The axle's bent," Gary explained, crawling out from underneath the quadricycle and sitting up on the dry ground south of the Ruined Forest. He looked back to the east, to the thick tree root sticking like a speed bump from the ground, the jolt that had caused the problem.

Mickey nodded and said, "Hmmm," though the leprechaun had no idea what Gary was talking about. "Well, can ye fix it, then?" he asked.

Gary sighed deeply and looked to the angled front wheel, and his expression was not hopeful.

"Ye got to fix it, lad," Mickey implored. "Or to be sure that Robert's going to find us sitting here in the open."

Gary reached over to take the spear of Cedric Donigarten, then slid back under the front end of the gnomish contraption and angled the spearshaft above the bent axle. He found rocks and placed them around the front wheels to keep the axle from turning as he applied pressure, then slid a large, flat rock under the back end of the spear to make sure that it didn't simply slide downward when he pulled the other end up.

"Young sprout," came a not-too-happy call in his head.

Gary ignored the spear, kept at his work.

"Young sprout." This time the call was accompanied by a tingling feeling in the metallic shaft, a clear warning that the spear might soon blast Gary's hands away.

We have to fix this, Gary telepathically replied.

"I am a weapon forged to battle dragons and fell un-lawful kings," the spear answered. *"I am the tool of the warrior, not the tradesman. I am the instrument with which . . ."*

All things in place, Gary put the top end of the spear over his shoulder and heaved upward with all his strength, pressing the spear between the bent axle and the front bumper of the gnomish vehicle. He felt the too-proud spear's anger, felt an energy charge beginning to build within the sentient weapon's shaft. But Gary growled in anger and pushed harder, pushed until a blue flash erupted from the spear.

And then he was sitting on the ground again, his hair dancing on its ends.

"Are ye all right?"

Gary nodded quickly to Mickey, then rolled to his hands and knees to inspect the axle. It still wasn't perfectly straight, but Gary's efforts had bent it back enough so that he believed the thing would drive.

"I am not pleased, young sprout."

"Oh, shut up," Gary said aloud, and he grabbed up the spear. Again he felt the charge building, and he instinctively started to drop the weapon to the ground. He stopped, though, with a determined growl. "You do it, and I'll leave you here on the plain," he promised. "Let the dragon find you and put you in his lair as a trophy, and see how much fighting you'll find there!"

The spear did not respond, but the tingling in its metallic shaft ceased.

Their progress was limited over the next few hours. The quadricycle bumped and bounced, and Gary kept it to as easy and level a course as he could find. The contraption wasn't built to handle this much weight, he realized, and with the axle already weakened, Gary feared that any hole or bump could buckle it once again.

They made it to Dreadwood, though, as twilight descended over the land, and even though the forest had seemed an evil place to Gary, he was horrified to view it now. Tangled boughs had been replaced by charred, skeletal limbs, and all the northern section of the forest glowed with residual heat. Orange embers appeared as mischievous eyes in logs lying prone, as though a hundred little goblins had climbed inside the fallen wood, daring Gary and Mickey to walk past.

"Now what?" Gary asked the leprechaun.

"Now we're going through," Mickey replied sternly, as though the answer should have been obvious.

Gary understood and accepted his companion's sudden anger. In looking at the devastation, Mickey could not help but worry about their friends, worry that Kelsey and Geno and Gerbil had not escaped the dragon fires. Blowing a deep breath, Gary set the quadricycle into motion, veering this way and that along the path to avoid fallen branches. Several time he had to get out of the seat altogether, to remove debris, and always, those orange ember eyes watched him, their glow intensifying as the night deepened.

"We'll camp on the other side of the forest," Gary decided after two hours of inching along. His hands were blackened from soot, his whole body was lathered in sweat under the armor from the residual heat, and he felt as though his lungs would simply explode.

"No, lad," Mickey replied grimly, "we'll keep going right through the night."

Gary looked at the sprite curiously. It seemed as if Mickey's euphoria at finding his pot had fully worn away, to be replaced by a level of despair that surprised Gary.

"I've a feeling that there's worse trouble brewing," Mickey explained. "We've a hundred miles to go to get to Braemar, and I'm wanting to be there before tomorrow turns to the next day."

Gary nearly laughed aloud. "I can't even see the path ahead," he complained.

Mickey spoke a quick rhyme and snapped his fingers, and a ball of light appeared, hovering a few feet in front of the quadricycle. "It'll stay out in front of us," the leprechaun explained.

"I'm getting tired, Mickey," Gary said bluntly. "I'm not a pack horse, and we've gone a long way already."

"No, ye're not getting tired," the leprechaun replied.

Gary scoffed at him.

"Ye're not getting tired," Mickey said again, his tone compelling. "Slip deeper into the seat, lad. Let yer body become a part of the gnomish contraption."

Gary eyed the leprechaun closely, but somehow, Mickey's words seemed to make sense to him. Without even thinking of the movement, he did indeed slip deeper into his seat.

"There's a good lad," Mickey said, and now his voice seemed incredibly soothing to Gary. "Ye can even close yer eyes." Mickey shifted so that he was sitting right on Gary's lap, and eased Gary's hands away from the quadricycle's steering bar.

"There's a good lad," Mickey said again, nodding approvingly at Gary's deep and steady breathing. "Just keep yer legs turning, turning easy."

Gary was soon fast asleep, caught in the throes of the leprechaun's hypnotic magic. His legs continued to pedal, though, and would throughout the night, as Mickey subconsciously compelled him, every so often whispering magical, coaxing words into his ear.

Many times that night, Mickey looked back anxiously to Gary. There was a very real danger in doing this to the

young man, Mickey knew, a danger that the exertion
would explode Gary's heart, or tire him to the point where
he would never recover. Mickey had to take the chance,
though, for he, unlike Gary, had heard the dragon's call
from the north, from above the Crahgs. Robert had sensed
his missing sword, Mickey believed, and when the wyrm
came back out of Giant's Thumb, probably the very next
morning, his mood would not be bright.

"Smooth and easy," the leprechaun gently prodded.
"Smooth and easy." Mickey looked to the slightly flip-
flopping wheel of the quadricycle and could only hope that
the thing wouldn't fall apart before they got to Braemar.

Wearing grim faces, Kelsey, walking, and Geno and
Gerbil atop the pony, made their slow way around the last
barrier of stone before the sheltered vale of Braemar on
the morning of the next day. They saw the lines of black
smoke rising out of the valley, and could guess easily
enough where Robert had flown off to. Half expecting to
find all of Braemar razed, Kelsey paused a long while before mustering the courage to step around the bend and get
his first view of the village.

Many of the structures remained intact, but many others
had been destroyed. Stone skeletons of farmhouses, their
ends pyramiding to a point, but not a piece of thatch left
atop them, dotted the landscape. The spoke-lock was a
one-story building now, with the top level flattened to kindling, cracked boards protruding from the edges of the
still-standing first level, and the roads and even a huge tree
had been ripped and torn by the angry dragon.

The normally stoic Geno let out an unexpected wail,
spotting two cairns piled high on hills beside the town.

"Are those the normal burial mounds of your people?"
Kelsey asked reverently, recognizing the source of his

companion's distress. "Are dwarfs buried under those piled stones?"

"Look closer, elf," Geno replied gruffly.

"The dwarfs are not buried *beneath* the stones," Gerbil, who knew the ways of the Buldrefolk better than the elf, explained, emphasizing the word "beneath."

"Look closer," Geno said again.

Kelsey stared at the distant mounds and discovered, to his amazement, that bodies of dead dwarfs had been stacked together with the stones, holding up their places in the piles as solidly as the boulders.

"Two mounds," Gerbil added, his tone unintentionally impassive. "Which means, by all dwarfish records, that at least six dwarfs were killed."

Geno grunted.

"The Buldrefolk will, of course, put no more than five of their fallen kin a single cairn," the gnome went on, speaking like a professor in some classroom far removed from so brutal a scene as Braemar after the dragon. "There is a belief among the dwarfs that . . ."

Kelsey held up his hand to gently stop the gnome. He knew that Gerbil wasn't intentionally being callous, but Geno, sitting dangerously close to the rambling gnome, seemed on the verge of an explosion, gripping the pony's bridle so tightly that Kelsey wondered if the leather tong would simply fall in half, squeezed apart by the dwarf's iron grasp. If Gerbil kept on going, Kelsey realized, the gnome might find that a dwarfish boot was nearly as strong a delivery system as his Mountain Messenger.

"Oh," Gerbil said simply, and apologetically, as he regarded the dwarf seated right before him, seeming to realize only then that his dissertation on dwarfish burial methods might have been somewhat out of place.

"Let's get down to the town," Geno offered, brushing off his moment of weakness. "It looks like it could have been worse. I see a few of the buildings still standing, and the Snoozing Sprite's up, if a bit blackened."

Kelsey nodded, and he held more than a little admiration for Geno at that moment. He had seen the dwarf's pain—perhaps the first time the elf had witnessed any emotion other than anger from one of the Buldrefolk—and had seen the dwarf sublimate that pain because Geno knew that they had no time for grief, not with Gary and Mickey wandering who-knew-where and with Robert still flying about, probably even then preparing to hit the village once again.

Braemar was bustling that morning, people rushing about, bringing supplies to various shelters, changing dressings on the nasty wounds, mostly burns, of the injured, and formulating defense plans should the dragon return. Braemar proper, like the actual town area of most of the outlying villages, was a small place, a cluster of just a few structures, with most of the people associated with the town living as far as several miles away. It seemed as if the majority of those farmers and miners had come in now, though, to help with the effort. These were admirable people, even to one of the Tylwyth Teg, who generally looked down their noses at humans.

Many sentries had been set, high on the slopes overlooking the town, and Kelsey's party was spotted and reported long before the three companions got anywhere near the village. No one rode out to meet them or to hinder them, though (Kelsey figured that no one would have the time), and few gave them more than a passing glance as they plodded along the street, muddy from the soaking rain and the firefighting efforts, into Braemar's central square.

Batteries of archers roamed the streets, pointing out angles of possible dragon descent and seeking out the best locations from which to strike back in the event of the wyrm's return.

One woman, three children in tow, cried out for her husband, trying futilely to get past the men blocking her entrance to her still-smoldering home. All three of the companions, even Geno, sent their hearts out to the apparent widow, and all three were truly relieved to see, unexpectedly, the supposedly missing man running down the street from the other direction, crying out for his beloved wife and children.

They were just turning their attention back to the road ahead when a familiar, plump face appeared from around a corner. Soot-covered, and lathered in sweat, Baron Pwyll seemed far less regal, seemed sobered, actually, as he walked solemnly out to greet his returning friends.

"You did not make the Giant's Thumb," the Baron reasoned.

"Have Mickey and Gary Leger returned?" Kelsey asked.

Baron Pwyll shook his head.

"Then they are still on their way," Kelsey said hopefully.

"They have the quadricycle," Gerbil interjected, smiling as widely as he could manage, given the grim scene all about him. "They have probably been there and are near to back again!"

Pwyll blew a deep breath, tried to turn up the edges of his mouth, but the smile would not come. "Perhaps that is why the dragon has not returned," he reasoned. "Robert flew in hard and fast, and was gone just as quickly. We spent a long night, expecting the darkness to be shattered by flaming dragon breath. But he did not come back."

"It is a hopeful sign," Kelsey agreed.

"How many dwarfs?" Geno said abruptly, and after a moment to digest the blunt question, Pwyll understood that

Geno wanted to know how many of his people had perished.

. "Seven," he answered.

"Kervin?"

Pwyll turned about and motioned to the Snoozing Sprite.

"Best place to be after a dragon attack," Geno agreed, and he handed the bridle to Gerbil behind him and slid down off the pony, cutting a beeline for the still-standing tavern.

"Even if the dragon does not return, there is much to do," Pwyll prompted the others, and Gerbil, too, slid down from the mount.

Kelsey removed his belongings from the pony's back and handed the reins over to Pwyll, bidding the Baron to find out where the pony would be of the most help to the people of Braemar. The simple gesture overwhelmed the Baron, for he knew how protective the Tylwyth Teg normally were of their precious steeds.

"Together we will not lose," Pwyll said firmly, right before he led the pony away.

Kelsey nodded, his fair features stern and determined. He was glad to see the normally quivering Pwyll apparently rising to the occasion, but his hopes were tempered by the grim reality. Robert was flying free, and even if Mickey and Gary somehow managed to replace the dagger and put the wyrm back in his hole (which Kelsey had never actually believed to be the fact of the matter), and escape with their lives, there was still the matter of King Kinnemore's gathered army, a new puppet ruler coming to power in Dilnamarra, so near Kelsey's forest home, and a witch coming out of her banishment in three short months.

At that moment, the future of Faerie seemed as bleak to Kelsey as the blackened kindling that had once been Braemar's spoke-lock.

A cry from down the lane turned the elf about, to see the frantic woman and her children locked in a communal hug with the man they had thought dead.

"Then again," Kelsey said aloud, his suddenly hopeful tone drawing a curious glance from Gerbil, "one never knows what might happen."

The quadricycle limped into Braemar soon after sunset that same day. Mickey steered it into the village square just outside the ruined spoke-lock, where it bogged down in the mud. A crowd of onlookers gathered about, keeping a respectful distance, but pointing Mickey's way and talking anxiously among themselves. Mickey had been farsighted enough to enact an illusion before he and Gary ever got close to the village, one that made him appear as a normal human boy and not a leprechaun. Greedy human hands seeking the fabled pot of gold would surely have engulfed him, even after the dragon attack, if the leprechaun had gone in undisguised.

"Easy now, laddie," the leprechaun whispered to Gary, who was sitting back with his eyes closed, his body, except for his pumping legs, limp with exhaustion. The semiconscious man kept on pedaling, apparently oblivious to the leprechaun's calls, or to the fact that the quadricycle's back wheels were spinning uselessly in the mud.

"Stop and rest," Mickey quietly implored Gary. Then came a great bump as the contraption's front axle snapped in half, dropping the whole front end of the thing into the mud.

"Oh," Mickey muttered, and he was certainly glad that the contraption had waited until now to fall apart.

Gary remained oblivious to it all, his legs turning the pedals, the rest of his body thoroughly drained to support the hypnotic effort, and his mind too shut down to even dream. He lay in blackness, unaware of anything at all, even the fact that he could very well, and very soon, work himself to death.

"Oh, my dear," came a wail, and Gerbil Hamsmacker bolted out of the crowd and rushed to his ruined contraption. "Oh, what have you done?" the gnome asked accusingly. He looked at Mickey curiously for a moment, at first not recognizing the sprite-turned-boy. "Oh, what have you done?" he said at length, finally figuring out the deception.

"I put three hundred miles on the damned thing in three days," Mickey replied. "Ye built it good, gnome, good enough to get ye on any plaque, by me own opinion."

The high praise calmed Gerbil down considerably. He fell flat to the mud before the contraption, trying to assess the damage, then nearly got run over as the continually turning back wheels caught some solid ground under the muddy trenches and lurched the contraption forward.

"Do make him stop that," Gerbil calmly said to Mickey, and once more, the leprechaun whispered into Gary's ear for the man to stop pedaling.

And once more, Mickey was ignored.

"What is wrong with him?" Kelsey asked curtly, coming over with Geno to join his companions. Both elf and dwarf crinkled their expressions when they regarded Mickey, but understood the matter soon enough. "And where have you been?" Kelsey went on.

"Hello to yerself, too," Mickey replied dryly.

Kelsey nodded and dipped a quick bow, as much of an apology as he would ever give. "You have much to tell us, I would assume," he remarked.

"Aye," said Mickey. "But first ye two help me to get Gary Leger out o' the seat, afore the lad pedals himself to death."

Geno offered a callous remark that Gary seemed near that point already. The dwarf stepped over, grabbed Gary's metal shoulderplate in one hand, and heaved the man from his seat, allowing him to fall unceremoniously into the mud. Mickey held his breath, and was relieved that Geno never looked into the low seat, never seemed to notice the stolen sword.

Gary lay facedown—it seemed as though he could not even breathe—but made no attempts to turn about. And still, his legs kept pumping.

Kelsey, Geno, and Gerbil, and many of those gathered about, looked to Mickey suspiciously, awaiting an explanation.

"Had to get to the dragon's lair," Mickey explained with a dismissive shrug. "And back fast. I'll put a spell o' resting on the laddie and he'll be all right after the night."

"You have been to the lair, then?" Kelsey asked anxiously, hoping that this ordeal with Robert was at its end. "And you replaced the stolen dagger?"

"Aye," Mickey replied. "Aye, to both." It wasn't quite true; once the pot of gold had been recovered, Mickey had forgotten all about the dagger, and had it still, in a deep pocket of his gray jacket.

"Then Robert is banished once more," Kelsey reasoned, "and the folk of Braemar can begin to plan for troubles from another direction."

"That'd be dangerous thinking," Mickey put in. All three of the leprechaun's companions eyed him curiously. "I seen the dragon, fast flying to the east," Mickey went on. "Whether he's to stay put in his hole or not, I cannot be saying. But I wouldn't take it as fact, nor should ye all, until we're knowing for sure."

"You said that the replaced dagger would ..." Kelsey began.

"I said an obscure rule in an old book," Mickey pointedly argued, for of course, the leprechaun knew that the wyrm had not been put back in his hole, knew all along that replacing the dagger would have no effect at all on Robert.

Only then did Kelsey, leaning forward on the gnomish contraption as though he needed the support, notice Robert's huge sword, lying in the seat where Gary had been sitting. Mickey watched the elf's face contort weirdly, knew that Kelsey was now, as Gary had done in the dragon's lair, putting the pieces together and figuring out the entire deception. Even if the dagger had been put back, the presence of the sword, a weapon that Kelsey knew all too well, would have defeated the whole purpose for the trip to Robert's lair.

To the leprechaun's relief, Kelsey did not mention the logical problem then and there, just offered a knowing smirk Mickey's way. "We will get him into a warm cot," Kelsey said, looking to Gary. "Be ready for a long night," he said to Mickey. "There is much to be done before the dawn."

"And much to be done after the dawn," Mickey added under his breath. "Unless I'm missing me guess."

22 ✝ Bait

The rains came heavy the next day, a soaking downpour under thick black clouds that stretched from horizon to horizon. Never before had the people of Braemar so welcomed such gloom.

"The wyrm'll not come forth in this," Mickey remarked to his four companions when the group gathered in the remaining, unburned area of the Snoozing Sprite for breakfast.

"But how long will the rains last?" Kelsey was quick to put in, and to Gary, it seemed as if the elf was on the verge of a tirade. Every time Kelsey had looked upon Mickey the previous night, and this morn, his eyes had been filled with hatred, and every word he spoke in response to the leprechaun was edged with venom.

Kelsey's obvious rage seemed to roll off Mickey's rounded shoulders. The leprechaun had his precious pot of gold back; nothing in all the world bothered Mickey anymore.

"The defense will be stronger the next time Robert arrives," Kelsey promised the others, looking individually to each of them, with the notable exception of Mickey. "Gerbil will aid in the construction of a catapult this day, and with Geno . . ."

"Save your breath, elf," the dwarf interrupted. "Me and

my kin are out of Braemar this day. With the dragon still about, we've got our own homes to worry about."

Kelsey started to reply, but stopped short and gave a resigned nod. He couldn't rightly judge the dwarf's decision, for the Firth of Buldre, the dwarfish homeland, was not so far from Braemar, certainly less distance than a flying dragon could cover in just a few hours.

"That might be a good place for all of us to make our stand," Gary interjected, remembering the dwarfish place, remembering the towering waterfalls and the continuous spray, and the thick-walled rocky caves that Geno and his kin called home.

All eyes turned to the young man—three of Gary's companions seemed intrigued.

The exception, Geno, was quick to respond. "You're not bringing a bunch of human farmers to the Firth," he snorted.

"You'd let them die?" Gary answered sharply.

"Yes." The answer was plain and comfortably spoken, and Gary eased back in his chair, his pending arguments deflated by Geno's callousness. The dwarf only gave the man a gap-toothed grin, further evidence that he was perfectly content.

"I think that the lad's on to something," Mickey said.

"No," Geno replied evenly, his clear blue eyes sparkling and his grin replaced by a determined scowl.

"Not to the Firth," Mickey went on. "Ye couldn't rightly be bringing human folk in such numbers to that place." Mickey was talking more to Gary than to Geno now, filling in the details that Geno hadn't bothered to add. "Never again would the dwarfs find peace, and if human greed is more than legend . . ."

"And it is," Geno added, and even Gerbil was nodding.

". . . then ye'd be sure to be starting a war, if everything else sorted out," Mickey explained. He looked to Geno hopefully, his dimples evident and all his face turned up in a hopeful grin. "But there be other waterfalls and other deep caves in wide Dvergamal where the folk o' Braemar might hide."

"And what of the folk of Drochit?" the dwarf asked, hints of sarcasm growing with every passing word. "And the hamlet of Lisdoonvarna, to the north and west? And Dilnamarra? Are you thinking to put the whole of Faerie's humans in mountain holes, leprechaun?"

"I'm thinking to steal us some time," Mickey replied curtly. "For, as Kelsey said, the rains won't be lasting too long."

Baron Pwyll came in then, looking thoroughly exhausted and perfectly hopeless. He grabbed a stool and brought it near the companions' table, then paused, as if awaiting permission to sit down. Kelsey shifted his own seat and motioned for the Baron to join them.

Pwyll's account of the progress in the town was bleak indeed, and the Baron informed them that Robert had been seen again, flying from the east to a roost in the mountains north of Braemar. "As soon as the rains end," the Baron reasoned grimly, meaning that there was no doubt but that the angry dragon would return.

Geno sent a stream of thick spittle splattering to the floor. "Round them up, then," he growled, at Mickey and at Kelsey. "I'll find you a hole—little good it will do you when Robert comes a-calling!"

The dwarf's last grim statement was true enough, they all knew, but the simple fact that Geno had made the concession at all brought smiles to the faces of both the elf and the leprechaun. Gary, too, gained some hope, and some faith in his stocky companion. For all the dwarf's gruffness, Gary liked Geno, and the dwarf's refusal to open his home to people in such dire need had disheartened the young man profoundly.

Kelsey quickly explained their plan to Baron Pwyll.

"We will be ready to leave before nightfall," the Baron promised hopefully, and he rushed out of the tavern soon after, to speak with Badenoch and make the necessary arrangements.

"It's a short-term fix," Mickey offered after a short period of silence. "And not to last the length o' time we're needing."

"I should have let Ceridwen out," Gary said.

"Ceridwen wouldn't be helping us any," Mickey answered.

They all sat quietly for a few minutes, pondering their predicament. Again, Mickey was the first to speak. "Ye'll not be taking the sword along for the walk," he said to Gary. "Suren it's a torch on a dark night to Robert's eyes, and if ye bringed it in the caves, the dragon'd find the folk soon enough."

Gary narrowed his eyes and ran his hand through his matted, straight black hair, digesting the information. "How is it a torch on a dark night?" he asked.

"I told ye before," Mickey replied. "Dragons know their treasures, and I'd put that sword's value above any other treasures that Robert holds—to Robert, anyway. He can smell the damned thing a hundred miles away, I tell ye."

"Then why did you bring it?" Geno growled at the leprechaun.

In response, Mickey looked to Gary, laying the blame where it surely belonged.

"I knew that we'd have to fight the dragon, sooner or later," Gary replied with some confidence, for he was beginning to formulate a crazy and desperate plan. "I figured that the sword would be the bait we needed to get Robert on our own terms.

"Are you sure that Robert will come for this?" he asked Mickey.

"Like a babe to its mother," the leprechaun replied.

"We have to count on that," Gary said evenly.

"I can use me magic to set the sword a-singing," Mickey said, but it was obvious that the leprechaun wasn't thrilled with his own idea. And who could blame him? Not many would willingly call an outraged wyrm, especially one as powerful and wicked as Robert.

Gary didn't quite understand what the leprechaun was talking about, but he figured that Mickey meant that he could somehow enhance the sword's signals to its hunting master. He had to let it go at that, at least for the time being, for the plan was flooding his thoughts then, and he had to speak it out loud so that he and his friends might help him sort through it.

Geno scoffed and Kelsey shook his head, his lips tight with obvious doubts. Mickey listened impassively, seeming more polite than interested, and only Gerbil, the gnome inventor who understood the possibilities of precise measurements, leaned forward in his chair, certainly intrigued.

Gary fought off all interruption attempts by Kelsey, and especially the doubting dwarf, attempts that came less and less as he stubbornly went through the mechanics of his plan.

"Oh, begorra," the leprechaun sighed when Gary had at last finished speaking. Mickey looked around to the others, Gerbil smiling widely, Geno eyeing Gary doubtfully, and Kelsey sitting back in his chair, his slender arms crossed over his chest and his magnificent golden orbs staring blankly off into space.

Apparently sensing the leprechaun's gaze, the elf turned to eye Mickey directly and offered a shrug.

"Might be that we've got nothing better," Mickey admitted, turning to Gary.

Not so long afterwards, Kelsey and Gerbil, atop the pony, charged out of Braemar, running fast to the north. Normally it would take four days of hard riding to make the trip from Braemar to Gondabuggan, but Kelsey had promised his friends that he would make it within two, despite the deepening mud.

Mickey, Gary, Geno, and Pwyll watched him go, the fat Baron shaking his head doubtfully, not fully understanding what the unpredictable and dangerous friends were up to. To Pwyll's thinking, splitting the forces in such dark times was not a wise move.

"And now where are you three off to?" he demanded, for it was obvious that the remaining companions were packed for the road.

"Kelsey said two days," Gary said to Mickey, both of them ignoring the Baron. "So in two days, you'll use your magic to start the sword singing."

"It'll hum a merry tune," Mickey assured him.

"I had thought that you would be helping me to make the move," Pwyll firmly interrupted. "The people of Braemar . . ."

"The folk'll get out on their own, don't ye doubt," Mickey interrupted, his tone casual. "And Geno's kin'll point them right." The leprechaun paused then, and scratched at his brown-and-gray beard, eyeing Pwyll all the while.

"What?" the anxious Baron demanded.

"Ye know, lad," Mickey said coyly to Gary. "I'm thinking that yer plan's to work—of course, it has to work, or nothing else is worth talking about. But I'm thinking beyond that plan o' yers, lad, thinking to what gains we might be making for the trouble that's sure to come even if old Robert is dead and gone."

The leprechaun's mischievous gaze then descended over Pwyll, with Gary and Geno gradually understanding and following the lead.

"What?" the Baron demanded again, looking from one hungry gaze to the other and wondering if he should, perhaps, turn tail and run off to find Badenoch.

"How are ye at mountain hiking?" Mickey asked.

It rained for the remainder of that day, and all night as well. The soggy companions, trekking gingerly but determinedly along slippery mountain trails, found the sky brightening the next morn, a sign that brought mixed emotions.

"Suren the wyrm's rested by now," Mickey reasoned, looking back ominously along the trails towards distant Braemar. Then the leprechaun looked up to the gray sky, the overcast fast thinning. "We've another few hours of rain, and then Robert'll be hitting the town all in a fury."

Baron Pwyll groaned, a common sound to the companions. Pwyll had argued to his last breath with Badenoch that he should remain with the townspeople, and not go running off on some wild adventure into the mountains. But Mickey and Gary had gotten to Badenoch first, and the leader of Braemar would hear nothing of "holding back the valiant Baron of Dilnamarra." Still, even with none listening to his whining arguments, it took a dwarfish hand tugging Pwyll by the ear to get his feet moving on the first part of the trip, the trail from Braemar into the foothills. To Pwyll's credit, after that he had kept the pace fairly well, but now, in the uncomfortably humid and warm air as the sun tried to bake its way through the stubborn clouds, the overweight man was sweating profusely, huffing and puffing with every step.

"At least the people won't be there when the dragon arrives," Gary added hopefully.

"Aye, but the wyrm'll fast figure the truth of it," Mickey said. "Then Robert'll go a-hunting. Even with all the rain, the dragon will sniff them out for sure."

Gary cupped a hand over his eyes to diminish the glare as he stared up into the thinning overcast. "A few hours?" he asked.

"If you care as much for the folk of Braemar as you make out, then you'll get your legs walking faster!" Geno, who had spoken very little since they had set out the day before, said unexpectedly, poking a stubby finger into Pwyll's ample behind. "I can get us to the spot in a few hours," the dwarf explained to Mickey and Gary, "but not if this one's meaning to stop every twenty steps for a rest!"

Mickey started to respond, words of comfort to Pwyll, it seemed, but Gary cut him short. "Go on, then," the young man said to Geno. "The Baron will keep up—or he will be left behind."

"Left behind?" Pwyll cried out. "In these perfectly awful mountains?" The Baron sucked in his breath immediately, realizing that it was not so wise a thing to insult Dvergamal in the presence of a dwarf.

"How would you like to take a perfectly awful flight?" Geno grumbled.

"Left behind," Gary said more forcefully, drawing a surprised "Oo" from Mickey. "I value the lives of the more than two hundred fleeing Braemar over the safety of a single man, even a Baron." Unblinking, uncompromising, Gary looked over to Geno and said, "Go."

The dwarf's stout legs churned powerfully, sending Geno rolling along at a great pace. They had been traveling a narrow path around the girth of a wide mountain, but now Geno led them straight up its side, then into a ravine, and up a wall across the way, this one almost sheer. They had no ropes, but Geno led the way, speaking to the stones and then jabbing his granite-hard hand straight into the rock wall, leaving a ladder of hand- and footholds for his companions to utilize. Despite the bulky armor, and the weight of Mickey, Gary went on tirelessly, hand over hand, reminding himself every few feet not to look down. Baron Pwyll came far behind, had managed to climb just a few rungs before he eased himself back down and announced that he simply could not go on.

"Carrying fat Barons will surely slow me down!" Geno growled, regarding the man, now a hundred feet below them.

"Leave him," Gary said firmly. "His chances here will be no worse than his chances beside us!" Mickey started to protest, but Gary's last statement, so terribly true, locked the leprechaun's words fast in his throat.

Geno yelled down directions to Pwyll, told him to follow the raving to the north, then fork to the east, where he would find a rocky vale below the intended pass. The Baron called up some typical complaints, but the friends, nearing the top of the climb, weren't listening. Just over the lip, Geno led them into a tight and dark cave, and Mickey put up a ball of faerie light as he and Gary followed the dwarf in.

Geno looked back at the sprite, scowling, and Mickey remembered how Geno felt about lights of any kind in his dark caverns.

"We can't be running along in the dark," the leprechaun reasoned, and the dwarf snorted and led on, and both Gary and Mickey were surely relieved.

They exited the tunnel more than an hour later, coming to a high and flat rock that afforded them a panoramic view of the region south and east. The sun was beaming by then, the overcast fully burned away.

Lines of gray smoke drifted lazily into the air far to the

southeast, painfully visible though the companions were more than twenty miles from Braemar.

"Alas for the Snoozing Sprite," remarked Geno, honestly wounded.

"Ye can't get a log wet enough to resist dragon fire," Mickey added grimly.

Even as they watched, another stream of smoke came up, rising to mesh with the unnatural cloud hanging over the ruined town. All three winced, Mickey shaking his head and Geno squeezing a rock that he held in his hand into little pieces. Gary, though, after his initial shock, found some welcome information in the newest column, for the smoke told him beyond doubt that Robert was still over the town.

"How far are we from the pass?" he asked Geno.

"An hour's walk," the dwarf replied.

"Half an hour's run," Gary corrected. He turned a wistful grin on Mickey.

"Lad, what're ye smiling about?" the leprechaun wanted to know.

"Set the sword to singing," Gary replied. "Let's pull Robert away before he can find the villagers' trail."

"We don't even know that Kelsey and the gnome have got to Gondabuggan," Mickey argued. "We can't go calling the dragon until we know!"

Gary understood the logic, understood that to call the dragon now would be gambling the lives of Braemar's folk against the entire success of his plan, against the potential for a complete disaster. But Gary wouldn't sit by and watch any more of Faerie's fine people be slaughtered. This was his plan, he trusted in Kelsey, and he was in a gambling mood.

"Do it," he said.

Mickey looked to Geno for some answers, but the dwarf just looked away. From the beginning, Geno had made it clear that he was their guide and nothing more, that he would be long gone into deep caverns at first sight of the wyrm.

Mickey let out a heaving breath, then reached down Gary's back to touch the hilt of the huge sword. He uttered an enchantment over the blade and tapped his finger atop the hilt.

"We'd best be running," Mickey said to Gary.

"Will the dragon hear it?" Gary asked.

"Already has," the sprite answered grimly.

Gary turned back to say some word of encouragement to Geno, and saw that the dwarf was off and running along the trail.

They came to the spot some time later with no sign of the dragon yet evident. Gary considered the layout of the place carefully, trying to fathom how he could choreograph this delicate situation. Geno showed him the marks he was looking for, deep scratches and scorches along the wall of stone. A wry smile crossed Gary's face when he noticed that this spot was conveniently located above a flat area that would serve as a perch, even for a beast as large as Robert. Gary pointed this out to the dwarf, then handed over the sword.

Taking the weapon, Geno scrambled up some stones and onto the intended perch. He moved under great hanging slabs of stone, resembling the enormous front teeth of some gigantic monster, but if the dwarf cared that tons of rock were hanging precariously above his head, he did not show it. Holding the sword out before him (he couldn't even reach the crosspiece to the hilt with its tip poking against the stone), Geno closed his eyes and began to chant quietly, a grumbling, grating sound, as though he was talking to the mountain itself.

And he was. A moment later, the dwarf gently pushed the weapon down, the stone simply parting around the blade as it sunk deeper and deeper. When Geno had finished, only the hilt and a couple of inches of steel showed above the flat area.

Mickey, meanwhile, had not been idle. Peering to the north and east, the leprechaun pulled out his umbrella and floated high into the air. He extended the fingers of his free hand and uttered a fast chant. Sparks erupted from Mickey's fingertips, drawing green and red lines in the air. He kept up the display for several seconds, then fell quiet, feeling incredibly vulnerable hanging in midair, with a flying dragon almost surely on the way.

"Come on, then," Mickey whispered to himself, peering towards distant Gondabuggan, and then all around anxiously.

A silver flash showed in the far distance, once and then again.

Mickey's smile took in his prominent ears. He snapped his umbrella shut and dropped like a stone, to be caught by a surprised Gary Leger.

"Kelsey got there, laddie!" the sprite cried. He grabbed Gary's ears and pulled him close, giving him a kiss on the cheek. "Oh, he got there!"

The mirth was stolen a split second later, by a roar that only a dragon—only a tricked and robbed dragon—could make.

"Time to go," proclaimed the dwarf, and, true to his word, Geno hopped down from the small plateau, rushed up to an opposite mountain wall and called to the stone. What had seemed just a small crack widened suddenly, and the dwarf, with a look back to Gary and Mickey, prudently stepped in.

"If you get killed," he offered hopefully to Gary, and he paused, as if fumbling to think of something positive to say. "Well, stonebubbles, then you'll get killed!" Geno bellowed, and he was gone and the stone snapped shut behind him.

"Loyal bunch, them dwarfs," Mickey said dryly. "But Geno would let us in, lad, if ye've changed yer mind."

That was among the most tempting offers Gary Leger had ever heard—and it only got more tempting when another roar, a closer roar, echoed off the mountain walls.

Gary shook his head resolutely. "We've got to do this," he said, reminding himself privately that he was part of something bigger, that there was a point to this that transcended his own mortality.

Another roar sounded, seeming to come from just beyond the next ridge.

Gary Leger set Mickey down on the ground and took up his spear. He hadn't come this far to turn and run at the moment of truth.

23 † Precisely Overpacked

Robert cut around jutting rocks, flying low and fast through rugged Dvergamal. The dragon sensed the magic of his missing sword, as though the weapon was crying out to him, crying out against the thieves who had dared to steal it away. Robert knew these thieves, had smelled their too-familiar scent when he had returned to his lair. If that scent wasn't enough of a clue, the missing pot of gold certainly was.

Now he would find the miserable leprechaun and his companions, find them and melt them away with all his fiery fury.

He came up over one low peak, then dropped fast into a ravine. He thought he saw some movement below—a large man scrambling—but he whisked away overhead, compelled by the calling sword.

Then Robert saw it, held aloft proudly by the man, Gary Leger from Bretaigne, with that miserable rat Mickey McMickey sitting on the ground beside him, counting the pieces of gold in his retrieved pot.

How dare they! the dragon fumed. Standing tall and proud on an exposed ledge, so open, so vulnerable to Robert's wrath. Their impudence drove the dragon on with all speed. He swooped high and issued a tremendous roar, then stooped powerfully and loosed his killing breath.

To Robert's horror, both his sword and the pot of gold

melted beside the thieves. The dragon started to bellow out a denial, and only then realized that he had been lured by a simple leprechaun illusion. Robert blinked his reptilian eyes, looking closer, as his dive brought him beyond the area, and there was only the empty high ridge, scorched by his fires, some of the stone bubbling still.

"I know you are near!" the dragon bellowed. "I will tear down the mountain," he promised.

For Gary Leger, looking up at the not-so-distant wyrm, seeing the unbridled fury and the bubbling stone, Robert's last words did not sound like any idle threat.

According to the plan, Gary had to call out, and Mickey, invisible in a deep nook behind him, prodded him to do so. Gary rationally reminded himself that he must, that Robert's fiery display had surely been seen across the miles and the plan had already been set fully into motion. But at that time, mere logic seemed a useless tool for Gary Leger in his battle against the plain horror of the dragon.

"Here," he started to say, but his voice cracked and he had to stop and clear his throat.

Robert banked sharply and rose straight up, breaking his momentum, his long neck snapping about so that he could look in the direction of Gary's meek call.

"Over here," Gary called again, more firmly. He stepped out from around a boulder, coming into a flat stone clearing just below the plateau that held the dragon's dwarfish-stuck sword.

Robert came in slowly, making an easy pass, eyes narrowed that he might better study the young thief. He noticed his sword, then, and issued a long and low growl.

"What tricks have you left, young thief?" he asked from on high.

"The deception was necessary," Gary replied, trying to hide his relief that the dragon had actually paused long enough to speak with him.

Wind buffeted Gary as Robert did as close to a hover as a massive dragon could.

"Of course, mighty Robert could fly past and burn us away," Gary went on, speaking quickly and glancing somewhat nervously to the northeast. "But that would ruin what you came to retrieve."

"What you stole!" Robert corrected.

"That, too, was necessary," Gary quickly continued, before the dragon's ire could gain momentum once more. "Stole, yes, but not to keep. You may have your sword back, mighty Robert." He held his hand out towards the embedded weapon and, to his relief, the dragon plopped down behind it, eyeing it curiously, suspiciously.

"It was I who took the dagger," Gary explained, his hand dramatically banging against his chest. His tone changed, deepened, as he recited the words, as though he was some actor in a grand Shakespearean production. "The dagger that allowed you to escape the terms of banishment."

"Again, a theft!" Robert interrupted, his drool sizzling from the edges of his dagger-lined maw.

"Again, necessary!" Gary shouted back, pointing an accusing finger the wyrm's way. "How else might I have lured Robert from his lair? How else might I have found the challenge that I deserve and demand?"

Robert's great head moved back, a clear signal that the dragon was somewhat confused.

"Did you think that I had come all the way from Bretaigne simply to play lackey to an overly proud elf?" Gary asked incredulously. "Of course I did not! It was my desire to see the spear reforged," he admitted, holding the magnificent weapon aloft. "But it was my greater desire to view mighty Robert, the legendary wyrm, whose reputation has come to all lands."

Gary sighed deeply, and snuck another glance to the northeast. What is taking so long? he wondered.

"I have defeated every knight in my land in honorable combat," Gary went on. "I have defeated the dragon of Angor."

"Where is Angor?" Robert demanded.

"It is an island," Gary replied quickly, trying not to get caught in his sticky web of lies.

"I know of all dragons," Robert sneered. "Yet I know not of any island called Angor!"

"A small dragon, he was," Gary stuttered. "Certainly of no measure against Robert the Wretch . . . Robert the Righteous."

The dragon chuckled, a curiously evil sound, at the apparent slip of the tongue. Old Robert knew well enough what the peoples of the land called him.

"I am Gary Leger of Bretaigne," Gary cried suddenly, proudly. "And I make my challenge against Robert honorably. Will you fight with me, mighty dragon? And will you withhold your killing breath?"

"Withhold my breath?" the dragon echoed incredulously, and Gary thought that the game was up, thought that Robert would fry him then and there.

"Unless you are afraid," Gary stammered. Again, he looked nervously to the east. "I have brought your sword, and the spear which I took from Dilnamarra. I had thought . . ."

"Behold Robert!" the dragon bellowed, and Gary's ears hurt from the volume. "He who killed a hundred men on the pass at Muckworst. He who cowed the painted savages of the Five Sisters, and who brought the humanoid newts under his protective wing. He who . . ."

The dragon's list of accomplishments—mostly horrible accomplishments—went on for many minutes. Gary was glad for the delay, but wondered what in the world was taking so long.

"Easy, lad," Mickey whispered from his hiding place behind Gary, sensing the man's distress. "These things take time."

Robert stopped suddenly, bellowed again—it seemed as if he was in some pain. And then, before Gary's incredulous stare, the dragon began to transform. He rolled his great wings in close to his sides, where they melded with his red-gold scales. His long neck contracted, as did his tail, and all his great dragon form hunched down and began to shrink.

The marks on the wall behind him became visible to Gary, and the young man nearly fainted.

Then Robert, the great red-bearded human, grasped the huge pommel of his stuck sword. Corded muscles flexed and tugged, and the stone itself groaned in protest.

Robert let go and rubbed his hands together, then grasped the hilt and tugged again, with all this strength. Amazingly, the stone held fast; the sword would not come free.

"What trick is this?" the dragon growled at Gary.

Gary shrugged helplessly, as surprised as Robert. "I did not think the simple dwarfish magic would prove the stronger," he said, slyly putting his emphasis on the word "simple."

Robert's eyes flared dangerously. "Stronger?" the dragon echoed. "Let us see who is the stronger!"

Gary was glad for Robert's roars in the ensuing moments, as the wyrm reverted to his gigantic dragon form, for they covered the man's heaving, relieved breaths.

"They better hurry," Gary managed to remark privately to the hiding leprechaun.

There came no reply, and Gary was surprised only for

the instant it took him to realize that the leprechaun, having lost faith in the plan, had slipped away for safer parts.

When Gary turned back to the higher plateau, he was facing the mighty dragon again, Robert the Wretched in all his evil splendor.

"Let us see who is the stronger!" Robert roared again. "I will melt the stone away, and then hack you down, foolish Gary Leger of Bretaigne."

Gary nervously clutched tightly to his spear, and the dragon, noting the movement, actually laughed at him.

"Would you like an open throw?" Robert invited, arcing his wings back and sticking his massive, armored chest out towards Gary.

"Throw, then, feeble human!" the wyrm invited. "A clear shot, but one that will do you no good. Do you believe that your puny weapon, though it be the most powerful in all the land, could bring harm to Robert?"

The dragon laughed again, his rumbling shaking the mountain stones, and Gary had no response, could find no words at all in the face of his terrible predicament.

"Shield your eyes from my breath," the dragon warned. "And make peace with whatever god . . ."

A hissing, whistling sound stopped Robert short. "What?" he demanded, turning his gaze, as Gary had turned his, to the northeast.

The M&M Delivery Ball, its cannon precisely overpacked to heave it at two hundred and seventy-three miles per hour, soared into Buck-toothed Ogre Pass, caught the dragon at the base of his left wing, smashing his seemingly impenetrable scales to little pieces. The wyrm's evil face twisted in sheer disbelief in the split-second he remained on the ledge before the force of the blow sent him tumbling, serpentine neck over tail, into the canyon west of Gary's position. The very ground shook under Gary's feet, and the sound of the falling wyrm outdid any thunder the young man had ever heard.

Stones dropped down behind the falling monster, Robert's weight bringing about a small avalanche. But these mountains of Dvergamal were old and solid, and the upheaval died away to dusty stillness in a few moments.

"Oh, ye got him, lad!" Mickey cried, becoming visible and leaping out from his nook. A crack on the stone wall opposite the target plateau split wide, and out hopped Geno, shaking his head in disbelief, his gap-toothed smile, the look of a mischievous little boy, as wide as Gary had ever seen it.

"Bah, I knowed ye wouldn't be going too far!" Mickey roared at the dwarf.

Geno laughed aloud—the first time Gary had actually heard the dwarf do that—and, to Gary's surprise, it came out as the laughter of a little boy, not the grating and grumbling sound the young man would have expected.

"Suren the world's a brighter place!" Mickey squealed, hopping a little dance all about the high pass.

A roar from below stopped the leprechaun's quick-steps and erased Geno's smile.

Gary rushed the ledge and looked down. There flopped Robert, sorely wounded, with one wing wrapped all the way around his back and a huge garish wound running the length of his side. He thrashed and kicked among the boulder-strewn debris of his fall, tangled along a row of low mounds. The sheer violence of the dragon's actions split the stones apart, but caused more injuries from the flying debris to mighty Robert.

"We've got to finish him," Gary said to his companions, who had come up beside him.

Both Geno and Mickey stared at the young man in disbelief. "You want to go down there?" the dwarf scoffed. Geno's face crinkled suddenly. "Oh," he said as if he had just remembered something. "The fat Baron's somewhere down there."

"Show me the path," Gary insisted, and Geno willingly obliged, pointing out a narrow trail leading down the canyon's side.

Gary spun to go, and bumped into a hovering dragon scale.

"Take it, lad," Mickey said grimly. "If ye're meaning to go. Take it and use it as a shield. Robert's hurt, but he's got his breath left, don't ye doubt."

Gary grabbed the thing out of the air, found it to be nearly as large as he, and wondered how in the world he was supposed to carry it along. He found it surprisingly light, though, and looking at Mickey, he understood that the sprite was still concentrating, still using his magic to partially levitate the thing.

Gary found a handhold along a crack on the back side of the scale, and, with a deep breath to steady himself and a silent reminder that they would never find a better chance to end this, he started off down the path.

"Oh, valiant young sprout!" came the expected call from the bloodthirsty spear.

"Oh, shut up," Gary mumbled back, feeling more stupid than brave and wanting nothing more than to wake up in the woods out back of his parents' home next to Diane.

Robert spotted him coming when he was halfway down the exposed trail. The wounded wyrm stopped its thrashing, its reptilian eyes narrowing to evil slits.

"Here it comes," Mickey whispered to Geno, and the leprechaun quickly ended his levitation of the scale and instead enacted an illusion to make Gary's position appear a few yards to the side.

Gary dropped the suddenly too-heavy scale-shield atop his foot, cried out in pain and fear, and fell back against the mountain wall behind the thing. Then he screamed in sheer terror as Robert's breath, the dragon not fooled by the leprechaun's illusion, completely surrounded him, licking at him from around the heavy scale.

Rock melted away; the hair on Gary's arm holding the shield disappeared, his skin turning bright red. He thought he was surely dying, then realized that he was falling, for the ledge beneath him had been burned to dripping liquid.

He crashed down among the stones, slamming hard, feeling as though he had broken every bone in his body, his lungs aching as though they would soon explode. His helmet flopped around so that he could not see, and he didn't want to see, expecting the dragon's great maw to fall over him, snapping him in half. He thought of the shield that had saved his life, but it was far gone, nowhere near the stunned man.

Gary lay dazed for a few moments, moments that passed too slowly, and then he realized that the dragon was crying out in pain. Gary slowly lifted his head and turned up the bottom of his backward helm. He saw Robert, thrashing again as a steady stream of hammers twirled through the air and banged against his unprotected, grievously wounded side.

The dragon's head came around to face the ledge, to face Geno and Mickey, and Robert hissed sharply, sucking in the air, fueling his inner fires.

A wall of protest rose within Gary Leger an outrage that stole his pain. He felt the spear lying beside him and grabbed it up, clambering to his feet and throwing aside his troublesome helm.

"No!" he cried, running as fast as he could go in the bulky armor. He went up the side of a mound and leaped ahead, spear extended as he flew for the dragon's throat.

The distracted Robert saw him coming at the last moment and tried to spin about as he loosed his fires. Gary was in under the line of the blaze, though, and then the huge tip of his powerful weapon was into the dragon's neck, caught fast under the creature's maw.

Gary felt the waves of energy running the length of the hungry weapon, coursing through its metal and into the roaring dragon. Robert thrashed about, sending Gary on a wild ride, back and forth. Up went the dragon's long neck, lifting Gary high into the air.

"Hang on!" the spear implored him, perhaps the most ridiculous request Gary had ever heard. Hang on? What the hell else was he supposed to do?

Then Gary felt a tingling rising from the bottom of his feet, like the pins and needles he might experience if he sat with his leg curled under him for too long. This tingling continued to spread, though, rising throughout his body, then leaving him altogether and, he somehow understood, climbing through the spear.

Robert screeched in pain, and Gary, to his own horror, came to realize what the sentient weapon had done. The spear was sucking out his very life force, converting it to energy and blasting it into the wyrm. And to Gary's further amazement, the ploy seemed to have had some effect. Down went the serpentine neck, bowed under the tremendous assault.

Gary felt his grip weakening, and suddenly he was flying free, crashing again against the rocky ground. It took him some time to reorient himself to his surroundings, some time to remember even that he was in big trouble.

When he finally looked back, he saw not a dragon, but a huge, red-bearded man, one arm hanging limply at his side, blood dripping from an open wound in his neck. Throaty growls erupted from Robert's bloody mouth as the beast stalked over and hoisted the fallen spear. Blue energy arced into Robert again, smoke rising from his hand and forearm.

On the ledge, Geno whipped his last hammer.

Robert only growled at the spear's impertinence, turned Gary's way, and lifted the weapon for a throw.

"Flee, young sprout!" came the call, and Gary understood that the sentient weapon could not match the dragon's willpower or sheer strength, and could not help him. Gary knew in that instant that he was doomed.

Robert's arm shot forward; the dwarf's hammer clipped his hand and the spear, and the throw went wild.

Robert looked incredulously to the ledge, then back to Gary. He gave an evil snarl and held aloft his working arm, clenching his hand so that his cordlike muscles bulged to superhuman proportions.

Gary nearly fainted. Robert would simply walk over and throttle him! Would just reach down and crush his skull as though it was some empty eggshell! Despair told Gary to lie back and close his eyes, get it over with as quickly as possible, but Gary, thinking once more of the fleeing folk of Braemar, of the carnage the dragon would soon cause, reacted explosively instead. He scrambled forward on all fours, got up to his feet just long enough to roll over one mound, then cut quickly to the side.

Robert did not hesitate, charging right for him.

With a wild leap, diving straight out, Gary got his fingers around the spearshaft. He spun and came up to a sitting position, and the dragon-turned-man skidded to a stop barely inches from the waving weapon's tip.

Robert's surprise showed clearly on his face, an instant of hesitation, a slight and short-lived opening.

Gary lurched forward, tucked one foot under him, and pushed ahead with all his strength. The spear's tip slipped more than an inch into Robert's massive chest before the red-bearded man could clamp his hand onto its shaft, abruptly stopping its progress.

Robert and Gary stood facing each other, gruesomely

joined by the metallic shaft, staring defiantly into each other's eyes.

Robert looked down to his newest wound. When he looked back, he was smiling evilly once more. "I will grind your bones," he promised.

Gary felt another tingle sweep through him, a pulse of energy that the spear had sent to blast the dragon's hand from the metallic shaft. Jolted and surprised once more, Robert reached back for the weapon immediately, but was too late to stop Gary's brutal surge.

"To make your bread?" the young man spat sarcastically, driving the enchanted spear through the dragon's heart.

Robert's breath went in, his chest heaving one final time. He grabbed up the stuck spear and yanked it free from Gary's grasp, stumbling back several steps.

"Well done," Robert offered, his tone full of surprise and admiration. He held in place for a long while, trembling, the shaft protruding from his muscled chest and quivering gruesomely, its end fast staining with the wyrm's lifeblood.

And then the dragon who had terrorized the land of Faerie for centuries fell down and died.

✝ Epilogue

"Young sprout." Gary heard the call in his mind, distantly, as though he himself was far removed from his own consciousness. It came again, and then a third time, leading him like a beacon back to the world of the living.

A myriad of pleasant aromas greeted him, and a thousand sounds, birds and animals mostly, and a quieter, more solemn humming that Gary knew somehow to be the song of the Tylwyth Teg.

Gary opened his eyes to the glory of Tir na n'Og. The sun was fast sinking in the west, but that did little to dull the vivid and beautiful colors of the magical forest. Mickey was beside Gary, and Kelsey, as well, along with the pony that had carried Kelsey and Gerbil to Gondabuggan, the valiant steed that had nearly given its life for the exhaustion. Like Gary, the pony was on the mend—who wouldn't be in the splendor of Tir na n'Og?

"Welcome back," Mickey said as Gary propped himself up on his elbows. He found that he was out of the armor, back in his clothes alone—and these had been sewn in several places to repair the tears and (Gary nearly fainted away again when he thought of this) dagger holes. The armor lay piled not far to the side, with the spear a short distance beyond it, leaning against a birch tree on the edge of the blueberry patch.

"How'd we get here?" Gary asked.

"We walked," Kelsey replied. "At least, some of us walked."

"Tommy carried ye, lad," Mickey added.

Tommy? It took Gary a moment to recognize the name, and then he glanced all around anxiously, dearly wanting to see his giant friend once more. "Where is he?"

"Not about," Mickey explained. "He and Geno went back to the east to prepare for the coming o' the witch."

Gary winced, and everything that had transpired over the last few days rushed back into his thoughts.

"Robert is dead?" he asked.

"Of course," answered the cocky spear, from its perch against the birch tree.

"Aye," Mickey answered. "Ye sticked that one good."

"Does that mean that he's banished for a hundred years?" Gary wondered.

"Robert is no witch," Kelsey answered. "The dragon is simply dead."

"Aye, and a good thing for all the land," Mickey remarked. "We taked his horns, lad, and a few o' his teeth."

Gary's face twisted with confusion. The last he had seen, Robert was a man, and no horned monstrosity.

"Of course the wyrm went back to being a wyrm when he died," Mickey explained, understanding Gary's confusion. "His human form was magic, and no more."

"Then where are the horns?" Gary asked. "And what happened to Baron Pwyll?" he added, suddenly remembering that the man had been somewhere about the vale wherein Robert the Wretched had met his doom.

"The two go together," Mickey replied with a chuckle. "We gave the horns to Pwyll, for 'twas he who slew the wyrm."

"Pwyll?" Gary balked. "I killed . . ."

"Pwyll killed the wyrm," Kelsey interjected. "For the good of Faerie."

Gary started to protest again, but stopped, digesting Kelsey's last statement. Baron Pwyll had been branded an outlaw by the throne, and Dilnamarra, by all accounts a strategic position, had been given over to a puppet ruler. But if Pwyll could be manufactured into some hero, some dragonslayer . . .

Gary nodded. "For the good of Faerie," he agreed.

"We knowed ye wouldn't mind, lad," Mickey said cheerily. "Pwyll will return the missing spear and armor, and return as a hero."

The words led Gary's gaze back to the pile of metal. He could see that the magnificent armor was battered. One of the arm pieces lay in plain sight, its metal torn. Gary looked down to his own forearm and saw a similar scar. He realized that to be the broken place in the dragon scale shield, a crack that Robert's fiery breath had apparently slipped through.

"Don't ye fear for the armor," Mickey remarked. "The Tylwyth Teg'll clean it up good, and any dent it's got, it rightly earned."

"Cedric Donigarten would be truly pleased," Kelsey agreed.

"It will look better if I'm in it when Pwyll brings it back to Dilnamarra," Gary reasoned.

"Aye, ye might be right," Mickey replied. "But that cannot be, since ye're leaving now." Mickey glanced to the other side of the blueberry patch, where a group of fairies had gathered and were now forming into their dancing ring.

Not so long ago, particularly at the moment he was forced to face the dragon, Gary would have welcomed those words. Now, though, his emotions were truly mixed. How could he leave, he wondered, with Ceridwen about to come forth, especially since he had been the one to release her?

"No way," Gary remarked firmly. "This isn't over and I'm not leaving."

"But ye are, lad," Mickey replied. "The witch'll be free in the next season, but she'll find a different world awaiting her. The folk're rallying around the Baron, both here and in the east, and, don't ye doubt, Connacht will find a fight on their hands that Kinnemore and Ceridwen never expected."

"I should be here," Gary reasoned. Looking for some support, he sent his thoughts to the sentient spear, reminding the weapon that he was the rightful spearwielder and that it was the only weapon in all the land which could truly harm the witch. To Gary's dismay, no reply came forth, and he could sense that the spear had broken off contact, even the continual subconscious contact, altogether.

"Ye go back to yer own place," Mickey said. "Who's knowing how long our next war will run? Ye've a life, don't ye forget, a life beyond the realm of Faerie."

For a moment, Gary couldn't decide if he wanted to remember that life or not. He was playing a monumental role here, in this land. He was the dragonslayer; he was making a difference. What could he do in his own world to possibly make any difference?

But the line of reasoning inevitably led Gary to remember Diane, and his family. He made a difference to them.

In the end, it wasn't his choice anyway. Kelsey helped him to his feet and led him over to the dancing fairies.

"Go on, then," Mickey said, and it seemed to Gary as if the falsely cheery sprite was on the verge of tears.

"This is not finished," Gary said determinedly. "I should be here."

"Ye never know what the wind will blow," Mickey answered with a smirk. "Now get yerself in the ring, lad, and go back where the fates determined ye belong."

Gary stepped in and sat down. He looked back to his friends and saw that Mickey had popped his long-stemmed pipe into his mouth. The fairy song compelled Gary to lie down, then, and close his eyes, and he fell asleep with that peaceful vision still in mind.

When Gary woke up, he found that he had left the realm of Faerie, but not the soreness of his exploits, behind. He was in the woods out back of his parents' house again, up in the blueberry patch, with the sky in the east growing lighter shades of blue.

"Diane," he breathed, and he rushed over the edge of the vale, heading for the mossy banking. To his utter relief, he found Diane sleeping still, groaning and stretching and about to awaken with the approaching dawn. Gary skittered down the hill and fell into place beside her, closing his eyes and pretending to be asleep.

Diane woke with a start, and looked all around, her face crinkling disgustedly. "Hey!" she said, and she punched Gary hard in the shoulder, then put her hand up to cover her nose. "I can put up with morning breath, but . . . did you get sprayed by a skunk or something?"

Gary opened his eyes and regarded her curiously, then took the moment to sniff at his armpit. He nearly fell over backwards. "No, just breathed on by a dragon," he replied with a chuckle.

Diane punched him again. "You must have been dreaming and kicking," she reasoned.

You run around for a week in heavy armor, under a summer sun and through soaking rains, Gary thought privately, and let's see how wonderful you smell! To Diane, he simply offhandedly replied, "Maybe."

Diane waved a hand in front of her face. She stopped short, though, her eyes locked on Gary's hip.

"What?" he asked, and when he looked down, he got

his answer. Across the side of his cotton shirt was a long stitch line.

"What happened to that?" Diane asked.

"It's an old shirt," Gary stammered, trying to tuck it in quickly and put the stitch line out of sight. Diane grabbed it from him and tugged hard, pulling the shirt all the way out and revealing, to her horror, the scar of a deep wound, a knife wound.

"What happened?" she demanded again.

"An old cut," Gary replied, though he, too, was obviously horrified to see the wicked scar.

"No, it's not!" Diane growled. "And don't you lie to me!"

"Do you think that you would believe the truth?" Gary replied evenly, his green eyes locking an unblinking stare into Diane's similar orbs.

She understood, then, remembered all that they had talked about, remembered the flowing script in *The Hobbit* and the tiny arrows on the windowsill. Gary had gone back!

"Don't ask," he said to her before her lips could form the obvious string of questions. "I don't believe it myself." Gary rolled to get up, and felt a lump in his pants pocket. He shifted and reached down, and produced a tooth, an incisor several inches long. He held it up, both his and Diane's expressions full of disbelief.

"Lion?" she asked, her eyes wide.

Gary shook his head slowly and corrected her. "Dragon."